GEORGE SHIPW

IMPERIAL GOVERNOR

sfwp.com

Library of Congress Cataloging-in-Publication Data

Names: Shipway, George, 1908- author.
Title: Imperial governor / George Shipway.
Description: Santa Fe, NM : SFWP, [2018?]
Identifiers: LCCN 2017059140| ISBN 9781939650832 (paperback : alk. paper) |
   ISBN 9781939650856 (epub) | ISBN 9781939650863 (mobi kindle)
Subjects: LCSH: Suetonius Paulinus, Gaius—Fiction. | Boadicea, Queen,-62—
   Fiction. | Romans—Great Britain—Fiction. | Britons—Fiction. |
   Queens—Fiction. | Iceni—Fiction. | Great Britain—History—Roman period,
   55 B.C.-449 A.D.—Fiction. | Great Britain—History, Military—55 B.C.-449
   A.D.—Fiction. | GSAFD: Biographical fiction. | Historical fiction.
Classification: LCC PR6069.H5 I47 2018 | DDC 823.914—dc23
LC record available at https://lccn.loc.gov/2017059140

Published by SFWP
369 Montezuma Ave. #350
Santa Fe, NM 87501
(505) 428-9045
www.sfwp.com

To Lorna

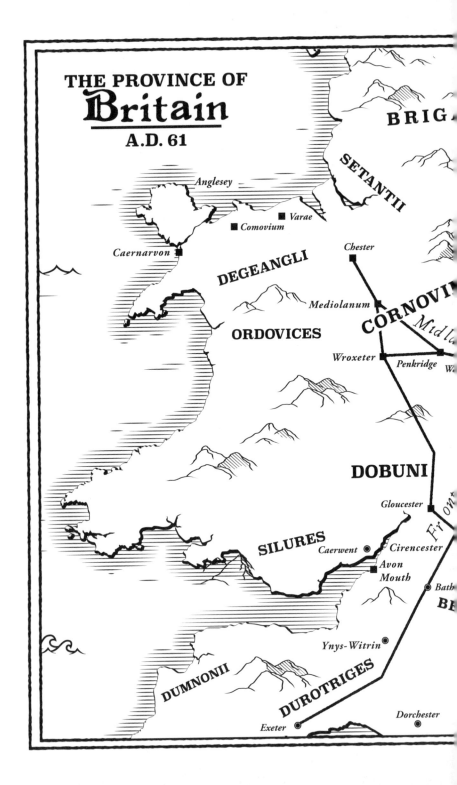

THE PROVINCE OF
Britain
A.D. 61

BRIG

SETANTII

Anglesey

■ Varae

■ Comovium

Chester ■

Caernarvon ■

DEGEANGLI

CORNOVI

Mediolanum ■

Midl

ORDOVICES

Wroxeter ■ Penkridge

W

DOBUNI

Gloucester ■

Fr on

SILURES

Caerwent ◉ Cirencester

Avon
Mouth ■

◉ Bath

B

Ynys-Witrin ◉

DUMNONII

DUROTRIGES

Dorchester ◉

Exeter ◉

Contents

Introduction

by Alan Fisk

One day in Montreal in the late 1970s, I was looking through a shelf of historical novels (my favourite genre). I was passing over a large number of bodice-rippers, a highly popular sub-genre at the time, when my eyes and fingers were arrested by a strikingly different title on a book spine: *Imperial Governor*, by one George Shipway, an author entirely unknown to me.

The book flap told me that it was about Boudicca's revolt of 61 A.D., and displayed a photograph of the rather intimidating-looking military man who had written it.

I went home and was soon gripped by my first reading of *Imperial Governor*. From then on, I bought all of Shipway's historical novels, which in later years went in and out of print before disappearing from the market.

Who, I wondered, was this masterly and engrossing author? A brief biographical sketch may illuminate his body of work.

George Shipway was born in India in 1907. At the age of seven, he was sent to boarding school in England, and at 18 he entered the Sandhurst military academy, which prepared him to become an officer in the Indian Army.

In 1928, Shipway was duly commissioned into the 13th Duke of Connaught's Own Lancers, a cavalry regiment. He would serve in a variety of roles for nearly 20 years, including commanding a force of irregulars on the Iranian frontier, and as a staff officer in Delhi. During one of his home leaves in England, he married his wife Lorna, who, like Shipway, was a strong personality. I suspect that the forceful female characters who appear in several of Shipway's novels, from Cartimandua in *Imperial Governor* onwards, owe something to Lorna.

George Shipway's Army career came to an end in 1947. At the Partition of India, the 13th Duke of Connaught's Own Lancers was assigned to Pakistan. It still exists, under the name of the 13th Lancers.

Shipway declined an offer of a transfer to the British Army. He and Lorna returned to England. They encountered an old friend who was married to another former Indian Army officer. The couple were now running Cheam School, a boys' school in Berkshire, west of London, and invited George Shipway to become a teacher there, specialising in history and geography.

Shipway had no formal teaching qualifications, but he was deeply educated, and he was interested in, and knowledgeable about, history. Many years later, his widow Lorna told me that she thought he might well have become a university teacher, instead of an Army officer, if his life had taken another path. Indeed, he used to joke that the only reason he had joined the Army was so that he could play polo, which he would not have been able to afford to do as a civilian!

George Shipway turned out to be a gifted teacher. He spent 19 years at Cheam, where his pupils included Prince Charles. The boys liked and respected him, and he would occasionally astonish them by demonstrating feats of physical strength. Shipway was a true scholar-athlete.

Meanwhile, he had begun to try his hand at writing. He had been encouraged by his friend John Masters, who was also a former Indian Army officer, and who is best known for his novels about the Savage family in India, particularly *Bhowani Junction*.

Imperial Governor was Shipway's first novel, and appeared in 1967 to immediate acclaim.

It is narrated by the Roman general Suetonius Paulinus, who is posted to Britain by the Emperor Nero in 60 A.D. to take overall command of all the Roman military units there. It is made clear to Suetonius Paulinus that this is to be no mere passive garrison duty. Newly conquered Britannia is a drain on the Empire's financial resources, and Nero wants to take over the still-unoccupied western and northern regions, where valuable mineral deposits are located.

Suetonius Paulinus plans a westward offensive, but he knows of two complicating factors, one in the east, and one in the north. In the east, the Trinovantes and Iceni tribes are unfriendly to Rome, and are restrained only by the policy of the King of the Iceni, Prasutagus, of cooperation with Rome. In the north, the pro-Roman Queen of the Brigantes, Cartimandua, is unpopular with elements of the tribal leadership, who see her as a dishonourable collaborator.

When Suetonius Paulinus does launch his operation in the west, his experience of mountain fighting in North Africa helps him to success, but he knows very well that sound tactics cannot overcome an unsound strategy. The weakness of that strategy is that the bulk of his forces are deployed in the west, while to his rear the east of Britain is dangerously sullen and unstable. That is not his fault, because he had been ordered to strike west regardless of current circumstances. Suetonius Paulinus knows that he will be holding the parcel if the music stops, and it will be he who will have to deal with what happens.

Suetonius Paulinus tells his story with plenty of military detail, and vivid pictures of the characters, both Roman and British, who figure in the narrative. This was the first demonstration of Shipway's style: dense, detailed, and full of violent incidents. Suetonius Paulinus prides himself upon being a strong commander, who can be ruthless towards both his enemies and his allies.

If Suetonius Paulinus has a dangerous fault, it is that he is impatient of any dissent from his own view of a situation. His strong will makes him an effective general, but he has a tendency to see anyone who questions his plans as being either a weakling or a coward or both. He sometimes realises that not all his officers and men admire him, and is puzzled by glimpses of their hostility.

The story drives on at a fast, but never confusing, pace, and Shipway's narrative style makes readers feel that they really are being taken into the confidences of Suetonius Paulinus.

Imperial Governor and its successors gained Shipway faithful readers and brought him admiration from other writers, who happily admitted his influence upon them. One such admirer is Bernard Cornwell, who has described Shipway's novels as "utterly brilliant and compelling," and adds, "I'm sure they served as a template for the sort of book I hoped to write."

George Shipway died in 1982. He had written nine novels over 11 years, and one can only wish that he had begun being published earlier than at the age of 60. As Bernard Cornwell says, "the only problem with Shipway was that he didn't write enough."

Read on and enjoy *Imperial Governor*.

Alan Fisk has written several historical novels, including *Forty Testoons* and *Cupid and the Silent Goddess*.

Prologue

A.D.
June 68

Nero is dead.

He had been stark mad for years and was hated by every member of the Senatorial order, but I must remember him as my friend. He let me live when he could so easily have killed me.

Now, from beneath the floor-tiles in my library, I can collect the papers I have written during the last six years and, after amending a sentence here and there and polishing a phrase or two, send them to the copying-offices to be published. I risked my life to write this book while Nero still lived: had he known of its existence I would not be alive today.

He was the last of the Julian line. Now I can tell the truth—the truth which yesterday was treason.

Who am I?

Eight years ago the name of Gaius Suetonius Paulinus was known to Romans from the Rhine to the Nile, from Euphrates to Severn, as one of the greatest generals in the world. A year later, after leading his army to the most resounding victory of modern times, he was recalled from his command and quietly relegated to private life.

I am that man.

Nero never gave any reason; he seldom bothered with explanations. Rumour and speculation abounded; then the matter was forgotten and the world at large saw only a man become famous and, perhaps, too powerful, plucked from his eminence and discarded. Such men in these times do not usually live very long. Yet Nero still showed me his favour and was content merely to have me watched lest my reaction to public humiliation drove me into conspiracy.

I am neither a hero nor overmuch afraid of death, yet I did not want to die. There were spies about me in those years, watching and reporting, listening for the incautious word that could be construed as treachery, looking for associations with disaffected men. I was very careful indeed. I stayed nearly all the time in Rome but lived in retirement, attending the Senate's meetings only as often as was necessary, voting exactly as Nero wished. It was a brave man who did otherwise. I entertained a little, inviting only those whose characters were exemplary in Nero's eyes. It was hard work for a man of my rank and family. My associates were financiers, swindlers, panders, harlots male and female, eunuchs, freedmen and a few patricians who, like myself, were determined to survive. I saw Nero frequently; he was always affable; in his presence I often forgot how mad and dangerous he had become.

Degradation had its reward. Soon after the Fire the spies were called off; but caution had become a habit and I took pains not to alter my behaviour. The following year Nero gave me the Consulship for the second time as a prize for good conduct and in recognition of the fact that he had finally decided I was harmless. At the end of my term I went to him and begged leave to retire to my country estates, pleading the weight of my fifty-four years as an obstacle to a proper performance of public duties. He assented cheerfully.

Now there is no need to hide anything any more. I can sit here in peace, looking over my vineyards and olive-groves to the green hills beyond, and tell fully and frankly of those hectic months in Britain which crowned and finished my career as a soldier. Most of this book concerns war or preparations for war. I am a soldier first and last, soaked in military habit and tradition during all the long years since my first, far-away campaign as a young tribune in the Mauretanian mountains. To politics, which undid me in the end, I gave less attention than I ought. I was ambitious, they said, watching me climb the Senatorial ladder. True enough; yet my ambition lay only in the field and camp, in the pursuit of military glory. Others of my Order, running the same race, turned their energies to law or politics, doing the minimum military service required, seeking, in the end, the same reward. They wanted a Province, preferably a peaceful one. What kind of man is it that wants to govern a *peaceful* Province?

Now I can explain what really happened, and show the world how it was that the great Suetonius Paulinus, Senator, Consul and Governor of Britain, descended to Suetonius Paulinus, Senator, twice Consul, lackey of a decadent Caesar, companion to his obscene companions; and further yet to Suetonius Paulinus, an old, broken soldier writing memoirs of old, dim campaigns.

Here it is, then: a tale of failure simply told, without embellishment or tricks of rhetoric. Try, in your kindness, to understand my difficulties and judge me leniently.

BOOK I

The Sowing

A.D.
October 59 – February 61

1

'Assume the honours which are justly due to your worth.'

HORACE

1

I was not in Rome when the Senate received the news that Veranius Nepos, Governor of Britain, was dead. The usual rumours of disaster followed the bald announcement, until an irritable message from the Secretariat revealed that he had died in his bed, in London, of congestion of the lungs and not, as had been surmised, under the chariots of a victorious Silurian army.

Soon afterwards a courier arrived at my headquarters in Lower Germany, where I had just assumed command, to recall me instantly to Rome. An immediate summons of this kind, even in those early days of Nero's rule, naturally caused a certain amount of nervousness in the recipient. My conscience was clear; my relations with the Prince were excellent and my speculations were not unduly gloomy during the journey home. There I heard from friends of Veranius's death and gathered some sidelong and exciting hints concerning my own future. I hastened to seek an audience at the Palace—the old Palace, not the Golden House.

The Prince received me. He was seated at the head of a long marble table, with Sextus Afranius Burrus, Prefect of the Praetorian Guard, on his right, Lucius Annaeus Seneca on his left and Claudius of Smyrna, Financial Secretary, standing beside him. Tribunes of the Guard flanked his seat; a soldier watched every doorway, and various Secretariat clerks, laden with reference-scrolls, crowded the background. These people were, in effect, the Government of Rome and her dominions; we Senators were the mouthpiece for decisions made in this unofficial but all-powerful Council.

Nero greeted me with all the charm of the Julian family, inquired shortly about affairs in Lower Germany and even apologized for my abrupt recall. Then he waved me to a chair and came to the point.

'You have doubtless heard,' he said, 'that Veranius has died in Britain?'

'Yes, Caesar,' I answered. 'I am sorry. He was a good officer and a loyal servant of Rome. I knew him when he was Governor of Lycia.'

'A sound man. More of a theoretical than a practical soldier, though. A great writer on military matters. He didn't accomplish much in Britain, though his intentions certainly had a wide enough scope. We have just seen his will: it arrived in the last batch of dispatches.'

I waited. This meant nothing to me. Nero tugged thoughtfully at his lower lip.

'Veranius thought he could conquer Britain—the whole of Britain— in two years. He spent his only year there fighting the—what are they called?—the Silures, as Gallus and Scapula did before him, and with just as much result. He never got anywhere.'

'What were his instructions, Caesar?' I asked quietly.

Nero frowned. 'His instructions were to subdue Britain as far north as the country of the—' He paused, stuttering, and Burrus murmured a word. 'These barbaric names! The Brigantes. As far north as the Brigantes and westwards to the sea. That was all I required. I still require it.'

Nero's protuberant blue eyes glared at my face without amity, remorselessly searching through flesh and bone for the quality beneath. I sat very still. He was very much a ruler during the golden years.

'Do you know anything of Britain?' he snapped.

'Nothing, Caesar, beyond what is known by any educated man in Rome.'

'So. Then Burrus here, and Claudius, can tell you later about the muddle and mess going on in that Province. You will need to know, because I am sending you there as Governor to put matters straight.'

I rose, stood at attention and thanked him formally for the honour. Nero grinned.

'I hope you will still thank me when you hear what you're going to. Listen carefully. Burrus, send everyone out. This is confidential.'

The clerks vanished from the room without further bidding. The guards remained. The Prince waved a document at me.

'This,' he said, 'is the latest financial return from Britain. We won't go into the details now: Claudius can do that with you some other time. These totals are the crux. Look.'

He tossed the papyrus over. I scanned the columns, rather at a loss. Claudius came to my side and ran a lean finger along a row of figures.

'You see?' Nero said. 'For the last financial year the costs of administration, occupation forces, navy, loans and everything else exceeded the income from the Province by a thousand million sesterces. A thousand million! The year before it was five hundred million, and the same before that.'

He beat the marble with his fist.

'This cannot go on. The Province is bleeding Rome dry. We have other expensive provinces; none costs so much as Britain.' He slouched, elbows on table, hands clasped before him. 'I had intended to withdraw our army and administration from the country, to abandon it entirely. Seneca dissuaded me.'

He turned to his old tutor and smiled somewhat maliciously.

'I took his advice, though I think he has special reasons of his own for giving it, and sent Veranius off with his orders. This was going to be Britain's last chance; if Veranius failed we should evacuate.'

Nero paused and frowned at his clenched hands.

'Veranius did very little in the time he had; but he could appreciate a military situation and he was no fool. He thought he could conquer Britain in two years. I believe it can be done.' He looked at me. 'I believe you can do it.'

I bowed my head. 'If you think it possible I will do it, Caesar.'

'A rash promise, Paulinus,' Nero said. 'You yourself declared you knew little of Britain. Listen. The country is rich in minerals: iron, copper, lead and tin. There is also gold. We get some of these metals but not nearly enough. Why? Because we have been in Britain for sixteen years and haven't yet conquered half of it. Sixteen years, and the Divine Julius subdued all Gaul in eight! The wealthiest mines still lie outside our area of occupation. We have made no serious effort at further conquest since our Governor Scapula died seven years ago. For seven years there have been no full-scale operations, nothing but frontier brawls. Consequently we've taken few prisoners and the labour force even for the mines we operate is now insufficient. So the revenue is steadily falling.'

Nero pushed back his chair and stood up. We all rose with him.

'I am sending you to Britain, Paulinus,' he said distinctly, 'to make war. I have examined all the evidence, all the reports from the Province, and have decided on the operations which you must undertake. You will not find them unreasonably difficult. Burrus and Claudius will give you your directive and any information you want.'

He paused, as though considering, and went on in a voice edged, ever so slightly, with menace. 'If you succeed your reputation will be second to no one in my armies. If you fail, you will have lost a province.'

2

The next month was turbulent. I retrieved all the household furniture, personal baggage and servants dispatched to Lower Germany in the expectation of three years' residence in that Province and overhauled and augmented it to accord with the greater splendour befitting a Governor of Britain. A considerable train of carts, wagons and draught animals had to be assembled for transport by the long route through Italy and Narbonne to the Belgic coast. As the month was October I had decided against travelling by sea to Marseilles. Dispatches went to military posts along the road so that escorts could be provided for each stage of the journey. My family was to remain in Rome: Nero's instructions, together with what I heard of climate and conditions in Britain, predicted that my life there had better be free of domestic ties.

Within a few days of my interview the Senate met and, for the second time in six months, conferred on me the Government of a Province and the gilded scroll which was my charter of office. The performance maintained all the gravity and solemnity of a former age when Rome's proconsuls were indeed chosen by the Fathers in Council and were answerable to them alone. The practical result of the official ceremony was a flood of applications for positions on my staff from Senators on behalf of their relations and friends. The candidates were nearly all Half-Year tribunes: young men who would clutter my civil offices and headquarter tents for six months, learning nothing and doing the minimum of work, before going elsewhere to continue their careers. I could have had a cohort of them if I had accepted everyone. However, they fulfilled certain useful, minor functions of an administrative nature and their turnover was rapid, so I chose a dozen of the best after interviewing each one personally and going through his records and credentials in detail. There was also one Broad Stripe tribune, going to serve his year with IX Legion, and three Narrow Stripe men about to start their military careers as prefects of auxiliary cohorts.

I was spared the cost of a troupe of gladiators, actors and dancers for the entertainment of my provincials. Nero had issued an edict only two years before which forbade governors to give gladiatorial, wild beast or other displays in their provinces, ostensibly on the grounds of expense. Cynical opinion whispered that really he feared lest his representatives might thereby attract to their own persons the popularity that should belong to the Prince alone. In truth, Nero at this time was very well liked both in Rome and in the Provinces and, to give him his due, I think it was not jealousy that caused the edict but a genuine care for the well-being of his subjects. Costly displays might well act as a kind of bribe to stifle accusations to Caesar of maladministration and corrupt practices on the part of a governor.

Amid these arrangements I found time to study most of the books written about Britain, from Pytheas through Diodorus Siculus, Strabo, the dispatches of the Divine Julius and the Divine Claudius's account of his brief visit. In addition I delved into the Senate's archives and read the dispatches of successive governors. These, naturally, were little more than news-letters containing information of general interest: all confidential material was confined to letters sent directly to the Prince or his Council. From these varied sources, and from maps of the Province kept at the Secretariat, I obtained a fairly detailed picture of the land which had to be converted, during my three years' term of office, from a wasting liability to a horn of plenty.

Flavius Vespasianus was in Rome at this time, making preparations similar to my own before leaving for Africa as Proconsul. During a meeting of the Senate I induced him to talk about his experiences in Britain during the Conquest. Everyone knows about his whirlwind campaign across southern Britain with II Legion; I was hoping to get his personal opinion of the quality and methods of the British warrior. He did not tell me much.

'How do they fight?' he grunted. 'Very well, for savages. Braver than any I've met. Tougher. Good physique. Catch them in the open and you'll have no trouble. They've no discipline. No knowledge of tactics. Attack in mass. No idea of manœuvre. No body armour. Give them the javelins and then charge. Hard work, though. Don't break easily.'

I tried to sort this out. Vespasianus's undoubtedly brilliant military intellect is not matched by his powers of conversation.

'Under what conditions do they fight best?' I asked.

He scratched his grey, scanty hair.

'Got to catch them in the open. Always have trouble otherwise. Shut themselves up in hill-forts. Very difficult. Remember a place I took with Augusta. Dorchester, they call it nowadays. Tremendous fort. Three lines of ditches. Stormed it all day. Lot of casualties. Took it in the evening. Hardest fight of the campaign.'

I gave it up. Vespasianus was out of date; conditions in Britain had changed since his day. I knew that nearly all hill-forts in the settled areas had been abandoned; they had lost their purpose when the land was pacified and tribes no longer indulged in private warfare. The forts still ringed the hilltops, their crumbling ramparts gradually filling the ditches, the stockades robbed for building-timber and firewood. Their former inhabitants, actively encouraged by the Provincial Government, had moved down the slopes into open villages and towns.

Vespasianus rumbled on. 'Hear you're going to Britain. Filthy country. Damp. Better off in Africa. Dry and hot. Might make a bit of money out of it.'

This last remark was unwise, to say the least. I knew Vespasianus was having money troubles; unfortunate speculations had reduced him almost to penury and city gossips declared that Nero had given him the African appointment to help him over a difficult period. But the good old days when a governor could make a fortune out of his province were gone. Nero himself had tightened up the existing regulations and introduced new ones which made corrupt provincial government difficult though not actually impossible. Moreover, the provincials were encouraged to make official complaints to Rome of any instances of venality.

'You should guard yourself, Vespasianus. These savages in the provinces love nothing better nowadays than to accuse their governors to the Prince. Don't you remember Pedius Blaesus, of Cyrene, who was condemned? Next week Acilius Strabo will be on trial. It shows how careful you must be. For myself, I hope only to finish my term without actually losing money.'

'You'll be lucky.' Vespasianus stretched his legs inelegantly, hitched his toga up to his knees and glanced irritably at an ancient Senator droning an interminable speech. 'Hope to live on your salary?'

'It seems ample enough. Besides, it's not money I hope to make in Britain.'

'Ambitious, eh? Afraid of being outshone in glory by Corbulo? Don't look so angry, Paulinus; you must expect common remarks from a common fellow, and it's what everyone in Rome says, anyway.'

He put a hand on my shoulder.

'Listen, young man'—there were exactly five years between us—'your career and mine so far are very alike. Both of us very fortunate very early. You in Mauretania. I in Britain. Sixteen or seventeen years ago. Since then neither of us have done very much. Lack of opportunity. Now we've each got our chance. Africa for me. No wars there. Might be some easy money: I want it badly. Britain for you. No cash. Plenty of fighting. Suits us both. Interesting to see how we come out, eh?'

He chuckled and belched. I surveyed him without pleasure.

'I prefer my own ambitions, Vespasianus. My advice to you is to live on your pay, accept only small and infrequent bribes, and keep your accounts straight.'

'So?' He eyed the aged Senator, now in the full flood of his peroration. 'How much longer is Thrasea going to keep us here? Well, I'll give you some really useful advice. Watch those Britons in what they call the "settled areas." Keep an eye on your Procurator and his taxes. Don't press the natives too hard. Beat them in the field and they respect you. Govern them well and they might even like you. Oppress them and they'll try to tear your guts out. I wasn't in Britain long but I learned that much. Good, the old fool's finished. I'm off. Farewell, Paulinus.'

In the outcome it would have been better for each of us had we heeded the other's counsel.

3

My written directive arrived during this time. The general tenor, though draped with all the verbiage and safeguards customary in Secretariat drafting, accorded well enough with Nero's succinct instructions. With it was a letter from Burrus asking the favour of a personal interview so that he might amplify certain points in the directive. He asked for a meeting at his own house instead of the Secretariat, which was unusual: I guessed that the Prefect wished to impart some peculiar and highly confidential interpretations.

I saw him the same day. When we were settled Burrus dismissed all his clerks and attendants.

'I hope your directive makes the broad outlines of our policy clear, Legate?' he asked.

'Clear enough so far as it goes, Burrus,' I assented. 'I should like some information which isn't in my orders and cannot be ascertained from official files in the Senate House. I know, for instance, the designations, strengths and localities of military units in Britain, but nothing of their fitness, morale or characters of their commanders. What is the temper of the people in the settled areas? How far can I rely on the co-operation or neutrality of friendly tribes on the frontiers? Litigation arising from taxation and revenue, which are not my direct concern, may require my judgment: are there local variants in the general system of provincial taxation? What are the army's commitments in the matter of revenue collection? These are a few points. I have others in mind.'

'They are matters of detail,' Burrus said with a touch of impatience. 'If, before you leave, you will list them I shall see that your questions are fully answered by the Secretariat departments concerned.'

He pushed back his chair, rose rather wearily and paced the floor. He looked tired and aged more than his years.

'What impression did the Prince leave on you?' he asked abruptly.

I looked uneasily over my shoulder.

'Have no fear, Legate. There are no witnesses and no eavesdroppers. I have a reason—a loyal reason—for asking you this.'

I hesitated, and spoke carefully. 'He is young, only twenty-two years old. He has ruled for five years. He has nearly conquered Armenia and kept peace on all our other frontiers. He has reduced taxes in the provinces. At the same time he has tried to curb extravagance in Rome. He has raised the Senate's authority. The State is prosperous, reasonably peaceful and the Prince is popular. In the conduct of both foreign and home affairs he is energetic and competent.'

I looked Burrus in the eye and went on:

'With his private life and family quarrels neither I nor any other citizen should have any concern until they affect the public welfare. So far, I believe, they have not. He is a fine ruler and I am proud to serve him. Have I answered you?'

Burrus came back to his seat and poured wine in my cup.

'Yes,' he said. He sighed heavily. 'I shall speak as frankly as you have not. All you say would have been true a year ago. Now the Prince is losing interest in ruling; less arduous occupations engage his time and Agrippina rules in his name.' His face hardened. 'Seneca and I are taking steps to put that situation right.'

He checked, and smiled ruefully.

'Forgive me. Indiscretions can be dangerous even between old friends. After all these years I am still too frankly-spoken for high politics. The Prince, in fact, has said so.'

'How does all this affect me?' I said.

Burrus's smile faded.

'In this way. The Prince is no longer consistent in his actions or his policy. Lately he wished to abandon Britain; today he is set on expansion.

The slightest setback to our arms might reverse his ideas once again, which would be very serious indeed.'

'Provinces have been lost before. Legions and legates have fallen in defeat. Rome still survives,' I said.

'True. What you don't know, and nobody, I trust, knows except the Prince, Seneca, Claudius and myself, is that the whole edifice of the State is threatened, not by foreign invasion and military defeat, but by financial collapse. It means little to you, I can see. Let me show you.'

He took some coins from his girdle and rang them on the table.

'Five denarii. How much do you think they are worth?'

'Twenty sesterces, I suppose.'

'So every citizen supposes. So do all the savages within our frontiers. They're all mistaken.'

I gazed at Burrus without comprehension. He shook his head.

'That, and other matters, Claudius will explain to you. The fact is that the State is insolvent. We must obtain raw materials, gold, silver, copper and so on to restore stability. Britain has plenty. It is for you to gain control of the sources and send the ore to Rome by the wagon-load. Do you now begin to see how much depends on your strategy in Britain?'

I tried to shake off a mounting depression.

'I at least understand the consequences of failure. Britain will be abandoned, as the Prince implied in his last words to me. He didn't actually say it would be better if I did not return—'

'You thought he made a personal threat? No. The Prince is not yet vindictive outside his family circle. Now,' Burrus added briskly, 'Claudius is here and will go into these financial matters more fully. Governors are not directly concerned with revenue but access to new resources in Britain will largely govern your military operations. Claudius knows them all.'

He went to the door and called a servant. Presently the Financial Secretary entered.

4

Claudius of Smyrna greeted me respectfully, as freedman to Senator. The exalted and responsible office to which he had risen had not produced that self-importance and insolence so often exhibited by many freedmen who hold high positions in the Secretariat. He was a quiet, lean man, self-possessed, dignified and obviously competent. Two clerks, bearing documents and maps, deposited their burdens on a table, arranged them swiftly, and were dismissed. Claudius looked inquiringly at Burrus.

Burrus said, 'I have told the Legate the bare facts—nothing more. If you would now be so good as to explain the immediate steps we are taking to prevent financial collapse, and then show him where the undeveloped mineral resources of Britain lie, we shall be able to discuss ways and means.'

Claudius turned to me. 'Most noble Paulinus, you must be shocked by this sad revelation of the unsound structure for which I am responsible. The fault is not altogether mine.'

He joined his finger-tips together and continued in his precise, old-fashioned, Greek-accented Latin, like a philosopher lecturing in the schools.

'You are aware that a comparatively small number of families, among the Senators and knights, possess between them an enormous amount of money. Because many of them are exempt from normal taxation very little of this wealth is returned to the State. Much money is spent on building, on displays, games and other quite unproductive affairs. Worse still, the possession of riches has led to a demand for luxuries on a vast scale. To the millionaire nothing that is common is luxurious; to him anything obtainable in Italy is common. Therefore he sends abroad for rare merchandise and spends huge sums to decorate his person, his table and his palaces. Nearly all comes from the East: silk from Asia, spices from India, incense and rare perfumes from

Arabia. Consequently Rome's imports from the Orient are immense; she exports nothing in return. There is no barter, no trade. Everything we buy has to be paid for in cash, in silver, and an enormous drain of silver flows eastwards. This has gone on for years. Now there is a scarcity of all precious metals in the State, and their value, in the State, has consequently appreciated.'

He rustled the documents lying before him on the table.

'I have some alarming figures here, though I doubt whether they'd interest you. I thought not. Well, the situation is not altogether new. It has happened before, though not quite to such an extreme, and there are two stock methods of dealing with it. One is to reduce the weight of new-minted coinage while retaining the same face value. This, you will realize, has little initial effect on internal trade, where the enhanced value of the metal about balances the loss in weight. Externally, however, where the value of metal has remained static or even, owing to a glut, slightly depreciated, the results must be disastrous. Foreign traders are quick to realize that a denarius no longer contains a denarius' worth of silver. Obviously, to safeguard themselves from loss, they must demand higher prices, not only for luxuries, which do not matter, but for necessities: corn, oil, wine, wool. Higher prices paid by our merchants mean higher prices in the shops in Rome. The denarius will buy less; the commons will be impoverished. Poverty means unrest, riots and disturbances. Meanwhile the millionaires will grow still richer, buying at ridiculously low prices the estates of lesser men who have failed.'

Claudius paused and coughed.

'The other way is better, but much harder. It is simply to acquire more precious metal from which money can be minted and to mint more money. With your assistance, most noble Paulinus, that is what we are trying to do.'

Burrus spoke. 'Be frank, Claudius. Tell the Legate the whole story.'

The Secretary nodded and smiled thinly.

'Politics and finance are closely linked,' he said. 'I try to avoid politics and find it difficult. One never knows how much to tell. You have commanded, Prefect.'

Like Burrus a little while ago, he suddenly produced a denarius from his person and put it in my hand.

'Is not that a fine coin?' he asked.

'Freshly minted and unused,' I observed, rather puzzled. I rang it on the table. 'And perfectly good.'

Claudius took the coin and tucked it away.

'It is worth slightly under three sesterces,' he said sadly. 'There are thousands being minted now.'

'You mean—'

'Yes. This is, we hope, a short-term policy. The Prince has decided to debase the coinage in order to carry us over the next two or three difficult years until the metal starts to flow from Britain.'

There was no hint of irony in his voice. I stared at him in horror.

'Is this money going all over the world? Are my legionaries to be paid in worthless ases? How do you expect me to keep discipline when this becomes known?'

'Not quite worthless,' Claudius said deprecatingly. 'Remember also that coins take time to circulate from the mint. The bad ones may not reach Britain for years, when our finances will once more be perfectly sound and all inferior money can be redeemed.'

I gulped some wine. 'Well, the Prince has decided. We can't change that. Where are these British mines which must restore our fortunes?'

Claudius unrolled a map and spread it on the table. It showed the irregular triangle which was the island of Britain.

'All our maps of this Province date from a survey made by Aulus Plautius soon after the Conquest,' Burrus said. 'They have since been amended by successive governors. Nevertheless I suspect that in many respects they are highly inaccurate. You might find it helpful, Legate, to institute a new survey as soon as your other duties permit.'

'It shall be done,' I said. A suggestion from Burrus carried the weight of an order from Nero. I bent over the map, a replica of others I had studied during the past week. Claudius's bony finger stabbed at the south-eastern corner of the triangle.

'You will know, most noble Paulinus, the mineral resources which are already the Prince's property. Here, south of London, in almost impenetrable forest, is much iron.' His finger moved across the map and rested south of the Severn estuary. 'Here is lead in quantity, but with a low silver content.' The finger travelled to the south-western tip. 'Here is tin. We don't really control these mines. This peninsula has never been conquered; the natives are warlike and independent; there are no roads. But these mines have long been famous and the tribal owners have traded for centuries with peoples from the Middle Sea. We have no monopoly, though they sell us their tin willingly; the traffic is all sea-borne and open to merchants from the whole world.'

'Iron, lead, tin,' I said. 'Useful but not exciting. Are all these mines being worked to full capacity?'

'The output of iron and lead has been dropping slowly but steadily for the last three years,' Claudius answered gravely. 'This is not due to exhaustion of the ore. Britain has been at peace, and peace doesn't produce prisoners for work in the mines. The death-rate is high; replacements have not kept pace with wastage although slaves have been imported from the German frontiers. My last report from the Procurator in Britain showed a deficiency of some five thousand workers in the mines under his control. Your predecessor, the most noble Veranius Nepos, had recourse to forced labour, which I understand caused considerable unrest among the provincials.'

Burrus nodded. 'The Belgae in the west threatened a revolt, which was uncomfortably close to our usual war going on against the Silures, so he revoked the decree. The Procurator was furious.'

Claudius went on, 'In short, the Prince's mines in Britain are not in full production owing to lack of labour. The other known sources, with one exception, are beyond our frontiers to the west and lie between the small island of Anglesey, here, and the Severn estuary. In Anglesey is copper. On the mainland east of Anglesey is more copper, and lead. Just beyond Wroxeter, to the west, is copper and lead. On the northern coast of the Severn estuary is iron.'

His finger wandered indeterminately over the country of the Silures and settled on its northern borders.

'And here is gold.'

I was surprised. 'We have all heard rumours of gold in Britain. No one, to my knowledge, has found any.'

'Gold is there,' Claudius said firmly. 'The deposits, so we believe, are small and don't compare in value with the potential yield from copper and lead farther north. The gold-mines, by themselves, are not worth a campaign.'

He stammered, obviously regretting a statement which verged on affairs outside his department, and bowed to Burrus.

'I beg your forgiveness, Prefect. I merely repeat an opinion you have expressed.'

Burrus tapped the map. 'Go on, Claudius.'

The freedman bent again over the sheet. 'Here, most noble Paulinus, are the richest lead mines known in Britain.' His finger rested between Lincoln and Wroxeter. 'They lie in this middle land, thickly forested, upland country, where our frontiers are vague, around a village called Anavio in the territory of the Cornovii. Unfortunately they are also claimed by a much more powerful, neighbouring kingdom known as Brigantia. Both the Cornovii and Brigantes are friendly towards us; the dispute is purely inter-tribal. We have leased some of the workings and a trickle of ore comes into the Province. The problem in this case, so I understand, is a political one: how to get possession of the lead-mines of Anavio without, at this stage, becoming involved in war against the Brigantes.'

Claudius leaned back. 'I hope I have made myself clear. Are there any questions which you would address to me, most noble Paulinus?'

'Only one,' I answered. 'With the State apparently tottering on the edge of economic chaos, how is it that only one small Province is to be drained of its wealth to restore the situation? Are the governors in Spain, Gaul, Africa, Pannonia and the rest receiving similar instructions?'

'A good point, but a political one. Perhaps you, Prefect—?'

Burrus rubbed his chin. 'Here is the answer, Legate. The Prince is determined that peace shall generally prevail in his provinces. He realizes that his policy in Britain will undoubtedly mean war. This he is prepared to accept providing his remaining provinces are quiet, which would not be the case if all the governors, like you, were to harass the provincials in search of precious metals. We already have a war on our hands in Armenia. If we are to have another let it be as far away as possible, in Britain.'

Burrus paused, frowned and picked his words carefully. 'You heard the Prince say he was once prepared to abandon Britain. The plan may still be in his mind and might easily be executed if the Province goes on losing money. The Prince, as the people's trustee and administrator of Rome and all her possessions, is bound to see his responsibilities largely through an accountant's eyes: a thing is either an asset or a liability. Britain, at the moment, is a definite liability.'

He hesitated, glanced sideways at Claudius and continued:

'He does not, if I may say so, quite appreciate the loss of prestige involved in leaving Britain. Although no military reverse had occurred the public would believe only that our troops had failed to hold the country. The reputations of the legions concerned would suffer and much discontent be engendered in the army generally. If the Prince has a fault, it is that he is not always entirely sympathetic with the military point of view. Do you not agree with me, Claudius?'

'Entirely, my dear Prefect.' Claudius rose. 'I have said all I had to say, most noble Paulinus. You will now doubtless wish to discuss strategical and political matters; of which, happily, I am entirely ignorant. I have your permission?'

5

I spent all next day at the Secretariat, part of the time with Burrus and part with his secretaries, delving into confidential records and dispatches dealing with our own and tribal forces and military administration in Britain. Much of this information I would normally have obtained from my predecessor, but Veranius Nepos was dead. Scapula's seven-year-old dispatches were most interesting. I regretted that he, too, had died in Britain; a talk with him would have been very helpful, for besides dealing with the Brigantes he had started an advance towards Anglesey. Both these were projects which I would have to undertake.

The documents made quite plain that the most troublesome opponents on our western frontier were the Silures. II Legion from the fortress of Gloucester barely held them in check and the whole area was the scene of constant raids and skirmishes. Until this turbulent tribe was either pacified or destroyed we could not safely start any operations in the north, towards Anglesey, where Scapula had already soundly beaten the Degeangli, one of my future enemies, who seemed to have little aptitude for war.

The independent kingdom of Brigantia hovered on the right flank of the Anglesey operation. Scapula, years before, had taken advantage of internal dissension within the realm to march in with a legion and re-establish the ruler, a queen called Cartimandua, firmly on her throne, thus securing a friendly power on his flank. The Brigantes were still amicable; but I remembered uneasily the business of the Anavio lead-mines and hoped that my political negotiations in that connection would not antagonize the tribe. Our intelligence reports showed the Brigantes to be a large, powerful and warlike race, the strongest of our potential enemies in Britain. Expansion of the Province was inevitable; sooner or later they must come into conflict with us. That moment lay in the future, beyond the scope of my directive.

No other tribes on the western or northern frontiers were likely to worry us. One theme which recurred throughout all these dispatches, from the Conquest onwards, was the inability or unwillingness of the various tribes to unite against a common foe. While the records of the Divine Julius's campaigns in Gaul show alliance after alliance formed against him, the nations of Britain, many of them akin to the Gauls, have never combined against Rome since the brief union of the Atrebates, Cantii, Catuvellauni and Trinovantes during Aulus Plautius's invasion. We have, needless to say, steadily exploited this peculiar British failing; one of the primary rules of successive governors has been to avoid any action, military or political, which might lead to a tribal federation.

The Order of Battle gave particulars of the weapon which I must wield in the struggle to restore the State's economic equilibrium. The striking force consisted of four legions, two at Wroxeter, one at Gloucester, one at Lincoln. Supporting these were the auxiliary forces: nine cavalry regiments, nine mixed cohorts and twelve infantry cohorts. This, on paper, made a total of twenty-two thousand legionaries and seventeen thousand auxiliaries. My own experience, confirmed by Burrus's wry look when I added up the figures, deduced that all the legions and most auxiliary units were under strength.

The unit confidential reports were rather discouraging. The discipline of the legions, except XIV Gemina, was indifferent. II Legion's morale was low; endless buffetings from the Silures had followed a straightforward defeat in the field seven years ago; the legion thereafter had never recovered complete ascendancy over the enemy. In XX Valeria there was friction between centurions and soldiers: this was a not uncommon occurrence, due to a well-known cause, that could only happen when a legion's legate was weak and her tribunes inefficient. The tough and vigorous commander of IX Hispana, in the absence of an enemy to absorb his energies, was driving his legion hard; the men apparently resented his interference with their peacetime routine.

The auxiliary regiments and cohorts, on the whole, seemed efficient; although the location chart displayed a remarkably haphazard distribution of troops both in fortresses and along lines of communication. Troop movements during Scapula's campaigns had upset the proper strategical dispositions and his successors, Gallus and Nepos, had failed to restore them.

Towards evening Burrus entered the office where I was immersed in papers and led me to another room, sparsely furnished with table and chairs. He closed the shutters of the single window and locked the door.

'The Prince has agreed you should be given highly secret information,' he said briefly. 'I needn't say this must go no further.'

I seated myself and prepared to listen.

6

'It's rather involved,' Burrus began. He spread out the map of Britain. 'Here, in this bulge above the Thames estuary, north of our colony at Colchester, lives a tribe called the Iceni. They have been allowed to retain their own ruler and run their own affairs and we have no military posts in their territory. Their king, Prasutagus, is old, extremely rich and has no male heir. He has made the usual will, leaving half his possessions to the Prince and hoping thereby that when he dies his successor will be left undisturbed in his inheritance and will continue to rule the Iceni as an independent, allied kingdom.'

Burrus flicked the map. 'As adviser to the Prince on military strategy I have other views. Icenia flanks one of our main lines of communication, the North Way from London to Lincoln. Moreover, with most of our field army stationed in the west, it is dangerous to suffer the existence of a wealthy, numerous tribe, completely free from any military or governmental control, so far in our rear. The Iceni must be brought under our dominion.'

'Have they ever caused trouble?' I asked.

'Yes, they have. Five years after the Conquest Ostorius Scapula ordered the complete disarmament of all tribes living in the settled areas. The Iceni pretended that this showed a lack of faith in their loyalty and, under this same Prasutagus, defied us and shut themselves in a hill-fort. Scapula's auxiliaries stormed and took the place without difficulty. The extraordinary thing was that though we then had every excuse to bring the Iceni under the Provincial Government's direct rule it wasn't done, and Prasutagus was allowed to retain his throne and the State its independence.'

Burrus sighed and shook his head. 'Odd things sometimes happened under the Divine Claudius. However, Prasutagus has given us no anxiety since.'

'The Prince has now decided to annex the kingdom?' I asked.

'Yes. Prasutagus is old, in poor health and his heirs are female. He may die any day. When he does we shall absorb the realm into the Province on the grounds that we do not recognize women rulers.'

'We recognize Cartimandua of the Brigantes,' I interjected.

Burrus waved an impatient hand. 'Surely you don't expect consistency in politics, Legate? Anyway, Cartimandua has a husband living, though in exile. Her situation is entirely different, and her tribe is far more formidable than the Iceni. But her time will come.'

He paused in thought and fiddled absently with a map.

'The reasons for Icenia's annexation are largely financial. We want Prasutagus's entire estate, not only half. And we intend to recover the Claudian grants.'

'What are they?'

'Soon after the Conquest the Divine Claudius made enormous money grants to certain tribes to gain their allegiance, to help build decent towns and generally civilize themselves. They were definitely grants but we intend, in the case of the Iceni, to treat them as loans and call them in when the kingdom is annexed.' Burrus tapped the table emphatically. 'The sum at stake isn't pocket-money. The Financial Secretary has calculated that recovery of the grants, plus Prasutagus's estate, will wipe out the expected deficit on the Province for the current financial year.'

'Will the Iceni submit?' I said. 'You annex the kingdom, seize the whole of the king's personal fortune and call in loans which the people understand to be gifts. Are these Iceni sheep who will merely bleat when they are sheared?'

'Far from it. They will inevitably revolt. That is why, when the time comes, you must be ready with sufficient troops near their borders to quell the rebellion instantly and, above all, prevent it spreading to other tribes.'

'The business must be carefully timed, then,' I said. 'My chief mission in Britain is to get control of mines beyond the western frontier. I cannot have a revolt in the east while my legions are fighting in Anglesey.'

Burrus answered, 'Exactly. The ideal would be to move against the Iceni directly Prasutagus dies. But should that happen when you are engaged in the west we in Rome will wait until your operations are ended, your forces regrouped and you send word that you are ready.'

I scratched an old wound on my ankle, a relic of Mauretania.

'You will have to keep this scheme very quiet,' I grumbled. 'If so much as a whisper gets to Britain—'

'Quite so,' Burrus interrupted. 'There are only four people who know of it: the Prince, yourself, myself and Claudius of Smyrna. Seneca doesn't know.'

'Seneca? Why not?'

Burrus raised his hand.

'Not so loud, Legate. These affairs can be dangerous.'

He walked to the door, twitched the hangings and came back. He said quietly, 'Seneca, too, has over forty million sesterces of his own invested in Britain, loaned to the provincials at high rates of interest, mostly to the Iceni.'

I gasped. 'Seneca, the Prince's Secretary of State! Unbelievable!'

Burrus smiled grimly. 'Yet perfectly true, Legate. Our moral philosopher is not quite so scrupulous as he appears. Nor, for that matter, are many other highly-respected men in Rome. But you see why we must conceal the plan from him?'

'Plainly enough. If he knew, he would immediately call in his loans. Not only would the Treasury be so much the poorer when the State foreclosed on the Iceni, but the refunding of such a vast capital sum might easily cause poverty and unrest all over Britain.'

Burrus stood. 'Secrecy, then, is absolutely essential. Remember that a banker of Seneca's stature has spies and agents throughout every province where he operates. Another point: the Procurator of Britain, Decianus Catus, owes his appointment to Seneca's influence and is probably his chief spy in the Province. The financial squeeze of the Iceni, when ordered, will be entirely in his hands. If he gets so much as a hint beforehand he will tell Seneca. Of that I have no doubt. But if we move without warning, Catus, as a government servant, will be compelled to collect debts due to the State before handling the affairs of private creditors, however eminent.'

'What sort of man is this Catus?'

'I have never met him. From secret reports I gather you won't like him. A self-important knight, high-handed, self-seeking, not very efficient. You have no jurisdiction over him in fiscal matters; he deals, through the Finance Ministry, directly with the Prince.'

'And sends Nero all sorts of other miscellaneous information, if I know anything of Procurators,' I growled.

'Of course.' Burrus grimaced sourly. 'You soldiers don't appreciate the workings of government. Catus's agents will certainly be watching you; he will report on your actions, as he sees them, to Nero; just as you will report on his. In this way the Prince has a double check on the two chief officers in all his Provinces. The men concerned know it; the provincials know it; so the Provinces are, on the whole, very well administered.'

He yawned and stretched. 'I'm used to it; I have been in the Secretariat so long I've almost ceased to be a soldier. The twisted machinations of politics stopped surprising me years ago.' He took my arm. 'Let's leave this dusty office. Will you sup with me tonight?'

Burrus saw me to my litter.

'There is nothing more I can tell you, Legate,' were his final words. 'You have seen every relevant document, dispatch and map. Nothing, however secret, has been concealed from you. I have given you all the knowledge of Britain that Rome possesses. I hope the island won't turn out very different from our conception of it.'

'Everything is different a thousand miles from Rome,' I said. 'But nothing in Britain seems very terrible except the climate.' I looked round; our attendants were out of earshot. 'Tell me, Burrus: why did the Prince choose me for this post?'

'He didn't,' said Burrus shortly. 'I did. You have been given a difficult Province and dangerous, delicate work to do. Only the best of our military talent is equal to it. The choice obviously lay between you and Corbulo; Corbulo is busy in Armenia. You are our foremost expert on mountain warfare since you made your reputation in the Atlas Mountains sixteen years ago; your British campaigns will be fought in mountainous country. The Prince likes you and respects your ability; he will therefore continue to support you even if things go wrong. Let's hope that will not happen.'

I clasped his hand and laughed. 'I thank you for an answer that is frank and without blandishment. Have you ever flattered anyone, Burrus?'

'Never, Legate. Farewell.'

'Farewell, Burrus.'

He turned and climbed the steps. I had refused his invitation to dinner; I never saw him again.

7

Ten days later I left Rome with sixteen tribunes, three secretaries, a score of freedmen, a hundred slaves and fifty baggage-carts. The Prince accorded me the unprecedented honour of a Praetorian century as escort on the first stage of my journey along the Clodian Way. The future was bright with promise.

2

'No government is safe unless it is fortified by goodwill.'
CORNELIUS NEPOS

1

We sailed from Boulogne on a windy day a fortnight before the Saturnalia. I embarked in the Fleet Commandant's flagship, and three transports, escorted by longships of the British Fleet, carried my retinue and baggage. I was thus technically afoot in my new Province, for the fleet was part of my military command. A vast ignorance of maritime affairs made me prefer this pitching, narrow warship to the steadier and far more comfortable merchantmen: I wished to study at close quarters the working of a ship of war.

The effort was wasted.

For seven hours I endured torment while the ship twisted and plunged like an unbacked horse, her sails reefed so that she should not outpace the slower transports. The other warships, hulls and sails painted blue-grey to harmonize with their background, were hardly visible behind the driving sleet-squalls. Drenched, shivering and sick, I sought refuge in an exiguous basketwork shelter on the poop.

The convoy moored at Richborough late in the afternoon and with the cessation of movement my sickness quickly passed. But I still felt weak and ill, in no condition to face the crowded wharves and the rigours of an official reception. I told the Fleet Commandant, Aufidius Pantera, to inform those concerned that all ceremonial must be postponed to the following morning. Then, in the wintry murk of a December dusk, I went ashore.

An elderly prefect of auxiliaries, a promoted centurion, commanded Richborough: I was quartered in a part of his house reserved for visiting officials. Warm wine, dry clothes and a little plain food so restored my health that I sent for Pantera and plunged into a brisk discussion of his command, the fleet that guarded the shores of Britain.

He confirmed the catalogue of ships that I had already studied in Rome: one trireme—a ceremonial vessel that put to sea only in a flat calm—thirty biremes, fifty single-banked pinnaces, twenty reconnaissance cutters, seven fleet transports and various small harbour craft. All were based on Boulogne, with a repair depot at Richborough.

I asked a question which had found no satisfactory answer in the Military Secretariat: 'Why is the British Fleet based on the coast of Gaul?'

Pantera shrugged. 'It always has been,' he said, 'since the Conquest. I suppose in the early days, before the land was pacified, to commit the fleet to a station on this side would have been risky. No one afterwards has bothered to make a change.'

'Has Boulogne any particular advantages?'

'Recruiting,' he said. 'I have a backbone of Middle Sea captains and navigators but most of my personnel come from the seafaring folk along the Gallic coast. We are not restricted to citizens, as you are in the legions.'

'The Britons do not make good sailors?'

'Fair. I've enlisted some Cantii from Richborough.'

I considered this. I had known, of course, that the fleet had its headquarters outside the Province. To my mind this was unsound. The twenty miles of sea between Gaul and Britain could, in bad weather, separate me from my warships as effectively as though they were in the Euxine. The fleet should operate from this coast unless there were strong contrary reasons. If seamen were the only problem then it was time the Britons learned to man their own ships.

'Would you have serious objections to transferring your base to Britain?' I asked.

'None at all,' Pantera said at once. 'There are as good harbours this side as the other: Richborough, London, Portus. I should prefer it. We're always having difficulties over supplies of timber, pitch, canvas and cordage in Boulogne. The Government of Belgica resents having to provide them, and the harbour officials can be very cantankerous.'

'Good. I shall refer the matter to Rome. In the meantime you can reconnoitre this coast for a suitable base.'

He smiled. 'I don't need to, Legate. We have to be situated opposite Gaul: most of our work lies in this area. Richborough is my choice.'

'That may be so,' I said. 'It won't do any harm to look further and make absolutely certain. I shall expect your report within a month. Now, what exactly is your work?'

'During winter, when the weather allows, we escort and transport Government stores and officials between Richborough or London and Boulogne. Ships seldom venture a longer passage. In the summer we have escort duties farther afield: tin transports from Exeter, iron and lead convoys from Pevensey and Portus; and routine cruises north to the Wash, west to the Lizard.'

'Are you ever attacked?'

Pantera nodded. 'Sometimes. There are a few pirates left, mostly operating from the Irish and Frisian coasts. It rarely happens. Our escorts are more in the nature of insurance against shipwreck than piracy.'

I remembered the role I had provisionally allotted to the British Fleet in my plans for the Ordovician campaign: tasks for which this harbour-bound, summer-cruising collection of warships without war experience seemed hardly fitted.

'Do you know anything of the seas between Ireland and Britain?' I asked abruptly.

'I once took a flotilla round Land's End and up the Severn estuary to Gloucester,' Pantera said, not without pride.

'No farther north? Well, your voyages in the future are going to be more extensive. Have you charts or maps of this island?'

He gave orders to an attendant, who returned in a little while with an armful of rolled papers.

'The Government insists on issuing us with official maps. We never use them; they are inaccurate and quite useless. Here is a chart of the sea enclosed by Britain and Spain, with Ireland lying midway between.' He unrolled a great sheet which nearly covered the floor.

I examined the map. The Commandant's strictures were justified; it was old, roughly-traced and bore little resemblance to the up-to-date, detailed drawings given to me by the Secretariat in Rome.

'When the winter gales have abated you will make yourself and your captains thoroughly acquainted with the western seas and coasts up to and immediately north of this island, Anglesey.' I followed the coastline with my finger. 'I shall want, in particular, a reconnaissance of the straits between Anglesey and the mainland. You'd better make your cruises in strength; we don't know what hostile ships, even fleets, may frequent these waters.'

The Commandant sat up, his face eager. 'That's livelier work than convoy-escorts. You shall have your report, even if we have to fight every pirate in the western seas. Am I allowed to know the reason for these instructions?'

'Not yet. And,' I added dourly, 'you are not to start a sea war in the process. Fight only if you must: the fleet must remain intact for more important work. This is only a warning order; you will receive full written instructions before the spring.'

'Very well, Legate.'

I rose, hitched my cloak about my shoulders and walked with Pantera to the courtyard. The wind raged in a black void. A few lights glimmered weakly near the wharves.

'I shall sleep well tonight,' I said. 'Sea voyages are a tiring pastime. Farewell, Pantera. My thanks for a safe crossing.'

2

The wind dropped at dawn and the rain dwindled to a light drizzle that beaded the cloaks of a cavalry troop and half-century drawn up on the dockside. A mounted tribune called the men to attention.

'Your bodyguard, Legate, reporting for escort duty,' he announced.

I returned his salute and walked down the ranks. A bit was badly adjusted; reins were cracked and worn; mud-smears stained a horse's shoulder.

'Why this, tribune?' I said, pointing to the dirt.

He looked surprised. 'It rained all night, Legate. The standings in the camp are waterlogged.'

'Which is why you should take extra care to clean arms and equipment before this parade. Look at that!' I pointed to a rust-pitted lance. 'Did that happen in a night?'

I passed slowly down the ranks, making no further comment. Nearly every man, and every horse, showed signs of a slack inefficiency intolerable even among auxiliaries. The half-century was little better, though its legionary training reflected a somewhat smarter turnout. The men themselves seemed either old or very young; their physique barely reached army standards. A suspicion regarding the composition of this force formed in my mind as I finished the inspection.

'What is the total strength of the bodyguard?' I asked the tribune.

'One troop and one century. The other half-century is on guard duties at your palaces in London and Colchester.'

'From what units are they seconded?'

'From no special units, Legate. Vacancies are filled by application to legions and regiments in turn.'

'Are there any stipulations as to length of service, character, skill-at-arms?'

'None that I know of, Legate.' The tribune shifted unhappily. 'I have only lately taken over command. I shall make certain that you have no cause for complaint in future.'

'You are a Half-Year tribune, presumably?'

'I am.'

'In that case you won't have very much time to show results. And I suppose your predecessor was also a Half-Year man? It explains a great deal. Are the wagons ready to march? Let us start.'

I strode through custom sheds to the road where the baggage-train and my companions of the long journey through Gaul waited by the roadside in the rain. The tribune left his horse and fussily conducted me to a curtained litter borne by eight Gallic slaves. I snarled at him:

'Do you think the climate of Britain has already so weakened me that I'm unable to ride? Where is my horse?'

My freedman head-groom produced my charger saddled and ready. The man failed to conceal a grin: I guessed he had tried to persuade the tribune that I loathed being carried, and received a rating for his presumption.

I trotted on, the troop clattering behind. Richborough presented the sad aspect of a deserted cantonment. Seventeen years ago the place had been our invasion base, holding reinforcements and supplies in vast quantities while the campaign progressed. Long lines of wooden huts had housed the legions; great warehouses, looming above the huts like forlorn citadels, had held their stores. Now they were empty and dilapidated, rotted by the rain, frost and pale sunlight of this inclement island. Only at the docks were the buildings in good repair; here the custom sheds and offices, the harbour-master's quarters and a shrunken reinforcement camp flanked the yards of the fleet's repair depot. The masts of our flotilla showed above the roofs. At this season sea-borne traffic with the Continent nearly ceased; in the summer most heavy merchandise was shipped straight to London to save the delay and expense of the road journey which we were now making.

From sea to sea across the neck of the peninsula stretched a bank, stockade and ditch, crumbling and sagging into ruin. We passed through a deserted gatehouse, crossed a narrow causeway; the road to London lanced far into the distance across a dark landscape oppressed by grey clouds. The rain ceased and the cold strengthened, biting through cloak and leather corselet. I pondered gloomily over my reception. No person of note, Roman or Briton, had welcomed me at the port, though news of my coming had been sent from Boulogne six days before we left. The pomposity of official welcomes can be abominably tedious, yet this total lack of ceremony was at least unusual. Only one tribune and his ragged command had so far recognized my arrival.

Something would have to be done about the bodyguard. It was clear that that unit, in Britain, was a refuse-bin for the unwanted nuisances of all the legions and cavalry regiments in the Province: a convenient receptacle wherein commanders could dump bad or useless men. A dull existence in provincial capitals far from the frontiers, with endless guard duties and processional escorts, was not the kind of life likely to appeal to an ambitious soldier. For the same reason the command was entrusted to Half-Year tribunes, who naturally gravitated to headquarters duties during their short appointments. I rubbed the chill from my cheekbones and cogitated on reforms. My bodyguard must become a crack corps, after the style of the Praetorians in Rome, though not—the Gods forbid!—with any corresponding political attachments. The establishment was too small. How long ago, I wondered, and under what Prince's edict, had it been formulated? I mentally drafted a new establishment on the basis of a mixed cohort of three troops and four centuries. It was a considerable expansion. Would Nero agree?

Entertained by these reflections I jogged through the desolate countryside, passing occasional groups of round, thatched huts and herdsmen guarding cattle. About midday we approached a large village called Canterbury, the capital of the Cantii. Timbered houses lorded it among the huts, and a small temple and a disproportionately large town hall, built after the Roman fashion, gave the place a seedily consequential air. My arrival was expected. People crowded the roadside; a venerable Briton, the senior magistrate, declaimed a welcoming speech in surprisingly good Latin to which I made a suitably gracious reply.

When we had left Canterbury behind I called the tribune.

'That, I understand, is the tribal seat of the Cantii, their most important town. I saw the remains of an old ditch and bank, obviously pre-Conquest. Why are there no modern defences?'

'None of the towns behind the frontiers is defended, Legate,' he said. He saw my surprise and added, 'I believe it is official policy, to show the natives that they need fear no raids from their countrymen while living under our protection.'

'I am aware of the official policy,' I said testily. Nevertheless this was a new aspect of our government. In Gaul, no less peaceful than Britain, ditch and stockade surrounded every town; palisades protected the meanest villages. Were the conquered tribes of Britain so utterly subdued, so completely trustworthy, that revolt was unthinkable? To encourage amity among the tribes was sensible enough; to hazard our security in the effort seemed overconfident. I could hardly believe that London, Verulam, Colchester, where thousands of Romans lived, were entirely without defences.

We reached Rochester at dusk, chilled and tired. The Government rest-house was passably clean and warm and provided a decent meal. The baggage-train was far behind, halting for the night at Canterbury, but pack-horses carried bedding for myself and my retinue. Though the rooms were crowded my second night on British soil was not uncomfortable.

We marched at dawn, moving high enough on the skirts of downland to catch a glimpse of the Thames estuary far away on the right. Then the road dropped into flat valley-lands and ran on a high causeway across mudflats and ice-hazed marshland. When a brief rise brought the river into view again we saw the roofs of London swarming on the far bank.

3

A great concourse blocked the approach to London Bridge. In front, seated awkwardly on a restive horse, a rotund, red-faced Roman saluted and announced himself as the Procurator of Britain.

'Well met, Decianus Catus,' I said.

'My greetings, Legate. Welcome to the Province. The council and magistrates of London are here to do you honour.' He waved a hand at the assembly behind.

'I am glad to see them. I had begun to fear that my arrival had passed entirely unnoticed.'

'The Province's custom,' he replied rather stiffly, 'is to receive her Governors officially in London. Richborough is somewhat remote and the facilities there are not suitable for ceremonial functions.'

This stilted language was typical of a petty official and the pompous delivery betrayed an over-sufficient self-importance. Burrus had been right.

I composed my features to a proper expression of benign interest. 'Well, better late than never. You may present the councillors of London.'

There were speeches, introductions, well-wishing and some priestly invocations before we could proceed. Then we rattled across the wooden bridge; Catus, having thankfully abandoned his horse, rode in a litter at my side. I followed the six lictors, inwardly cursing myself for failing to foresee this procession. My horse, cloak and clothing were stained and splashed with mud: all could have been cleaned, and myself and my escort put to rights, in a brief halt a mile from the bridge. The spectators, happily, ignored my travel-stained appearance and cheered me heartily into the town.

Catus accompanied me to the Governor's palace, a huge red-brick agglomeration set in a clearing, as it were, amid the timbered, grass-thatched hovels which formed the bulk of London's buildings. There he left, assuring me that all was ready for my comfort, promising to wait upon me at dawn next day. Certainly nothing was wanting: I found a competent staff of servants, good baths and excellent food. The house was even warm.

My first governmental action was to summon the Provincial Council to a meeting at Colchester in two months' time. The Council represented all the tribes in the Province, with an elected president who assumed the title of Pontiff of Britain in recognition that the Council's primary object was to encourage the official Roman religion. To this assembly I would have to announce my edict on taking office.

The drafting of this edict took considerable time and gave my staff much file-hunting for precedents and forms. It was based, of course, on the Provincial Law, a code formulated after the Conquest by Aulus Plautius, approved by the Divine Claudius and periodically supplemented to accord with current practices. The terms of the edict bound me closely during my period of office. Much of it was merely a repetition and affirmation of the Provincial Law. Another part, by custom, dealt with town finances and moneylenders' rates of interest, and on this I took Catus's advice, who recommended that rates for private usury should be raised in order to encourage provincials to borrow from Government funds at lower interest. A third section covered points of private law concerning such matters as inheritance, bankruptcy and deeds of sale: my legal secretaries delved into the books and prepared a draft which needed little correction.

The only ticklish part of the edict concerned the provision of corn during my tenure of office. We requisitioned corn from everywhere in the Province to feed the army and civil service. Rates of payment, based on the current average corn prices throughout Rome's dominions, were fixed in Rome and not by me in Britain. If this price were above the local market rate everyone was happy and I was entitled to pouch the difference; but if below, the provincial farmers naturally had good reasons for discontent. I found Rome's price had lately dropped well below that which prevailed in British markets. Here was a possible source of trouble; a piece of grit whose friction might cause a spark to flare in the settled areas. The thought displeased me and I again consulted Catus.

'You cannot alter the Government price, Legate,' he said comfortably. 'It has been tried—by Gallus, I fancy. The Prince's reply is in the records: as smart a rap over the knuckles as any Governor could wish for.'

'But how do the farmers react? Surely this leads to all sorts of evasion: concealment of stocks, short planting, illegal smuggling of grain to other markets and so on?'

Catus grinned. 'You underrate my agents, Legate. While the town councillors are responsible for grain collection from town demesnelands, and tribal chiefs for other areas, we do not necessarily accept their assessment of the annual yield. My men know to a bushel what every arable field in the Province should produce, and take pains to keep their information up to date.'

'So you expect no complaints?'

He shrugged. 'Rome's price fell below the market rate only three months ago, too late to affect the last harvest. The Britons will grumble—they always do—but they'll produce the corn. They have no choice.'

'I don't want insurrections in the settled areas, Catus,' I said with emphasis. 'Any fighting in this Province must be confined to the frontiers.'

His watery blue eyes opened wide in surprise. 'Fighting? Why, Legate, the natives would never dream of rebellion! They have become quite civilized under our influence and, besides, they're a spineless lot.'

I remembered Vespasian's estimate of the Britons, and his warning, and looked at this fat knight with distaste. 'You should be careful about compulsion, Catus. I'll not be able to spare troops to extract corn from recalcitrant peasants, nor to kill them should they become violent.'

'That won't be necessary.' He oozed self-confidence. 'We have methods of persuading difficult farmers. For instance, let's suppose that you, a Briton, farm a few fields near Canterbury. Normally you would deliver your requisitioned corn to Richborough, or possibly London. Then I offer you less than market rates. You refuse to sell and, after some argument, I agree to pay market rates and order you to deliver the corn to, shall we say, the legion at Gloucester. Wouldn't you rather accept my price than have to travel the breadth of Britain to fulfil your contract?'

I moved impatiently. 'That is merely another method of coercion. Is there no better way of avoiding hardship to the provincials and possible trouble for us?'

'There is,' Catus said thoughtfully. His eyelids flickered. 'It is said, Legate, that you are a man of considerable personal fortune. You might be able to afford to pay, yourself, the difference between the two rates. That, at least, would keep the natives happy.'

I stiffened in anger. The trap was obvious and crudely set. 'Thank you, Catus. I don't wish it said, in Rome, that I am bribing my way into favour with the provincials. The Prince might misunderstand my motives.'

I got to my feet, really furious that this little vulgarian, so early in our relations, should try to snare me in his gutter politics. What a letter he would have written to Nero had I been idiot enough to agree to his proposal! Now he saw my rage and waddled after me, disclaiming and apologizing. I interrupted with cold thanks for his advice and a colder farewell.

He flushed a deeper crimson and snapped like a cornered fox. 'If you really want to remove a grievance, Legate, I suggest you examine the methods of your own department. It's common knowledge that the legions and auxiliaries use false grain-measures to weigh the requisitioned corn on delivery. Barefaced robbery, Legate, by your soldiers!'

'If that is true, Catus, I shall correct it,' I said stonily. 'Farewell.'

4

Before leaving London I wrote three letters, each to a different addressee, which were my first dispatches to Rome. The first, to the Prince, contained a detailed report on confidential matters affecting policy, and requests for decrees in cases that were either beyond my powers or for which precedents were lacking. The second, to the Secretariat controlled by Burrus, dealt with routine administration concerning strength—returns, equipment, pay and promotions in the army and fleet. The third was a situation report addressed to the Senate. The letter to Nero I drafted myself and wrote in my own hand; secretaries prepared the others. I took this opportunity of pointing out the paucity and incompetence of the Governor's bodyguard in Britain and asked Nero's permission to disband the existing formation and recruit afresh on a mixed cohort basis. I also requested approval of my plans for shifting the fleet base from Boulogne.

Then, summarily postponing petitions and lawsuits, I left for Colchester.

Members of the Provincial Council began to arrive from the nearest tribes, each with his retinue of advisers and supporters. Some lodged in the Government rest-house; others were guests of Trinovantan nobles; and men of exceptionally high standing, like Cogidumnus, King of the Regni, set up their own pavilions on the fields outside the town. I received each one in audience, tried to estimate his character and ability and, at the same time, exerted all my charm to make a favourable impression. The smooth working of my government depended largely on the goodwill of the Council: it had Rome's authority to appoint inquisitors to investigate complaints against me and could, if so minded, instigate a formal prosecution leading to a trial before the Roman Senate. Such cases were not uncommon, as I had pointed out to Vespasian. So far the Council of Britain seemed to have approved of their Governors and I had no intention of becoming the first exception.

I adjudicated in several lawsuits, none of any interest, and then, suddenly sick of the dreary atmosphere of courts and offices, decided to pay a flying visit to Lincoln, the nearest legionary fortress. Accompanied only by three tribunes, a secretary, the freedman chamberlain of my household and a few slaves, all mounted, with pack-horses carrying rations and spare clothing and escorted by my ragged troop of bodyguard cavalry I pounded up the North Way at a fair speed, sleeping at three road stations on the route and arriving at Lincoln on the morning of the fourth day. The great fortress stood on a slight eminence, looking, under lowering clouds, like some dark, squat monster of British fable returned from the dawn of time. The four-square rampart, each side a quarter-mile long, rose steeply from a stupendous ditch to a stockaded crown, twice a man's height, made of oak trunks hewn from the forests. Along this the watch-towers straddled at regular intervals; between them loomed earth platforms mounting ballistae and catapults, whose stark timbers reared skywards like questing fingers.

I had sent a dispatch rider ahead to warn Quintus Petillius Cerialis, legate of IX Legion Hispana, of my arrival; I did not wish him to think I was trying to catch him unaware. He received me at the gate, led me straight to a well-appointed bath-house and provided an excellent meal. Afterwards, clean and refreshed, I went with him to the parade ground outside the stockade to inspect his command.

Besides the legion, Lincoln's garrison comprised three cavalry regiments and four infantry cohorts. The total strength, legionaries and auxiliaries, was just over nine thousand men. Except for a mixed detachment a thousand strong, sweeping the countryside to the north on a routine patrol, all the men were on parade. I spent an interesting afternoon watching the drills and exercises and was pleased with what I saw. It was clear that the soldiers under Cerialis could use their weapons, knew their battle-drill and were physically fit. I could see no signs of the discontent indicated in Burrus's intelligence reports, but when I congratulated the legate in his quarters that evening he mentioned the matter himself.

'The men are efficient enough,' he said moodily, unbuckling his sword and throwing it to a servant. 'They ought to be after all these months of concentrated training. Now they're beginning to get stale. What's the use of keeping your javelins sharp if you never use them?'

'Tell me your troubles, Cerialis,' I said gently. 'I know a little about this and perhaps could help you.'

Cerialis sat down, elbows on knees, hands clenched, the muscles on his forearms rippling like angry snakes. 'A year ago,' he said, 'I put into practice a training programme for this garrison far more strenuous than is customary in the service. You can imagine just how tough it was. The men responded because I told them that when they measured up to my standards they would see action. They are now, at a guess, the best-trained force in Britain, and have been so for months.'

He paused and stared into the brazier.

'But operations in Britain have ceased; the situation on all frontiers is static; and you have been forbidden to probe far into tribal territory?' I said.

'Yes!' he shouted. 'Not only that, but my patrolling range has been steadily reduced. I suppose the Government is afraid the sight of a Roman soldier might hurt the natives' feelings.'

'There is a policy behind all this, Cerialis.'

'Is there?' he asked bitterly. 'I wish you'd explain it to me. I'm not trying to be offensive, Paulinus; these things were decided before you arrived. But are we to remain fortbound for ever? In the west there seems to be a stalemate, which is not surprising: difficult, mountainous country which will take years to subdue. Why shouldn't we hold in the west and strike in the north? I've thought it all out. Look—!'

He jumped to his feet, anger drowned in enthusiasm, and shook a map from its metal tube. With a sweep of his arm he unrolled and pinned it to the table with a dagger. It was an enlargement of the standard maps, showing Britain from the Wash northwards, with many additions provided by patrols and spies.

'This is the plan which I sent to Veranius Nepos: a strong column, one legion and supporting auxiliaries, to push due north from Lincoln fifty miles up this valley to a Brigantian town called York. My native agents say it's the usual tribal fort, ditched and stockaded, and can easily be stormed. That would be our first objective. I think, at the same time, another column should move from Wroxeter through Chester, parallel to mine but west of the hills, to divert some of the tribal forces. When York is taken it can join us to build a fortress there as an advanced base for the next move.'

He waited, eyes sparkling, face shining with eagerness and sweat.

'And who would your enemies be, Cerialis?' I said.

'First,' he answered, 'we'd meet a tribe called the Parisi just north of us. They fight mostly from chariots. An auxiliaries' battle. Then we hit the Brigantes.'

'Ah,' I said. 'The Brigantes. A very different proposition. You know all about them?'

'Yes,' he said impatiently. 'Some of my centurions and veterans marched into the hills with the legion under Nasica. They stormed Brigantian forts when we were shoving that woman Cartimandua back on her throne a few years ago. They're a strong tribe; they're well-armed and fight like wolves; but we've met better savages and won. What about them?'

I drummed fingers on the map and sought words to restrain this brilliant, headstrong soldier, words which must disappoint but would not sour him. Sooner or later he would have to know of my forthcoming operations in the west; he might as well be told now. I dismissed guards and servants from the room. In outlining my plans I stressed the importance of his task in guarding the backs of my armies, alert to deal with any signs of unrest in the settled areas. I did not tell him about the proposed annexation of the Icenian kingdom but implied that insurrection could be expected in the east while I was marching to Anglesey. I indicated that his troops would find plenty of occupation; in this, at least, I was more right than I knew.

Cerialis was not happy when we sought our bedrooms. He seemed, however, fairly resigned to his secondary role with its vague promise of minor skirmishes and police work. I turned at the door and laid a hand on his shoulder.

'A last word of advice, Cerialis. I don't think we shall engage in major operations this year, probably not until next spring. It's a long time to keep men keyed up to operational fitness. Let them relax for a bit; send some of them on leave. And give yourself a bit of rest. You'll fight all the better when the time comes.'

He sighed, then grinned. 'Of course you're right, Paulinus. I've been overdoing it. But you'll keep my plan in mind? After all, when you've finished with the Silures and Ordovici no one but the Brigantes will be left.'

'I'll not forget it, Cerialis,' I assured him gravely. 'Sleep well.'

5

In Colchester the Provincial Council had fully assembled. I arranged a private interview with the Pontiff, Epaticcus of the Atrebates. Son of Tasciovanus of the Catuvellauni, and younger brother of the famous Cunobelinus, he ruled the Atrebates by right of conquest. Cunobelinus had sent him, when a young man, to invade Verica's realm and hold it as an ally of the Catuvellaunian kingdom whose capital was then at Colchester. Epaticcus, in a brief and brilliant campaign, defeated Verica, drove him into exile, subdued the Atrebates and occupied the throne. When Cunobelinus died, in the year of the Conquest, he became for a short time an independent ruler until his kingdom was overrun by Vespasian's ruthless sweep through southern Britain. Wisely recognizing that Rome was here to stay he came to terms with his conquerors, swiftly adopted for his capital at Silchester our system of municipal administration and, as magistrate and councillor, continued to direct tribal affairs, under our surveillance, with hardly less than his old kingly authority.

He was now nearly seventy years old, a staunch friend and citizen of Rome.

I liked him on sight: a fine, upright, hawk-nosed old man with piercing blue eyes and a shock of white hair. We discussed the forthcoming meeting in a friendly conference and settled points of procedure. Afterwards, strolling together in the frost-bound gardens of Government House, I led the conversation to the affairs of the peoples in the settled areas in their relations with the Government. I found him free in his opinions, frank and direct.

'We Britons behind the frontiers are resigned to Roman rule,' he said. 'Most of us find life easier than in the old days. We can sow our crops with the certain knowledge of reaping them, and hardly notice when half the harvest is lost in taxes. It's a fair price to pay for living in peace with our neighbours.'

'You sound almost regretful, Epaticcus, that you can no longer engage in private wars when you feel inclined. Are the old animosities really dead? Do your people, for instance, emigrants from Gaul, settled by conquest in Britain for little over a century, feel easy among the aboriginals you dispossessed?'

'We still distrust them, Legate. They're unreliable, these descendants of the ancient Britons, dark-minded under their fair skins, full of old hatreds, always recalling dim glories of the past. We subdued them; Rome conquered them; but they have never, in their hearts, accepted either.'

'I think you're prejudiced, Epaticcus,' I said thoughtfully, for this viewpoint was new. 'The Trinovantes, in whose territory we stand, are peaceable, co-operative, good taxpayers and one of the most civilized tribes in Britain. They do not brood over old enmities.'

'You think not?' He looked at me sideways under bushy eyebrows, halted and leaned heavily on his staff, head bowed in thought. 'Legate, you have not been here long. Perhaps you'll forgive advice from an old man who has seen all the flaring, wide-flung fires of hatred, Briton against Briton, stamped under the iron heels of your legions. You think the sparks are quenched. It's possible. But the embers may have solidified under the weight to a glowing fireball ready to burn the feet that press them down. Your precious Trinovantes are not so happy as you think.'

'Why, Epaticcus?'

'Ask your veterans in this colony. Ride round their farms and compare the land they have seized with the official allotments granted by your Government. Ask the Augustals of Colchester. Whence comes the money to support the Temple of Victory, a bigger and more magnificent shrine than any in Gaul? Then send your spies among the Trinovantes, to their villages, and let them listen to the unguarded talk in wine shop and cornfield, in tannery and brickyard.'

The old man compressed his lips, thumped his staff abruptly on the ground and looked at me askance, obviously fearful of having said too much. I laid a reassuring arm about his shoulders.

'All this, Epaticcus, I shall do. Tell me what I shall find.'

'I have chattered enough, Legate. It is time to return to my encampment. Have I your permission?'

He could be induced to say no more and took himself off, leaving me puzzled and worried. The conversation was disturbing enough to send me straight to my Secretariat, where I summoned the secretary in charge of intelligence and told him to compile, from the Colchester Council's archives, a statement of official land grants made to every veteran in the colony. Then, from the Financial Magistrates's files, he was to enter individual holdings as assessed for tax. A comparison of the two would reveal whether unauthorized land-grabbing was as universal as Epaticcus had hinted.

The second point required delicate handling. The Augustals of Colchester, who not only directed official religion in the colony but generally superintended worship of the Prince's Divinity throughout Britain, were the Province's leading supporters of Rome's authority. Their prestige in Britain was immense and their influence in Rome not inconsiderable: to interfere directly in their affairs was to invite a complaint to the Prince in his capacity of High Pontiff. In the end I decided to assemble the six Augustalian magistrates on the pretext of discussing religious ceremonies in connection with the Provincial Council's meeting.

When we had ploughed through the details of complicated and interminable rites I turned to the most talkative of the magistrates, a cheerful freedman who had amassed a fortune from the local metal-workers' foundries.

'Sacrificial offerings on the scale that you propose will be very expensive,' I said. 'I trust the Temple funds will not suffer unduly?'

The man grinned. 'Have no fear, most noble Paulinus. The Temple of Victory can afford all that and more besides.'

'I confess I am surprised. Celebrations on such a magnificent scale would tax the resources of Ephesus. You must be rich men.'

The flattery took effect. 'The Augustals are not paupers, most noble Paulinus. We contribute our share, and the priests help as well.'

I affected surprise. 'The priests? Are your priests also millionaires? This is surely unusual?'

'It is.' He leaned forward confidentially, oblivious to the disapproving glares of his brother magistrates: they plainly thought this low-born fellow capable of any indiscretion. 'We choose most of our priests from the princes and chieftains of the Trinovantes. They are rich, and loyal to Rome, and desirous of showing their loyalty not only by priestly service but also by generous contributions of money and land to the worship of the Divine Nero.' He smiled. 'We find this a considerable help to our finances.'

'Undoubtedly. Yet your statement is most remarkable. I've always understood your countrymen to be somewhat retentive of their possessions and especially reluctant to part with land. The Trinovantan nobles must be exceptional.'

Another magistrate, a Roman, interrupted the freedman. 'You may rest assured, Legate, that the Trinovantes regard their contributions towards our temple as no hardship, but as an honour.'

I looked at him, a lean, hard-eyed man who realized and disliked the trend of my questions. I turned the conversation to safer channels and dismissed the men soon afterwards. Then I summoned my chief of intelligence, Valerius Celsus.

'You are relieved of all other duties for a special task which is altogether too delicate to entrust to our internal security section,' I told him. 'Listen carefully. The Augustals of Colchester are levying taxes on the Trinovantan nobility. I am certain the chieftains resent this intensely—but that is not your concern. Your business is to intrude an agent who can gain access to the Augustals' accounts, discover how much land the Temple owns and the names of the previous owners, together with the names of the Trinovantes whose religious contributions are particularly large.'

Celsus scratched his head. 'This will be hard, Legate. You know how difficult it is to pry into the affairs of any guild, let alone a powerful one like the Augustals. The scribes are carefully chosen, sworn to secrecy, and have fatal accidents if they are indiscreet.'

'I know,' I said impatiently. 'Nevertheless it must be done. Pick your spy well and make quite certain that, if he is caught, nobody can trace his connections.'

'Very well, Legate.' Celsus saluted and left, a perplexed and thoughtful man.

6

Two months later I received a report on this matter: it may as well be set down now. The Temple was, indeed, immensely wealthy, possessing farmlands bequeathed or transferred by Trinovantes in all parts of the territory. Celsus could obtain no evidence of compulsion in the acquisition of these properties; they all appeared on the account rolls as voluntary gifts; no single chieftain had made any outstandingly large contribution. He had tried to pry into the motives stimulating such unusual generosity and had found nothing beyond ordinary loyalty, a keen religious sense and his agent, strangled, in the river.

Inquiries into the veterans' holdings were completed about the same time. Here the proof was definite: almost without exception the ex-soldiers held land far in excess of their original grants, acquired by simple dispossession of British peasants. In some cases the previous owners had been allowed to remain on their farms, working now as servants of the colonists; in others the natives had been evicted entirely. Council archives recorded lawsuits brought by Britons against their oppressors which were invariably abortive; the Provincial Law ruled that if a native sued a Roman, or vice versa, the judge must be of the defendant's nationality. This operated in favour of the veterans, whose magistrates were not only their own comrades but were themselves probably guilty of the very offence which they judged. In recent times there had been no actions at law, for the natives had realized the futility of expensive litigation which always failed.

Though much of this information was vague and unsatisfactory one thing was plain. The Trinovantes, chieftains and peasants, were steadily being despoiled of land and livelihood by methods which had no legal backing and smelt strongly of blackmail and oppression. What was done could not be undone; but I made up my mind to tolerate no further injustices of this kind, not so much out of compassion for the Britons—they were, after all, a vanquished race and must expect to provide the fruits of victory—but because in the settled areas I wanted no fires smouldering that could burst into flames when the legions were warring at the ends of Britain.

How fiercely, if at all, the spark of rebellion glowed I had not discovered, and intelligence gave no help. I pondered for long over ways and means of probing the Trinovantes' blank wall of outward friendliness, though my internal security experts complacently insisted that I fought with shadows. I just could not believe that a people suffering such widespread persecutions could feel anything but hatred for Rome: a loyal Trinovant seemed to me a contradiction in terms.

3

'The safety of a kingdom depends more upon its alliances than upon armies or riches.'

SALLUST

1

The Provincial Council met in Colchester's basilica. I delivered my edict, which aroused no immediate reaction because the proceedings were bound by a rigorous tradition and intensely formal. After each member had risen in turn to make his speech of welcome I called on tribal representatives in order of seniority to present petitions or complaints on behalf of their tribes. Every man, amid lesser grumbles, protested against the price fixed for requisitioned corn. Although it was unusual for a governor to answer points raised during the conference—they were noted by scribes and dealt with at leisure—I felt it wise to reply at once. I pointed out that for many years the world prices of corn had been higher than British prices and that most governors had acted generously in paying British farmers the Imperial rate. Britons who for years had not hesitated to sell corn to the Government for more than their own countrymen would pay, and grown rich in the process, should not object when the market temporarily operated against them. The remedy, I said, was in their own hands: to grow more corn by more efficient methods until they could sell to all at the new rates and still make a satisfactory profit.

The faces showed dissatisfaction and disbelief. I cursed them silently; the meeting dragged on; I endured without relish the discomforts of a cold and draughty chamber and the boredom of long speeches whose Latin was often barely comprehensible. Orators of Gallic origin, such as Atrebates and Belgae, spoke fairly good Latin because their language was in many respects akin to ours; but aboriginal tribes like the Regni, who used the Old British tongue, sibilant unlike any civilized speech, found much difficulty in expressing their ideas in the Roman language.

Soon after dawn next day began the Temple rituals and sacrifices that continued throughout the morning. Epaticcus, as Pontiff, conducted the rites with dignified precision; the ceremonies were impressive and splendid. The recitations of poetry and trials of eloquence that occupied the afternoon were neither. I was heartily glad when the last of the worst orators was led away to be ducked in the river—a strange but condign custom—and I could retire to my house for a badly-needed cup of wine.

Athletic contests, chariot races and a huge market and fair occupied yet another day. Both Romans and Britons took part in foot races, jumping, discus and javelin throwing, and the Romans usually won. But the chariot-drivers were all Britons who drove light two-horse cars which they handled with remarkable skill over an oval course marked on the frozen fields outside the town.

On the last day the councillors in turn paid me state visits in order to discuss in private any matters which specifically concerned their tribes or towns. In this way I met Prasutagus, King of the Iceni. Allied rulers were not members of the Provincial Council and attended its deliberations only by courtesy, but those who wished to be regarded as our friends made a point of attending the annual meetings, particularly when a new Governor was present. Prasutagus showed few traces of the warrior who had defied Scapula; though courteous, gentle and eager to please he was feeble and obviously in poor health. His queen,

Boudicca, a brawny, mannerless woman who smelt of sweat, kept aloof and took no pains to hide her dislike of my Roman surroundings, my Roman companions and my Roman self. The Britons commonly allow their women much more freedom in speech and action than is tolerated in civilized countries, a failing that Boudicca took full advantage of. I found her, then and later, quite detestable.

Now for the second of these allied monarchs: Cartimandua of the Brigantes. I had, needless to say, previously studied the secret dossiers of every tribal representative: Cartimandua's file was a long one. She was now a woman of thirty-five who could look back on a queenly career, mostly discreditable, of seventeen years. As I watched her state procession approach the basilica I remembered the main details inscribed in the rolls: '...Queen-regnant of Brigantia, made peace with Plautius within a year of the Conquest...four years later Scapula reprimanded her for Brigantian raids into Government territory, probably instigated by her anti-Roman consort Venutius; her efforts to control her subjects fired a rebellion. Column under Scapula invaded Brigantia and restored order...three years later C. surrendered to the Government Caratacus, son of Cunobelinus, British war-leader and hero, who had taken refuge in Brigantia after defeat by Scapula...three years later became mistress of Vellocatus, her husband's armour-bearer, and killed Venutius's brother and kindred. Venutius publicly assumed leadership of anti-Roman nationalist party and rebelled. Gallus sent legion, defeated Venutius, restored Cartimandua...'

Betrayal, murder and adultery. These were not all. Entries dated after the departure of successive governors were written in cipher in her dossier: '...mistress to Aulus Plautius...became mistress of Ostorius Scapula during first Brigantian revolt; liaison continued until his death...fled to Wroxeter at outbreak of second Brigantian revolt, when Didius Gallus became her lover...' It was clear that our loyal ally Cartimandua had embraced certain Roman usages with progressive fervour. I was prepared to dislike her on sight.

2

She alighted from a litter draped in cloth of crimson and gold and greeted me simply in the Roman fashion.

'Greetings, most noble Paulinus.'

I stared, manners forgotten. My mental image of a raddled, middle-aged strumpet dissolved before the reality of this slim, beautiful queen with a girl's face. The mellow sheen of old bronze glowed in her hair; her eyes were dark sapphires set wide above high cheekbones; her lips tilted at the corners in a smile to loosen the knees of Mars himself.

Lest any should think me easily inflamed, here let me say that in the business of love I behave neither like a callow boy, prostrated by any beautiful face, nor a middle-aged fool in search of romance. In my youth I have pleasured many a senator's wife and beguiled his daughter; such behaviour is no more than fashionable. Certain young men I have also loved but never to the point of infatuation. The passing years, continuous service in the field and the chill blasts of death and wounds and fighting have cooled the lava of desire; my interests of heart and head have become my military career. Not that I am incapable of relaxation; my household still contains expertly amorous slave girls and personable boys, but these frolics are incidental as a visit to the latrines.

So I was totally unready for Cartimandua.

I returned her greeting with, I hoped, elegance and dignity. Cartimandua presented her councillors of State and a good-looking, sulky youth of indeterminate office whose name was Vellocatus. I wondered where this unimpressive individual concealed the attributes that had ousted from Cartimandua's precarious affections the formidable Venutius, successor to Caratacus and the first warrior in Britain. I came to a vulgarly inescapable conclusion and then, looking at the Queen's radiant and youthful face, revolted from a mean and sordid thought. This is truth: she had that effect on men.

The interview followed a normal, polite, conversational course while I sought an excuse for a more private meeting without arousing scabrous comment. Presently, on the pretext of elucidating a minor problem of boundary limits that required a reference to Plautus's original treaty with Brigantia, I led her within the basilica and we paced the hall, side by side, while the papers were being fetched.

Cartimandua said softly, 'You understand the Greek language?'

She spoke in Greek and looked for the surprise in my face, without success: my powers of astonishment were already numb.

'In discussing matters of State we have to be careful, most noble Paulinus,' she went on, still in an undertone, while pretending to admire a bust of Nero that dominated the eastern apse. 'My attendants speak only their own tongue and a little Latin. And yours?'

I looked at the gaggle of tribunes and guards which had entered the hall with us. Most of the officers spoke Greek as their second tongue. I hesitated. Secretaries approached, carrying the long, closely-inscribed scroll that governed Brigantia's relations with Rome. I pointed to the magisterial dais in the apse; they flattened the papyrus on a table, weighted the ends, withdrew. Curtly I told the duty tribune to keep guards and attendants at a distance and invited Cartimandua to the dais. With a sharp word to her own guards, muscular Brigantes in glittering mail who seemed reluctant to release her beyond sword-length, she mounted the steps, sank gracefully to the marble seat and became to all appearances intensely interested in the treaty's preamble.

Beneath Nero's stony glare, the incurious gaze of her warriors, the speculative glances of her councillors and Vellocatus's glower we talked for a long time, always in Greek, of frontiers, high politics and, finally, of love. Under the circumstances I found the last very difficult, and the strain of presenting an appearance of equanimity while making amorous advances to a beautiful, intelligent woman in the very language of love became too severe. Luckily the advent of Cogidumnus of the Regni and his train gave me an excuse to end our communion. I led the

Queen back to her entourage, began the ceremonial leave-takings. In Cartimandua's eyes, as she said farewell, dwelt a grave amusement and complete appreciation of my embarrassed relief.

I had a good deal to think about.

3

A night's sleep restored my senses and put the Queen of Brigantia into perspective. Since her betrayal of the British partisan leader Caratacus she was probably the most unpopular woman in Britain, but she still ruled the country's most powerful people and still remained friends with Rome. This was statecraft of a high order, political dexterity in the tradition of Cleopatra. Cartimandua, according to the ciphered minutes in her dossier, used the game of love as an agreeable means to political ends. A morning's cold reflection decided me that yesterday's affair, budding and promising a rosy growth, could follow the same useful pattern.

We had discussed, cautiously, the matter of the Anavio lead-mines. I had shown Cartimandua that the potential wealth of the district was grossly under-exploited because any large-scale attempts by either the Cornovii or her own people to mine the ore immediately led to inter-tribal bickering over rights of possession. With this she agreed. I had pointed out the advantages of leasing the mines to the Roman Government. She would be assured of a steady income; her subjects would not have to work in the mines at the expense of agriculture; contention with her neighbours would cease. The proportionate rights to the minerals could be settled, I suggested, at a conference between the Government and both tribes. She had affected to doubt whether we would pay as much for the leasehold as the Brigantes already obtained by their own efforts—a normal prelude to the commercial-political haggling inevitable in this kind of treaty.

I had made no approaches to ensure her neutrality during the coming Ordovican campaign. Her personal loyalty to Rome, rooted in hard self-interest, was unquestioned; the doubtful element was a small but powerful anti-Roman party in Brigantia, subdued but not eradicated during Venutius's rebellion. At present, according to our reports, the Queen was in complete control. Whether she could restrain her fanatics from raiding the flanks of Roman forces engaged with another foe was dubious. And where was Venutius? He had fled, five years since, far to the north beyond Brigantia's borders, beyond reach of our intelligence, which could nevertheless trace his hand and direction in several minor upheavals, which disturbed the kingdom from time to time. He was not a man to relinquish easily the power and wealth of Brigantia and, for all we knew, might be able to gather forces and strike while my legions were involved elsewhere. I resolved, on our next meeting, to seek some information from the Queen about her late consort.

We met the following morning when I was exercising my horses on the Lincoln road. A cortège approached at speed, Cartimandua in the lead driving a two-horsed chariot. I signalled my escort to give her passage. She reined her horses with a neat, almost imperceptible motion of hands and wrists and greeted me merrily.

'Most noble Paulinus! May we have the honour of your company to Colchester, or are you at this early hour already engaged on State business?' The deep-blue eyes sparkled like dewdrops in dawn sunlight.

'Greetings, Queen of Brigantia.' I dropped into her mood of raillery. 'I'm exercising my stud—a far more important occupation than matters of State.'

The grooms, at a command, displayed their horses: four matched Asturian greys, four big German bays and two Illyrian stallions of lovely conformation and uncertain temper. My own mount was a strapping chestnut, a crossbred Gallic-Asturian with beautiful manners, superbly trained. I pride myself on my string—no better horses are stabled in the Roman Army. Their contrast with the small, shaggy-coated British ponies of Cartimandua's Brigantian guard was the gulf between Bucephalus and a backyard donkey.

Cartimandua saw my quick, scornful glance of comparison. Her lips tightened; then she laughed.

'Would it please you, most noble Paulinus, to ride in my chariot and try my team? In size, looks and breeding they can't begin to match your beasts, yet for their poor purposes they're not inadequate.'

The protocol governing relations between Roman governors and allied rulers, though lengthy and comprehensive, did not define the etiquette enshrouding invitations to chariot rides. But I did not hesitate for a moment. Cartimandua's challenge was unmistakable.

'Nothing would give me greater pleasure.' I dismounted and told my escort to stand fast. The Queen drove an elaborate version of the tribal war-car, a light, two-wheeled, ash-framed chariot with a body of plaited willow-wands. The pole was encased in sheet-bronze intricately chased; silver medallions and bright enamel plaques studded the frame. Spokes and felloes were alternate gilt and scarlet, and the axle hubs ended in square, empty sockets, worn with use and iron blacked at the edges.

I put my hand on the wooden mounting-horn projecting from the car's body. Vellocatus, standing beside Cartimandua, made no move to dismount and muttered angrily in her ear. The Queen turned on him. Her beautiful face, all her features, altered for one terrifying second and I saw the fearful ferocity of a Medusa and understood, for the first time, why Cartimandua remained Queen of Brigantia. She said something, very quietly, in her own tongue and Vellocatus dismounted without another word.

I took the man's place; Cartimandua spoke to her horses—lean-headed roans, standing higher than most British animals, whose coats were shaved and singed and brightly glossy—and they sprang to a canter. My escort stood fast, as ordered, but the Brigantian warriors clattered after us in an untidy crescent. The Queen smiled slightly, flexed and shook her reins. The team leaped to a gallop like bolts from catapults and raced down the road towards Colchester. The light chariot swayed and bounced and, as the pace increased, seemed about to take wing. The

Queen's guard, shouting, hallooing and flogging their horses, dwindled to dancing specks.

Tightly gripping horn and guardrail, I reluctantly tore my fascinated gaze from the highway that poured frenziedly towards the chariot and glanced at Cartimandua. Tawny hair and emerald cloak streamed behind her like twin banners; her outstretched arms and supple hands guided the reins, flexed the bits which caressed the horses' mouths like loving fingers; a colour like the flush of dawn light touched her cheeks and all the joy of living was in her eyes. She met my look and laughed. 'Take the reins. Show me how a Roman drives!'

I am no charioteer. Like most senators I have, when young and foolish, frequented the racing stables of the Blues and Greens and aped the manners and style of popular champions and practised with my companions while the great men watched condescendingly. Sometimes Hierax or Antilochus would even offer a titbit of advice to his noble emulators. That was a long while ago; I felt no assurance of controlling this hurtling eggshell. But the horses were balanced and collected; their mouths responded to the pressure of my hands like cushioned silk. I could handle this team.

Then stupefaction stunned relief. Cartimandua stooped, loosed her sandals, released the golden brooch that secured her cloak, let it fly like a windblown leaf. In the wink of an eyelash she vaulted the guardrail, balanced for a dizzy second and ran barefoot along the pole. She touched her horses between the ears and danced back so lightly and surely that the bucking, swaying sliver of timber that she trod might have been the solid rock of Petra beneath her feet.

She dropped into the car, snatched the reins, checked and swung the pair in a horrifying arc that turned the chariot within the margins of the road. The car slithered to a standstill.

Astonishment and shock held me speechless as a gangling rustic. I gazed at her mutely. The Queen's eyes were bright with tears; her lips quivered. She flung towards me, strained her body to mine.

'Now!' she whispered. 'Now!'

I looked along the highway, to north and to south. The road was empty.

4

Snared like a callow boy, I told myself morosely as I rode back to the capital. Subdued and enchanted by a lovely, wilful woman who adds unusual weapons, a charioteer's acrobatics, to her powerful armoury. Tricks, I reminded myself sourly, which were so old that the great Caesar knew and noted them in his history of the British expeditions.

We had retrieved our escorts, taken polite farewells and gone our respective ways. But Cartimandua, after our eccentric coupling in the well of the chariot, had made me promise to see her that night, to visit her pavilion in the Brigantian encampment during the second watch. Her guards, she had said, would be picked for their discretion and warned of my attendance. My own escort must be small, otherwise her people might take alarm. An obvious precaution, I reflected glumly: one does not fulfil amorous assignments with a cohort and band. At the least I might combine pleasure with business and, with luck, make some political capital out of the night's transactions.

After dark, accompanied only by the centurion of my bodyguard and a trusted freedman-horseholder, I rode through a hailstorm to Cartimandua's encampment. Her attendants were few; the ceremonies on arrival were limited to those necessary for my comfort; soon we were left alone together. I had spent the afternoon studying in detail departmental literature concerning the Anavio lead-mines and copies of correspondence between the Procurator and Claudius of Smyrna, in Rome, about the annual sum to be paid for the lease. I was fully prepared with facts and figures for some hard-bargaining business.

I could have saved the trouble.

Cartimandua was in no mood to discuss politics: the most I could extract from her was a promise to clinch the matter if I visited her at Aldborough, her capital. Thereafter we passed the hours until dawn in a manner that would certainly earn a ciphered entry in her dossier after I had left Britain.

5

With Cartimandua's going I was feverish to leave Colchester for the frontier. Daily I resented the work which still kept me in the capital. First I issued an edict announcing the holding of a census throughout the whole Province, a quinquennial event delayed by Veranius's death and much overdue. The census, a thorough-going affair which included a survey of the extent, character and ownership of land, served as a basis of assessment for land tax and also demanded details of other forms of wealth for computation of poll tax. No individual, whether citizen or native, chieftain or colonist, escaped its investigations. And the time and circumstances made it a convenient means of assaulting again that stone faced Trinovantan secrecy.

It was my business to appoint a census officer of equestrian rank who, with information and co-operation from local magistrates, would appraise each fiscal district. The district of Colchester included all Trinovantan territory. I reckoned that an able census officer, under cloak of revenue assessments and with the assistance of trained intelligence agents, should discover a lot that had nothing at all to do with taxation. In consultation with the Procurator I drew up a list of officers, some from his own department, others seconded from the army.

Among the latter I selected Gnaeus Aurelius Bassus, prefect of the 2nd Asturian cohort stationed at Gloucester, a young man starting his equestrian career whose record in command of his cohort on the turbulent Silurian frontier was distinguished by audacity and cunning. Bassus rode express to Colchester in response to an urgent summons. My confidential clerks had prepared a written summary on the phenomenon of the Trinovantes' apparent contentment under every form of unbridled extortion, which I let him read. I then asked for his comments.

Bassus countered with a question. 'Expropriation of land by the colonists is confirmed. Oppression by the Augustals is suspected but not proved. Is there any evidence from the Trinovantes themselves of their reaction to either?'

I turned to the secretary in charge of internal security for an answer.

'There is nothing which we can reasonably translate as conspiracy against the State,' the freedman said, fumbling among his papers. 'We have noted a good deal of grumbling, chiefly against taxes, which is not unusual. Much traffic comes and goes across the Icenian border: that is not unlawful and there are no signs of smuggling on a large scale or other attempts to evade customs duties. We have found nothing suspicious, except perhaps one incident—' He broke off and put a scroll on the table.

'I have seen that report,' I said. 'To my mind, it touches the fringe of what we are trying to discover.' I addressed Bassus. 'One of our native agents was found, terribly wounded, on the outskirts of a forest not far from here. He babbled of Druids and human sacrifices before he died. He may have been delirious: I personally think he stumbled on one of those outlawed religious conventions, was set upon and left for dead.'

Bassus said, 'What do you want me to do?'

'Primarily, conduct the census of this district,' I answered. 'Your instructions for that will come from the Finance Department. You will, as census officer, have the help of magistrates, chieftains and village headmen throughout the territory. You will be able to travel to every hamlet, forest and field and ask questions of anybody and everybody without exciting remark. These people have met census officers before and are accustomed to their inquisitiveness. I want you to find out anything—I repeat, anything—which may indicate the existence of anti-Roman societies, Druidical sects, traffic in armaments or treasonable links with the Iceni. Am I clear?'

'Yes,' Bassus said. 'What assistance shall I have?'

'You'll have the usual military escort, clerical staff and servants, including six of our best agents, all natives.'

'I can send them to confer with you whenever you wish, noble Bassus,' the secretary added. 'In secrecy, of course.'

'I'll see them tomorrow,' Bassus said. 'Legate, may I send to Gloucester for three of my own troopers who have some aptitude for this work and take them as part of my escort?'

'You may,' I replied. 'And I think, Bassus, you will find the answer, if there is one, not in the villages or fields or wineshops but in the forests near the Icenian border.'

'Yes, Legate. I think so, too. If treason is there I shall discover it.'

'I hope you find your quarry. May Diana speed your quest.'

My secretary gathered up his papers, looking glum. He was a valuable, faithful servant, easily hurt by the slightest rebuff. I knew what he was thinking and tried to reassure him.

'Because I'm employing the Prefect on work that properly belongs to your department you needn't think you have failed me,' I told him. 'You haven't yet had time to reorganize the internal security service. Otherwise this procedure would be unnecessary. We face an unusual situation calling for extraordinary measures: the census officer has opportunities for probing into tribal affairs which are denied to your men. Go with him and give him that invaluable help in his mission which only your experience can provide.'

6

The tribunals further delayed my departure. I always found litigation a bore. My legal knowledge, acquired in the practical school of the courts during my time as praetor and consul, is adequate though not profound, and my inclinations have never led me to specialize in the study of jurisprudence. Time spent in the courts, in my view, is mostly wasted.

In Britain civil cases were dealt with by magistrates and only came before me on appeal or when the legal arguments were so involved that a magistrate's decision was likely to create a precedent. Such instances were not rare: British advocates, particularly those of Gallic origin, were a tedious fount of rhetorical tricks but surprisingly quick in fastening upon any points of law likely to help their clients. I also had to appoint juries and keep a careful watch on any inter-tribal arguments which came before the courts. Though these were mostly of a trivial nature—disputes over boundaries, straying livestock, water rights and so on—it was essential to see that justice was done. The tribes did not love each other overmuch and an inequitable decision might easily lead to bloodshed.

Judgement in criminal cases involving the death penalty was my prerogative alone. These cropped up less frequently. Offences against the person of a citizen or security of the State were exceptional among a population which had settled down and learned to respect Roman authority. As the months passed, however, I found far too much of my time spent either at the tribunal or considering judgements in my offices. Like the Prince, I made a habit of obtaining my counsellors' and assessors' opinions on each case in writing and then, after a night's interval spent in studying their conclusions, delivered my verdict.

The work was onerous. I began seriously to consider drafting a paper for Nero's consideration, advocating provision of a Law Officer for Britain to relieve the Governor of judicial work.

I left Colchester for Gloucester, which I proposed to reach along the West Way. Here, perhaps, because Romans generally are disgracefully ignorant of the geography of Britain, I should give a brief sketch of the Province's main military highways. All radiate from London: the North Way ends at Lincoln; the Midland Way reaches Wroxeter by way of Verulam and the great forests of central Britain; the West Way runs to

Gloucester through Silchester. The main lateral road, the Frontier Way, runs from Exeter through Cirencester and Leicester to Lincoln; its title nowadays is a misnomer because the frontier has since advanced to the line of a road joining Gloucester and Wroxeter, bordering the countries of the Silures and Ordovices. Other highways connect important towns: Colchester to Verulam, Silchester to Bath and Dorchester, to Winchester and Portus; and more are being built. The roads, incidentally, are planned and made under the supervision of our military engineers; the tribes through whose territories they pass provide labour and become responsible for their subsequent maintenance.

I travelled with a large retinue which included the whole bodyguard and most of my staff, leaving only a skeleton staff in Colchester to deal with routine administration. We marched roughly fifteen miles a day and halted for successive nights at Chelmsford, London (whence Catus was fortunately absent on a tax-hunting expedition), and Staines and arrived at Silchester on the fourth evening. Even this moderate rate of travel sorely tried some of my civilian officials. My immediate predecessors, it seemed, had conducted their tours in more leisurely fashion. I was unsympathetic. I warned the grumblers that physical unfitness might disqualify them from further employment and, though we often moved faster afterwards, had no more complaints.

At Silchester I was ceremoniously received by Epaticcus, supported by his town councillors and six magistrates whom the tribal assembly elected annually by popular vote. Because many members of this assembly lived a long way from the capital their meetings were seldom fully representative, so that magistrates, and hence the councillors, who were all ex-magistrates, were a close confederation of the royal family and Atrebatan aristocracy. This was an idiosyncrasy common to most tribal capitals which I found not unwelcome: these British noblemen were, on the whole, an improvement both in bearing and manners on some of the vulgar knights and Roman merchants who governed places like Verulam and London.

I liked the surroundings of Silchester. They suited its name, 'Town in the Wood', and these woods were pleasant, sunlit copses very unlike the dark forests of the north. The town itself was no more than a cluster of mud-and-timber huts, some tiled, some thatched, and an unimpressive market-place and town hall and three brick temples built with some pretensions to Roman style. The site was on a promontory, falling away on three sides, protected on the fourth by the remains of a native bank and ditch.

Although Epaticcus offered me the hospitality of his house I declined politely and slept in camp. His palace was the largest house in Silchester but differed little from the others in design: I suspected an absence of baths and central heating. Spring was in the air, touching bare branches with her green wand, but the nights were still too raw to court unnecessary discomfort. In the morning, accompanied by the old chieftain, I made a tour of the town and its environs. The place had most impressive possibilities.

I pointed out to Epaticcus that he was missing his opportunities. A focal point in the road system, with fertile soil and plentiful water, Silchester could be developed into a flourishing town worthy of an Atrebatan capital. A town of straight, well-paved streets, with offices, shops, warehouses, granaries, inns and law-courts would attract trade and traders, many of whom might set up in business there. Trade meant prosperity and a higher standard of living for all the Atrebates. I brushed aside his objection that the people were farmers, living mostly in widely scattered farmhouses in woodland clearings. Arguing and cajoling all the way, I led him to his house where, with tablet and stylus, I made a rough drawing of an outline town plan.

'Here,' I said, 'is the line of your bank and ditch. A gate here, and another, and a street connecting them. A central square, with town hall and market-place. A great temple in this square, and public baths in this. I myself will build a mansion; let it be here, across the road from the temple. And you and your aristocracy shall raise houses worthy of your standing, embellished with paintings and mosaics, set among shrubs and flowered gardens.'

Epaticcus studied my scribble with an inscrutable face.

'Where,' he asked, 'do poor farmers raise the money to finance this programme?'

I reminded him that our revenue registers contradicted the idea of Atrebatan poverty, but agreed that the capital cost would exceed his resources.

'The Government,' I added, 'will lend you what you want, by issuing loans to individuals and, for public buildings, to the corporation. Moreover, I shall write to Rome asking for a grant—a grant, not a loan—to be made to the Atrebates for public works. I cannot promise you that it will be made, nor the amount, but I will try.'

'My thanks. And who will prepare the plans, the designs? Are we to use these?' He indicated my scrawled tablet.

I laughed, and told him that I would provide an engineer officer and men to draw up plans and do the preliminary work. I had the very man in mind: Sextus Julius Frontinus, a tribune of good family who was travelling with headquarters staff on his way to join XIV Legion. During his tenure as prefect of a cohort he had shown a pronounced bent towards engineering and surveying and had written a brilliant little manual on the tactical siting of marching camps.

Epaticcus was not yet convinced, and I had to promise him that I would use the environs of Silchester as a training ground for the new British cohorts and for my bodyguard, and would build barracks. This, and a further assurance of making Silchester a leave centre for my troops, seemed to persuade him.

'Think of the profits to be made from wineshops and brothels patronized by furlough-happy soldiers with money in their fists!' I argued.

He agreed to call a meeting in the senate-house next day, and I knew the controversy was finished. His government followed the rules and motions of municipal law, but the old king's word was still the ultimate ruling in anything affecting the tribe's internal welfare. His reluctance subsided further when I promised not to leave Silchester until detailed plans had been drawn and work was ready to begin.

I explained the business to Frontinus and gave him authority to obtain a staff of qualified engineers, skilled workmen and technical equipment from II Legion at Gloucester. I also warned him that the new town was to be fortified with a twenty-foot embankment and an outer ditch ten feet deep. I intended to found the new Silchester on a pattern which other towns would afterwards be urged to follow.

Finally, in my monthly dispatches to the Prince, I asked permission for rebuilding Silchester. This was only a formality. Many decrees, dating back to the Divine Claudius, had pressed Governors to settle the natives in towns built after the Roman fashion, for the very reasons which I had summarized for Epaticcus. According to my promise, I asked Nero for a grant of one million sesterces: a request that was wishful rather than optimistic, though backed by persuasive and cogent arguments. I remembered the economic condition of the Province, not to mention Rome herself, and expected no more than a polite refusal.

7

Leaving Silchester in her birth-pangs I resumed the march to Gloucester and arrived on the third day to find the legate commanding II Legion Augusta a very ill man. He was dying from a congestion of the lungs caused by three years' service in Britain's damp and pestilential climate. I saw him on his sick-bed and had a talk with the legion's doctor, who opined that, while he could offer no hope of recovery, the invalid might linger on for months. This was a nuisance. I had plans for the garrison demanding a capable and energetic commander, and Paenius Posthumus, prefect of the camp, who had taken over command when the legate fell sick, did not in my view fill this role. A report to Rome with a request for a new commander was no help: the posting might take months. More probably my application would be refused; Nero was always reluctant, except for disgraceful conduct, to deprive high-ranking officers of their commands.

Besides Augusta the fortress held three thousand auxiliaries: three cavalry regiments and five infantry cohorts, one of them milliary. Detachments from all these units, amounting to nearly a thousand men, were scattered without regard for regimental homogeneity at road stations along half the highways of Britain.

I inspected the fortress and watched the men at drill and battle exercises. There was nothing much wrong either with the fortifications or the training of the men who manned them: the aggressive habits of the Silures demanded a high standard from both. Only when I talked with centurions and legionaries did I discover an attitude of mind which was less creditable than normal healthy respect for a vigorous foe. They told unbelievable stories about these dark-featured, stocky savages: they never suffered from rheumatism or pneumonia, they could exist for days bodily under water, they could run sixty miles in mountainous country between dawn and sunset.

The Silures were formidable enough without legendary embellishments. They had formed the backbone of Caratacus's forces when he made his last stand against Scapula; their utter defeat on that occasion encouraged the legate to believe they were a conquered people needing only a watchful eye to keep them in submission. He withdrew his field army and dispersed II Legion in working parties over the trans-Severn countryside to build forts at strategic points. The Silures rose again without warning; detachments were attacked and destroyed, the unfinished forts burned. The legion's main body, hurrying forward in support, was fairly and squarely beaten with the loss of the camp prefect, eight centurions and seven hundred men. The remnants fled to Gloucester and sustained a bitter siege until harvest-time drew most of the tribesmen away to their homes. The legion, licking its wounds, recruited its strength from reinforcement depots and established the Severn as the limit of Roman-dominated territory in this area.

Even that limit was hard to sustain in the years that followed. The Silures, now convinced of their superiority in battle, harassed the garrison without respite. Foraging parties were overwhelmed, which often led to further losses when rescue parties of cavalry and auxiliary infantry were in turn cut up and routed. Time and again legionary detachments were dispatched to retrieve these disasters; the tribesmen easily evaded our heavy infantry and escaped into the hills. Their forays became more extensive; they depopulated the Severn plain on our side of the river and raided over the escarpment to the downland pastures beyond, even threatening Cirencester. These attacks were profitable; they carried off prisoners, cattle and plunder, destroyed everything and were seldom intercepted on the way back. Their successes began to affect tribes hitherto submissive. The Dobuni, for instance, who were the chief sufferers from these incessant raids, quite reasonably despaired of protection by their Roman conquerors and attempted to make separate terms with their tormentors.

Under Didius Gallus matters improved. He brought XX Legion from Wroxeter to support Augusta and waged a regular campaign to clear Dobunian territory of raiding-parties. He was partially successful; his forts, raised at close intervals on the edge of the escarpment overlooking the Severn, gave early warning of raids and provided forces for quick retaliation. Silurian losses mounted; many bands were cut off and exterminated and not a single survivor returned across the river. Gradually we regained the upper hand. The Silures remained aggressive and still harried the river plain, though they found this progressively less rewarding as the few remaining settlements were destroyed. Seldom now did they venture across the escarpment. But all land west of the Severn was Silurian; our forces entered it at their own risk and with the threat of instant retaliation.

Such was the situation when I arrived.

One thing all the men I talked to agreed about was the Silures' astounding intelligence service, a system whose workings had never been discovered but which accounted for most of the disasters suffered at their hands. The tribesmen, so a centurion said, seemed to know the destination, route, strength and composition of every patrol before the rearguard had cleared the fortress gates. This, if true, smelt of treachery within the camp. I set my own intelligence to discover what foreigners were employed in Gloucester and soon had ample confirmation of my suspicions. Many slaves belonging to centurions and legionaries, usually employed on land farmed by soldiers near the fortress, were Silurian prisoners of war. There was only one answer to this. I had all Silures in Gloucester collected, chained and marched under escort to the lead-mines near Bath, and forbade the future employment of enemy tribesmen in or near the fortress. This order was, naturally, tremendously unpopular; the slave owners swore that their servants were so well guarded that communication with their kin across the Severn was impossible. I replied grimly that the loss of a few slaves was a cheap price to pay for the lives of Roman soldiers, bade them watch results and made plans to prove my reasoning valid.

Ten miles west of Gloucester, on the hostile bank of the Severn, where the plain ends at broken, craggy hills typical of the country, were iron-bearing rocks worked by the tribesmen, whose mining villages lay in steep valleys protected by forts on the heights above. Posthumus told me that any incursions into the hills were fiercely resisted; the Silures were most tenacious of an area where armament factories forged swords and spears for their warriors. Previous attempts to raid the mining villages had a regrettable history. The natives seemed invariably forewarned, deserted the mines and manned their forts, whence they issued to harry the withdrawal of our columns to the river. We burned the villages: they were wooden huts which could be rebuilt in a day. Storming the forts was a laborious, expensive and interminable task—there was always another on the next hilltop. The only way effectively to damage the enemy was to catch them unprepared in the valleys. This we had never done.

I judged that now was the time, when the tribal intelligence system lay in ruins and they had not had time to create another, to strike a useful blow at the mining communities. I ordered normal patrolling and camp routine to continue as usual, so that scouts across the river should see nothing untoward, and meanwhile settled the details of a compact striking force for a limited raid.

I chose two thousand men, legionaries and auxiliaries, and spent a hard fortnight exercising them in night operations. Then, after nightfall of a blustery, rain-swept day in late April, I led them across the Severn ford into Silurian territory.

Our objective was three large mining-villages lying close together in the same valley, whose exact location and approaches were well known to certain veterans of Augusta who had taken part in Scapula's extensive operations against Caratacus. The valley was twelve miles distant from Gloucester: we reached it before dawn, after a difficult night march, and surprised the villages while the inhabitants were still bleary with sleep and quite unprepared. We cut them to pieces, burned all the huts and took no prisoners. Over two thousand Silures died; we lost two men.

The news of our success spread through the fortress at arrow-speed: this was the first real blow the garrison had dealt the enemy for over three years. The uplift to morale was enormous; the men were keen to emulate their comrades' deeds and envious of their boasted exploits. I took advantage of this wave of enthusiasm and, at a centurions' conference, expounded the merits of secrecy, surprise, aggression and hard training. Lastly, I warned them that the Silures would certainly try to retaliate for our raid, and that the centurions must immediately prepare plans for an ambush.

Six days later the Silures did indeed return, making at dusk for a ford upriver. They were allowed to cross, were set upon before they could re-form and nearly annihilated. Hardly a man escaped.

I left for Wroxeter with a light heart. The years-long malaise that affected Gloucester's garrison was waning.

4

'So let us have some fighting now, and no more speeches.'
THE ILIAD

1

Wroxeter, the most powerful fortress and largest settlement in Britain, dominated the upper Severn from a small plain encircled by foothills that rose westwards to the mist-shrouded peaks of Ordovicia half a day's march distant. The rampart, two miles in perimeter, contained seventeen thousand armed men: XIV Gemina and XX Valeria, four cavalry regiments and six auxiliary cohorts.

The legions' legates met me at the Praetorian Gate and, before entering, we made a circuit of the defences. Ditch, embankment and stockade conformed in dimensions with the regulation requirements for static camps. Additional touches showed the direction of an imaginative mind: the bottom of the ditch was planted with pointed, fire-hardened stakes; deep pits, spiked at the bottom and lightly covered with turf or brushwood that toned with the natural vegetation, were set as snares across likely approaches. Lime-washed rocks at varying distances from the ramparts acted as ranging marks for catapults and ballistae. Best of all, the native settlements that clung like a parasitic growth to every other military post, whether road-station or fortress, did not exist at Wroxeter. The dwellings of shopkeepers and soldiers' concubines alike were confined to the tribal capital a mile away, so that their untidy sprawl was no menace to the garrison's safety, neither masking targets nor acting as a screen where an enemy could assemble unobserved.

The gatehouse trumpets saluted my first entry to the fortress. I rode straight to the regimental altars in front of headquarters, made the customary offerings and entered the legates' quarters opposite. Relieved of helmet, sword and cloak and comforted with a cup of passable wine I made desultory conversation with the two legates about matters of current interest.

Though technically equal in status, each commanding the fortress for a month in turn, their personalities were quite dissimilar. Valeria's legate, T. Pomponius Mamilianus, was a senatorial aristocrat of long lineage, courtly manners and small ability, a lazy dilettante who seemed grotesquely misplaced in this grim fortress on the uttermost frontiers of Rome. His languid courtesy and unruffled politeness, his supreme lack of interest in any topic but the latest gossip from the Prince's court or the newest writings of Petronius did not impress me as characteristic of a vigorous commander. I mentally dismissed him as a nonentity, an unremarkable man who would leave no mark on history.

Marcus Vettius Valens, the lean, seamed, leathery legate of XIV Legion, was the real power in Wroxeter. He had risen from the ranks of the Praetorian Guard to become tribune of the 3rd cohort, in which he accompanied the Divine Claudius to Britain and took part in the capture of Colchester. Thereafter he saw service in Pannonia with XIII Legion, where he greatly distinguished himself, and later in Asturia. Officers commanding legions who have themselves been legionaries are rare in Rome's history: the mere narration of Valens's career marks him as a most exceptional soldier. During my British campaigns he excelled as a master of administrative detail, a skilled tactician and an iron disciplinarian adored by his men. He hid these qualities under a sourly pessimistic exterior which only changed in battle, when his cheerful confidence was a tonic to faint-hearts and a gage for the brave.

2

One of my first tasks at Wroxeter was to investigate the disturbing reports submitted to Burrus about Valeria's morale. I made a few tentative inquiries of Mamilianus which he met with an irritating compound of bored ignorance and lazy excuses. Therefore I instructed my inquisitors, who were housed in legion barracks in daily contact with the troops, to sound the men discreetly and find out what their grievances were. They submitted a report within two days. But a second-hand account is always unsatisfactory: cautious reservation and unlimited exaggeration were both obvious; so I told the inquisitors to find a responsible man to whom I could talk in private. They produced G. Mannius Secundus, legionary of the 7th cohort, whom I interviewed in my quarters with only the chief inquisitor in attendance.

After some preliminary chatter designed to put him more at ease—an inquisitorial summons to the Governor is not conducive to peace of mind—I went to business.

'I have heard, Secundus, that our men of XX Legion Valeria are not happy. I believe also that the reasons for their discontent, if true, are sufficient grounds for a thorough investigation. But we don't want to hunt boars which turn out to be sows. Before I do anything I must know, from the lips of a responsible legionary, that I shall be acting not on suspicions but on established facts. That is why you are here. Our talk is private; nobody else will hear what you say nor, indeed, will be aware that you have spoken to me at all. Tell me, why is there more petty crime, insubordination, leave-breaking and suchlike in your legion than in any unit in the Province?'

Secundus shifted his feet unhappily. 'I didn't know there was, Legate. We grumble a bit, like all soldiers. Maybe our centurions are a bit tighter than most.'

'More than XIV Legion? Discipline is pretty strict there, you know.'

'Ah, Gemina—! They don't let the centurions—' He compressed his lips.

'Yes?' I inquired gently. 'They don't allow the centurions to do what? Come on, Secundus. This won't be repeated.'

He considered, took a deep breath and spoke with a rush. 'Well, it's like this, Legate. You know there are always unpleasant duties to be done about a camp, hewing timber for stockades, cutting firewood, barrack repairs, washing latrines and so on. These things have to be done; we don't mind doing them so long as the fatigues are equally divided and everybody takes his proper turn.'

'Aren't century and cohort duty rosters kept?'

'They're kept all right but many names never appear unless something agreeable like a wine-ration party crops up. Then the lucky ones fill the whole detail.'

'Why?'

'They bribe the centurions,' Secundus said bitterly. 'There are fixed rates for fatigue-exemptions. Street-cleaning costs least; then the scale rises with additions for the dirtier jobs.'

'Let me get this clear, Secundus,' I said quietly. 'A soldier is paid ten ases a day—225 dinarii a year—from which he has stoppages for bedding, food, clothing, burial-club and compulsory contributions to the savings bank, not to mention payments for his first issue of weapons and armour. Not much can remain for bribery. Do you pay your centurion?'

'Yes,' he answered, 'a little: I only miss street-cleaning. I'm an unlucky gambler and own no tillage outside the camp. A lot of men can afford to pay more; they sell vegetables to century messes, for instance.'

'I see. What happens if you can no longer afford to pay your bribe, or decide to stop?'

'You don't,' Secundus said, 'otherwise life becomes unbearable. A centurion's flogging is no joke.'

'A centurion, on his own authority, can only beat a man for stealing from a comrade, giving false evidence against a comrade, or for culpable physical unfitness,' I said sternly. 'Are the centurions disobeying standing orders?'

'Oh, no. They know their regulations very well. But, Legate, they are their own judges of a man's unfitness. They don't have to prove their case before the tribunes.'

'And I suppose a legionary who defaults in his tribute is suddenly found to be below standard in physical training, arms drill, swimming and route-marches? A flogging a week, or more, until he resumes payment?'

'I've known men to be beaten every day,' Secundus said. 'Even the strongest surrender eventually.'

'How much do you yourself pay?'

He told me. Assuming only half his century paid as much the centurion must receive a comfortable annual increment from this source. He certainly made more—Secundus paid the minimum possible.

'I shall deal with this matter,' I told him. 'You have done your century, your cohort and your legion a service by telling me what you know. As a reward I shall make you an orderly on my staff. The official posting will be made tomorrow. You can tell your comrades that the reason for your summons here was in connection with the transfer. Dismiss.'

I sent away the inquisitor and considered my next step. Secundus's story was not new; bribing centurions was so common in the army that it was almost a custom of the service. Rarely, however, did it assume the proportions of a compulsory tribute enforced by beatings; when this happened something was grievously wrong with the unit concerned. The blame normally lay in one quarter. I sent for a nominal roll of the legion's tribunes.

Five out of the six were Broad Stripe tribunes. Broad Stripe men were not necessarily bad officers; they were simply inexperienced, never having served in the army before. The Narrow Stripe equestrian officers, however, must have commanded an auxiliary cohort before coming to a legion, which imbued them with a sense of responsibility, discipline and some military knowledge. Mamilianus, a man of ancient patrician descent, obviously preferred staff officers of his own senatorial class. Not that legates had much say, officially, in tribunes' postings: they were supposed to take what they got and make the best of it. Unofficially, though, a legate with senatorial influence usually persuaded the military secretariat in Rome to appoint the tribunes he wanted.

From my confidential files I checked the careers of Valeria's tribunes. They were all rich wastrels; even the equestrian had narrowly escaped dismissal for having his cohort insufficiently trained. I handed the files back to the secretary, investigated certain regimental records in the praetorium and went to the legate's quarters.

'I am going to carry out some cross-postings of your staff officers,' I told him, and added a summary of my discoveries without disclosing their source. 'Your tribunes have failed in their duties. Your nominal rolls are both inaccurate and out of date. The discharge lists of time-expired men are incomplete, service records are often missing, gratuity receipts are unsigned. Punishment books are badly kept. Applications for furlough, on the other hand, are minutely noted—I suppose this aspect of military administration holds the strongest appeal for your useless officers. All these are routine duties, requiring little energy and no intelligence. The more important ones have been equally neglected. Your tribunes have shirked guard rounds; they have failed to be present at the men's mealtimes to check the quality of their food; they seldom inspect the sick-quarters. Most important of all, they have lost touch with their men. They have neither listened to legionaries' complaints nor kept a check on the conduct of centurions. You, yourself, cannot escape responsibility for their dereliction of duty. Admittedly you have been given a very poor lot. That at least can be rectified.'

This diatribe disturbed Mamilianus's languid serenity but did not stir him to an energetic protest. I returned to headquarters and forthwith drafted orders distributing the tribunes among other legions, sending three to Cerialis with a private note urging him to treat them rough.

A sequel, amply confirming Secundus's tale, came the very next day. A legionary on patrol had contrived to leave his century, hide in a ravine and make for a village beyond the frontier. He was caught, brought back and now awaited trial. The evidence disclosed that the man, most brutally treated by his centurion over a period of months, had finally decided to risk a tormented death rather than endure the centurion's vine-staff any longer. Insufficient bribery was, of course, the reason. Deserting the standard is a capital offence and I could do nothing for the man; but I deprived the centurion concerned of his rank and then cashiered him without discharge emoluments.

This episode, by bringing the scandal into the open, gave an excuse for direct action. I called together all Valeria's centurions and summarized in simple, virulent sentences the ill-effects of their venality on the legion's happiness and fighting spirit. Accustomed to the laxity of useless tribunes and a feeble legate, they did not take my words kindly. There were angry scenes around the tribunal. Discipline wavered: an ugly surge dismayed my guards and sent my officers' hands to their swords. But one does not publicly castigate fifty pugnacious and arrogant veterans without precaution. The double century of Thracian archers that I had paraded near the armoury suddenly notched arrows to bowstrings, and the centurions saw and subsided. I scourged them in soldiers' language and dismissed them to barracks.

All that could be done to help XX Legion had been done. Active service should complete the cure. For that it must wait awhile.

3

Imperial couriers brought dispatches from Rome in reply to my first letters sent three months before. The Prince wrote amiably and granted all my requests save one. He said:

'Naturally, my dear Paulinus, I do not expect you to provide a comprehensive report on the state of Britain after only a fortnight in the Province. I am only pleased that you have noted so much in so short a time, and commend your observation.

'I agree that an escort befitting your position is essential for prestige alone, not to mention your own safety, a matter always near my heart. The establishment you suggest seems entirely suitable provided the experiment of mixing auxiliaries and legionaries in one unit turns out successfully. Have you considered training legionaries as cavalrymen?

'The British Fleet is under your orders, and I am sure you will use it with your usual skill to assist your operations. The programme of cruises is approved. Let all forays into the western seas be made in strength sufficient to overbear any opposition, for you will find losses in ships and sailors not easy to replace.

'I do not, however, think that the fleet's base should be moved from Boulogne. That port has many advantages which will doubtless occur to you after further reflection.

'I was unaware that no statue of myself existed in Colchester; your intention to repair this omission is thoughtful and timely. Have you an artist in Britain capable of the work? It seems unlikely; perhaps I had better send you a sculptor from Rome.

'I await your further dispatches with interest and the certain knowledge that they will report progress in those special duties for which I sent you to Britain. Meanwhile, take every care of yourself in that unhealthy climate. I am told there are clever physicians in London: do not neglect their advice should any disease afflict you.'

If Nero's refusal of the fleet base project seemed a little terse a note from Burrus, written in a cipher arranged between us for particularly confidential correspondence, explained why. He wrote:

'Your request to move the fleet to a harbour in Britain was tactless. Surely you must realize that a Governor who has complete control of his warships can, at will, render the Province virtually inaccessible? Do you think any Roman ruler would allow such a risk? The lessons of history must surely teach you otherwise.

'In every action you contemplate you would be wise to consider the political implications as they might affect highly-placed persons in Rome. Please be more careful, for your own sake.'

I must confess to a moment of stark fright when I deciphered this. Burrus was quite right. A generation before I might have been recalled and made to open my veins for very much less. I wiped my brow and turned to other letters.

From the sheaf of routine administrative instructions, senatorial decrees and juridical rescripts emerged a sheet of military secretariat orders concerning armament. Army commanders were directed to strengthen the soldier's body-armour by the addition of iron shoulder-pieces and belly-bands. I studied the appended diagrams with interest. Four curved iron strips, attached by studs to the leather cuirass, protected each shoulder; five broader strips guarded chest and stomach from nipples to navel.

This decision was the culmination of many years' argument in military circles. The heavy armour of the Civil Wars, those old-fashioned solid bronze cuirasses and cumbrous greaves, had slowly yielded to lighter, variegated patterns dictated by experience, the soldier's individual preference and the whims of legionary legates. The overall trend favoured lightness: leather body-armour replaced metal. Contemporary opinion held that the soldier's main protection was his shield; the thick leather cuirass, reinforced by leather flares at the shoulders, with dangling metal strips protecting his lower belly and private parts, could only be strengthened at the expense of mobility. It was a convincing argument. A fully-armed-legionary on the march carried helmet, cloak, shield, sword, dagger, two javelins, two palisade stakes, corn rations for a fortnight, cooking-pots and entrenching tool. The total weight was around sixty pounds. The new iron body-armour, besides adding a good ten pounds, would hinder movement and weapon-handling. I, personally, believed in keeping the weight down and considered the new instructions a retrograde step. They had probably been dictated by Domitius Corbulo as a result of the damaging losses he had lately suffered in Parthia.

Another instruction which concerned javelins was my own idea, conceived many years before. The regulation pair of javelins, seven feet long, are heavy weapons of equal weight with a maximum killing range of twenty yards. I had always considered this too short for the first volley; the momentum of his charge often carried an enemy to sword-length before a second flight could be delivered. Hence, I argued, the need to replace one of the javelins by a lighter weapon with longer range. I had succeeded in having prototypes issued to selected units for trials. Reports were generally favourable, but the light javelins became a subject of controversy among the authorities and no decision was made. Now, fifteen years since my original suggestion, all legions were ordered to adopt them. The armourers were in for a busy time.

Only one more letter was of interest in the light of after events. Among a dozen applications for military appointments from patrons on behalf of their protégés was one from Burrus himself, recommending a young man called Gnaeus Julius Agricola, son of the Senator Lucius Julius Graecinus executed by Caligula. Burrus, in his laconic way, conveyed that Agricola was a youth of exceptional qualities who would be an asset to the staff of a legion. One did not refuse Burrus's requests: I wrote accepting Agricola for a vacancy occurring in October in XIV Legion.

4

I worked far into the night, dictating to my secretaries letters and orders consequent on the mail from Rome. Each legion was directed to supply a century for my new bodyguard. I wanted the four cavalry troops to be representative of each race, Gallic, Spanish, Pannonian and German, supplying the bulk of our horsemen, so I chose them from Indus's Horse, 1st Asturians, 1st Pannonians and 1st Nervana respectively. All these were to be picked men, not less than twenty-five years of age, with five years' service, battle experience and exemplary characters. The five centurions and four decurions I selected by name, basing my choice upon their conduct sheets and, in most cases, on personal knowledge.

The bodyguard would assemble at Silchester, where Sextus Julius Frontinus, whose work in connection with rebuilding that capital was by now purely advisory, would command and train them.

Next I wrote to Aufidius Pantera, giving him detailed instructions for the fleet's summer cruises. I told him first of all to reconnoitre the Severn coast near Caerwent with a view to landing a sizeable force near by: this was in connection with a project forming in my mind to deal really effectively with the Silurian problem. I confirmed and amplified my warning orders, delivered when I first arrived at Richborough, to explore the Anglesey straits and Ordovican coast. Mindful of Nero's warning, I directed that the full strength of the fleet, less one flotilla for routine escort duties, must be used on these voyages, and that, to avoid losses by shipwreck, he should not leave port until assured of reasonably calm weather. As for the fleet base, I told him that, on consideration, the advantages of Boulogne outweighed those of any harbour in Britain.

My directive on appointment as Governor had contained a suggestion that auxiliary cohorts might be raised from British tribes for service outside the Province. I had so far done nothing about this because I preferred to wait for a closer acquaintance with the tribes in order to choose the right material and, if possible, to enlist men who might be used with advantage in my Anglesey campaign. This, admittedly, was not our normal practice: we seldom used auxiliaries in the provinces whence they were recruited because of the risk of employing them against their own kindred. I proposed to break the rule for two good reasons. The Army of Britain's auxiliary strength was low, 17,000 men compared with 22,000 legionaries, whereas a properly balanced force needed at least parity in numbers. Also I intended to recruit only from the Dobuni and Cornovii, two aboriginal tribes who, dispossessed of valuable territories by the invading Belgae to the east and harried for generations by mountain tribes from the west, were the natural enemies of every other Briton in the Province. They should, I judged, prove entirely reliable whether employed on internal security duties or the frontier.

Secretaries wrote energetically while I dictated my requirements to the magistrates of these tribes. The Cornovian centre was Wroxeter: they were told to assemble thirteen hundred men (allowing three hundred for wastage) of fighting age and good physique at Wroxeter within thirty days for enlistment in the Roman Army. At the fortress they would be medically examined, provided with arms and equipment and an instructional staff and sent to Silchester for training. Similar orders went to the Dobuni at Cirencester, with a copy to Paenius Posthumus telling him to equip the men, find instructors and dispatch them to Silchester. The instructional staff for each contingent contained a centurion in command, an option for each century or troop, a standard-bearer, tesserar and duplicar. I urged the legion commanders concerned to select the very best men they had.

The tribes had to include among their men a proportion who by ability or birth were fitted for command and could be promoted to centurion or decurion as training progressed. Given good material an auxiliary unit, within six to eight months, can be fully trained and, except for the commanding tribune or prefect, provide its own officers. It was therefore in the tribes' interests to provide suitable officer material. I underlined this point to the magistrates and finished the letters with an exposition of the honour bestowed upon their peoples in being the first Britons accepted as Roman soldiers, indicating that the choice had been made by the Prince himself in recognition of their loyalty and fighting qualities. I bestowed titles upon the two units: the Cornovian contingent became the 1st Britannic Cohort (milliary) and the Dobuni the 1st Britannic Cavalry (milliary).

The secretaries went on writing. A letter to Frontinus at Silchester directed him to design and build fortified barracks for three thousand men and a thousand horses on the heath west of the town. Another to Epaticcus demanded timber, tiles and labour for the same purpose. A third told Posthumus to send two hundred legionaries to Silchester as overseers and gangers. I wrote to the remount depot near Canterbury for horses and followed this with a note to Cerialis at Lincoln, where the local inhabitants were great horse breeders, telling him to pick a few hundred of the best mounts and send them south.

Trumpets sounded the end of the fourth watch before I signed the last document. I went to my quarters, leaving the tired clerks to seal and deliver the mail to dispatch riders whose horses stamped restlessly in the chill gusts of a May dawning. The scribes never understood my urge to work to a finish. My chief secretary, companion of many wakeful nights on campaign in diverse lands, had once ventured a faint remonstrance:

'Could not this letter wait until tomorrow, most noble Paulinus?'

'Tomorrow?' I had answered. 'Why, tomorrow we may both be dead!'

5

As at Gloucester, I accompanied patrols across the frontier into tribal territory. A longer expedition took me to Chester, a native village standing at the conjunction of Setantii, Cornovii and Degeangli. Here, ten years before, Ostorius had built a lines-of-communication guard-post during his campaign against the Degeangli. The ruins now gave shelter to native hutments and a flock of sheep. Thoughtfully I regarded the river which flowed beneath the site.

'Is this navigable to the sea?' I asked Valens.

'Yes, with care,' he said. 'The water is full of shoals and shifting sandbanks. The estuary eight miles downstream is a productive fishing-ground. Fishing boats get here without any trouble.'

Westwards lay the route to Anglesey. When the Degeangli and Ordovices had been conquered Chester was bound to become a key position in the Province's strategical layout. I examined the place, mentally enlarging the ruined century-post to fortress size: the ground answered the purpose well.

'Valens,' I prophesied as I turned my horse, 'one day a legion will live here.'

'So? It's not much use on our present lines. Is anything afoot?'

Valens knew nothing of my intentions. In such matters I was a disciple of old Metullus Pius, who had declared that if his tunic knew his plans, he would burn it. So I laughed and turned the conversation to the dangers of prophecy and the quibbles of soothsayers, whom we both disliked. Valens gave instances of promising operations being thwarted by unfavourable auspices and railed against the troops' superstitions which demanded these rites as a preliminary to battle. I agreed.

'As you know, Valens, I have priests and augurs permanently attached to my staff. On occasions that really matter they are not entirely free agents.'

He sniffed. 'It's as well. Even the Divine Julius was not above faking the auspices when it suited him. You tell the fellows what to find?'

'I tell them whether I want the signs to be favourable or not,' I said shortly. 'I don't believe in allowing eclipses, chance meteors, diseased livers or a flight of geese to deflect me from my purpose. These things have to be interpreted as I command. That's why I have my own augurs.'

Valens looked at me curiously. 'You do not fear the wrath of the Gods?'

I smothered a sneer, remembering in time that Valens, plebeian by birth, probably still held to old-fashioned beliefs.

'No,' I answered quietly. 'What I do is done for the good of Rome and thereby may earn the Gods' forgiveness. We have a long way to ride and evening is near. Let us hasten.'

In Wroxeter our legionaries were fitting the new armour. Equipment progressed as fast as the armourers, hampered by a shortage of iron, could forge the plates. Ingots in fortress reserves were insufficient to meet the demand: the stockpile was only designed to cope with battle losses and routine repairs. London's arsenal was already distributing its large supplies to the legions and the stocks of iron under military control were draining away. All other iron, in London warehouses or at the mines, was controlled by the Procurator, to whom I sent urgent indents backed by the authority of Burrus's signature. Catus, while asserting his willingness to supply the ingots, pleaded export priorities, short production, lack of escorts for pack-trains and a dozen other excuses for delay. The metal trickled slowly into fortress stores over the months; it was not, in fact, until after I left Britain that every legionary had the new armour.

The men grumbled, of course, saying they were swaddled like Egyptian mummies. Actually the plates hampered them very little, though experience compelled minor adjustments. Shoulder-flanges, as designed, were too long at the back, hindering free play of the shoulder-blade when the arm was drawn back for a javelin cast; the plates had to be shortened behind by a couple of fingers'-breadths on the throwing side. The soldiers soon became used to the extra weight; it made no visible difference to their endurance on the march. The centurions brooked no excuses stemming from the new equipment; always something of a law unto themselves in the matter of military dress, many of them already used armour far heavier than the new issue. This, often of their own design, varied from sheet-metal back- and breast-plates to scale armour copied from the Parthians.

The new javelins demanded a change in drill. For the benefit of those unversed in military technique I must explain that a cohort in battle order is drawn up ten ranks deep, though lesser depth is sometimes permissible to cover a wide front. Each man in line has two yards' fighting space; rear rank files, two yards behind, cover these spaces, both to present the appearance of a solid front to the enemy and to avoid the butts of the front rank's javelins on the back swing. When the preparatory order to throw javelins is given, every front rank man passes one of his two javelins to the man on his right rear, so that, with only one javelin in hand, he is unencumbered for the throw. When this is delivered he swings his arm back and grasps and hurls the second javelin in one motion. The front files, having cast their two javelins, now step to the rear and by a series of diagonal backward paces take position behind the original rearmost rank. Meanwhile the erstwhile second rank, now in front, has its first javelins ready and the process is repeated.

This simple drill was unsuited to the purpose for which the light javelin was designed. The basic idea being to kill the enemy at longer ranges it was necessary for light javelins to be thrown first. Valens suggested a solution.

'Arm your first five ranks with light,' he said, 'and the rest with heavy.'

'It won't do,' I answered, watching a cohort doing javelin exercises. 'What happens if the enemy gets to close quarters before the heavy-armed ranks have reached the front?'

'Yes. Awkward. Well, give the light weapons to the first two ranks only.'

'We can't work on hard-and-fast suppositions that the enemy will be at certain ranges when certain ranks are ready to throw. There's only one answer. The two front ranks alone will be the javelin throwers, changing places after every second throw in the normal way. Ranks in rear will stand fast, passing javelins to the front as the throwing-range requires.'

Valens rubbed his chin. 'They'll get very tired after a while.'

'In action, Valens, how many successive volleys have you seen thrown without a pause? Six? Seven? That's about the limit. After that either the enemy have been stopped or they're on our swordpoints. Don't you agree?'

'True. And any trained man can throw a dozen heavies without tiring.'

'There is also the advantage that you can always have your best marksmen in front, which is impossible with the present system. Anyway, let's try it out.' I called up the centurions of the cohort at exercise and gave them instructions.

The men fumbled it at first, with the obstinate awkwardness of old soldiers called upon to perform a new and untried evolution. Gradually the movements acquired smoothness and rhythm; changes from light to heavy javelins followed without check or confusion. The two front ranks, during this trial, merely went through the motions of throwing; actual discharge was impossible on the congested parade ground. When the men showed reasonable proficiency I ordered the centurions to march the cohort to the javelin ranges.

They formed up on the throwing-line, ten deep, facing the figure-targets of packed earth at distances of ten, twenty, thirty and forty yards.

'Light javelins at the far targets,' I told the senior centurion, 'and heavy at the nearer ones. Change the type at every third throw. Continue the volleys until all javelins have gone.'

The centurion took position. 'Light!' he roared. 'Poise! Throw! Light—poise—throw!'

Points thudded into targets; javelins passed in a steady stream to the front. Soon the last volley went home.

'Steady—rest!'

I looked critically at the two ranks of throwers. They were panting from their efforts; the rate of discharge had been high and each man had flung twenty javelins. But the marksmanship remained good to the end though the last two volleys were possibly a little ragged. Valens, at any rate, was satisfied.

'That's the right answer,' he said. 'I'll have this practised by every cohort. I congratulate you, Legate, on solving the problem so quickly.'

I smiled to myself. The solution was hardly a spur-of-the-moment brainwave: I had worked it out many years before in readiness for the original field trials of my new weapon. 'Simple ideas are usually the best,' I said sagely. 'When your centurions and options are proficient you must form a cadre to supply instructors for other legions.'

6

About this time I started making arrangements for my visit to Brigantia. An exchange of letters with Cartimandua fixed a meeting at York, a village in Brigantian territory forty miles north of Lincoln. Peaceful visitations by Governors to trans-frontier territories, even when they were allied kingdoms, rarely occurred; and Valens, when the expedition was mentioned, pursed his lips and opined that I was taking an unnecessary risk. I admitted an element of uncertainty: Brigantia contained a powerful anti-Roman clique which would delight in violating the Queen's safe-conduct in order to create friction between our two governments. However, Cartimandua promised to send a strong escort of native troops to meet me near Lincoln and I intended also to take a Roman guard sufficient to deter anything but attacks on a tribal scale. For this purpose I wrote to Cerialis, telling him to warn a cavalry regiment, three legionary and two auxiliary cohorts to accompany me from Lincoln.

The chief object of my visit, of course, was to conclude a treaty giving us control of the Anavio lead-mines. I told the Cornovii, who claimed part possession, that they would have to argue their case at York and that their ambassadors must travel in my train. The Procurator was also concerned, for if the mission were successful he would immediately become responsible for working and staffing the mines. I laid the whole project before Catus by letter and invited his company on the journey. He declined, but promised to send representatives from his staff capable of dealing with all the perplexities of law and finance which would certainly arise. He assured me that he held complete records of the Anavio mines which gave yield capacities whereon we could base our financial estimates. As a precaution I asked him to send an expert to the district forthwith, preferably one of the contractors who would eventually lease the workings, so that he could make a last-minute assessment and ensure that our information was entirely up to date.

Arrangements, then, were well in hand to accomplish one of Nero's most important directives. My stay in Wroxeter was coming to an end; I must soon exchange the uncomplicated pleasures of a soldiers' camp for the complexities of administration and politics. The prospect was uninviting; the temptation of making one last patrol in a new area was irresistible.

Valens highly disapproved of my trans-frontier forays, maintaining that scrambling on hillsides in tribal territory was no part of a governor's duties. In answer I pointed to the vast difference between this district and Gloucester, where patrols ventured into Siluria only in considerable strength and with a definite expectation of fighting. Here, thanks partly to a vigorous commander and garrison, partly to a less intractable enemy, the country for many miles westwards was quiet and the tribesmen seldom opposed our periodical reconnaissances. My arguments were wasted: he always came with me and always doubled the patrol strengths irrespective of tactical requirements.

Valens was away inspecting road-stations on the morning when I rode out with two centuries of Valeria, the 2nd (C.R.) Vascones cohort, one troop of the 1st Loyal Vardulli and a bodyguard troop. The plan was to follow the Severn valley upstream for a dozen miles due west, turn south along the course of a tributary and complete the circuit by striking across the hills eastwards to Wroxeter. The whole journey, little short of thirty miles in hilly country, was strenuous work for any infantry; yet the tribune of Vascones, hardy mountaineers from the Pyrenees, cheerfully informed me we would return to the fortress well before dusk.

Our objects were to impress the tribes by showing the standard in their territories, to prevent secret concentrations near the border and to acquaint officers and men with terrain where they might have to fight. Secrecy and surprise were vital if we wanted to avoid ambush. We were a routine patrol, but success and safety depended on the antithesis of routine.

Fortress commanders planned their patrols carefully, seeing that they went out at irregular intervals and followed different routes. Valens had ordered this particular reconnaissance, which he did not know I would join, with a definite purpose. He had intentionally left the area of this day's search unvisited for some time in the expectation that the Ordovices of the region, encouraged by immunity, might get up to mischief.

His appreciation was correct.

We followed the right bank of the Severn. The cavalry deployed four hundred paces ahead and a century flank guard skirted the wooded foothills on our left. We met only occasional herdsmen, who invariably deserted their charges and ran for cover. By the fifth hour we reached our turning point at the river confluence and swung south past the deserted hutments of a native village, overlooked by the inevitable hill-fort. The tribune reined his horse and surveyed the scene.

'Most peculiar,' he observed. 'The place is empty.' He stared at the fort, shading his eyes from the noonday sun. 'Doesn't seem to be anyone up there either. Very odd.'

'Is this village usually inhabited?' I asked.

'Yes, Legate. I've been here before. The people scatter to the hillsides or fort when they see us coming. They've no cause for panic: we don't worry them unless we've had trouble on the way. So far as I know this lot has never been harmed.'

'Well, they are not here now. What do you make of it?'

He shrugged. 'Maybe they've evacuated for some reason of their own. Religious festival, perhaps. Perhaps not. They've probably sent their families and livestock to one of the big forts in the high mountains. It's a habit of these small communities when trouble is brewing.'

'What sort of trouble?'

'War parties,' the tribune said briefly. 'They're always fighting among themselves. Occasionally they decide to raid a road-station or village in Roman territory. We break them up on sight, either way.'

He called his centurions and gave instructions. The patrol advanced, van and flank guards set, the main body deployed in square and alert to meet any sudden attack. Trees and undergrowth shrouded the hillsides and spilled into the valley; clefts and gullies could have screened a dozen ambuscades. None materialized. We marched for some hours, tense and cautious, until we reached another settlement, likewise deserted.

The tribune sighed. 'There's a war party around, all right. Lucky we didn't meet it in the valley. I hate those gullies. Now we can get on the hilltops; the track from here follows the ridge back to the Severn.'

A trumpet blared. The centuries wheeled left and began to climb the rocky slant towards the guardian fort that lowered silently from crags two hundred paces above. The slope was too steep for riding. The Vardulli, leading their horses, entered the infantry square. We climbed silently and, for my lungs, all too speedily. The vanguard reached a false crest and vanished from sight.

The harsh bray of war-horns and a yell like splitting thunderclouds tore the sunlit stillness.

'That's it!' the tribune snapped, sword suddenly in hand, and stormed upwards bellowing commands. The Vascones, breaking swiftly from column into line, leapt after him with the agility of Pyrenean goats. Legionaries and dismounted cavalry plodded grimly on while the auxiliaries streamed past. Helmets were pressed down, shields unslung, javelins hefted thoughtfully in hand.

The false crest saved us. The enemy launched his attack from the topmost ridge directly our vanguard, in extended line, cleared the rise. The slope between false and true crests, a hundred paces wide, was so gentle as to be practically level. The Britons charged the vanguard directly it set foot on this platform and smashed it back. A brief resistance checked the tribesmen's impetus and saved the main body from the full force of a downhill charge. With a last desperate burst the auxiliaries reached the heights: Vascones and Ordovices met shield to shield on the platform's edge.

I paused and regarded the mêlée above. The crest heaved and boiled like an angry volcano but our line seemed to be holding. Should we go straight up in support or come in from a flank? To the right the rock-piled walls of the native fort effectively commanded any approach on that side. I gave a signal; the legionaries changed direction diagonally to the left, behind a rocky spur which hid them from the fight. I signalled again; the men, turning right, formed line from column, mounted the hump and found themselves overlooking the battleground.

We surveyed a scene of strenuous confusion. The auxiliaries, losing cohesion during their uphill charge, had engaged, in considerable disarray, an enemy who habitually fought in a rabble. There was no battle-line. Knots and groups of men hacked, shouted, dissolved and swirled one about the other. The Vascones' long swords were difficult to swing amid the press of bodies; they stabbed short throwing-spears and jabbed spiked shield-bosses into enemy faces. It was an untidy engagement, without front or flank or rear.

Nobody seemed to notice our arrival, though the outer surges of the struggle lapped the base of our mound not fifty feet below. I hesitated. The legionaries' javelins, in this mess, would kill both friends and foes. The senior centurion, at my elbow, also recognized the problem and solved it instantly.

'I think we can separate them, Legate. Have I your permission?'

I assented. The centurion barked an order. The front rank's javelins reared and poised for the throw. The legion's trumpets blared in unison.

'Disengage!' the brazen voices roared. 'Disengage! Disengage!'

His stratagem was successful. The auxiliaries recognized a military command and saw, in the line of levelled javelins, the consequences of dawdling. They broke from their antagonists and scattered briskly to the flanks, while the Ordovices, shocked into awareness of a new enemy, tried frantically to change front. The centurion did not give them long.

'Throw!'

The range, though helped by a downhill trajectory, was nearly beyond killing-distance. Two swift volleys whipped into the throng without doing much damage. The nearest enemy were running out of distance; those farther away showed signs of recovering from the paralysis of our appearance.

'Down javelins!' I yelled. 'Out swords!'

The ranks stooped, grounded javelins, jerked upright. Blades rasped from scabbards.

'Charge!'

We went down the short slope at a steady run. I had time to wonder if yet another consul's career was finishing in a squalid frontier skirmish; then all thinking ceased in a flurry of action. I was never in danger; my bodyguard had thrown their reins to the Vardulli and surrounded me so closely that I hardly crossed blades with a Briton. Which was probably as well, for I had no shield.

The business did not last long. The Ordovices found heavy mailed infantry, locked shield to shield in battle line, a different proposition to light-armed auxiliaries dispersed and winded after a long uphill sprint. The tribesmen broke. Some sought refuge among the crags, others in the fort. The Vascones rallied and converged, cutting down the fugitives or felling the running figures like stricken deer with well-aimed slingshots. The legionaries halted briefly, dressed ranks and stormed the fort. There was no ditch in that rocky ground; the only barrier was a boulder wall, chest-high, hastily manned by desperate survivors. Stones and heads rolled indiscriminately under the feet and blades of Valeria, who then contentedly slaughtered everyone within the ramparts while Vascones, sweeping round the hillside, cut off any who escaped.

I took no part in this assault, being too busy recovering my breath after the stress of close-quarter fighting. The din on the hilltop died away. Romans moved purposefully among the scattered bodies, pulling out our own dead and wounded, prodding at any Briton who still showed signs of life. I told a trumpeter to sound the assembly, posted sentry-groups in case of a counter-attack and demanded casualty reports.

Twenty-two auxiliaries and five legionaries had died. Some of the wounded were too badly hurt to walk. Medical orderlies attended to serious cases, applied salves and bandages and made litters of leather corselets taken from the dead and stretched between javelin shafts.

We could not dig graves in that hard ground nor wait until pyres had consumed the bodies. We stripped the dead of weapons and armour, heaped the corpses together and piled a huge cairn of stones on top. It was the best we could do.

With fifteen miles to march in the remaining four hours of daylight we could not afford to linger. The Britons, adept at using every scrap of cover in their native mountains, had vanished utterly. This did not necessarily mean we had seen the last of them: the Vascones' tribune, wounded and morose, assured me they might easily reappear and harass us all the way home.

'We didn't do that bunch enough damage,' he growled. 'They only left eighty dead. They'll be celebrating the affair as a famous victory by morning.'

'It was a well-laid ambush,' I observed. 'The tribes must have known we were coming.'

The tribune shook his head vigorously. 'No, Legate. I don't think so. Our security is pretty good: the Britons knew about us when they saw us, not before. Remember also that they had to evacuate those two villages we passed and gather their warriors. All that takes time. And, if they'd been hunting us they would have used many more men. Ten Britons to one Roman is regarded as reasonable odds in this part of the world.'

'Why, then, did they attack us?'

'I believe this was a war-band setting out on a raid. We probably bumped them quite by accident; they spotted us first, weighed the chances, decided the ground was heavily in their favour and quickly set the trap. A pity we didn't save one of their wounded and squeeze the truth out of him.'

'No time for that,' I said. I studied our little force, marching in line of century columns, three up, along the broad crest of the ridge. 'Not much chance of being surprised here,' I continued. 'The top of the hill is the place to be in this sort of country. We proved that in Mauretania many years ago.'

'You can't march along the tops of Ordovican mountains, Legate. Too narrow, too broken, too much scrub. This roundbacked one is exceptional: you could build a road along it.'

'We probably will, one day,' I grunted, and fell silent, absorbed in my own thoughts. That skirmish had revealed the damage that could be inflicted by a determined enemy on a Roman Army as it heaved its cumbrous length along these narrow, treacherous ravines. The same problem had irked us in the Atlas, though there everything was on a larger scale: the mountains higher, the lowlands broader, the country comparatively barren. An onset there could not develop with the devastating rapidity possible in this land where steep, wooded hillsides brushed the elbows of men walking in the valleys. We would have to evolve new tactics, some specialized form of mountain warfare, to counter the hazards peculiar to our frontier terrain. This was the kind of military puzzle I loved, a riddle to relieve many tedious hours of travel on Britain's roads.

The tribune's pessimism was unjustified: we saw no hostile tribesmen and reached Wroxeter during the first watch, three hours overdue. Valens, returned from his inspection, furious when he discovered my absence with the patrol, was already parading a search-party. He let no consideration of rank blunt the force of his remarks. I felt he had some justification and listened meekly.

'And what excuse do you think I should make to the Prince, had you been killed while wandering round the countryside with that patrol? Do you fancy that Rome considers her Governors expendable, like centurions?' he finished.

'No, Valens,' I answered, 'but I do fancy a little fighting now and then, even if I have to play truant like a schoolboy to get it.' I clapped him on the shoulder. 'I deserve your reprimands, and apologize. I have learned a lesson and been set a problem. I also have a dry throat and aching bones. Let's go to the baths. While I get clean and massaged you shall tell me everything you know about fighting in the mountains.'

We drank and talked far into the night, dissecting our existing tactics for hill fighting and trying to fit the pieces into a new pattern. No complete solution emerged, but we decided on the broad principles of certain battle-tactics which Valens agreed to try during the summer. Reminiscence began to embroider discussion, and while the wine-flasks emptied and trumpets heralded the changing watches from midnight towards sunrise our memories meandered through far countries and forgotten fights and long-dead comrades. We parted very amicably indeed.

At dawn, with a severe headache, I took the road for Lincoln.

5

'Riches, the incentive of vice, are dug out of the earth.'

OVID

1

That journey, through some of the dreariest countryside in all Britain, took six days. We went through forests heavy with summer foliage where the trees, close-packed and forbidding, unrolled to the skyline a monotonous canopy divided like a sword-cut by the road whereon we travelled. My staff, baggage-train and escort, strengthened by a century of XIV Legion, stretched from one milestone to the next. No one lived in these midland tree-wastes; until we entered the river valley cradling Leicester, capital of the Coritani, we saw hardly a soul. We marched twenty miles a day, halting each night at road-stations cowering like forgotten outposts in a sullen, abandoned land. Some forts, like Wall, were too small to shelter my entire retinue; legionaries and bodyguard threw up marching camps near the ramparts and bivouacked in the open, seldom bothering to erect tents, for the nights were warm and rainless.

On the third day we reached Leicester. This was the poorest tribal capital I saw in the Province, a mere drift of thatched and mud-walled huts without one significant building. On this ignoble hamlet we had imposed the laws and councils of urban government: I was received by the magistrates and decurions proper to a township. They made no resplendent spectacle; the officials were hardly to be distinguished in appearance or dress from the peasants they ruled.

The Coritani were Old Britons who had survived only because their land was so inhospitable that nobody else wanted to live there. They were the poorest and, according to some doubtful census figures—the forests hide many tax-evaders when revenue officers arrive—numerically the weakest of all tribes in the settled areas.

I halted a day at Leicester, heard the inevitable lawsuits and conferred with Coritanian magistrates and elders. It disturbed me to find a tribe we had ruled for nearly two decades in such a primitive state. Revenue returns, passed to me for information from the Procurator's department, had more than hinted at their poverty, but I was unprepared for the abysmal misery depicted by this barbarous settlement. There was no chance here, as at Silchester, of inducing the people to scrap their hovels and build decent houses in the hope of attracting trade. Few merchants ventured into these sombre woodlands, where pastures were sparse and poor, where the natives barely produced enough to sustain life and had no residue left for barter.

I found that their staple foodstuff was beans which, introduced years before from the Continent, flourished improbably in this damp, heavy soil. This gave me a chance of offering some practical help. As beans form a considerable part of army rations their cultivation is encouraged throughout the Province. I made a formal contract with the magistrates whereby the Government would buy an agreed percentage of the annual crop, without limit in quantity; and paid a small subsidy from my treasury—well aware of the actuarial disputes that would later arise with Catus—to help begin the good work.

We left this depressing place with relief and entered Lincoln two days later. The Procurator's representatives had arrived. While it was not surprising, in the nature of Catus's work, that some of his highest officials should be freedmen, I thought it insufferable that he should appoint one as head of his mission, knowing that I was bound to seek his advice and guidance almost daily throughout the course of our Brigantian negotiations. Catus doubtless intended, by this petty device, to damage my prestige with the natives. For it must be remembered that provincials on the world's outer rim do not understand the increasing use we make of freedmen in important government posts. They know slavery and its degradations and cannot understand how ex-slaves can hold authority over freeborn men.

I had already learned, through spies in Catus's household, that he thought my naturally chilly demeanour indicated a scornful disdain of everyone of inferior rank, including himself. This was nonsense. Every man of senatorial rank nowadays has to associate on more or less equal terms with equestrians and, on occasion, with distinguished freedmen such as Claudius of Smyrna. But there is a vast difference, as Catus knew well, between Claudius and a second-rate provincial official. Being fully aware of all these nuances I took good care, throughout the negotiations, never once in a Briton's presence to address Catus's secretary directly.

2

Cerialis, like Valens, frowned upon my expedition. With characteristic vigour he suggested the worst possible eventualities and, when he saw I was not to be dissuaded, tried to bend the project to his own pet purpose.

'Three thousand men are ready to march, Paulinus, as you ordered. Quite a strong escort. Have you any idea of Brigantia's armed strength?'

'Yes,' I said, unbuckling my corselet. 'Somewhere between twenty and thirty thousand. We've fought them, you know, and intelligence keeps us quite well posted.'

'Exactly. Heavy odds even for three cohorts of Hispana. Have you any guarantee of coming out alive?'

'Only the Queen's word,' I said lazily, lying back on the couch, 'and political common sense. Brigantia and Rome are very good friends. Why should they be after my head?'

'Common sense rates low in the British character; otherwise they'd have united and slung us out years ago. You have Cartimandua's safe-conduct. What about Venutius?'

'He's not in Brigantia.'

'His supporters are, though,' Cerialis said grimly, 'and extremely active.'

'And thoroughly suppressed,' I yawned. 'It's no good, Cerialis. I'm going to York without any worries or doubts. If I had any I'd take two legions, not five cohorts.'

Cerialis pinched his lip, eyeing me thoughtfully.

'I wish you would,' he exploded. 'Don't you see what a magnificent opportunity this is? I could follow you at a day's march with the remaining garrison; we would take York, render the Brigantes leaderless by seizing the Queen and her captains and march on the capital before the tribe could organize any opposition. We might conquer Brigantia in a fortnight!'

'Cerialis,' I said impatiently, 'you can't undertake major campaigns at a moment's notice. Apart from twenty other flaws in your scheme, who is going to garrison Lincoln in Hispana's absence? You have an obsession about Brigantia. We shall take the kingdom, but all in good time. Not next year; maybe the year after. Now be a good fellow and let me have a nap: the fleas at the last road-station gave me no sleep at all.'

He went out, shaking his head lugubriously. I sighed and pulled the blankets thankfully to my chin. Quintus, like all men who theorize without inner knowledge, could be tedious. But he was an admirable soldier.

I stayed several days in Lincoln preparing myself and my party for the journey north. Catus had assented to my request for a new survey of the Anavio mines. The man he sent, a competent Roman mining engineer and contractor, submitted an excellent report showing that the known deposits were capable of a tenfold output and still richer fields awaited discovery. The lead had a higher silver content than that found near Bath. He ventured an estimate of the Anavio field's annual yield when properly worked: I pictured a satisfied smile upon the Financial Secretary's melancholy face when the news reached Rome.

'You have kept this secret?' I asked.

'I had two assistants helping with the survey, Legate,' he answered. 'They have not talked. No one but you has seen that report.'

'Good. You and your men must keep your mouths shut. Now listen. The Brigantes will know you have been nosing around the mines; they will guess I sent you. This report stays here. Prepare another, equally detailed, showing poor yields with little likelihood of improved output. Don't overdo it: cast the estimate very slightly above the figure already known to the natives themselves. Be prepared to produce this statement when we meet the Brigantes at York.'

'I understand, Legate.'

'You must be ready to argue a case based on a bogus survey. From this you must work out, with the Procurator's representative, a financial statement computing an equitable annual payment for the leasehold. Don't let the Procurator's people, or anyone else, know that the report is not genuine.'

'Very well, Legate.'

Poor Cartimandua, I thought. Only a Roman could love you and swindle you in the same breath.

3

We left Lincoln on a glittering morning in early June. Cerialis had given me, besides three cohorts of IX Legion, Petra's Horse, the 1st Celtiberians and 4th Dalmatians. Though this was a peace march we took routine precautions: cavalry detachments scouted ahead and watched the rear; the Celtiberians threw out flank guards. I rode at the head of the main body, followed by the bodyguard and legionary cohorts, between whom and the Dalmatians in rear were the baggage-train, my clerical staff, the Procurator's men and the Cornovii with their lawyers. The wheeled transport found progress difficult; the North Way ended at Lincoln and we followed a native trackway, broad and well-defined but rough-surfaced. It followed the spine of a ridge throughout the day's march, giving us views of rolling forests extending unbroken over the plains below. This was the country of the Parisi, famed as charioteers throughout Britain.

The dust of our passage attracted many sightseers who gathered by the roadside and watched, calling to our men in a guttural dialect. We saw nobody afoot; even the herdsmen rode small, shaggy ponies. These people were cheerful and friendly; their curiosity and eagerness to examine our appearance and accoutrements at close quarters was such that the flank guards had difficulty in preventing them from mingling with the column. They had, as yet, no reason to fear Roman soldiers.

Towards late afternoon the ridge descended to flat marshlands and the cavalry reported a broad river ahead, apparently guarded by native warriors in strength. Forewarned of this estuary, nearly a mile wide at the crossing, I had previously arranged with Cartimandua that ferries should be provided for our passage. The natives, I guessed, were the tribal escort she had promised. I cantered forward and was astounded to see Petra's Horse storming into battle line at a furious gallop while trumpets frenziedly sounded the alarm. I shouted inquiry at a decurion as he hurtled by.

'Enemy!' he yelled. 'Enemy cavalry attacking!'

I set heels to my charger and rode full tilt. A white cloak showed the Prefect, sword out, marshalling his troops to action front. I slithered to a halt beside him.

'Where is this enemy, Prefect?'

'There, Legate.' He pointed with his sword.

Five hundred paces away a fluid crescent of horsemen approached us. Sunlight gleamed on lance-points, helmets and harness.

'They've slowed up now. A moment ago they were charging,' the Prefect added.

'Sound the "Stand Fast",' I ordered. 'Stay in battle order but don't advance.'

I rode on with my bodyguard cavalry. A group detached itself from the concourse and came to meet me, headed by an enormous chieftain gay in red-painted helmet, yellow cloak and bright-blue shield. He jumped off his horse and saluted with upraised spear.

'Queen Cartimandua sends me to greet you and escort you safely to her presence, Legate of Rome,' he said in broken Latin.

I replied briefly, sweat prickling my backbone. His first welcome from Rome's emissary had nearly been the spear-points of a tempestuous cavalry charge. My bodyguard relaxed; I sent orders to continue the march to the estuary, where ferries were ready. It was too late to cross that day so we made camp, the Britons amusedly watching our sweating legionaries while they dug. I spent a difficult evening entertaining Brigantian chieftains in my tent. They showed little appreciation of vintage wine and swilled, instead, a fiery concoction brewed from barley, the very smell of which turned my stomach.

At dawn the troops were ferried across the estuary, a long and irksome business requiring many journeys in rowing-boats and small fishing craft. Precautions were difficult in this amicable setting but I managed, through tactful interpreters, to ensure that approximately equal boatloads of Britons accompanied each relay of our own men, so that at no time did tribesmen greatly outnumber Romans on either bank. The swarm of Brigantian warriors made tactical dispositions for the march impossible: I compromised by detaching a rear party five hundred strong who, after demolishing our marching camp, crossed the river last and followed warily half a mile in rear, whence they could strike swiftly if anything went wrong. For the rest it was a parade march with massed standards and trumpeters.

The British warriors rode ahead, around and amongst us, shouting, chattering and singing, with no pretence of order or formation. Physically these Brigantes resembled the natives of our settled areas: tall, powerful men, fair-skinned and red-haired. The chieftains' helmets and shields were brightly enamelled, their cloaks brilliantly variegated like summer wildflowers, while intricate designs in gold and silver decorated sword-hilts, scabbards, baldrics and saddlery. Jewelled brooches fastened cloaks and belts. Their followers, in contrast, ran mostly half naked, wearing only rough woollen trousers bound criss-cross below the knee, armed with either sword or spear and a square wooden shield. The swords were long, without points, used only for slashing. Two-horsed chariots, painted in garish colours, whirled back and forth; spearmen rode bareback on small, rough-coated ponies, nimble and easily handled despite their rude appearance. All, leaders and led, displayed a boisterous cheerfulness contrasting remarkably with the subdued demeanour habitual to our own Britons. Does Rome, I wondered, kill laughter when she conquers?

All day we tramped across rough moorland in broiling sunlight, fording several streams and rivers. By late afternoon when, according to the Brigantian leader, York was only a mile or two ahead, I halted the column and ordered arms and accoutrements to be cleaned and burnished. I rode back to the baggage-train and changed from my usual legionary corselet to ceremonial dress: helmet and cuirass of hammered bronze, chased and engraved and washed with gold; scarlet crest and cloak; tunic, breeches and boots of red Spanish leather; gold-plated scabbard and jewel-hilted sword. Then, with helmets donned, shields on arms, we swung at parade step into York.

We were met by Cartimandua wearing a shimmering azure robe ablaze with gems and riding in a magnificently ornate chariot. At her wheels rode Brigantia's nobility, a blazon of colour, and her royal guard, huge warriors in horned helmets and brazen armour. A native village, ditched and stockaded, timbered and thatched, formed the background to this splendour. Cartimandua made her formal speech of welcome in precise Latin. I answered her in the same language and, through interpreters, replied to other orations from clan chiefs and headmen. These ceremonies over, the Queen led me to a low plateau overlooking a river, crowned, to my astonishment, by a fortified camp built in the Roman fashion.

'I thought to save your men the labour of digging,' she said. 'Does it meet your requirements?'

I quickly assessed dyke, ramparts and timber stockade, with gates correctly sited and watch-towers set at proper intervals.

'Perfect,' I said. 'The exact dimensions for three thousand men. Who is your engineer?'

She smiled. 'Go inside.'

I rode into the camp. Timbered barrack-huts bordered stone-paved streets; store rooms and horse lines were precisely disposed. I poked thoughtfully with my sceptred staff at a clay manger. The earth was bone-dry all through. This camp had been made days ago, long before we left Lincoln.

I signalled the column to march into the fort and rejoined Cartimandua. 'Your intelligence service is magnificent,' I said grimly. 'How long ago did you learn the exact force I was bringing?'

She laid her hand on mine. 'No, Paulinus; we must not quarrel. I knew to a man how many followers you would bring to Brigantia; I knew it before you, yourself, came to Lincoln. You and I are rulers; we have to keep ourselves informed.' She pointed to the camp. 'Have I misused the information? And does it matter whence it came?'

'To me, very much. Never mind: I shall find out in time. Who laid out this fort?'

'I did.' She smiled demurely. 'Ostorius Scapula was a most militarily-minded man and talked of nothing but cohorts and camps. I could not help learning a little.'

I grinned. 'A little! You ought to be training my engineers! Do we meet tonight?'

She shook her head. 'Tomorrow, at noon, a banquet. Then a formal meeting to begin our negotiations, which will probably last till evening.'

'And then?'

She pointed to a crowded encampment in the distance. 'The royal household. My own pavilion is set some way apart. My servants will wait at the Decuman Gate after dark to lead you there.'

I met her eyes and shivered in all my limbs. She twitched the reins; her chariot rolled forward.

'Very soon after dark, Paulinus.' Her voice sank to a whisper and drowned in the clatter of hooves. 'The nights are short in summer.'

<h1 style="text-align:center">4</h1>

Negotiations for the Anavio lease began next day when the Queen and I each formally presented our cases. Discussions went on for a fortnight. I was spared attendance except when some point of policy or principle was involved; most of the wrangling was conducted between lawyers and accountants on both sides. The contractor's faked report carried weight, for he had been cunning in pitching his estimates quite high, by British standards, and in disclosing some unimportant ore-bearing veins hitherto unknown to the natives. The Cornovii created many obstructions, not without reason; their claims tended to be crushed between those of the two greater contenders.

I blessed the Cornovii. During these weeks I roamed the moors with my beautiful queen, riding beside her chariot, attended only by a handful of guards. Day followed golden day. Sometimes we rode out early from her pavilion—for I no longer bothered to return to the camp before dawn—and returned at dusk, after eating beside some clear, tumbling stream with the guards at a discreet distance, making love under skies of Grecian blue, while the soft warmth of Britain's summer sunlight caressed our naked bodies.

Did I love Cartimandua? Can any man of two-score years and more unravel the fragile threads of love from the warp and weft of passion? I think not. This only I know, that when her infrequent letters reach me here in Rome (as they still do, intercepted by the Prince's spies, read and marked by grubby fingers) my heart aches and for days my household goes upon tiptoe.

The conference ended at last. From our viewpoint the settlement was highly satisfactory and the Cornovii had fared not too badly. Once more Cartimandua and I met in council of state and together signed the treaty. My tribunes and chief centurions organized a feast in the camp for the Queen and her nobles. At this I presented Cartimandua with gifts on the Prince's behalf: a racing chariot of Roman pattern, the carved woodwork inlaid with gold and silver tracery, and four Asturian stallions, mettlesome yet instantly obedient to voice and rein. For the chieftains there were rare and delicate woven fabrics, vases and goblets, engraved swords and decorated bridles. To her, that last night, I gave my own offering: a small, beautiful statuette of Aphrodite, created long ago in Hellas by a poet in bronze.

Next day we paraded before the camp, ready to depart. The ceremonial farewell speeches came to an end; trumpets called; cavalry filed down the track. I faced the Queen and raised my sword in the Royal Salute.

'Farewell, Queen of Brigantia.'

Her lips trembled.

'Farewell, Legate of Rome.' And, like a wind-torn sigh in the trumpets' voices: 'Farewell, my beloved.'

5

The weather, changing suddenly to rain-charged gales, fitted my mood of black depression. Through mud and swollen fords we marched to the estuary, where racing tides delayed our crossing. In Lincoln I waited only long enough to conduct a searching inquiry into the garrison's security system, sparing neither Cerialis nor his staff in efforts to trace a Brigantian connection. The efforts were unsuccessful. Two suspected British spies, a groom and wine-vendor, were caught and examined but died under torture without disclosing any clues worth following. I brusquely told Cerialis to extend his inquiries to road-stations between Lincoln and Wroxeter and to interrogate dispatch riders on that route; after which I departed fuming for Colchester.

My temper in the days that followed was not improved by the suffocating piles of documents which demanded attention. I sent copies of the Anavio treaties to Nero with a covering letter that carefully ascribed the successful outcome to the far-reaching authority of his name. In these dispatches I reported the formation of two British cohorts; complained with deference about my exiguous auxiliary force and sought the equivalent of eight cohorts as reinforcements. Nor were auxiliaries our only lack. In a letter to Burrus I stressed that all legions were under establishment, some by as much as five hundred men, so that legionaries who had completed twenty years' service and were unwilling to re-engage as veterans for a further five were being forcibly retained with the standards. Even veterans found discharge difficult. Grievances among old soldiers re-echoed quickly down the ranks and tended to unsettle entire units. Moreover, I added, the quality of the recruits we did get was deteriorating: fewer and fewer were Italians, more and more were Gauls from Narbonne, or Spaniards, with odd jetsam from Macedonia and Asia. The Army of Britain was maintained largely by drafts from Rhineland depots over which I had no control: I asked Burrus, in succinct language, to address instructions to these depot commanders reminding them that Britain was not a rubbish-dump for provincial recruits.

A secret report from Aurelius Bassus, census officer of Colchester, made me frown and send for the author.

'Bassus, there is nothing concrete in this,' I said, flicking the roll. 'Hints, suspicions, doubts, that is all. You were told to report under three main heads: anti-Roman elements in Roman territory, traffic in armaments, treasonable links between Iceni and Trinovantes. You suspect all these but can prove nothing. Why?'

'Because getting proof in these matters is like grasping water, Legate,' he answered composedly. 'My palms are damp. I *know* the Trinovantes have secret societies plotting against us; I *know* the Iceni and Trinovantes have anti-Roman connections. But my hands are empty: I cannot prove these things.'

'Tell me.'

'A multiplicity of incidents paints the picture, Legate; a recital of the whole would last till sundown. For example: my men found, in a forest, a Trinovantan woodsman wearing a sword. This is against the disarmament edict and so he was arrested and questioned in secret. After some pressure he confessed himself a member of a gang smuggling armaments across the Icenian border, named certain fellow-tribesmen working with him and agreed to reveal a secret cache in the forest where they hid weapons. We acted. The men he betrayed had vanished, presumably across the border; the cache, a pit beneath an oak-tree, had been emptied before we arrived. We buried our native in it.'

'Go on.'

'One of my Asturians, a fellow I chose for this mission because he spoke the Old British tongue, obtained employment on a chieftain's estate near the Icenian border. We had a message from him saying that Icenian nobles frequented the house and conferred in secret with the owner and other Trinovantan aristocracy.'

'That might mean anything.'

Bassus sighed. 'It might. The Asturian also said he was hoping to discover what went on at these meetings. Three days later his head was deposited on my threshold during the night. The Druids' sign was carved between his eyes. I decided not to make a fuss, all things considered.'

I stared at his impassive face.

'This is impossible, Bassus! Do you mean to tell me that our expensive, highly-organized security system cannot get evidence of conspiracy between two whole tribes?'

'No, we cannot,' he answered heavily. 'The natives watch us very cunningly and with enormous patience. Every man, from chieftain to slave, is a potential spy. How can we tell friends from traitors?'

'Have we no friends among the Trinovantes?'

'Practically none.' Bassus spoke with an air of desperation. 'Listen, Legate, because you'll not find this in my report. I'm convinced that both Trinovantes and Iceni hate Rome and everything Roman. I believe they have been in secret alliance for years. Only one man restrains them.'

'Prasutagus?'

'Prasutagus of the Iceni. He is old and wise and has already felt the strength of Rome's arm. When he dies anything may happen. This territory is totally unprotected, Legate. We need a legion stationed permanently in Colchester.'

'You are not yet my military adviser, Bassus.'

The Prefect suddenly looked very tired. 'I am sorry, Legate. Perhaps this mission has overstrained my faculties. Have I your permission?'

When he had gone I sat head in hands for a long time. I believed Bassus. His reports accorded too well with my own conceptions. We had here a dormant volcano whose explosion might blast us out of Britain. At its molten core lay the Iceni, our friendly allies. Must we wait for Prasutagus to die? The kingdom should be annexed forthwith. On what grounds? How could we reverse our policy towards a familiar neighbour with no evidence beyond the unsupported convictions of a cavalry prefect? Useless to write to the Prince. I took stylus and slowly ciphered a letter to Burrus.

'Persuade the Prince to let me march against the Iceni before winter. They are ready for revolt and are sowing disaffection widespread. I am certain of this but can offer no definite proof. I cannot spare troops to police this area; you know why. Use all your influence. This matter is vital.'

The days went by. I dealt with multifarious business: routine returns and reports from legions, audits, indents and fiscal problems from the Procurator, queries from local authorities and tribal magistrates arising out of projects initiated during my tour, and everlasting judicial work. Daily, before sunrise, I held an audience interviewing petitioners, merchants, landowners, magistrates and chieftains, settling grievances or merely exchanging compliments. Much time was wasted, for the Britons are a garrulous race who attain their ends only through a maze of verbiage.

Amid such distractions I completely reorganized our lines of communication. The haphazard distribution of road-station garrisons, their indifferent discipline and the dilapidated condition of many forts had filled me with increasing irritation throughout my travels. The only exceptions were stations between Cirencester and Wroxeter which, girdling the frontier and controlled by fortresses, were rigorously efficient. In order to bring about a similar unity of command and responsibility I issued orders withdrawing all the heterogeneous garrisons from other roads and replacing them by single units responsible for policing definite sectors. Thus the Frontier Way was allotted to 1st Nervana and 2nd Nervii; the West Way to the 3rd and 4th Gauls; the Midland Way to 1st Vangiones and the North Way to 1st and 2nd Lingones. Some of these were milliary units and all, except the Nervii, were mixed cohorts, horse and foot, and so could provide mounted detachments for patrolling. Certain specially trained legionaries also were seconded to important stations near towns or at road junctions to serve as intelligence and customs officers.

Each cohort had to maintain a main headquarters and reserve force at the most important point in its sector, with detachments at stations sited, on an average, twelve miles apart. On the Midland Way, for instance, the 1st Vangiones, a mixed milliary cohort, kept four hundred men at High Cross, the intersection of Midland and Frontier Ways, with eleven other garrisons varying in strength from a century at Verulam to twenty-five men at Towcester.

As a postscript to these instructions I directed the repair and, in some cases, the complete reconstruction of the stations themselves, with stringent commands against civilian settlements abutting the defences. These mushroom growths sprang up wherever we built a permanent post, often housing more people than the fort itself. I did not formulate any minimum separation, leaving this to be decided by sector commanders in accordance with local topography and tactical requirements; nor, unfortunately, could I direct the removal of temples and shrines. This edict, intended to clear a proper fighting-space around each fort, was generally effective. Some garrisons, however, were most dilatory in razing hutments and, in more civilized and therefore litigious areas, the demolitions gave rise to many vexatious claims for damages and compensation.

Largely dependent upon road-stations were the military dispatch riders. The Imperial Post from Rome, whose riders were civil service slaves of the Prince's Household, plied only from Richborough to Colchester. Government correspondence elsewhere in the Province was carried by messengers seconded from cavalry regiments, who rode in thirty mile relays between alternate road-stations. This system had become slack and was slower than it should be. The messengers were unrestricted by regimental discipline, formed undesirable attachments with Britons on their routes and often lived with native families in roadside villages, preferring the laxity of civilian existence to military austerity in a fort. Under these conditions mails could be tampered with; from this source, I felt certain, Cartimandua had secured her foreknowledge of my escort's strength.

I therefore filled the post stable with fast, high-quality horses and replaced doubtful men with hard-riding horsemen of proved integrity who normally worked to a schedule of fifty miles a day. In addition, I instituted an emergency timing on all main roads whereby urgent letters could travel at eighty miles in the day. Only messages franked by legates commanding legions or the Procurator could be sent by this service: I did not relish some young tribune galloping my post-horses to death because his minion had a colic.

My internal security network was now functioning with reasonable efficiency. Agents sent out during the winter to enrol spies among the tribes had returned and reported their tasks completed. Intelligence reports from the settled areas, apart from the usual grievances connected with taxation, made dull reading; everyone seemed happy and contented under Roman rule. I thought grimly of the loathing and intrigue seething around the capital, unmentioned in any agent's report, and wondered how much our system was really worth. Harassed by doubts and fears I nagged my secretary in charge of intelligence, devised checks and counter-checks, spies to spy upon spies, increased secret service grants, all without apparent effect. More reports flowed in, that was all; their comforting tenor stayed unchanged.

I started a new survey of Britain, apportioning the Province between twelve parties chosen from legionary surveyors. This was a long-term measure whose results would be collated years hence by my successor. (The map of Britain lying before me as I write is the outcome of this achievement.)

Early in July Aufidius Pantera wrote that he had found a good landing place near Caerwent, though he made certain reservations about weather and tides. In reply I wrote:

'Your news is encouraging, dear Pantera. Now you must find an inlet or creek on the Severn estuary's southern shore, nearly opposite Caerwent, to shelter a fleet capable of embarking two thousand men. You must then reconnoitre a safe passage across the estuary between this haven, when you have found it, and the Caerwent beaches, and make your master mariners so familiar with it that they will be able to cross safely by night. Do this with circumspection so that the Silures are not disturbed by constant cruising near their coasts.

'You must also calculate for me a period of, say, seven days in late August when tides will favour a crossing.

'I warn you now that you will have to find ships for this operation. Tell me how many will be required and whence they can be found. You shall have my authority to commandeer merchantmen from London and other ports; but do nothing until I give you word.

'Keep this matter secret. Let no hint of my plans reach even your captains. Farewell.'

I had been in Colchester for a month, working twelve hours a day, bad-tempered, haunted by memories of Cartimandua. The note from Pantera with its promise of battles to come was like a breath of the clean sea-wind that drove his ships. I threw my reply to a dispatch clerk and bellowed for the tribune on duty. Within minutes the Secretariat buzzed like a tumbled hive; next day I started for Silchester.

6

Frontinus had done his work well. The main streets were already paved, foundations of town hall and market-place laid and walls rising. The public baths were almost finished and Epaticcus's own house, designed by an Italian architect from London, wanted only roof tiles. Rebuilding elsewhere was scanty; six or seven houses were slowly rising at street corners. Otherwise the original mud and thatch cottages, where they had not been demolished to make way for streets, still made the bulk of Silchester. The surrounding ditch and bank were not yet dug; only a token furrow between surveyors' stakes marked their course.

With Frontinus and Epaticcus I strolled to the site of my own mansion, whose walls rose unevenly like broken teeth. The architect was busy with measuring-rod and plumb-line among toiling bricklayers and masons. I conned the work with approval, particularly the bath-house adjoining the forecourt: this, so far as I knew, was the only house in Britain outside London with its own baths. A range of stables was being built for my private stud, for I liked to keep my horses under my own eye.

Acres of scrub had been cleared around the camp to make parade-grounds, and here my newly formed guard and British auxiliaries were exercising. The latter were still in the individual training stage. I halted before a Dobunian squad who were doing sword exercise with double-weight drill purpose weapons to strengthen their muscles.

'How are they faring?' I asked the option instructor.

'Well enough, Legate. We'll make faster progress when they understand more Latin.'

'Very likely.' The tribes who spoke Old British were slow in learning our language. Even Gallic expressions in the drill-books meant nothing to them.

I turned away to watch other squads, some doing physical training at the double under heavy packs, others bumping in the riding-schools to scathing comments from hard-bitten decurions. Movement, noise, pounding hooves, clash of iron and jingle of harness, dust, oaths, the smell of sweat and leather: all the senses were assailed and delighted in this factory of the Roman Army, this machine turning ferocious savages into cold, disciplined fighting-men. I grinned with pleasure.

'Let's see your command, Frontinus.'

We rode to the bodyguard's parade-ground. I watched, in critical silence, a very different scene. These were men of outstanding quality, fully trained soldiers before they came to Silchester. All that remained for Frontinus was a process of integration and perfection so that the result should be a pattern for every other unit in the Army of Britain.

'And that,' I murmured, 'you have done, Frontinus. I shall inspect the guard in two days' time and see them exercised in parade and battle drill. If all goes well they will be given their scarlet crests.'

The bodyguard's passing-out parade was watched by the British auxiliaries and also attracted many spectators from the town. After a minute inspection of arms and equipment, with which I could find no fault, the cohort marched past in line, four cavalry troops leading six centuries. Frontinus then drilled the centuries, putting them through a variety of manœuvres: line to column, column to square, square to line of columns, reinforcing front and many other movements, finishing with a javelin volley and charge. The performance was immaculate.

The cavalry's brightly coloured tunics and fringed saddlecloths made a lively contrast to the legionaries' sombre russet-and-iron. Their drill was good, surprisingly so for auxiliaries. Dashing, vigorous horsemen; yet I could not visualize them breaking heavy infantry like the iron-clad legionaries who, leaning on tall, half-cylinder shields, watched their manœuvres with sardonic amusement.

7

During July and early August I made an extensive tour of southern Britain from Winchester to Exeter. This was a slow journey broken by many prolonged halts, for I made a point of visiting every town and important village and conferring with magistrates, chiefs and elders. The country was mostly downland broken by marshy, forested river valleys, the tribal centres being no more than large native villages unadorned by any specimens of Roman architecture. My travels had more than a political purpose. The army required quantities of wool for clothing, leather for shields and tunics, tents and boots; and depended on the civilian population to provide both. The open plateaus of the south were the great stock-rearing lands of Britain, abundant in cattle and sheep, and in the forested valleys pigs were bred, equally important for the lard and fat in army rations.

I played the farmer among farmers, inspecting stock, suggesting ideas for improvement, arranging for pedigree rams and bulls to be sent from Roman farms to improve breeding strains, granting small money subsidies where the result might be to our advantage, appointing expert overseers in backward communities.

These farmers, growing little corn, were comparatively unaffected by adverse corn prices. I found them contented, co-operative and reasonably prosperous, particularly as they all, but for a few town-dwellers, escaped poll-tax. Land tax they had come to accept as an unpleasant but inescapable necessity. Hard cash is the best incentive to greater effort: though lacking powers to remit taxation I contracted that the Government would always buy, at prices giving farmers a good profit margin, a fixed proportion of their pigs, wool and hides. A ready market encourages expansion; production in this part of Britain increased by a third within two years.

Near Winchester was a large estate confiscated by Aulus Plautius when the owner, a Belgic noble, was executed for treason. This now belonged to the Prince, being supervised by a freedman of Caesar's household. Here I found a weaving establishment which produced clothing, cloaks and blankets for the army from the raw wool provided by Belgae and Durotriges.

Such matters, and the inexorable litigation awaiting me in law courts at Winchester, Dorchester and Exeter kept me fully occupied. Military affairs were in abeyance in this peaceful, ungarrisoned district. On the main roads, however, I took the opportunity of inspecting the lines of communication troops, already moving to their new stations, and enforcing demolition of civilian encroachments: an obnoxious measure which increased my popularity with neither soldiers nor natives.

One day we turned aside from the highway to visit a disused British temple on the plain near Old Sarum. I had heard much of this monument. The reality was somewhat disappointing because the great stones were dwarfed in the flat immensity of their surroundings. Nevertheless the concentric circles of hewn rock, encircled by bank and ditch, were not without grandeur. Melancholy and forlorn, they stood intact except for one of the tremendous inner portals, overthrown, as ancient digging showed, by human agency. I was unwillingly impressed despite a firm disbelief in gods and religion, Roman or barbarian.

'Does anyone know the history of this place?'

A man stirred in the bodyguard ranks.

'Permission to speak, Legate?'

'Your name?'

'Dossenius Proculus, centurion, seconded from II Legion Augusta.'

'Go on.'

'I was a recruit with the legion, under the legate Flavius Vespasianus, when we fought and conquered the southern tribes seventeen years ago. I accompanied a detachment sent to destroy this temple.'

I slid from my saddle and sat on a fallen stone, idly tracing with my finger some characters carved in a long-forgotten language.

'Tell me the story.'

'The legion was encamped at Winchester, which we had entered without resistance and found unoccupied. Cavalry were probing westwards, trying without success to find enemy. The countryside seemed deserted. We found later that many refugees had fled to the great Durotrigan fortress at Dorchester.

'One cavalry troop caught a Briton and brought him in for questioning. His story we only half understood: a garbled description of a war-band gathering at the Temple of the Sun. None of us had heard of this temple, then, nor knew where it was. The legate decided investigation was worth while and detailed a cohort, with auxiliary infantry and cavalry, to destroy both war-band and temple, if it existed. We took the native as a guide.

'The place was a day's march distant, an unpleasant journey in freezing weather with a bitter wind howling under lowering clouds. We came to the plain and passed solitary huts, small settlements, round burial mounds. All were desolate, grey and lonely. In the afternoon it began snowing.

'We plodded on. The clouds descended, black and heavy. The snowfall turned to a blizzard. Visibility closed to a few yards; we lost sight of our cavalry, scouting at head and flanks. The tribune halted and closed the formation. Then our guide became reluctant, struggling and shouting. I put a javelin to his back and forced him on. We had no time to waste on remorseful traitors.

'Presently a cavalry scout reported something ahead: vast buildings, he said shakily, fires and hundreds of people. The guide was making a lot of noise, obviously trying to give warning. No one could have heard him beyond a javelin-cast in that gale, but he had done his job and was now a nuisance. We cut his throat.

'The tribune took me forward to the cavalry, halted in a fold of ground. We saw these monstrous stones and a great crowd filling the enclosure to the bank and beyond. Fires, whipped by the wind, sparked and flared within the inner horseshoe of lintelled pillars. The assembly was still, watching, intent upon something hidden from us behind the huge black rocks.

'Our preparations were short. Cavalry and auxiliaries moved silently to positions surrounding the temple. One century the tribune held in reserve; the other four formed line and drew swords. When all was ready the trumpets sounded.'

Proculus paused, rubbed his nose and coughed.

'I tell you this as it happened, Legate, believe me or not. In the snap of an eyelid the wind rose and hit us like a wave, screeching like a million demons. It was terrifying. The temple pillars, I swear, rocked before my eyes. The fires flicked out like candles. The crowd swayed; a crawling moan rose to an agonized shriek which drowned the gale.

'Well, the signal had been given. I was only a recruit, blinded by snow, wind-deaf and frightened. The veterans weren't feeling too sure of themselves, either, judging by the language. But it takes more than tempest to stop Valeria. We cleared the ditch at a run; our sword-points jarred on bone. After that it was all right. The first Britons died without knowing what killed them.

'The rest was panic and slaughter. We worked inwards from the circular bank, pushing the crowd together with our shields, shaving the outer edges with our blades like peeling layers from an onion. Women and children died with the rest; we had no orders about prisoners. There was practically no resistance until we reached the inner stone circle.

'Here, around these huge pillars, we had a proper fight. They made a tight ring, filling gaps between the stones with their bodies, fighting like men at the edge of hell. Within, above whooping trumpets, iron-clash and battle-yells, I heard men singing, high-voiced and despairing.

'It was soon over, and we were inside, where we are now: the inner sanctuary, I suppose you might call it. We found priests dressed in wolf skins, faces painted blue and yellow, bunched together, still chanting their death-song. The sight was so unexpected, unreal, that our men paused. Only then did I realize that the wind had dropped, suddenly and completely, and everything was still. The snow drifted down gently.'

Proculus kicked the stone on which I sat.

'This was an altar, Legate. Seventeen years ago two naked bodies lay on it, a boy and a girl. They were most delicately carved, like capons at a banquet, neatly decorated with their own tongues, breasts, genitals and entrails. Yet they still lived; their eyes moved; they knew.

'The tribune, a young fellow, saw and was sick. He was then angry and told us not to kill the priests. He put guards over them, and sent the auxiliaries hunting for timber, difficult enough to find in this treeless plain. They cut stakes, and we dug holes and planted the stakes five paces apart in a circle between the outermost stone ring and the bank. Then we bound the priests to the stakes, fifty-six in all, and stacked wood around them. It was full night by the time we finished.

'The wood was wet, green and burned badly, so that our torchbearers were busy keeping the fires going. The priests died slowly, burning a little at a time, smouldering, moaning until the fires were rekindled, screaming when the flames leapt and bit. The horrors on the altar still lived and watched. None of us dared touch them.

'By morning all were dead. We worked all day to drag down the stones but they were heavy, the bases buried deep. We toppled only one of the portals. It lies there now.'

I rose stiffly. My fingers felt sticky where they had touched the stone; I bent and scrubbed them on the turf.

'Were these men Druids, Proculus?'

'As to that,' the centurion said, 'I cannot say, knowing nothing of barbarian customs. The tribune said they were not; he thought they were priests of an old religion, older than the Druids, as old as Britain itself.'

'Well, we have ended it.' I mounted and surveyed the stone circles, silent, brooding, evil. 'This place is accursed,' I added violently. 'Accursed and indestructible. If we cannot raze these pillars they must stand for ever. Yet two thousand empty years will not free their tormented ghosts. Let us go.'

The column swung across the plain. Dust rose beneath our feet, drifting in the sun behind the marching men, hiding the temple behind a dancing tapestry flecked with gold.

8

A dispatch from Pantera called me to Silchester. I sent messengers to him and to Vettius Valens, summoning them to conference. I sent my civil secretariat back to Colchester and stripped military headquarters to the essential minimum, leaving superfluous personnel in Silchester. On a rainy morning in mid-August I rode for Gloucester, sniffing like a questing boarhound at war over the horizon.

6

'This sort of stratagem is to be used, not merely against those whom we deem simple-minded, but much more when the ruse invented is such that it might seem to have been suggested by the Gods.'

SEXTUS JULIUS FRONTINUS

1

The main room of Augusta's praetorium contained a long oak table, three chairs, benches, armour stands and wall racks stuffed with metal roll-containers which held the legion's documents and files. Here the legate directed his legion's affairs, heard complaints, conferred with tribunes and centurions and dispensed summary justice. The door, closed and guarded by a sentry, faced an inner entrance to the clerks' room, now unoccupied; the shutters of one window were open to the fortress's forum; at the opposite end a dun-coloured dawnlight struggled through thick glass panes. Papers, maps, tablets and an abacus littered the table where, relaxed and tired, I sat and blinked at the guttering lamps. Here I had spent the night alone, collating, amending, simplifying the intricate details of an operation that was to clear the ground for more ambitious campaigns in the coming year.

I had committed myself to this project, the reduction of the Silures, with considerable reluctance, for it is never my habit to exact by force what can be obtained by negotiation. But the Silures, almost alone among the tribes we encountered in Britain, understood none of the principles of diplomacy, disregarded treaties at their convenience and were consistently treacherous. They were a race different from and older than the cis-Severn tribes: survivors, I think, of those shadowy people who built the great stone circles near Old Sarum and who, defeated by successive waves of invasion, retreated sullenly to the western mountains where they now lived. Their tribal rule and organization contained certain peculiarities unique in Britain: although, like all tribes, they were divided into septs and clans each ruled by a minor chieftain who, from a hilltop stronghold, held dominion over a few valley pastures, their kingship was hereditary, wielded supreme power and was worshipped as a deity. Their ancient religion, dark and obscure, reluctantly accepted the Druids, who were tolerated rather than venerated; the priests of the golden sickle had less influence among the Silures than anywhere else beyond our frontiers.

Our dealings with the tribe had been unfortunate. Ostorius Scapula had defeated them in the field, but indecisively, and their subsequent harrying had prevented all his efforts to establish forward posts in their mountains. Scapula was the first Governor to try diplomacy, but the sketchy negotiations collapsed abruptly over the question of hostages: the Silures, in effect, replied as the Helvetii answered Julius Caesar a hundred years before, that they were accustomed to taking hostages, not giving them. Scapula's successor, Didius Gallus, exhausted by ineffective efforts to bring the tribal army to a decisive action, tried to secure peace by bribes. The Silures readily accepted the gold, promised everything that Gallus demanded, and promptly renewed hostilities with redoubled vigour.

With such a savage and intractable people persuasion and bribery were equally useless. Conquest would be a protracted and expensive business. But they could, I thought, be brought to terms by striking at their heart, at their most precious and revered possessions. No other course seemed possible.

The sentry's javelin-butt grounded in salute; the door opened for Vettius Valens, Paenius Posthumus and Aufidius Pantera. When they were seated I called the option of the guard.

'Admit nobody and keep everyone well away from the windows of this room.'

I drank a cup of wine and rubbed my smarting eyes.

'What we shall discuss,' I began, 'is secret and must not be mentioned by any of you beyond my presence. Understood?'

They nodded assent.

'Next spring the army will undertake a major offensive whose scope and direction I do not at present intend to reveal. Our immediate concern is that the Silures, as matters stand, could disrupt those operations either by direct participation or by invasion across the Severn into our settled areas.

'My object is to neutralize the Silures until our spring offensive is over. To do this I propose to mount an expedition, with duration and objectives both strictly limited, against the Silures early next month.'

'At this season?' Valens interjected.

'With particular intent. For at this season the tribesmen have gathered the harvest and no overriding distractions prevent them going to war. They will react to a Roman invasion by a large-scale mobilization that will strip every town, village, fort and valley of fighting men. I propose to send a legion across the Severn at Gloucester in the hope of attracting the entire armed strength of Siluria.'

Posthumus said, 'We'll still be fighting by midwinter.'

'Wait,' I interrupted. 'The legion will be no more than a magnet, a lure to draw and hold. It need not, and must not, advance more than a few miles across the border. There, in Silurian territory, the legion will fortify a camp, an impregnable base whence it can lay waste the countryside within a day's march. The tribesmen will rally to this outrage like wasps to rotten fruit.

'But our main blow will be struck elsewhere, by a small sea-borne force crossing the Severn estuary well below Gloucester and directed on the Silurian capital, Caerwent. They should find this fortress almost undefended, its garrison facing the legion many miles away. Their task is to capture members of the Silurian royal family and high nobility, whom we shall hold as hostages against the tribe's good behaviour.

'To prevent Gloucester being ungarrisoned while our forces are in the field, I propose to transfer a legion here from Wroxeter until the operation is over. Probably a superfluous precaution—but you never know. Perhaps by some unlikely stroke of tactical genius the Silures may decide to by-pass our rather obvious bait and attack Gloucester.

'That is the outline of my plan. What do you think of it? Valens?'

The legate pondered, pulling at his beard. 'What if Caerwent is strongly held?' he said at length.

'We retire to our ships and the attempt has failed,' I answered. 'It's a risk that must be taken. Posthumus?'

'Caerwent is unknown ground. How shall we discover the defences and approaches?'

'I have provided for that. We shall have a guide who knows the place well.'

There was silence for a few moments. Valens, deep in thought, idly rattled the abacus beads.

'Then I have your approval in principle?'

'Yes,' said Valens. 'It's a bold plan and packed with dangers as a dog with fleas, but I don't see why it shouldn't succeed.'

'Right,' I said briskly. 'Then here are the details. XIV Legion with one cavalry regiment and two infantry cohorts will move to Gloucester and take over from II Legion who, with all attached auxiliary troops, will cross Severn and establish a fortified camp in the plain just short of the foothills, whence they will ravage the surrounding country and attract as much opposition as they can. Two thousand men of XIV Legion—the best you have, Valens— will march by way of Cirencester to a point on the estuary roughly opposite Caerwent. Thence, after some training in assault landings, they will be ferried to the Caerwent beaches. Tell us about the ships, Pantera.'

'I can provide twenty-five biremes and fourteen cutters for the operation. The voyage across the estuary is short; we can cram seventy men on each bireme and twenty-five on the cutters. All these ships are now harboured at Exeter and can make the passage to Severn within a fortnight.'

'Good. I'm glad you didn't have to commandeer merchantmen. Describe what you have discovered from your reconnaissances.'

'About thirty miles down the coast from Cirencester,' Pantera continued, 'a river flows into the Severn estuary. The natives call it "Avon".'

'Old British for "river",' Valens grunted. 'Nearly every stream in the western Province has that name.'

'So?' Pantera suppressed, not too successfully, his impatience with the interruption. 'There are shoals and sandbanks near the mouth, and of course it's tidal, but I have found an embarkation point where ten ships at a time can be moored at high tide. The whole force can embark within two hours.'

'How about the crossing?'

'The sea shoals quickly two miles from the Silurian coast. We shall have to sail due north to a promontory jutting into deeper water. It's a straight voyage of about six miles.'

'And how far is this promontory from Caerwent?' Valens asked.

'Five miles,' I said. 'I'll tell you about that later. What about tides, Pantera?'

'We shall embark at Avon mouth at the flood, Legate: stand offshore during the ebb and start crossing when the tide turns so that we can arrive at Caerwent beaches with the next flood. I have tried that beach at high tide: a bireme grounds fifty yards offshore in four feet of water.'

'The men will get wet but won't drown. How long for the crossing?'

'With a fair wind and calm sea, using oars and sails, under two hours. With a contrary wind and choppy sea it might be six. Remember the ships will be heavily laden.'

'We'll plan for the worst,' I said. 'We want to disembark off Caerwent three hours before dawn so that our men can assault the fortress at first light. We must therefore embark at Avon mouth the previous afternoon, set sail at sundown and cross by night. Now, Pantera, on those timings, what dates give the most suitable tides?'

'Between the seventh and twelfth of September, Legate: in three weeks' time.'

'Well, there you are,' I said, turning to Valens and Posthumus. 'II Legion will invade Siluria on the last day of August and build its camp. You, Valens, will pick your striking force, two thousand legionaries and a hundred infantry scouts, and start for Avon mouth at once. The rest of your legion and auxiliaries must reach Gloucester one day before Augusta marches. Pantera, the ships will assemble at Avon mouth by the first of September. There is much more to arrange; but send these orders at once. Is all understood?'

Valens grinned happily. I went to the window and flung the shutters wide. The dawn sunlight, fresh and glorious, cascaded into the dingy room.

2

By noon gallopers were riding to Wroxeter and to the fleet at Exeter. Valens left soon afterwards, swearing he would rejoin his legion within thirty-six hours. Pantera, who had brought two biremes and a cutter to Gloucester, embarked for Avon mouth where he intended to meet his ships. The Prefect of the Camp nagged me to elaborate on my orders for his legion; he seemed nervous and over-anxious as though oppressed by the responsibility of his imminent command in the field. I became irritated, uneasy and regretful that the legate of Augusta, now desperately ill, was unable to lead his legion.

Posthumus's chief concern was the weight of opposition that he would encounter. I explained that I did not anticipate any great resistance to his march into Silurian territory because the tribesmen would be unprepared for so strong an invasion. That was the reason, I told him, why II Legion must march as soon as Gemina had arrived, so that the natives might not be forewarned and prematurely alarmed by massive troop movements.

'And when you are out there, Posthumus,' I went on, 'you've got to dig deep and fortify a camp capable of resisting a determined siege for at least ten days. That should not be difficult against an enemy who, though numerically strong, is without siege weapons or artillery. Remember, you are only a bait to draw the tribal army from Caerwent. I neither expect nor desire you to meet them in open battle.'

'That's clear enough, Legate,' he said. 'But what of our withdrawal? If your appreciation is correct I shall be cut off from Gloucester and surrounded for days by a superior force and shall have to fight every yard of the way back.'

'I don't think so, Posthumus. If the enterprise against Caerwent is successful the news will scatter your opponents. You know what rumour can do. They will suppose a large army has landed in their rear and is ravaging the land. They will disperse to defend their homes, leaving, at most, a token force to contain your legion. And, don't forget, I have Gemina in Gloucester ready to extricate you if you should run into serious trouble on the way home.'

The barb failed to wound him. Posthumus, still dubious, departed to draft his orders. He was not, I felt, a man of decision. For a moment I contemplated going with Augusta myself; then dismissed the idea. With operations in three different places requiring my direction I could not afford to be isolated in a besieged camp.

Five days later three cohorts of XIV Legion swung into Gloucester, Valens at their head. I was surprised to see him because I supposed he would have remained in Wroxeter to organize the main body's march. My surprise turned to exasperation when I learnt that he proposed to lead the Caerwent expedition himself. I had already nominated one of his tribunes, an experienced and efficient officer, for this command. Valens remained unmoved by my protests.

'This is as difficult and dangerous an expedition as you'll meet in a lifetime,' he said caustically. 'My legion's reputation and my own honour are involved. Besides, you must have the best leadership you can get. I'm providing it.'

I surrendered at last, secretly not altogether displeased. Valens had brought his First Cohort, a thousand strong, all veterans of over twenty years' service, and twelve picked centuries and a hundred Vascones, tough companions of my unfortunate patrol from Wroxeter. To mislead tribal intelligence we had concocted, as the official reason for their move, a reinforcement of Exeter's garrison. In reality the vexillation was to march through Cirencester to Bath and thence disappear over the escarpment into the coastal plain near Avon. Before they left on the following day I took Valens to my quarters—I lived in a wing of the ailing legate's house—and introduced him to a key man in the operation.

'This,' I said, indicating a young British peasant waiting respectfully by the door, 'is Vepomulus of the Dobuni, your guide and adviser on the Caerwent defences. He speaks Latin quite well.'

'Where did you find him?' Valens said, eyeing the man doubtfully.

'Some months ago, when I conceived this operation,' I explained patiently, 'I realized we could not blunder around Siluria in the dark without the help of someone who knew the country. I told my intelligence agents in Dobunian territory to find a friendly native who was familiar with the Caerwent district. After a deal of searching they produced Vepomulus, who was captured three years ago in a Silurian raid and enslaved in Caerwent, where he remained for two years before escaping again to the province. He knows Caerwent and its environs as intimately as his own village, and he has no love whatsoever for the Silures. They killed his wife and children.'

'Very well,' said Valens. 'What has he to tell us?'

We went into the court where a sentry stood on guard. I sent the soldier out of earshot and showed Valens a map in relief, delicately modelled by Vepomulus in the damp earth, of the Caerwent coast and hinterland.

'Study this,' I told Valens, 'and listen carefully to his explanations. Vepomulus will go with you to Avon mouth and later, when you have revealed the project to your men, he will reconstruct this map and a model of Caerwent fortress itself, so that you can show your centurions what to expect.'

Valens spent three hours with Vepomulus, absorbing in slow detail all the information the latter had to impart. Then, with the Briton standing silently watching, he brooded over the model, chin in hand, while he formulated his plans. Finally he sought me out and expressed himself satisfied.

'The operation is not, after all, quite so fantastic as I thought,' he declared frankly. 'The terrain is difficult, but there is a clear route from sea to town. The defences are formidable but so extensive that a strong garrison is needed to make them impregnable. I hope Posthumus will lure that garrison away and keep it occupied elsewhere.'

'He will do both,' I assured him. I gestured towards the Dobunian. 'Treasure Vepomulus as you would your mistress: his work is not ended when you have stormed Caerwent. Two years' captivity has made him familiar with the face of every member of the Silurian royal family and palace nobility: he will be able to recognize the hostages I want.'

Valens and his force marched away next morning. I spent three more days in Gloucester supervising Posthumus's preparations; then followed Valens to Avon mouth. I found him in a fortified camp overlooking the estuary, conferring with his tribunes, centurions and options over an enlarged replica of Vepomulus's relief map. I listened with growing approval. Valens's plan was simple, clear-cut and thorough to the most minute detail, yet flexible and amenable to rapid and orderly adjustment against all foreseeable contingencies. Every officer was thoroughly rehearsed, not only in his primary mission, but in an alternative role to meet accidents and reverses. This was professional military planning at its best.

It was the 27th of August. The invasion fleet had arrived and lay at anchor in the river. Every night a few biremes and cutters were moored inshore and the men practised disembarkation drill. They marched for long hours across country in the dark, learning by hard experience the art of silent movement. They discovered that iron striking iron or stone creates noise; so hobnails were extracted from boots; apron-strips and scabbards wound with wool and muffled, javelins carried point to butt. A stumble or whispered word brought swift retribution from a centurion's staff. Valens was taking no chances.

We perfected our communications. I appointed from the bodyguard strong riders on good horses in a chain of short-stage relays which ran through Bath and Cirencester so that a dispatch from Avon mouth to Gloucester could be delivered within twenty-four hours. Valens could embark at any time between the 7th and 12th of September, both dates inclusive; the actual day depended upon favourable weather. He was to send a message when he started and another directly he returned.

I rode back to Gloucester. The day after my arrival the rest of XIV Legion and three auxiliary units tramped through the Decuman Gate. The fortress became, for a short while, very crowded. At sunrise II Legion crossed the Severn, with two cavalry regiments—1st Thracian and 1st Pannonian—and four cohorts, 1st Morini, 1st Baetasii, 3rd Bracarii and 2nd Pannonians, a total of eight thousand five hundred men.

Long dust-plumes trailed the vanguard horse as they fanned out on the far bank; grey cloud-light of a sullen dawn glinted dully from helmets and javelins; the long column, like a russet, speckle-backed python, coiled over the plain. The faint chorus of a marching song competed unprofitably with screeching wagon axles lurching along rutted tracks. The rear party's last scouts turned, waved lances in farewell, and disappeared into the woods.

I left the ramparts, returned to headquarters and sat in the empty office, staring unseeing at the racks of dusty cylinders. This was the start of waiting. My part was finished. My forces were committed to battle on widely divergent fronts, against all the hazards of disjunction, a sea crossing, unknown country and an unpredictable enemy. Had any general ever conceived a madder scheme?

3

A messenger from Posthumus, escorted by a section of horse, reached Gloucester the following midday. Surprise had been complete: he had encountered no opposition during the march and made camp without interference. He proposed to spend the day strengthening his fortifications. Two more dispatch riders came through on successive days, reporting successful forays in his immediate neighbourhood and destruction of villages and hill forts. The last message said that tribal opposition was increasing and that the camp was being gradually invested. Thereafter I received a brief daily situation report by carrier pigeon. This means of communication, known in antiquity and used with success a hundred years before by Decimus Brutus at the siege of Mutina, had been suggested by Posthumus, who trained the birds himself. I was sceptical but, as we foresaw that within a few days all normal communications with Gloucester must be completely severed, raised no objection to the experiment. To my surprise and gratification the pigeons provided scanty though sufficient news of the legion's doings throughout the operation.

By dawn of the 7th, the first of the six days allotted for Valens's crossing, the pigeons' tiny scrolls had informed me that Posthumus, on his estimate, was surrounded by thirty thousand Silurian warriors. We had no accurate information of their total manpower and could only base our calculations on the numbers known to have engaged Ostorius during his campaign against Caratacus, and these calculations were further complicated because at that time a large Ordovican contingent, indistinguishable from their Silurian allies, had fought on the British side. Still, thirty thousand was a solid force for one tribe to put into the field: most of the settlements, including, I hoped, Caerwent, must have been drained of men.

Posthumus, in his curt messages, did not seem unduly perturbed by the concentration against him and the daily, even nightly, attacks made upon his camp. Indeed, as I discovered later, he quite enjoyed this passive role, so suitable to his temperament. Augusta's camp was well sited and as strong as engineering skill and equipment could make it; the men had little trouble in beating off the most determined attacks. They were well supported by the 'wild asses' of the legion's artillery; a type of engine which Posthumus preferred to ballistae. The 'wild ass' was indeed less cumbersome, could shoot more quickly and was, perhaps, more suitable for breaking up massed attacks at short range. Its drawback, to my mind, was an inherent unreliability in the mechanism which made it liable to burst without warning on discharge, when flying splinters of disintegrated timbers killed and maimed the crew. Posthumus was lucky: during the siege only one 'wild ass' unleashed the vicious backlash of its namesake.

Nor was the garrison entirely passive. Three well-timed sorties, two at dawn, one at dusk, gave the defenders breathing space and inflicted notable losses on the tribesmen. I had forbidden major attacks. II Legion, their morale entirely restored since the winter by a series of successful raids, were probably capable of giving the Silurian Army a sound beating in open battle. This, however, was not my object at the moment. Firstly, with an eye on the Anglesey campaign next spring, I did not want to risk heavy losses among our troops; secondly, anything short of annihilation, which was unlikely, would leave the Silurians free to regroup and fight a protracted campaign among their own mountains; thirdly, I would still have failed to compel their tractability during the coming year. Posthumus had been told to contain the tribesmen, not scatter them; I must give him full credit for doing his duty very well.

By the 9th of September no message had come from Valens. I was becoming anxious. The weather during those days was stormy; I stood on Gloucester's ramparts, gathering my cloak against slanting rain, and glumly watched the tattered clouds racing overhead. I imagined, with painful clarity, the tempest confining Pantera's ships to the shelter of Avon mouth. Such, indeed, was the case. But the 9th dawned clear and still and continued calm all that day and the next. I hoped again. Two days later an exhausted rider on a spent horse hailed the gatehouse guard and presented Valens's report on his mission.

<h2 style="text-align:center">4</h2>

Valens's message gave only a brief account of the onfall at Caerwent, and I have compiled the history that follows from the legate's description after his return. On the 7th of September men and ships were ready to go; but the wind which lashed the stockades at Gloucester tore the Severn sea across and across, driving spume-capped rollers into the estuary at Avon mouth and forcing the ships up-river for shelter. On the 8th the wind still blew unabated. Valens, chewing his fingernails impatiently in the fort, made sarcastic comments about windbound mariners to Pantera; in reply the Commandant took him to a headland and showed him the breakers thundering shorewards.

'Even in this weather I can get you to the Caerwent beaches,' he said. 'The gale is southerly and favourable. If you think your legionaries can struggle ashore through fifty yards of raging water I am ready to try.'

Valens regarded the six-foot waves, and apologized. The men, keyed-up in expectation of battle, moped inactively in the fort where their leather tents were flattened by the gale and their straw bedding soaked by driving rain. The ships, line ahead in midstream, stretched away out of sight round the river's curve, sails furled, yards aslant, oars inboard, tugging at anchor cables. So two days and a night dragged by.

By midnight on the 8th the wind was dropping; the 9th dawned calm and sunny, the sea still choppy in the storm's aftermath. Pantera, after a highly technical discussion with his master mariners, told Valens that he believed the lull would continue for at least another twenty-four hours. Armed with this assurance Valens hurried back to the fort and, at the altars by the standards, where an augural tent had been pitched and the ground consecrated, took the auspices in front of the assembled soldiers. Needless to say I had provided three of my personal augurs. Their chickens, well-trained, left the cage with alacrity and greedily swallowed the scattered grain; and a stray crow which appeared, cawing vigorously, well to the left, added a fortuitous confirmation to these favourable omens. The tense silence which always prevails at augural ceremonies was broken by a growl of applause. The assemblage dispersed; centurions barked orders; by midday embarkation had begun.

The tide was on the flood. The ships, ten at a time, were rowed to the line of piles driven into the mud by Pantera's men and made fast. The soldiers scrambled aboard. Two-thirds of the fleet's complement of marines remained ashore in order to make room for the legionaries and to garrison the Avon mouth fort during Valens's absence. Valens had wanted all marines disembarked but Pantera, insisting that he must have a minimum fighting force in each vessel to repel possible attacks while his fleet was anchored off the Silurian coast, flatly refused. In this he was doubtless wise, but the ships were very crowded.

After each galley had embarked her complement she was rowed downriver and anchored offshore. The tide was ebbing rapidly before the last men were aboard; one or two vessels grounded on mudbanks and had to be towed off. But by evening the embarkation was finished and the whole fleet, thirty-nine vessels large and small, anchored in the estuary, rocking gently to a diminishing swell.

Valens, whose military experience had not hitherto included a sea-borne assault, anticipated the voyage with fidgety apprehension. The ships, comfortingly solid when moored to the piles, suddenly seemed small and frail in open water. He himself was on Pantera's flagship, a half-decked bireme with fifty oars a side. Before the tide turned again at dusk he had time to inspect the galley from her bronze-sheathed ram-beak and gilded boar's head snarling at the prow to the fish-tailed ornament that curled above the helmsman's shelter on the poop. Forward of the single mast was a wooden fighting tower, crammed perforce with legionaries who also packed the entire deck except where handling of anchor, sail and rudders demanded work-room. Below decks the rowers lounged on the two-tiered rowing benches where the oars, drawn inboard, formed multiple barriers athwartships. As Valens, on his tour of inspection, stumbled and ducked between rowing benches and oars he discovered, by the hilariously outspoken comments on his antics, that fleet discipline was rather less stringent than a legion's.

The legate's acid comments on this point drew from Pantera some explanations that astonished him. He learned that up to two hundred men lived in the confined space of these war galleys. The bulk were rowers who were, so to speak, the equestrian class of this queer society wherein the sailors, comparatively few in number, who navigated, steered and sailed the ship, were the senators. Lowest in the hierarchy came the marines, some seventy to a bireme, who guarded the ship in port and repelled boarders if attacked at sea. The marines were armed very much like our auxiliaries with iron helmets, leather corselets, round shields and swords. The sailors were unarmoured and unarmed, except for daggers, but every rower had a scabbarded sword strapped to his bench.

'The rowers are part of the ship's fighting force,' Pantera said in answer to Valens's query. 'The marines are too few to carry a powerful adversary by boarding after we have rammed her, or to repulse a determined counter-attack from her decks.'

'Surely you lose manoeuvrability when you throw your oarsmen into battle?'

Pantera, intently watching the tide rip plucking his anchor cable, leaned far over the wicker bulwarks. 'Not really,' he replied absently. 'With ship locked to ship the rowers are temporarily superfluous. Generally we only have to call the upper bank oarsmen on deck, still leaving twenty-five oars a side. Tide's nearly on the turn,' he added.

They walked to the poop, picking their way among congested soldiers, some of whom were already suffering from the ship's uneasy motion at anchor and were miserably seasick, oblivious to the crew's joyful taunts.

'All seamen will unite against a soldier,' Pantera observed dryly. 'In every crew rowers will bicker amicably with sailors, and both badger the marines, but the differences are more imaginary than real. Each depends on the other to work or fight the ship, and they all resent the higher status of the army.'

'Whence are they recruited?'

'Mostly from the Gallic coast: Belgica and Lugdunensis.' Pantera glanced at the sky, darkening rapidly eastwards, where a few faint stars glimmered like drowned pearls. Seawards some trailing clouds smeared the blood-red banners of a dying sunset. 'A ship's officers—master mariner, helmsman and master rower—are usually Romans, sometimes Greeks.' He looked overside. 'On the turn now. Time to move into formation.'

A pipe shrilled. The rowers sprawling below decks, arguing, gambling or sleeping, jumped into silent activity and manned oars, untethering the straps which secured them inboard. The pipe squealed again; simultaneously the oars thrust outboard and poised above water, each bank level and steady as a legion's spears. Other ships repeated the signal until Pantera, watching in the gathering gloom, saw all were ready.

'Up anchor.'

The master rower trilled again on his pipe. A line of sailors heaved rhythmically on the anchor cable, dragging it hand over hand through the hawsehole. The master rower watched anxiously, pipe to lips, ready to order a stroke of oars should the hook be fouled. All over the estuary cable crews chanted in mellow unison as ships weighed anchor.

'Stand by to hoist lantern.'

A huge lantern, half a shield's height, was lighted and hooked to a running halyard from the topmast.

'Hoist.'

The lantern climbed jerkily upwards. The pipe yelped. A hundred oars struck water together. The bireme shuddered and lifted. The pipe settled into a steady rhythm, a low note mounting suddenly to a wild screech, from which the rowers took their time. Around each ship the thrashing blades churned water to foam. The fleet moved seawards.

When the coast astern was swallowed in the evening's gloomy haze the lantern dropped and rose twice. Pipe and oar-beat ceased. The bireme nosed gently onwards, losing way.

'Now we take up station,' Pantera explained.

The serried lines astern merged and diverged as ships found their cruising stations. Out of seeming confusion a pattern materialized: four chevrons, precisely spaced like flighting wild geese, covered a mile of sea from front to rear. Biremes held point and centre; cutters guarded the wings. A lantern crept to masthead at the point of each chevron. Oars dropped and flailed; the fleet swept forward.

It was now quite dark, only a pale glimmer remaining in the western sky. Flying tendrils of broken cloud obscured the guiding stars and drew rich sea-oaths from the navigator. The waves, choppy and white-crested, snatched at the oars. The rowers' curses could be heard on deck.

'Steady breeze, dead astern,' Pantera said. 'Sea moderate. We've plenty of time. Master, hail the messenger cutter. Tell her to command the squadron to stand by to hoist sails and rest lower oars.'

The fleet messenger, a small open decked vessel with a single bank of oars, turned swiftly and vanished into the darkness. Soon Valens heard faint hails from the flotillas in rear as commands passed from ship to ship.

Presently the messenger returned, took up station astern and reported, in a stentorian bellow, that orders had been given and understood.

'Execute.'

The lantern dipped and climbed. Sailors already clinging to the swaying yard forty feet above deck unfurled the great sail, dropped it gently on the halyards and sheeted home. The pipe squealed on a different note, and cut; the oar-thrash ceased. The lower bank rattled inboard; the upper, commanded by the pipe, resumed the eternal dip, pull and lift.

Pantera turned to Valens, standing silent beside the helmsman. 'Now we are settled for the night, unless the weather changes. Why not go to the cabin and rest, Valens? There is nothing you can do for the next four hours.'

'Rest in this pandemonium? Just an excuse to get me out of the way. Don't blame you. Never felt so useless since I was a recruit.'

He stumbled over the rows of legionaries swathed in their cloaks and went into the tiny cabin beneath the poopdeck, a perquisite belonging only to flagships, a little box not much larger than a coffin. Here, after removing helmet and sword, he lay flat on his back in a narrow bunk, wedging knees and elbows against the heave and sway of the ship. A leather curtain separated him from the rowing deck. Fifty sweeps creaked in unison against leather-bound tholes; the timing-pipe howled like a tormented ghost; timbers groaned; waves smacked the planks beside his head. Valens, pulling cloak to ears, swore vigorously and fell asleep.

5

'The Commandant reports land in sight, Legate.'

The orderly handed him helmet and baldric; Valens went outside, still only half awake. After the cabin's stuffiness the night air struck chill. The moon, newly risen, cast a livid sheen on the crowded decks. Sharp-voiced centurions were rousing their men, who stumbled to their feet shivering and grumbling, groping in the half-dark for shields and javelins. The sail had been furled and the lantern, Valens noticed, no longer glowed at the masthead. The oars moved in slow concert to subdued chanting from the master rower; his piercing pipe was still. Valens climbed to the poop and found Pantera in low-voiced consultation with the master.

'We've made the ships as invisible and inaudible as we can,' he said. 'Lanterns were dowsed directly the moon rose, half-way across Severn. There's the Silurian coast.'

Valens followed his pointing arm and distinguished a darkening loom on the vague horizon.

'Our lookouts have seen no lights on shore, which is a good sign. The natives sometimes fire beacons as alarm signals.'

The compact mass of legionaries rustled and shuffled while men sought their allotted places. A metallic clink loosed a centurion's hissing vituperation. The soldiers handed cloaks and neckcloths, tied in neat bundles, to their section leaders: these garments would only hinder their struggles with the surf. An option made a tidy pile by the mast; a marine took charge.

'Eighty-four cloaks I give you,' the option growled. 'Keep them dry and keep your thieving fingers off. I'll slit your nose if so much as a scarf is missing when we get back.'

'If you get back, soldier,' the marine jeered. 'Suicide squad, that's you! I won't be seeing your ugly face—'

'Quiet, there!' Valens snapped. He stared astern. An occasional glint of moonlight on oarblades revealed the following flotillas. Otherwise, with sails furled, they were hardly discernible.

'Not much chance of the enemy seeing us at this distance,' he grunted. 'It might be different closer in. No change in the debarkation plan, I suppose?'

'None,' Pantera answered. 'Our flotilla will row in until bows touch bottom. When your men are overside we will back, turn and clear the way for successive flotillas. As I've told you, we had trouble in finding a landing beach unobstructed by either rocks or sandbanks. This one is only a few hundred yards long so we cannot ground the whole squadron together. You needn't worry: there are still three hours before dawn.'

'You must know this coast very well.'

Pantera laughed. 'I should. I have made two daylight and six night crossings since Paulinus told me to reconnoitre. I could make this land-fall blindfold.'

The galleys crept forward, oarbeats slowing, while leadsmen in the bows called soundings in hoarse undertones. Soon Valens could hear the rustle of surf and see a silver-white thread of foam. The hills beyond rose in turgid humps and were swallowed by the sombre sky.

'Not long now,' Pantera murmured.

Valens said, 'We shall be back before nightfall. Stand in close and pick us up as we come.'

'The Gods go with you.'

Valens left the poop and forced his way through the legionaries who clustered, tense and silent, at the bulwarks and peered uncertainly towards the moonlit beaches. He reached the prow, where stood the century's standard and escort. The leadsman's voice held a warning tone.

'Are your men ready?' he asked.

The centurion's answer was drowned in the rattle of lifted oars. The bireme coasted slowly ahead. Rollers raced past the hull and lifted her shoreward. With a sudden splash the oars dropped to check her way; the keel grated faintly on shingle.

Valens glanced overside. The sea looked cold and menacing; the rollers thundered high and fast. If Pantera had miscalculated the power of the undertow an armoured man would drown horribly in this swirling blackness. He turned to the standard-bearer.

'Over you go!' he growled, and jumped.

Minutes later he stood on the beach, gasping and retching seawater. Soldiers stumbled from the breakers and collected round the standards. Centurions and options counted and cursed and belaboured laggards.

Without waiting for stragglers the first wave advanced three hundred paces inland in extended order, forming a screen to cover the landing against surprise.

The leading flotilla backed water and turned broadside to the shore, timbers and cordage creaking as helmsmen swung the giant tillers which controlled twin steering-oars. The ships passed in procession to the left, immediately disclosing the second chevron's approaching prows. Valens, with grim enjoyment, sensed its passengers' sensations at that moment; then he turned to the tribune, centurion and orderlies of his small staff.

'Where is Vepomulus?'

The Briton, shaking with cold, stepped forward unhappily.

'Go to the outpost line and make certain of the route from the beaches,' Valens told him. 'You, centurion, go with him.'

More men came from the sea, grouped and marched inshore. Time passed. The moon dipped to the horizon and darkness increased. Valens, looking anxiously seawards, imagined a faint lightening of the eastern sky.

'Hurry!' he snarled at the panting men squelching over the sand.

Vepomulus returned, warmed by his walk, brisk and confident. The last flotilla decanted her load, bringing a centurion with a tale of misfortune. Three ships, carrying nearly two hundred men, had run aground on shoals in mid-crossing. Valens, blaspheming at this depletion of his force, hurried along the beach to the centuries, ranged by their standards, and gave the order to move. Vepomulus, a centurion in close attendance, was in the lead with a small band of Vascones. Two centuries, left to guard the beach-head and cover the vexillations' re-embarkation, were already digging the fosse of their fort, wielding pick and shovel with quiet urgency.

For the first mile the march was a nightmare. The firm sand of the beaches quickly yielded to wide mudflats where men sank thigh-deep at every step. The pace dropped to a crawl; the legionaries, soaked in the landings and then chilled to the bone, now sweated and panted from their exertions. The darkness, in this hour before dawn, was absolute; a man straying from the ranks could only regain his bearings from the laborious noises of the column's passage. A dirty copper tinge marked the eastern sea-rim before they reached firmer ground and found the main course of a rivulet which split into a hundred channels through the mudflats. They followed the brook inland.

After a time the vanguard stopped, and the column, files bumping files, shuddered to a halt in a flurry of smothered imprecations. Vepomulus returned from the head and found Valens.

'The diversionary party leaves us here, lord Valens,' he murmured.

Valens turned to the centurion at his side. 'Do you think you can find the route?'

'If the sand model at Avon mouth didn't lie I shall have no trouble,' the centurion answered. 'I follow this brook, keeping it on my left, for five thousand paces. I shall then arrive beneath the Silurian hill-fort, in full view from the summit if the dawn is up and their sentries are alert. If not, I wait in the open until I am seen.'

'Correct,' Valens said. 'And then?'

'I feint an attack on the fort, up the steep slope from the south, making a noise uproarious enough for you to hear a mile away.'

'Off you go,' said Valens. 'The Gods be with you.'

The centurion led his little detachment, three centuries and thirty Vascones, away into the darkness, and the column left the brook and forged straight towards the distant loom of hills that, like stormclouds in a starless sky, could be sensed rather than seen. Eyes accustomed to the dark could now distinguish their immediate surroundings: straggling coppices broken by openings cleared for cultivation where the prickling stubble underfoot told of crops recently harvested.

The way began to slant gently upwards, and the ground became rocky, the dim silhouettes of trees less frequent. The men moved faster, silent and intent, while the world grew grey about them. The slope grew steeper; the dark bulk of the mountain advanced like a gigantic shadow. They marched steadily upwards, following a shallow dip in the hillside that, rock-strewn and tree-scattered, concealed them from all eyes save those—and Valens devoutly prayed there were none—on the precipitous slopes directly ahead.

Presently Vepomulus came back to the legate, who was striding at the head of the leading century.

'If you halt the column, lord Valens,' he said, 'I can show you Caerwent.'

6

The centuries halted in the gully. Men whose throats were parched by sea-brine and the travails of the march drank thirstily from rain-puddles among the rocks. Vepomulus and Valens and his officers climbed warily from the dip to a ragged tree-clump on the crest. Vepomulus pointed.

A vaguely defined hump loomed obscurely in the distance. In that light no details could be observed. Valens clucked impatiently.

'Nothing to be seen from here,' he snapped. 'How far away is it? What is the route?'

'The fort is nearly a mile ahead, lord Valens,' Vepomulus said. 'We follow the hillside to a wooded dip, twin to the one we are in now. If we can get there unseen we shall be hidden from the ramparts and only five hundred paces away.'

Valens glanced at the sky. 'We'll have to move, then. Centurion, lead the column up here. Stir your legs!'

Scrub and stunted trees covered the hillside where they marched. Progress was difficult; files tended to straggle as each man tore his own route through the bushes; but there was now sufficient light to see the ground and choose a path. Valens set a fast pace, his jaw grimly set. The rearguard was running. The distant mound of Caerwent grew nearer and clearer in the growing daylight. Then Vepomulus pointed to their objective; a scrub-ridden scar in the hillside, a useful screen for an assembly area. Valens ploughed on, head lowered, feeling utterly exposed to hostile eyes peering from the heights ahead, expecting any moment to hear horns braying the alarm. At last the rounded crest hid him from Caerwent; he turned, panting, to watch his men come in, urgently beckoning them to close up beneath the reverse slope. No sound came from the fortress.

He summoned his centurions and climbed cautiously; they lay concealed among bushes and surveyed the place they must storm. Pallid shafts from a hidden sun flicked colour on a background iron-grey in early dawn. They saw the stronghold across a narrow plateau: a formidable rock-walled fort, ditched and stockaded. A haphazard pattern of round thatched roofs showed above the stockades; scattered smoke drifts proved that some of the inhabitants were already astir. A cock crowed, faint but clear in the stillness. Vepomulus pointed to a cluster of long rectangular rooftops; these, he whispered, formed the royal precincts.

Low-voiced and succinct, Valens enumerated the features, now visible in actuality, which had so often been studied and memorized on models. Caerwent gripped the end of a spur which fell steeply on three sides; the fourth sank gently to an isthmus of high ground connecting spur to parent hill. Along this neck the Romans had come in their final breakneck advance, so approaching the fortress on its single vulnerable side. On this face was Caerwent's only gate, a massive structure flanked by wooden towers and protected by drystone curtain walls which blocked the causeway. Sentries kept watch; spearheads glinted on the gate towers; helmeted heads peered from guard-posts set at intervals along the stockades.

In frantic haste, ears cocked all the while for Roman trumpets from the hill-encircled plain below, Valens issued his orders. He made some minor adjustments—chiefly consequent on the loss of three valuable centuries which were sitting at that moment on a sandbank somewhere in the Severn estuary—in the broad plan for the assault that had been discussed and decided during the daily conferences above Avon river. He had with him six centuries of the first veteran cohort and four others, giving a total strength of roughly twelve hundred men. Of these he kept two centuries in reserve outside the fortress, ready to give help where required or cover the withdrawal. The remainder would assault the stockade on either side of the causeway. When the ramparts were stormed Valens, with three veteran centuries, was to strike directly at the halls of the royal household where, he hoped, he would find the hostages he sought. The rest of his men must seek the defenders, create confusion and do all the damage they could.

Centurions returned to their commands and, with an urgency all the more intimidating because it was utterly silent, flung their men into assault array. The legionaries crouched voiceless in the scrub, seeing nothing but the ragged crest of the plateau, hearing nothing but the hurried breathing of their comrades and the shrill pipe of wakening birds, sensible of nothing but battle-tension and parched lips and dry mouths.

Valens, conscious of mounting panic, lingered on the crest. No sound came from the faceless void of the valley-plain below. Where was the centurion's detachment, that all-important diversion that was to attract the hill-fort's garrison to the southern ramparts, to fasten their attention until the real attack crashed upon them unawares? Had the party gone astray? To Valens's fevered eyes the hills were bathed in broad sunlight and the day was far advanced—surely, if the centurion had followed his orders, he must be seen by now? In truth, as the legate admitted afterwards, the long hours of darkness had so sharpened his night vision, and anxiety so tangled his brain, that the first faint gleams of dawn seemed like the radiance of high noon. For the night-gloom was only just lifting, and the valley-plain was shrouded in mist.

But such afterthoughts came later, and now he was racked by doubt. Had our ruse succeeded? Were Siluria's fighting-men really facing Posthumus and locked in a hopeless siege? Were only old men and palace guards left in Caerwent, as he hoped and expected? Or would he find a strong, alert garrison capable of hurling his storming-parties into the ditch and hunting the broken remnants into the sea?

The legate sighed. His sword irked him: the scabbard had rubbed his hip-bone raw during the march. He jerked savagely at the baldric and resumed his intent scrutiny of the black, rocky ramparts.

A sudden movement flashed behind the stockade. A sentry leapt from a watch-tower and disappeared, spear aloft, from sight. A sharp commotion disturbed the watchers on the gate towers. Shouts rang faintly in the thin morning air and echoed in the hills. And simultaneously, hazed by distance but unmistakable, Roman trumpets howled from the plain.

Valens waited and watched. Warhorns ripped the stillness. Half-seen figures cascaded from the gate towers, vanished within the fort. The turmoil carried to his ears like the bellowing of distant cattle. Carefully he inspected towers, sentry-posts and stockade on the perimeter, on the wide arc of rock-wall defending the narrow plateau across which he must attack. He saw no watchers, no movement anywhere. The ramparts were deserted.

Valens turned to the waiting centuries, drew his sword and held it high.

7

No trumpets gave the signal. In tight-lipped silence the centuries climbed from the gully and moved at a jogtrot up the gentle slope beyond, the columns diverting to their objectives like fingers from an opening fist. The Vascones bounded ahead, making for the gateway, swinging their loaded slings. They slid into the ditch, found foot- and hand-hold on the wall and skipped to the top. A quick heave and push from their comrades flung the leaders over the stockade.

The gate-wall was not quite deserted, after all. A few half-grown boys, left there as unwilling lookouts, yelled in panic before they were trampled underfoot. The centuries poured over the wall, javelins poised, searching fruitlessly for targets. A section detailed for the purpose unbarred the heavy oaken gates, iron-strapped and bronze-studded, and flung them wide. Valens and his veterans swept through.

The men paused an instant to take stock. The great stone-walled oval of Caerwent, two hundred yards from end to end, lay at their feet. Round, grass-thatched huts, stone granaries and rickety shelters were planted thick about the enclosure, and in one quarter a fenced corral harboured cattle and sheep, not yet released for the day's grazing in the valley pasture-lands. In a central clearance stood a long, low house, rock-walled, with window-holes only at the two ends, and a smaller, square building, abutting it at right angles. A slender palisade, a barrier for straying livestock rather than armed men, surrounded the whole. This squalid edifice was the 'palace' of the King of Siluria, the man who led thirty thousand warriors and for seventeen years had defied the legions of Rome.

The place was full of movement. Between the huts scurried women and boys, children and old men; an occasional belated warrior, spear in hand and never a glance for the iron-shod wave that broke silently over the walls at his back, ran for the farther ramparts. There, shouting and blowing warhorns, jostling and brandishing weapons, Caerwent's garrison prepared to repulse the centurion's puny detachment that crawled up the steeps towards them.

The centuries leapt from the ramparts and quartered the enclosure, killing as they went. The Silures at the stockades heard the death-cries, tried to face about, swirled in cyclonic confusion—during the few chilling moments before the javelins flew and the sword-blades struck. Then it was all cut and parry, guard and thrust, and the Britons died on their walls, and died on the steep hillsides where they were flung, and died in the huts where they fled.

Valens and his personal guard and Vepomulus and his attendant centurion followed the veteran centuries, who charged straight for the palace. They smashed through the flimsy palisade. Two centuries, as rehearsed, promptly surrounded the enclosure. The third ran for the doorway of the main hall and, in an alley between the two houses, met five warriors of the royal guard, five battle-crazed barbarians seeking death.

The Britons held the narrow passage as, in ages past, the famous Three held Tiber bridge. Four times shields met and clanged, and swords and spearheads whirled and darted, and four times the veterans of Gemina recoiled, cut and bleeding, and dying men writhed on the rocky floor. Then the centurion, a huge, black-bearded giant whose muscles corded arm and thigh like rippling ropes, gave an exasperated grunt, flung javelins and followed fast. A brief swirl and clash, and the way was clear.

'Extra sword-drill for you useless turds,' he snarled to his men. 'Come on!'

They plunged for the door. Valens raised his voice in a warning shout.

'No more killing!' He thrust Vepomulus forward. 'Go and bring your hostages out. Take your men with him, centurion.'

They hustled forty moaning captives, male and female of all ages, from the rock-walled building. The centuries closed about them, formed ranks and made for the gate. They passed through bedlam. Men, women, children, cattle, horses and dogs ran riot in witless panic. A century crossed their path, sweeping in line through the enclosure, hurling blazing torches into huts, leaving a litter of bloodied bundles in their wake. A wild-eyed Briton hurled a spear, turned and fled. Helmets flitted among the huts where legionaries hunted shrieking fugitives to their deaths. Smoke spiralled lazily upwards; banners of flame, pale in the dawning sun, fluttered eagerly on thatch.

Valens saw no fighting anywhere. The sack had begun.

He mounted a gate-tower and watched his orders meticulously obeyed. The soldiers killed every living creature, human and animal.

Soon the Silures were all dead, and the agonized crying ceased; but cattle are laborious slaughter, and the bellow of stricken kine was a bizarre funeral-dirge for the death of Caerwent.

'Seven days' training, a sea-crossing and a five-mile night march, all for half an hour's fighting,' the legate murmured to himself. 'Such is war.'

A joyous whoop from the burning palace interrupted his reflections. A fire-party of the First Cohort, expert pillagers all, had discovered a treasure-cache beneath the rock floor of the palace. Labouring like field-slaves beneath the tottering roof, scorched by sparks and falling embers, they scooped up gold and silver plate, bracelets, brooches, leather sacks abulge with coins, pearls and jewels, and bore the loot triumphantly to the gate.

'No time to assess this now,' Valens said. He raised his eyes to the distant hills, where three separate smoke-columns coiled sombrely into a cloudless sky. 'The alarm is out. The hornets will be about our ears if we don't move fast.'

Horns sang the Rally; the notes floated like liquid jewels above the crackling roar of a burning town. The legionaries stripped their dead, pitched the bodies into the blazing huts, laid the wounded on stretchers. The force assembled, counted casualties, received quick orders for the return march. The weeping prisoners, mercilessly harried by unsympathetic guards, stumbled pitifully in their efforts to match the legionaries' swinging march-step. A few children, too young to walk, were lifted on ironclad shoulders where, their terrors soon forgotten, they crowed and played happily with helmet crests and bloodied javelins.

Before the column dropped into the valley Valens looked back. A sluggish smoke pall hung over Caerwent and embraced the spur as though reluctant to disclose the havoc beneath. The legate rubbed a hand over his face, tugged his beard. A sour, metallic taste, like congealed blood, tainted his tongue. He hawked and spat.

'Paulinus should be pleased,' Valens observed to no one in particular.

8

Posthumus had orders to break camp on the 12th of September; on that same evening his legion marched into Gloucester. I had Gemina standing to, ready to support him if the withdrawal were hard pressed; but Posthumus said the enemy had melted away two days before, leaving only small detachments to watch his movements. Soon afterwards Valens and his gallant little force arrived, their prisoners intact except for one old man who had died at sea. I put the captives under close guard in a barrack room and asked Vepomulus for their identities. It was a rich haul. We had taken the Queen of Siluria and her entire brood, together with the King's mother and uncle and other royal relatives and elder statesmen. No doubt the Silures already mourned them as dead and were hatching plans to exact a bitter revenge.

I quickly disillusioned them.

One of the councillors, an unimportant man, was given a horse and put across Severn with instructions to bring the King of Siluria, his chieftains and no more than a small personal escort to Gloucester within seven days. They arrived surly and suspicious, anticipating treachery, ready to gallop for the foothills at any least sign of a snare. We then wasted two whole days while emissaries came and went in efforts to arrange a meeting in circumstances which would not endanger the King's safety. Finally, becoming tired of these vacillations, I took a body-guard troop, crossed the Severn and rode to the British camp. After the consternation caused by our arrival had subsided we sat down quite amicably to complex and prolonged negotiations.

I dictated my terms, which were not excessive. For one year from that date the Silures were to refrain from hostilities of any kind against Rome. In return Roman forces would restrict patrolling to a line five miles west of the Severn and would send no foraging parties across the river. I reiterated, with suitable sternness, that aid given to a tribe at war with Rome would be regarded as a hostile act; if any Silures were found fighting in the ranks of our enemies the pact would be void. In the meantime our prisoners would be housed and attended as befitted their high position and would be returned unharmed a year hence. If the treaty was broken they would be instantly killed.

The arguments continued for hours, with Vepomulus as interpreter—a position which, remembering the degradations of captivity, he thoroughly enjoyed. I knew the Silures were in a hopeless position: if they valued their royal house—whom they revered as gods—they had no option but to agree. And Valens's ruthless extermination at Caerwent, a massacre without a single survivor, had shaken their resolution more than any reverse we had inflicted on them in seventeen years of war.

Agree they did, in the end. It was a sad procession that trailed into the sunset, towards the stark mountain fastnesses that reared like precipice-walls of a lost world.

I summarized the results of the expedition in a dispatch to Nero. At the cost, all told, of seven dead legionaries and fifteen auxiliaries we had immobilized, for a year, a tribe of our most intractable enemies. The threat to my southern flank during the campaign planned for the following spring had vanished. In fact, the consequences of Caerwent's destruction were more far-reaching than I could have imagined. The disaster seems to have broken the Silures' spirit. From that day—now eight years ago—the tribe has been comparatively subdued, and my successors in Britain have enjoyed virtual peace on the Severn frontier. I recommended Valens for a Golden Crown and Vepomulus for citizenship; both awards were eventually granted. For myself were less tangible rewards. Burrus demanded a detailed description of the sea-borne expedition's planning and execution and, with suitable comments, embodied my dissertation in an official manual which he issued for the guidance of military and naval commanders. The pamphlet earned widespread approval and has, in its small way, become a classic. And Sextus Frontinus, who, as I write, is compiling a handbook of military stratagems, tells me he means to include this little operation alongside the brilliancies of Alexander, Alcibiades, Marius and other famous generals.

Success breeds fame; failure begets oblivion. We could so easily have failed.

7

'To how many mischiefs does not religion persuade?'
LUCRETIUS

1

The storming of Caerwent was but preliminary to a campaign still six months away. I had other preparations to make. To this end I rode with Valens to Wroxeter and, soon afterwards, visited Chester again. This time we made a more thorough inspection and discovered a native village on a hillock by the river bank, not far from the ruined fort. The inhabitants were Cornovii who got their living partly by agriculture and partly by fishing in the river and its estuary. In those waters they were expert navigators.

Our party, a strong mounted patrol formed from my bodyguard cavalry and the 1st Tungrians from Wroxeter, included a pilot and some seamen, supplied by Pantera, and an engineer detachment of XX Legion. We camped at Chester for three days. The sailors voyaged down the river in flimsy native fishing craft; the engineers examined timber supplies in the surrounding forests and reconnoitred the river banks for shipyard and launching sites. Reports from both parties showed my project to be feasible. We returned to Wroxeter, where I gave Valens his instructions.

'I want you,' I told him, 'to establish a fort at Chester straight away.

As the place is in friendly territory we must tell the Cornovian elders of our intention: we do not want to offend unnecessarily. If you have to include any cultivation within your fortified area see that proper compensation is paid for the crops.

'You shouldn't have any trouble from the Setantii across the river; they are, I understand, tributary to the Brigantes and so, in a way, our allies. The Degeangli of the western hills are a different matter. They may react sharply to a military outpost so close to their boundaries. But we know that they are neither numerous nor truculent. You will probably be raided, but seldom with any determination or strength.'

Valens said, 'Ostorius walked through the Degeangli ten years ago with nothing more serious than a skirmish. He had an army with him, though. Makes a difference. Will Chester be a normal frontier post, or have you any special role in mind?'

'The garrison will carry out watch and ward duties, of course; but that is not your only task. During the winter you will have to build ships—flat-bottomed barges—sufficient to carry a legion.'

The grey tufts of Valens's eyebrows climbed his forehead. 'Barges? For what?'

'I shall tell you later. Now, details. Your fortifications must cover a stretch on the river bank where shipwrights can work. You must be strong enough to repel raids on both fortress and shipyard. A thousand infantry and a cavalry regiment should be enough. Agreed?'

'Agreed.'

'Detach the units from your garrison here. You will also want an engineer party and some naval architects. I have written to Pantera; he is sending half a dozen shipbuilders.'

'We'll need them. I've never had to build a fleet before. How many barges do you want?'

'Each one should carry thirty men, fully armed. That makes a hundred and seventy barges for a legion. We must have a reserve. Say two hundred, to be ready by the end of March.'

'That's better,' Valens said with relief. 'Six months. Plenty of time. Anyone special you want to command this post?'

'No. Appoint a competent tribune. Remember, Valens,' I added seriously, 'the barges must be ready without fail when I want them. Make no mistake about that.'

'Never fear. I shall keep a watchful eye on Chester myself. If that's all I had better go and get the detachment organized at once.'

They left next day. Soon afterwards I paid a visit of inspection and found Chester active as a trodden ants' nest. Vedettes of Proculus's Horse ringed the site at warning distance, and ten troops—a mobile striking force—stood to their horses under arms. Under this protection the 1st Tungri, a milliary cohort, laboured with pick, spade and axe. Beneath the relentless eyes of their centurions the toiling auxiliaries added a second and third ditch to the standard defences of the marching camp constructed when they first arrived. Sweating soldiers, stripped to their breeches, cut thorn bushes to fill the outer ditch, felled timber for revetment and for stakes which, sharpened and fire-hardened, they planted point-outwards on the scarp. Beyond the ditches they cleared a wide space of trees and scrub and dug 'lilies': a riddle of concealed manholes each armed at the bottom with a pointed stake: a replica of Valens's snares at Wroxeter.

On two sides of the fort the defences extended to the water's edge, enclosing a space where our barges would be built and dry-docked. Compact fighting towers, timber-built on packed earth foundations, guarded these curtains. Within the fort carpenters built wooden barrack-huts to replace lines of leather tents. The thatched roofs might later be replaced by tiles; meanwhile fatigue parties dug capacious water-tanks alongside as an insurance against incendiary arrows.

The granary alone they built of stone, roughly dressed and mortared; and they raised the floor above-ground on pillars to guard against damp and vermin. Three months' supply of corn had been carried in wagons from Wroxeter. The natives would provide more grain for which, being

Roman subjects, they would either receive cash on the spot or credit in taxation dues, until the fort had a year's stock.

Between the curtain ramparts soldiers were piling timber hewn from the forests. Under terse directions from Pantera's shipwrights they trimmed logs and laid the frameworks of the first vessels. When the garrison had finished the fortifications everyone not on watch, patrol or foraging would take part in this work until the whole yard was stacked with barges. Even for the Roman soldier, accustomed in the course of a day's march to lay a road, build a bridge or construct siege engines, this was an unusual task. However, the novelty might help to relieve the bleak tedium of winter in an outpost fifty miles removed from the comparative luxury of 'legion' at Wroxeter where bath-houses in the fortress and wineshops and women in the native town all helped to alleviate discomfort and monotony. Here, as in a hundred other auxiliary posts, the short, dark, rain-sodden days depressed the spirits of men raised in happier climates around the Middle Sea. For this reason I have always tried to garrison my outposts with Germans, Northern Gauls and the like, men accustomed to weather approaching Britain's in severity. The Tungri, for instance, should find midwinter conditions in Chester no worse than their native Belgica.

2

I had to return to Colchester by the 13th October for the anniversary of the Prince's accession. The celebration, starting at dawn with prayers and sacrifices at the Temple of Victory, continued until dusk in manifold ceremonies during which the oath of allegiance to the Prince was administered to all citizens and provincials in the Colony. This was a fitting occasion to dedicate my statue of Nero. True to his word, the Prince had sent sculptor and materials from Rome; the product, a larger than life image in coloured marble, barely justified the trouble and expense, for the artist's charges were exorbitant.

I went to London as soon as the accumulation of paper work and legal business allowed. At a daybreak reception soon after my arrival a young tribune, come from Richborough on his way to join XIV Legion, waited to pay his respects. This was Julius Agricola, the youth recommended to me by Burrus. After an exchange of courtesies Agricola handed me a roll sealed within a buckskin covering.

'The Praetorian Prefect ordered me to give this into your own hands, Legate.'

I took the roll with an inward tremor. Only a letter containing very confidential, not to say dangerous, matter would travel by hand of a trusted courier in preference to the Imperial Post. After the audience, alone in my chamber, I broke the seals. Burrus wrote:

'I put your proposals for a speedy annexation of the Icenian kingdom to the Prince. He did not approve. As you know, in foreign affairs his emphasis is on peace: he desires no wars, insurrections or outbreaks on the frontiers other than operations deliberately undertaken with a particular end in view. Corbulo has finished off the war in Armenia; the Temple of Janus is closed and will remain so, Nero hopes, until you march to Anglesey next spring.

'Against this background your suggestion, although it agrees with official policy to the extent that the territory must eventually be annexed, was coldly received. The Prince does not favour the continuance of these allied kingdoms within our frontiers. Nevertheless he maintains that the right moment for the arrogation is directly Prasutagus dies, and not before. Not only will there then be a legal pretext but also, with no male heir to the throne, the Iceni will be left without a leader to cement opposition against us. This, you must admit, is a material argument against immediate action.

'About the Trinovantes the Prince is not so restrained. The suspicions voiced in your intelligence reports of disloyalty and intrigue amongst them, unproved though they may be, have angered him because the Trinovantes were among the first peoples in Britain to submit to our rule. He has decided to call in forthwith the grants made to the tribe by the Divine Claudius on the pretext that they were only loans. You will remember that when you were in Rome we discussed with Claudius of Smyrna similar measures to be taken against the Iceni when we annexed the kingdom; there was no suggestion at that time that the Trinovantes should likewise suffer.

'How this will affect you I cannot guess. The Trinovantes, I imagine, after nearly twenty years under our direct rule, are hardly likely to rebel. I have seen to it that Nero's orders to the Procurator meet with delays in drafting; so this letter should precede his instructions and give you sufficient warning. It might, possibly, be wise to provide Catus's officials with strong escorts when they travel to collect the grants.

'Other consequences of the edict, which Nero has made no effort to keep secret, may be more serious. Roman bankers with money invested in Britain must already know what is afoot. Already, I feel sure, private messengers are spurring across Gaul with instructions to their agents in London and Colchester to call in all outstanding loans from the Trinovantes. Seneca is deeply involved. I believe that he is alarmed for his British investments and will try hard to elicit from the Prince whether such measures are likely to be extended to other tribes. He might succeed. Should he do so the results, so far as the Iceni are concerned, might be disastrous.'

Disastrous indeed. To reveal to Roman financiers our intentions towards the Iceni could start a chain of events culminating in an uprising which might be very difficult to suppress. Public and private financial interests would make a racecourse of the road to Britain, descending on the tribe like a flock of vultures, each seeking to drag his own morsel from the writhing entrails. The money had long since been spent. Therefore distraint of property, livestock, corn, land and slaves must inevitably follow. The Iceni were a fierce and independent people, as we already had reason to know. Nothing seemed more unlikely than that they would submit meekly to legalized pillage. The only alternative was open rebellion. Was I to take the legions to Anglesey with this dagger at my back?

I read on: 'Damaging rumours are circulating in Rome about affairs in Britain. The gossips say that slave labour in mines and government farms is so short that revenue suffers; yet throughout the summer campaigning season you have made no move against the enemy, gained no victories and taken no prisoners. It is not hard to guess the source of these slanders: Catus bears no love for you and sends malicious reports to his patron Seneca. The Prince, knowing and approving your plans, should be unaffected by such talk. Yet Seneca is persuasive and has much influence with him; so much so that he has managed to convince Nero that your profitable bargain over the Anavio mines was largely due to Catus's skilled diplomacy.

'I tell you these things merely to show you how the currents flow in the City. Do not be discouraged. All will be well when your legions overrun Ordovicia next spring: the spate of lead, copper and slaves resulting from your conquests can never be diverted to anyone's credit but your own.'

Glumly I re-read the last paragraph. Burrus's hint was plain. Nero was impatient for results: any postponement of the projected campaign might have, for me, most unfortunate consequences. Well, so be it. Whatever trouble might be brewing in the Province I would march from Wroxeter in April.

3

The road to Silchester, lying like a sword-blade on the snow-flecked earth, was shrouded in an opalescent curtain of flying sleet. Sudden gusts whipped the screen into whirling fury and ripped the last decaying leaves from sodden trees. The forests heaved and thrashed like fleets storm-driven under bare poles. We buffeted our way head down, face stung by slanting needles. I maintained a difficult conversation with

Agricola, sometimes yelling above the wind, for I had ordered the young tribune to take the longer road to Wroxeter: his company might thaw the numbed weariness of a long, cold ride. Moreover, I could benefit from the freshness of his perception. I had been ten months in Britain, ten months so stretched by head-racking work and constant travelling that my own percipience, through over-close familiarity with this peculiar country, was in danger of being blunted. His first impressions were startlingly similar, I remembered, to my own.

'It seems strange,' he said, 'to find unwalled towns in a province so recently pacified. Very different from Gaul. A great credit to our firm administration here.'

I shook my head, and raindrops flew like spray. 'It's no credit to anybody. These open towns are a menace and an invitation to loot for any rebellious Briton with a grievance and a handful of followers.'

Agricola looked surprised. 'This is not directed by policy, then?'

'No. A fool of a tribune told me the contrary, when I first landed. My secretaries searched the records and found no edict, no hint of anything which might explain the inexplicable. The towns have just been allowed to grow like that.'

'Most of them,' Agricola mused, 'are of course resettlements from tribal strongholds. It might be preferable to keep well in the background anything, even ditches and stockades, which might remind the natives of their former warlike habits.'

'Nonsense, boy. You won't talk like that when you've been here a bit longer and have got the feel of the country. All Britons are savages at heart. We've managed, in the settled areas, to smear a thin coat of Roman behaviour over their natural barbarism. The varnish is already cracking in some places.'

I raised my arm; the bodyguard trumpeter took up the signal; the column swung into a canter and drummed onwards.

Silchester made Agricola raise his eyebrows, for it had become a town with defences. These were crude enough, no more than a bank thrown up from the spoil of an encircling ditch, the gates mere gaps unguarded by curtain ramparts. Nor were they finished: the mounds were uneven and unpacked; the ditches unrevetted. Gangs of labourers—local tribesmen and squads of British auxiliaries—still toiled with shovel and basket.

'My work, Agricola,' I said. 'This town, under the Prince's pleasure, of course, is my creation. Hence—' I waved a hand expressively at the ramparts.

Epaticcus, his magistrates and councillors received us. We rode to the town hall, now all but completed, for the official speeches of welcome and exchanges of compliments. The new Silchester rose around us. Hard, pillared outlines, clean-angled roofs of rose-red tile stood proudly aloof among the shapeless native huts, ignoring their neighbours like lords among a rabble. My own mansion had been made ready by household staff sent ahead from London. The grounds, trim and cleared of builders' litter, wore the withdrawn, desolate look of gardens in winter. A friendly warmth—token of a skilfully designed hypocaust—greeted me as I entered; walls freshly gay in new colour wash and mosaics in intricate red-green-gold designs defied the grey-fogged daylight.

There was much to be done in Silchester, yet that sense of importunate urgency which harried my work in Colchester and elsewhere was absent. Possibly the town itself, precious to my eyes though raw and quarter-built, girdled by gentle forests beautiful even at this season, quieted my nerves. Perhaps the Atrebates helped: a slow-moving, slow-thinking people, friendly and easily moved to laughter. Here, alone in Britain, could I imagine that we Romans were not only respected but almost liked.

I postponed all official business for several days. With a few lictors I roamed the town, approving or amending building plans, chatting to architects and masons, encouraging gang-overseers on the ramparts. With Frontinus, Agricola and others I hunted boar, using those huge

British hounds to drive our quarry from the woods to the open heath west of the town, where we rode great tuskers to a fighting end on our lances.

4

I continued to spend a minimum of time on official business. After receiving, at dawn, the usual petitioners and visitors I hurried through reports, returns, intelligence summaries and other papers until noon. Then, ignoring my secretaries' despairing grimaces, I threw aside rolls, tablets and maps and spent the rest of the day as I willed, walking or riding in Silchester's countryside, boar hunting, or superintending the interior decoration of my house. Agricola described a newly-invented process, all the rage in the City, of artificially staining and colouring marble to produce tinted statues. The expensive sculptor Nero had sent from Italy was still hanging about my household: I commissioned him to execute various figures and groups from what remained of the Ligurian marble imported for the Prince's statue at Colchester.

Agricola had also brought from Rome a recently-published manual on mounted archery by G. Plinius Secundus. This, though no more than a codification of the methods used by our Thracian auxiliaries, served as a useful guide and check for prefects commanding horsed bowmen, for which purpose I ordered it to be reproduced. Stimulated by Plinius's deceptively easy instructions we ourselves practised archery at a gallop, using javelin targets as marks. The results considerably increased my respect for Thracian dexterity in this art.

Dispatches from Rome aroused me from idleness like a shock of icy water. A copy of a letter from Nero, addressed to me for information, ordered Decianus Catus to recover the Trinovantes' grants. Within a day I received a routine message from Catus requesting military escorts for his agents. A detachment of some two hundred elderly legionaries, seconded from various units; was permanently stationed in London for duties of this nature. Usually I merely countersigned the Procurator's message and sent it to the centurion commanding, who detailed the escorts necessary. This time I withheld my authority and, instead, wrote to Catus:

'I have received a copy of the Prince's edict concerning the grants made by the Divine Claudius to the Trinovantes. It is just possible, according to my information, that there may be unpleasant repercussions when this decision becomes known. I do not really anticipate any violent reaction from the tribe but, to be on the safe side, I am ordering a detachment from Lincoln to march at once to Colchester, where their presence should remind the natives of the loyalty due to the Prince.

'I am sure you will agree that this is a wise precaution and that dispatch of your collectors had better be postponed for a fortnight. It is unnecessary to remind you that meanwhile none but ourselves should know what is going to happen.'

Following this I sent an immediate message to Cerialis directing him to send a cohort of Hispana, a cavalry regiment and an auxiliary cohort to Colchester forthwith. I considered returning to the capital myself, and decided against it: if Catus kept his mouth shut nothing could happen for fourteen days. If, on the other hand, so much as a whisper should reach the moneylenders they would descend on the territory in a swarm to recall their loans, leaving little for the Government agents. Hence the Procurator, yoked under an Imperial edict, was bound to realize that he could do no favours to his mercantile friends in London without creating immense difficulties for himself. All should be well until the Lincoln detachment arrived at Colchester and Catus loosed his agents. Unless, of course, there had been a leak in Rome.

I pulled my chin, remembering Burrus's last letter. Indiscretion in Rome would be revealed only by complications in Trinovantia. I wrote a third letter, to Aurelius Bassus at Colchester.

'Financial measures are impending which may unsettle the Trinovantes. For at least a fortnight they must not be allowed to suspect that anything unusual is in hand. Use your authority as Census Officer to restrict movement into the territory to all, except soldiers and Government officers. In particular, forbid entry to merchants and bankers and their agents. Keep your fingers firmly on the tribal pulse. Send me daily intelligence reports by express messenger. This is most secret.'

These activities returned me to the full flood of official business. I heard law cases in the new town hall and delighted my secretaries by reading, dictating and signing documents for eight hours a day. The British cohorts suffered under exacting inspections; I confirmed plans for a new road linking Silchester to the Midland Way; an embassy from the Regni was persuaded to relinquish toll and custom rights at Portus and Pevensey. And my chamberlain reported sedition among my domestic staff.

He was a worthy freedman with a mighty paunch and no imagination, and so chose the end of a very tiring day to seek an audience.

'Well, what is it?' I growled.

'A matter affecting your household, Lord. I have found two servants plotting against the State.'

'Servants! By Apollo, can't you deal with them yourself? Why pester me with trifles?'

'Lord, I would not dare, unless the circumstances were exceptional.' He paused. 'One is Verecunda.'

'Verecunda—'

The woman was a dancer, an actress, a Spaniard. Quintus Veranius brought her to Britain with his troupe of entertainers in the days before the edict that forbade Governors to give displays in their provinces. Left destitute when Veranius died in Britain, unbequeathed in his will, she had attached herself to my household. A chance summons to my bed had revealed her as a skilful exponent of the intricacies of love: her eccentric subtleties had intrigued, fascinated and finally wearied me. She was a beautiful sheath for masculine tumescence: I could not visualize her as a political schemer.

'And the other?'

'Lucius, the gladiator.'

'Who is he?'

'Another, like Verecunda, who belonged to the Legate Veranius. He joined our household at the same time.'

'Yes, I remember.'

The man was a Gaul of Aquitania. I had once called him in to settle, by way of demonstration, an after-dinner argument regarding the relative merits of vertical and lateral parries against spearthrusts.

'What have they been doing?'

The chamberlain shuffled uneasily. 'Lord, they are members of a religious secret society.'

'The Shades take you! That need not be a crime! What society? What religion?'

'Christians, they call themselves. They worship a god called Christ.'

'And why not? The province has a thousand gods. As long as they're not Druids—'

'That is the point, Lord. Like Druids, they refuse allegiance to the Prince.'

I pondered. This sounded more serious. It might bear investigation. I sent for the inquisitor in chief.

'Two of my domestics,' I told him, 'are suspected of belonging to an anti-Roman society involving the worship of some obscure god. Examine them, find the truth and report to me. The woman is not to be tortured; treat the man as you like.'

I then forgot the incident until, a few days later, the inquisitor stated the results of his inquiries. He said, 'There is a secret society in London, Legate, calling themselves Christians, and these two are members. So far as I can find out the bond is predominantly religious. They seem to be of the Jewish faith except that, besides the Hebrew god, they also worship a certain Christ.'

'What is the nature of this Christ?'

'He was, so they say, a criminal executed by us in Judaea about thirty years ago.'

'How extraordinary! Why do they worship a felon?'

'They say he was the son of the Jewish god.'

'Mad! But no matter: have you found anything treasonable in this association?'

'Yes, Legate. The religion has not received State sanction under the Law of Associations; the members meet oftener than once a month, which is forbidden by the same law; and they refuse to recognize the Divinity of the Caesar.'

'So! Here we have a gang of seditious law-breakers operating in the Province's largest town, recruiting confederates under our very noses, and this is the first we hear of it. How long has this society existed?'

'Not long, Legate. The association was founded in London a year or two since by some foreign sailors from the East. Their numbers are small, little more than fifty.'

'What kind of people are they?'

'The lowest orders, Legate, the poorest men and women, slaves and criminals. There are no Romans amongst them.'

'Did Verecunda tell you that?' I asked.

'No, Legate. She told me nothing, and you forbade—' He gestured expressively. 'The man Lucius, under pressure, supplied all I have told you.'

'Do you know anything else about these Christians?'

The inquisitor hesitated. 'Nothing more was admitted by the two accused. But, since starting the inquiries, I have heard rumours.'

'Such as?'

'It is said that they practise magic, commit sacrilege against our Roman Gods and their ceremonies include ritual cannibalism and incest.'

'Cannibalism!'

'They are said to eat the raw flesh of murdered children. These matters,' he added hastily, 'I have not verified.'

'No, but I shall,' I said grimly. 'This sect must be stamped out mercilessly. Keep the prisoners confined but see they do not die: they must be brought to trial.'

I summoned my secretaries and started a check in the files for any edicts bearing on Christians. Records in Silchester revealed nothing; the secretaries swore that the subject was unmentioned in the provincial archives. Nevertheless I sent an immediate message to Colchester for search to be made among documents there; and directed our intelligence agents in London to hunt down members of the sect.

The hunt, improbably enough, led them far to the south-west, to the country of the Durotriges. In a remote, marshy plain about twenty miles south of Bath the agents tracked down a headquarters of the cult, a tiny settlement on an island among the marshes where the Christians lived in poor reed huts. The island—called, in the Celtic tongue, Ynys-Witrin, or Isle of Glass—was hastily evacuated before our men could land. The sect scattered, some taking refuge not far away in a peculiar lake-village whose inhabitants lived in huts built on reed platforms. The villagers, when our men went there to seek the fugitives, were distinctly unfriendly; they denied all knowledge of strangers in their midst and obstructed any investigations of their strange dwellings. Our agents' escort was small; they could not persist without danger. They destroyed the wretched hovels on the Isle of Glass and came away.

In this manner, as I learned much later, slipped through our hands a certain Josephus of Arimathaea who had recently landed with twelve disciples and assumed leadership of the Christians in Britain. My information about him is scanty and unreliable, the product of bath-house gossip and the type of intelligence item that is marked 'unconfirmed'. It seems that Josephus knew Christ personally and was concerned in some way with his burial. I always thought it a pity that we lost the man, for he, if anyone, could have explained to me the mysteries of his odd religion, the contorted beliefs which exalt an executed criminal to divinity, and the Christians' arrogant refusal to recognize the existence of older and far more respectable gods. Josephus has since disappeared, for we never found him again—indeed, we never tried—and he may even have reunited the sect on his miserable island.

Fuming over my ignorance in a matter of such potential danger to the State, I inquired of Agricola. He was full of information.

'Christians, Legate? They have become quite a nuisance in Rome these last few years. Don't you remember Pomponia Graecina, wife of Aulus Plautius, who was tried by a family tribunal four years ago for what they called foreign superstitions? The wretched woman had got herself mixed up with Christianity. She was certainly involved, but was acquitted because the tribunal could find no difference between Christianity and Judaism. The latter, of course, is not a prohibited religion.'

'Well, is there any difference?'

Agricola shrugged. 'Not much, though the Jews hate the Christians for adding another god, and an executed felon at that, to their own religion.'

'Jews! They're trouble enough. I don't understand much of this, Agricola. Why should these people make a god out of a man condemned by a Roman official? Surely that alone is defiance of our authority?'

'Possibly, Legate. Nobody knows very much about them, except that they're the scum of Rome—Pomponia was an exception—and acknowledge no god but their own, not even Caesar.'

'They could be a menace. Slaves and suchlike muck agitating against the State. Are the Roman authorities worried?'

'I believe the magistrates are beginning to keep a watchful eye on them. We don't want another Spartacus.'

'Exactly. And they must be well organized to have established cells in Britain already. Poisonous weeds: they shall be rooted out.'

The Colchester archives yielded nothing. I thought of writing to Rome for guidance but, on consideration, decided that the matter was too trifling for the Prince's notice. Moreover, while I awaited a reply the sect in London might scatter and escape.

They did, in fact, get warning of my intentions because only seven were arrested and brought to Silchester for trial during the first week of December.

We had lost Josephus but we caught in this gang one Aristobulus who was, so to speak, his second in command. Aristobulus was quite frank about himself and his objectives in the Province. A Christian, so my inquisitor told me, seldom needed any persuasion to talk about himself, his conversion and his creed, but the most rigorous torments usually failed to make him incriminate other Christians. Aristobulus, so he said, was a pupil of one of Christ's disciples, a namesake of mine, who had trained him as a missionary and sent him to Britain. The man's job, in effect, was to convert our subjects to Christianity; whereby he automatically denied them belief—or at least acceptance—of Caesar's godhead and divinity. The man was a self-confessed traitor, a wrecker and a menace. I was determined, before the trial began, to kill him.

The charges against the accused were illegal association, treason, magic, conspiracy and sacrilege. The first charge they all admitted; the second they denied in fact if not in law; the rest, to my disgust, could not be proved. Hostile witnesses, collected by my agents, could only attest that the Christians met secretly before dawn to sing hymns to Christ as a god. They partook of communal meals; the food, at these impoverished gatherings, was not even meat, let alone infant corpses. The prisoners agreed with our spies' assertions that they took oaths not to commit fraud, theft, adultery, lying or breaking trust.

Under examination their bearing was confident, almost proud. They gave evidence with the ring of truth, without cringing, despite their low origins and servile occupations. They had, it seemed, perfect faith in their gods and their religion. They seemed, without arrogance, to convey a steadfast propinquity as members of a union which gave some kind of common aspiration now and for the future, whether on this side of the grave or the other. It was all most disappointing.

After hearing the evidence for prosecution and defence I addressed the prisoners:

'You have been found guilty of breaking the Divine Augustus's Law of Associations, in that you have formed a guild without sanction and have held meetings at too frequent intervals.

'You must understand that I am not bent on persecution: I care not a whit for the tenets of your belief. Rome embraces many religions and ten thousand gods. One extra more or less matters nothing. But we demand that all faiths must be united in a common allegiance to a Supreme God, Caesar. This you refuse.

'You are therefore also guilty of treason in that you deny, or have abjured, any faith in the Divinity of the Prince.'

I glanced at Verecunda, standing white-faced, eyes downcast, and went on: 'I am disposed to be lenient. Provided you repeat an invocation to the Roman Gods, offer adoration to the Prince's image and make suitable offerings; and publicly curse your god Christ, you shall be pardoned. Otherwise—'

The prisoners' eyes were upon me: I read no fear in them. Aristobulus, lips hardly moving, said quietly: 'Courage, brethren. He watches over us. His everlasting mercy shields us.' Then there was a long silence.

I suddenly felt tired of the whole business. What use in killing these misguided wretches? Besides, Catus needed labour.

'Very well,' I said. 'For you, Aristobulus, and your treachery, I can find no more suitable reward than the death suffered by your disreputable god. You shall be scourged and crucified. The rest of you are condemned to lifelong servitude in the Prince's mines at Anavio. Remove the prisoners.'

Months later I learned that Verecunda the actress and Lucius the gladiator escaped together from the slave-train somewhere near Leicester. They were never recaptured.

5

The necessity of my attending the Prince's birthday celebrations recalled me to Colchester before the 15th of December. I was glad to return: the Trinovantes worried me like an aching tooth, though Bassus's daily reports contained nothing disquieting. Cerialis's detachment had made camp outside the Colony and the Procurator's men were reaping their financial harvest. Bassus, when I met him, was puzzled by the mild reaction to Catus's demands.

'The natives grumble, Legate,' he said, 'which is only to be expected. Some of the Trinovantan nobility are being broken in this process. The bankers, too, are around like hungry sharks. Yet I can find no open sedition, no word or act which might be a token of awakening resistance.'

'We must have a better hold on them than we realize,' I answered. 'Or possibly fifteen hundred soldiers in their midst has a soothing effect.'

'Either that, or they're being careful that premature action does not ruin some secret villainy which they are hatching.'

'Nonsense, Bassus. I remember your years: they still lack visible foundations. In fact the evidence points the other way. There have been no refusals to pay? No riots?'

'Nothing, Legate. A few minor chieftains with small possessions and little to lose have fled across the border to Icenian territory. We shall hunt them, of course, as soon as you have demanded their extradition from Prasutagus.'

That seemed to be that: my anxiety was as groundless as Bassus's premonitions. Catus, who was in Colchester to supervise recovery of the grants, was also satisfied.

'A stroke of genius on the Treasury's part,' he declared. 'Not only are we getting several millions in money but also much land, cattle and slaves forfeited by debtors unable to meet their dues in cash. The Prince's personal estates in Britain will be vastly enlarged.'

For a moment I felt uneasy. A Briton deprived of his money could restore his fortunes by hard work; if we took away land and home we removed the bedrock of his existence. From such material revolutionaries are made. I would tell Bassus to keep track of the dispossessed.

As the days went by intelligence summaries mentioned more flights across the border. Prasutagus, pressed for extradition of the fugitives, promised by letter to repatriate any of the Trinovantes seeking refuge at his court and willingly granted safe-conduct for military detachments sent in pursuit. Nevertheless the runaways evaded our soldiers; the Iceni in village, field and forest denied any knowledge of their whereabouts. Prasutagus, to my suggestion that his people were sheltering them, returned hurt and evasive replies which I found most exasperating.

Shortly before the Saturnalia the Procurator reported that all the grants had been recovered in full. I returned Cerialis's men to Lincoln and settled down to the everyday routine of administration, nursing my health in the comparative warmth and luxury of the capital against the journeys to be made later in the bitter depths of a British winter.

In January Agricola arrived from Wroxeter, carrying special dispatches from Valens. These contained a report on the results of his experiments in mountain warfare tactics. He had evolved a system of static and mobile guards which, though slow and cumbrous to operate, seemed at least to promise a reduction of those costly ambushes common to this type of warfare. Agricola, in his short time with XIV Legion, had thoroughly grasped the principles of these tactics and had seen them successfully worked in trappy hill-country across the frontier. After careful study and long discussion with the tribune I approved Valens's methods, ordered him to put them into practice with the Wroxeter garrison and promised to conduct a personal trial when next I visited the frontier in February.

Valens also wrote of a serious recrudescence of Druidism in his area. This information emanated chiefly from his native spies; concrete evidence was difficult to obtain. Patrols sent to localities where gatherings were reported almost invariably had a wasted journey. He had, however, rounded up a dozen suspects who, under torment, admitted attending the forbidden rites. These men were held in the fortress prison and awaited my judgement on a capital charge. It seemed, from their depositions, that Druid priests were filtering across the frontier from Ordovican territory, bent on restoring the old faith among our Cornovii.

The news coincided with my own intelligence, vague though it was. There were signs of a Druid revival stretching eastwards beyond the Cornovii across the black midland forests to Coritania. The tale seldom varied: wandering priests from the western mountains, slinking by hidden tracks and byways from village to village, persuaded small, timidly acquiescent congregations to celebrate savage sacrificial rites in dark groves. Road station garrisons of the Midland Way, warned to be especially vigilant on their patrols, had caught nobody.

Yet Government agents—Britons of the district, some of whom I had questioned myself—were positive in their assertions. Or they had been at the beginning, about six months before. In the meantime several spies had disappeared without trace and reports from the remainder dwindled to a trickle. I had to face the disconcerting fact that these Druids, proscribed, hunted and persecuted for nearly twenty years throughout the Province, still wielded some mystic power over the people: a power sufficient to overcome their fear of all the terrible penalties which Roman justice could inflict.

I unrolled a map of Britain, sent for the intelligence files and marked the localities where Druid activities had been reported since June. While there was hardly a territory free from suspicion—even the Cantii were incriminated—the crosses on the map radiated eastwards like probing fingers from the country between Wroxeter and Chester. The Ordovices were undoubtedly the nucleus. Apart from the sudden renewal of proselytism this was not altogether surprising: Druidism was the chief religion of the mountain tribes and Anglesey itself was the sacred centre of the cult.

I dismissed the secretary and looked at Agricola.

'Now, Tribune, What do you think about it?'

'The source of the trouble seems to be beyond our reach, Legate. Short of invading Ordovicia—'

For a moment I was tempted. My intentions for hostilities in the spring were known to nobody except the Prince, Burrus and myself. Often I felt the need for an independent, inquiring mind to survey the entire plan of campaign and support or criticize my assessments. This attractive, friendly yet discreet and reliable young man was a natural repository for confidences. I liked him immensely. A fortnight of his company in London and Silchester had revealed a keen discernment and common sense, even though his military qualities remained untested. Could I trust him? Undoubtedly—but I was no idiot girl to be blabbing secrets. With that decision I took another.

'Agricola, I am considering your appointment to my staff. Would that please you?'

'It would be an honour, Legate.' He hesitated. 'May I remind you that I have served less than a month with the legion and have no knowledge of war?'

I gauged the distress plainly written on his face.

'I know. Naturally you would prefer learning your trade with troops on active service. You need not worry. I can promise you plenty of fighting very soon. You won't find my headquarters a banqueting couch.'

He flushed. 'No, Legate. I hardly imagined that. I accept with gratitude.'

'Excellent. I have in mind that you should be my personal assistant, to share my quarters in barracks and my tent in the field. You will have a great deal of hard work, some responsibility and my entire confidence in everything both official and private.'

Agricola said nothing. His eyes sparkled. I smiled at him.

'We are both of senatorial rank. You may address me by name

when we are alone. Now, about these deferred discharges in the fourth cohort—'

So I took a messmate, my first and last in Britain; and never regretted my choice.

6

At the end of January I summoned the Provincial Council to its annual meeting. Proceedings were mercifully less prolonged than those of the previous year. A new President had to be elected and I managed, with great difficulty, to get Epaticcus chosen for a second term.

Continued resentment about corn prices was partly allayed by a slight rise in Roman rates and by the suppression, during my tours of military posts, of fraudulent dealing in the matter of grain requisitions. The common practice, I had discovered, was that centurions in charge of rations used measuring jars holding appreciably more weight of grain than their markings indicated. Moreover, it was quite usual for officials, both military and civil, deliberately to requisition corn at a season when, though army granaries were amply stocked, the local farmers had none. After arguments and threats the Romans found a solution highly profitable to themselves: the army would provide the corn, sell it to the natives, and then accept it back in fulfilment of the requisition. The corn, naturally, never moved from the granaries throughout a transaction which seldom appeared in any account books.

I had also tried, without infringing the Procurator's authority overmuch, to ensure that deliveries of grain should be made to the nearest collecting centre. Many unfortunate farmers, owing to some former recalcitrance in providing their dues, had been compelled for years to deliver to stations many miles from their homes.

I saw no prospect of attending to local administration and justice for several months after the Ordovican campaign had opened; so it became necessary, early in February, to make a protracted tour of the Province, visiting most places of importance. This was a journey whose details I prefer to forget. The ultimate vileness of Britain's climate was displayed in every miserable day on the long, straight roads. We were chilled by still, gripping cold which clutched our bodies like iron claws; we were lashed and soaked by rain, sleet and snow, sliced by winds which pierced wool, metal and leather and froze our very entrails. Brief respites in reasonably civilized surroundings hardly compensated for nights spent in repelling cold and bugs at bleak, inadequately heated road stations and rest-houses. The soldiers' lot at these isolated posts was unenviable. Only routine patrols, mostly confined to roads by the all-pervading mud, relieved the tedium of short, foggy days followed by dreary nights in unheated barrack-rooms. Hypocausts were rare; bath-houses almost unknown. The rigours of a British winter revealed to me the shortcomings, where our troops' welfare was concerned, of Roman military administration.

We passed through London, where I met Aufidius Pantera and settled with him the composition, strength and date of readiness of an operational squadron. I did not reveal the theatre of operations. Thence we plunged westwards to Silchester, Winchester and finally Exeter. Here I encountered that outlandish tribe the Dumnonii. So isolated were they by the remote wilderness in which they lived that, though technically under our rule, they were actually more independent than the Iceni or Regni. A strange, aloof people: survivors of many invasions dating back into the mists of time, seeming hardly aware of our existence in the Province, indifferent but not hostile. With this attitude, as matters stood, I was content: they were unlikely, in this critical summer, to rebel against a yoke which they barely recognized.

From Exeter I struck northwards to Bath, taking my half-frozen bodyguard and staff across the bitter uplands through Cirencester to Gloucester. The legate of II Legion died of his wasting sickness shortly before I arrived, leaving Paenius Posthumus in full control. I wrote to

Rome for a new commander, knowing full well that no replacement could possibly arrive before midsummer.

Gloucester was quiet. Since Valens's blow at Caerwent our patrols had seen hardly any Silures: the fortress wore the relaxed air of a peace station in a settled land. Though somewhat doubtful of the effect of such prolonged inactivity on our men's morale I enjoined on Posthumus a policy of strict non-provocation.

Thence we followed the chain of stark outposts guarding the border roads, thankfully anticipating the delights of winter quarters at Wroxeter. Dispatches from Colchester awaited me at the fortress. I read them: all thoughts of relaxation vanished like midsummer mist.

Prasutagus of the Iceni was dead.

BOOK II

Harvest

A.D.
March – May 61

8

'Now peals the clarion; through the host hath spread
the watch-word.'

VIRGIL

1

March was two days old. The King had died soon after I started
my tour of southern Britain nearly a month before. I crumpled
the dispatches in my hand and strode angrily into the legates' quarters,
cursing the idiocy of the Colchester secretariat in classifying this news
as routine and sending it to Wroxeter to await my arrival. They knew
well enough that urgent messages had to find me, without fail, wherever
I happened to be. A furlough application from an importunate tribune,
I remembered grimly, had been considered weighty enough to follow
me to Exeter. Apparently the death of an allied king was not, in their
eyes, a matter of any importance. I promised myself a savage readjust-
ment of the Colchester secretariat's scale of values.

Meanwhile, how did this new factor affect my plans? I restlessly
paced the floor of my room and brooded on the problem while a servant, unlacing my corselet, pattered anxiously alongside. Catus must
certainly have mentioned Prasutagus's death in his dispatches to Rome.
The Imperial Post averaged thirty days between Rome and Richborough; therefore Nero would know before the middle of March.

I saw the implications with vivid horror and hurled my helmet into a corner. The Prince's orders to annex Icenia could reach Colchester by mid-April, when I hoped to be half-way to Anglesey.

I swore at the unfortunate slave and wrenched free of the corselet. Would the Prince hold his hand until the Ordovices were conquered? I very much doubted it. Burrus, knowing my difficulties, would try to persuade him; but Burrus, judging by the tone of his last letter, seemed to be losing his power to sway Nero. Rome needed money desperately: Nero would snatch a windfall like Prasutagus's inheritance as a toad snaps a fly. Anyway, to count on the Prince's forbearance would be dangerous: I must base my plans on the worst assumptions and not delude myself by optimistic fallacies.

I flung myself on a bed and lay hands behind head and stared at the beams overhead. Slaves removed boots and massaged my legs. By mid-April, then, Catus and his vultures might be pillaging the Iceni, vigorously assisted by Seneca's agents and a score of greedy bankers. All the royal possessions, treasure, land, stock and slaves would be forfeit. The Claudian grants would be recovered and private loans recalled. Not many of these debts could be repaid in money: property must be confiscated to make them good.

I called for a beaker of wine, swallowed it at a draught and resumed my blind examination of the rafters. The Trinovantes had lately suffered in the same way without apparent resentment. Yes—but they were long accustomed to subjection and had no king, no royal family whose spoliation and deposition could focus their anger. The Iceni, on the contrary, were independent, pugnacious and, like most British tribes, regarded their chieftain as little less than a god. Were they likely to revolt? Perhaps not. They had tried it once and been soundly beaten.

I kicked the slaves away, wrapped myself in a cloak and paced the floor again. Foolish to assume anything but the worst. They would certainly revolt. Should I then postpone the Ordovican campaign until all

Icenian property was safely in the Procurator's treasuries, granaries, warehouses and stockyards, until the kingdom was formally annexed and fortified garrisons held the people in subjection? The process might take all summer, and might, at a chance, be done without a hint of revolution while the legions idled on those frontiers which I had been commanded to advance, while that financial salve for the State's tottering economy, the mineral wealth of Ordovicia, remained untapped for yet another year. I recalled Burrus's oblique warning and grimaced wryly: nothing would better ensure the Prince's displeasure.

Then the campaign must go forward, whether the Iceni rebelled or not. I halted my pacing and gazed through a window at the gaunt bulk of the praetorium. They were changing the guard on the standards. The mass of glittering insignia encircled the altars like jewels in a diadem. A centurion barked an order; javelin butts thudded.

I turned away. The decision was taken—a decision that was to bring the grimmest fighting that Roman arms had seen for half a century.

2

Now it remained to ensure that, even if trouble were brewing in the east, an uprising could be swiftly and destructively quelled. I summoned a confidential secretary and dictated a letter to Petillius Cerialis:

'I have certain misgivings about the security of the territories peopled by Trinovantes and Iceni. During the coming spring and summer our legions in the west will be fully occupied with operations on their frontiers, operations which unrest in the settled areas could bring to a standstill. As a precautionary measure, therefore, I want you to send a strong vexillation to Colchester. The force will not leave Lincoln before 1st April. You will detach every man you can spare from the fortress: the vexillation's strength, in any event, must be not less than five legionary cohorts, a cavalry regiment and two auxiliary cohorts.

'I realize that a loss of four thousand men will nearly halve your garrison's strength and that the tactical balance between legionaries and auxiliaries will be unsound both in the vexillation and the garrison. This, unfortunately, is unavoidable. I can spare no men from Gloucester or Wroxeter. You have the comfort of knowing that, on your own frontier, Brigantia is quiet and on friendly terms with us.

'This is a warning order. I shall send, later, a detailed directive on your role at Colchester. At the moment I can tell you only this: rebellion is possible. If you think the situation at Lincoln sufficiently secure you may, with advantage, command the detachment yourself.'

The last sentence was more than a sop to Cerialis's warlike proclivities. With his hand directing operations I could be certain that, if action against the Iceni became necessary, counter-measures would be instant, rigorous and ruthless. I sealed the letter and gave it for dispatch to Mannius Secundus who, since attachment to my headquarters after the bribery scandal in XX Legion, had graduated to the post of personal orderly.

'To Lincoln by special messenger,' I told him. 'Find the prefect Aurelius Bassus and send him to me.'

Bassus, after nearly a year's work, had finished his census of the Colchester district and been granted permission to resume command of the 2nd Asturians in Wroxeter. He entered and saluted.

'Greetings, Legate.'

'Greetings, Bassus. I trust you have found your cohort in good order after your long absence?'

'As good as ever.' He smiled. 'Under the legate Valens's eye they could hardly be otherwise.'

'I am glad to hear it. Be seated, Bassus.' I beckoned the orderly. 'Secundus, bring wine for the Prefect; then leave us and see we are not disturbed.'

When Bassus had spilled his libation I said, 'How long since you saw Colchester?'

'Seven days, Legate. I have barely arrived.'

'You knew, then, of Prasutagus's death?'

'I knew. He died more than ten days before I left.'

'Bassus, during the special mission covered by your census activities you eventually took control of our intelligence system over the whole area around Colchester. You also, from time to time, reported undercurrents in the Icenian kingdom. How finely did your security network cover Icenia?'

Bassus shifted his baldric and toyed thoughtfully with his sword-hilt. '"Covered" is not quite the word, Legate. Much of the country is marsh or forest; the people still live in hill-forts, in small communities where strangers are instantly remarked. To introduce agents was difficult, sometimes impossible. Many disappeared; we never discovered how or why. Only from the capital, Norwich, did we get reports with any frequency.'

'I understand. We still have agents in Norwich?'

'Yes.'

'Good. Now, Bassus, I want you to summarize for me, as you saw it, the political situation in Icenia immediately before and after Prasutagus's death.'

Bassus frowned at the floor, marshalling his thoughts.

'The King,' he began, 'had been bedridden for a month before he died. The nation realized he would soon join the Shades. The provisions of his will had been known for some time; all were aware that, since half his possessions had been left to the Prince, Rome would secure his family in their inheritance. That is so, is it not?'

'Those are the facts,' I answered impassively.

'There is no male heir,' Bassus continued. 'The intention, within the kingdom, is that Queen Boudicca shall rule as regent until her elder daughter comes of age and marries a nobleman who will be chosen for his military and political abilities. The pair will then, in effect, found a new royal dynasty.'

I listened with interest. Intelligence had mentioned nothing of this.

'Prasutagus was a friend of Rome. Boudicca,' Bassus said definitely, 'is not. You have seen her?'

I recalled Prasutagus's muscular, coarse-featured consort at my first Provincial Council meeting, and grimaced. 'I have.'

'She makes no secret of her contempt for what she calls the luxurious and effeminate degeneracies of Roman civilization. More practically, she leads and fosters a clique of nobles with similar ideas. She instigated the King's evasive replies to your demands for extradition of absconding Trinovantan debtors: replies which would never have been sent had Prasutagus been in full health and command of his faculties.' He paused. 'So much my agents reported without reservation. They also passed on certain rumours.'

I poured more wine. Bassus slowly withdrew his sword and tapped it sharply home.

'Boudicca is supposed to shelter Druid priests in secluded islands among the marshes, and to be a secret participant in Druid rites. Encouraged by the priests she communicates with disloyal elements in the settled areas: the Trinovantes, in particular, and the Catuvellauni. When Prasutagus was alive he kept a firm check on such activities, even to the point of quarrelling violently with his queen. Now that he is gone—'

'All this is unproved?' I asked.

'And unprovable, Legate. But, in intelligence work, you cannot disregard rumours, especially when they have persisted for a year or more.'

'That I grant you. Assuming, then, that Boudicca hates us, can she influence the Iceni sufficiently to incite open rebellion?'

Bassus shook his head. 'No, I think not. She is a woman of considerable personality: we shouldn't underrate her. But the Iceni haven't forgotten that we defeated them in battle, and that we used only auxiliaries to do it. They have no desire to test a legion's strength. Moreover, except for the royal guard, they are disarmed. Or so we hope.'

'What do you mean?'

Bassus shrugged. 'Every house, hut and hovel in Iceni probably has sword or spear buried under the floor or hidden in the thatch. Every nobleman and magnate drives a chariot; most farmers own horses. They could raise an army, horse, foot and chariots, within three days.'

'Of what strength?'

'We estimate the males of military age at about forty thousand. We take no census there, as you know.' The Prefect showed some surprise. 'But this assumes a national uprising, of which there isn't the least likelihood. I trust I made that clear?'

'You did, Bassus.' While he talked I had been thinking: now I made up my mind. 'Listen very carefully.'

I related the whole complex history of our relations with the Iceni, of Nero's plans for annexation and the dangerous chain of events unleashed by Prasutagus's death. I told him, without being more specific, that the legions in Wroxeter and Gloucester would be engaged in operations during spring and summer; and that Cerialis had been warned to reinforce Colchester.

'The essence of these precautions,' I finished, 'is that we should strike as soon as, or even before, rebellion becomes overt. The Iceni must be given no time to assemble an army, still less to cross their own borders. They must be destroyed long before they are fully mustered: we can put only four thousand men against them, remember.'

Bassus listened in horrified astonishment.

'To do this we must know Icenian intentions almost before they are aware of them. You, Bassus, are thoroughly acquainted with our intelligence system in the area. You must return to Colchester immediately. Use all your ingenuity to penetrate Boudicca's inmost councils. Spare neither effort, money nor lives. The Province's safety may well depend on your success.'

Though the evening was chilly and icy draughts rustled hangings over door and window the prefect wiped sweat from his brow before replacing his helmet. 'I go at once, Legate.' He paused, gathering cloak and sword. 'I am only a humble soldier. To criticize my superiors in Rome who formulate and direct policy on the Imperial frontiers is almost treasonable. Yet I say the Gods have made them mad. Do they know nothing of Britain?'

He went out. I sighed, called servants and prepared for bed. Bassus, with his limited horizons, could not judge otherwise: he knew nothing of the economic canker driving Rome to perilous remedies. As for myself, I had made every possible preparation, by early warning and swift counter-blow, to guard my defenceless back from the deadly dagger-stroke of insurrection.

3

I started preparations for war. Orders sent to Richborough directed Aufidius Pantera to assemble his ships at Chester by the 1st of April. I could not set the date any earlier: galleys could not be expected to navigate eight hundred miles of turbulent ocean between Boulogne and Chester during the height of the winter gales. Pantera, fearing irreplaceable losses by storm and shipwreck, had in fact been most reluctant to put to sea before March was out. I had brusquely observed, when he raised objections during our conference in London, that the fleet must be prepared at need to face bad weather, the only serious enemy it was likely to meet in British waters.

He had spent the previous summer reconnoitring the route round Anglesey to Chester and would not be sailing into uncharted seas. As a safeguard I had increased the fleet's operational strength to provide reserves against disaster and had promised him a whole month in which to make the voyage. Both precautions, as it transpired, were necessary and fortunate.

Secret warning orders went to Posthumus at Gloucester and Frontinus at Silchester. These required certain auxiliary units to muster at

Wroxeter on the 1st of April. From Gloucester I selected two cavalry regiments, the 1st Pannonians and Indus' Horse, and two cohorts, the 1st Morini and 3rd Bracarii. Frontinus was to bring both his milliary cohorts of British cavalry and infantry. I was somewhat reluctant to use native forces so near their homes—our troubles in Pannonia fifty-five years before had revealed how dangerous this could be—but three factors had decided me to include them in the field army. Although I had told Rome the cohorts were ready for service no posting orders to the Continent had been received, and they were merely idling in Silchester; they would be used only against their hereditary enemies, the western hill-tribes; and Cerialis's commitments in Icenia prevented me, as I had originally planned, from taking fifteen hundred auxiliaries from Lincoln.

In Wroxeter I mobilized XIV Legion Gemina and four cohorts of XX Legion Valeria; three cavalry regiments, 1st Vettonian, 2nd Asturian and 1st Tungrian; a mixed milliary cohort, the 1st Loyal Vardulli; and three infantry cohorts, the 6th Thracian, 2nd Vascones and 1st Frisiavones. These units, together with those called from Gloucester and Silchester and 1st Tungri at Chester, provided an army against the Ordovices of eight thousand legionaries, nearly four thousand cavalry and five thousand auxiliary infantry: a total of seventeen thousand.

Wroxeter, left with one auxiliary and six legionary cohorts and a cavalry regiment, would be the only fortress seriously weakened when the army marched. This I judged to be of little consequence: the Ordovices, fully occupied with an invasion, could spare only limited forces for raids outside the theatre of operations.

Of course, when my orders passed to cohort and regimental commanders and thence to centurions there was no longer any secrecy about a spring offensive. The fortress awoke from winter's lethargy like a lion roused from sleep; although snow still flecked the foothills and shrouded distant peaks the men moved briskly on routine tasks and drilled and marched with a vigour enhanced by expectation of battle. Speculation concerning our objectives was rampant; some favoured a combined operation with Gloucester's garrison against the Silures; others swore we were going to conquer Brigantia. Bath-house betting was free and furious; tongues wagged in Wroxeter's wineshops and brothels. I realized that both the Ordovices and Degeangli knew that war was coming; I was equally certain that neither had any idea where the blow would fall.

I spent long hours with my staff calculating our requirements of supplies and transport, collating the results and dictating administrative directives. At that season we could not rely on seizing either grain or forage from enemy sources in the barren hills of Ordovicia. The insignificant tribal granaries, widely scattered in a hundred hill-forts, would be almost empty by the end of winter. Therefore we had to carry with us enough rations to last until the fighting was ended, the country consolidated and our lines of communication open to supply trains. Fourteen days' rations on the man and a further forty days' reserve on the baggage-train was the safe minimum.

The estimated weight of reserve supplies divided by an average wagon-load gave the transport necessary to feed men and horses. In addition we had to carry artillery, tents, engineer equipment, armourers' tools, medical stores, spare swords and javelins, boots, clothing, armour, officers' baggage and a hundred other items. Every cohort bore on establishment sufficient wagons to carry first reserves of equipment; but stores required for prolonged campaigning were beyond the capacity of unit transport. So every commander, after receiving from me a list of reserves of all natures which his unit must take, was told to indent for additional transport. My staff examined the indents very closely indeed and pruned them to the ultimate donkey-load. The amended totals dictated the number of carts which we must buy, requisition or set our carpenters and wainwrights to construct.

Wroxeter hummed from dawn till dusk. Armourers hammered and sweated at their furnaces and forged repairs to weapons and mail. Grindstones sang in strident harmony and whetted swords and javelins to hairline keenness. Carpenters chopped and sawed raw timber into axle, spoke and yoke. Butterfly-winged leather tents were taken from store and greased, pitched, repaired and repacked. Artillerymen dismantled ballistae and catapults and lowered the huge baulks from the ramparts into carts specially strengthened to stand their weight. Natives in long files, laden with corn, trudged daily through the gates to refill granaries—sullen-faced creatures, these, for requisitions at this lean season were unpopular. The men built fences and corralled draught animals for our baggage train, oxen and mules, also prescripted from the local inhabitants. The close-packed wagon ranks lengthened like evening shadows in the baggage-park. And every day, for hour upon hour, centurions marched and counter-marched their men until the rawest recruit knew by heart every manœuvre that battle-drill demanded.

After a week, when I was satisfied that the flood of preparation was in full and methodical spate, I took my bodyguard cavalry and rode to Chester. Valens had told me the barges were ready and I wanted to test their seaworthiness. The shipyard was stacked to capacity. I had each barge, a rectangular box thirty feet long and ten wide, hauled in turn to the riverside on rollers and launched. Thirty fully-armed Tungri clambered aboard, sinking the boat to a six-inch freeboard, and with paddles and long quant poles manœuvred it clumsily up- and downstream.

The inspection took two days. I boarded every barge myself and found the majority made a little water during the short cruise. For security reasons I could not explain that these vessels, unladen, must make a seventy-mile sea voyage lasting a week or more. I contented myself with a wholehearted castigation of shipwrights and centurions, and followed it with orders to boil pitch and caulk the seams so thoroughly that not a drop of water could seep through. This work, and the subsequent trials, took four more days; finally I was satisfied that the flotilla was as watertight as human hands could make it.

The fort had suffered some raids during the winter. After one or two experimental attacks, easily repelled without much loss to either side, the Degeangli had flung storming parties, at night, against the shipyard's curtain walls. The tribesmen had overwhelmed the fighting towers on one wing, penetrated the yard and damaged a number of barges before a counter-attack from the fort ejected the survivors after confused fighting in the darkness. Casualties in this short, brisk action had been quite heavy: the tribune commanding, outraged at his losses, strengthened the post's defences and prepared reprisals.

He was confident that the tribesmen, encouraged by success, would repeat their raid. After dark, for night after night, he laid an ambush in a gully favoured by the enemy for their approach. Eventually his persistence was rewarded: he waylaid and cut to pieces a strong war-band and hunted the remnants into the river by the light of a waning moon. Thereafter Chester was left in peace.

4

April's advent brought to Wroxeter the cohorts I had summoned from Gloucester and Silchester. From Lincoln came an unexpected and far less welcome arrival: a Brigantian mission escorted by two troops of Classus's Horse, which clattered through the gates and sought an urgent audience. The escort commander gave me a message from Cerialis that almost made me weep with vexation.

'Venutius has reappeared. He has been lurking in the far north, among a tribe called the Selgovae, where he built a fort and collected a band of warriors. Now he has marched south, entered Brigantion territory and is fortifying a stronghold in the plain forty miles from York. His adherents at Cartimandua's court have fled to join him.

'Cartimandua sent Vellocatus to Lincoln to ask for help. She is very afraid. Vellocatus wants IX Legion in York at once. I told him that only the Governor could order Roman troops across the frontier. He insisted on seeking you.

'This, I submit, is all the excuse we need for peaceful annexation. I am ready to march whenever you give the word. Presumably you will detach another force to garrison Colchester if you think the situation there is still precarious.'

Typical of Cerialis, I thought irritably, to pursue his own impossible fantasy beyond the bounds of all military and political realities. I threw the letter aside and summoned the Brigantian mission to audience.

Vellocatus, in stating his case, shed a good deal of his sulky reserve. The possibility of Venutius regaining his throne clearly terrified him. This did not surprise me: that redoubtable warrior would exact a rough and summary retribution from this youth who had made free with his consort and his kingdom. When he had finished I tried to elicit a few facts.

'How many men has Venutius?'

'We don't know exactly, most noble Paulinus. Some say he has attracted more than twenty thousand freebooters from Selvogae and Votadini, promising them rewards and loot.'

I grunted disbelief. 'They must know he is unlikely to sack his own realm. A dispossessed chieftain hiding among strangers could hardly persuade so many to join him, however great his reputation. I consider your estimate much exaggerated. How long has Venutius been in Brigantia?'

'Since the new moon, most noble Paulinus.'

Fourteen days. 'Has he tried to approach York?'

'His foraging parties have come within a day's march. The army remains in his stronghold.'

'What precautions have you taken?'

'We have mustered our tribal levies at Aldborough. We shall have difficulty in keeping them under arms, most noble Paulinus; fields have to be sown and cattle pastured. Already many clansmen grow restive and are asking their chiefs for permission to return home.'

I studied the young man with pensive dislike. 'Why,' I asked him, 'do you want our help? Why does the Queen not lead her army immediately against Venutius, before her men wander back to their farms? Surely her forces outnumber whatever mercenaries Venutius has collected?'

Vellocatus flushed, lowered his eyes and mumbled unintelligibly. An old chieftain at his side spoke with forthright vigour: 'The Queen cannot rely on the loyalty of Brigantes in battle against a famous warrior who was once their king. That, most noble Paulinus, is the truth. If Venutius marches she is lost.'

I nodded. 'Exactly as I thought. Now listen to my judgement. At present no Roman soldier will enter Brigantian territory. By force or bribery you must keep your army in being until either Venutius strikes at York or, as is more likely, his levy grows tired of waiting and disintegrates. Should he move south in full array you will at once inform the legate Petillius Cerialis at Lincoln, who will come to your help with all his resources. Make sure Venutius is informed that Cartimandua's army will be supported by eight thousand Roman troops.

'If, however, the Queen's authority over her own soldiers is insufficient to keep them in the field you can expect no assistance from us. That is all.'

It was not quite all, because Vellocatus and his companions, with verbose and complicated arguments, tried hard to obtain immediate reinforcements. I finally lost patience and, with the terse comment that our army was not stationed in Britain to bolster a nation unwilling to fight for its own survival, dismissed the embassy. I then wrote to Cerialis informing him of the conditions I had imposed on Vellocatus, and added:

'You are now faced with the unhappy possibility of having to fight on two fronts, for the threat in the Colchester area has in no way diminished. Obviously there can be no question of dividing your forces until you see how the situation develops.

'My previous orders are therefore cancelled: you will not at present send any detachment to Colchester.

'The storms gathering north and south of you are equally menacing. I can allocate no hard and fast priorities. If Venutius attacks

Cartimandua she will, without our aid, inevitably be defeated; and we shall have an implacable enemy on our borders who may, in the flush of victory, decide to ravage the Province. If, on the other hand, the Iceni and Trinovantes rebel and are not immediately crushed they might lay half Britain in ruins.

'The pots are simmering: they may come to the boil successively, simultaneously or not at all. Early information of developments on both fronts is essential. Keep in close touch with Cartimandua; and I shall tell Aurelius Bassus to send you intelligence reports from Colchester every few days.

'My own armies will soon be fully committed, so you can expect no immediate aid. Any vexillation sent from my theatre of operations will take, I estimate, at least ten days to arrive anywhere in eastern Britain. Should you be desperately pressed I shall, of course, reinforce you. We must hope that matters do not arrive at that pass.'

Let nobody suppose that I failed to recognize the terrible dangers of my determination. All too frequently have my friends of later days insisted that this was the point when I should have altered all my plans: I should have abandoned the Ordovican invasion and led my men, instead, against Venutius, leaving Cerialis to deal with Iceni and Trinovantes.

To this I can only retort that no Governor can make war beyond his frontiers without the Prince's mandate, which, in Britain, takes two months to seek and obtain. If, on the other hand, I treated the Brigantian threat as an emergency imperilling the Province's safety, and marched straightway to York—for I was not compelled to have Nero's permission to act in self-defence—to defeat Venutius might carry us beyond midsummer, dangerously late for resuming the Ordovican campaign, which must then be postponed for another year. And if, withal, the Iceni did not revolt I should be accused by Nero of procrastination, timidity and failure to accomplish the design for which I had been sent to Britain, with the ineluctable penalties of recall and disgrace or worse.

It is better, I think, that a man's reputation should perish in the furnace of resolution than suffocate in a morass of inanition.

5

April entered in a scurry of wind and rain. No message came from Chester reporting the fleet's arrival. I fretted, visualizing fearful disasters at sea: gales had been too frequent of late. The men grew restless; materially and mentally they were ready for war and chafed at delays whose causes they could not be allowed to know.

On the fourth day of April a tired trooper on a foundered horse brought a brief note from Pantera announcing his landing. I wasted no time. Within the hour tribunes, prefects and senior centurions assembled at headquarters to hear my orders.

'The Prince,' I began, 'has committed me to exterminate the Druids in Britain.' (I had decided that the men would more easily understand this ostensible reason for fighting than the tortuous economic compulsions which really drove our army westwards.) 'This religion's foul contagion emanates from the country of the hillmen. Thither we shall march.

'The enemies we shall meet are Degeangli and Ordovices. Roman soldiers met and defeated both tribes twelve years ago: some of you have already sheathed your swords in their bodies. The natives do not know what we intend; they will, as always, be slow to unite against us. In any event their numerical strength is not great: the roughness of their country will give you more trouble than their prowess in battle.

'Our conquest must be thorough and permanent. We shall march to Chester and thence into enemy territory, road-building as we go. Our progress will be slow, probably not more than five miles a day. Near Chester lies a fleet of galleys and other vessels whose purpose will arouse speculation in your minds. Forgive me if I do not at present enlighten you: a wise general whispers his plans not even to his pillow.'

I detailed the order of march and administrative arrangements, finishing with a word of warning: 'To Druids we show no mercy; they will be exterminated like vermin. But remember that when we have conquered we shall make these people our subjects and, I hope, civilize them. So, in battle, kill when you must and spare when you can—we want slaves, not corpses. Nor will you permit your men to loot or ravage those communities which offer us no resistance. The tribes, after our conquest, will pay tribute, and the soldiers will get their share.'

We marched at dawn next day on the road Valens had made to Chester. I anticipated no opposition until we left Chester and was chiefly concerned at this early stage with settling the troops into field routine and discovering weak links in our baggage train. I threw out a small advanced guard—the 1st Morini with an engineer detachment, two legionary centuries and two cavalry troops—whose chief function was to reconnoitre fords and, at the day's end, select and mark out a camp site. Force headquarters, escorted by my bodyguard, headed the main body, for I always followed the Divine Julius's precept that a commander should be at the forefront. Headquarters' baggage followed the bodyguard. Then came Gemina's legionary cavalry and command group—Valens, his tribunes and senior centurions. The legion's Capricorn standard, escort and massed musicians followed. This was my own innovation. When action was improbable I usually ordered century hornblowers to march together and play in unison. The music enlivened weary hours of monotonous travelling.

The legion pounded behind, six abreast, undulating like some monstrous armoured crocodile escaped to these frigid regions from Euphrates' sultry waters. Those within earshot of the horns kept parade step, matching their pace to the music's beat. The rest used the normal route march free-step, each man suiting his stride to his own convenience and physique.

The artillery and siege train creaked on cumbrous wagons between XIV Legion and Valeria's four cohorts. This sequence was dictated by a bitter experience in Mauretania, when a sudden raid on the baggage had destroyed a large part of my engines which, in those days, customarily marched with the transport.

Behind Valeria came four auxiliary cohorts and four cavalry regiments, followed by the baggage—a long string of wagons, carts, pack-mules and donkeys and their attendant drivers, drovers and servants. No horn-band for these: they tramped to a strident march-tune of screeching axles and braying mules. The 3rd Bracarii escorted this mile-long train, marching alongside and striving, by exhortation, curses and blows, to maintain close order and a steady pace. The baggage train, often chaotic, always vulnerable, liable to panic disintegration at the first alarm, is the bane of every commander's existence.

My rearguard duplicated the advanced guard: legionary infantry and cavalry with an auxiliary cohort. On either flank, at distances dictated by the terrain and varying from a hundred paces to half a mile, marched a cavalry regiment with troops dispersed to cover the column's entire five-mile length.

We pitched camp after twenty miles. I followed my invariable practice and rode ahead with the advanced guard to confirm their selection of a site; then the engineers stake-marked gates and angles and pegged the alignment of ditch and rampart.

Guides met XIV Legion and led it without pause to line three faces of the camp; Valeria's cohorts filled the fourth. Auxiliary units on duty for the day threw a protective screen around the site, a ring of cavalry vedettes backed by infantry picquets. Cavalry filed to horse lines, dismounted and stood to their horses. The baggage-train meandered in and was herded to its allotted sector. When all was ready trumpets gave the signal. Eight thousand legionaries discarded shields, helmets, javelins and packs, seized pick, spade and mattock and attacked the ground like dogs digging for a badger.

The cavalry picketed horses, off-saddled, watered and groomed. Auxiliary cohorts worked under the Camp Prefect's direction, unloading baggage, pitching tents. Within two hours, timed by headquarters' water clock, the legion had dug the regulation ditch, nine feet broad and seven deep, shaped and packed the rampart, erected a palisade, pitched tents and mounted guards. The camp was fortified and ready.

6

Another twenty miles next day brought us to Chester, where we made camp near the auxiliary fort. Directly headquarters' pavilions were pitched Pantera sought me with news both good and bad.

'My ships are anchored in the estuary six miles downriver,' he reported. 'We've had some losses during the voyage.'

'How many?' I asked anxiously.

'We sailed from Boulogne, according to your orders, with thirty ships: twenty biremes and ten cutters. Two biremes and two cutters went ashore in a gale on the Dumnonian coast before we could run for shelter. We again met bad weather before we rounded Anglesey; the fleet was scattered. Two more biremes and four cutters are still missing, either foundered or driven ashore.'

'Most unfortunate, Pantera. Still, that leaves you with twenty warships. Are they undamaged?'

Pantera compressed his lips. 'Far from it, Legate. Every ship suffered materially to some extent, and some have lost men overboard.'

'You can make them seaworthy?'

'We are doing so. We have to replace broken oars, step new masts, renew stove-in planks and patch sails. Fortunately there's plenty of timber on shore near our anchorage.' He looked at me gloomily. 'I don't think, Legate, that you appreciate the strain my men have undergone during this terrible voyage. Never before has a Roman squadron been asked to cruise in these oceans at this season. I was prepared for hardship and danger: I did not expect seas like raging mountains, nor gales that flung ships from the water like blown spume. We're lucky to have lost only a third of our force.'

I listened with my mind elsewhere. My private estimate of probable casualties during the voyage had been exact. Twenty ships remained, the minimum necessary for my purpose. A bireme, given calm weather, could tow ten or a dozen barges and a cutter six; so I could still use about a hundred and eighty barges of the two hundred available. Not too bad.

'How soon will you be ready to sail?'

The Prefect stiffened. 'Our last straggler arrived in the estuary two days ago. The ships will be seaworthy within another two days.' He paused. 'My crews' morale is low, Legate. They may be unwilling to sail until the equinoctial gales are over.'

I faced him in astonished anger. 'Unwilling? Do you mean they're mutinous? Explain yourself!'

'Legate,' Pantera pleaded, 'you have never, I think, been in a galley when the waves run high enough to smash oars to slivers and tear them from the rowers' hands; when the wind shreds stout canvas like mildewed parchment; when treble-manned steering oars hurl the helmsmen across the decks like empty sacks; when only a frail sea-anchor holds prow to wind and the spouting rocks drift steadily nearer. We have had this and more, Legate, not once, but for days together.'

I rubbed my chin. 'Such things are part of your trade, Pantera, as death or mutilation by sword or lance are part of mine.'

'Would you parry a spear-thrust with a paper shield, Legate?' he said quietly. 'As well ask your sailors to face the horrors of outer Ocean in their frail galleys. Our ships are not designed for these waters.'

'That may be so. Your next voyage, luckily, is much less hazardous: you should never be far from shore and can run for shelter at need. Tomorrow,' I added briskly, 'I shall speak to your men. Assemble them ashore at midday.'

'Very well, Legate.'

I unrolled a map. 'You reconnoitred this coast last summer. Show me the most favourable anchorages and let us work out a movement programme.'

When the discussion was ended and Pantera gone I summoned Agricola. 'Leave at dawn tomorrow and ride to the estuary,' I told him. 'Mix with the fleet's officers and men. Talk to them, gauge their temper and discover their grievances. Report to me when I arrive.'

Trumpets sounded the second watch—but there was no rest for me yet. I conferred with Valens and auxiliary commanders, arranging duties for the next day. Our main task was to move the barges to the fleet anchorage, for shallows and sandbanks prevented the galleys from cruising upriver to fetch them. 2nd Vascones provided crews for the barges—a fatigue that absorbed the entire cohort—for I had planned that these same men, made familiar with the task by paddling and poling six miles to the estuary, should eventually propel the craft across the Anglesey straits.

I directed all available troops to build the first six-mile section of our road to the river mouth. Strong protective detachments guarded the working parties, though so far no Degeangli, hostile or otherwise, had shown themselves. The route did not coincide with that taken by Ostorius Scapula twelve years before: he had entered Degeanglia farther south and marched across the hills. I, on the other hand, with a forward base established at Chester, intended to follow the flat coastlands for fifteen miles before turning inland. Even when we joined Ostorius's route I knew, from perusal of his careful records filed in Colchester, that we would find no road: he had merely levelled native tracks to make them viable for his baggage-train.

I ordered Proculus's Horse, garrisoning Chester fort, to be relieved by the 1st Britannic Cavalry. Proculus's, a good, experienced regiment, would be a welcome addition to Wroxeter's attenuated garrison; and I had not been impressed by the British cavalry's discipline and horse-mastership during the march.

That march had also exposed certain administrative weaknesses, chiefly in the baggage train, where ill-conditioned vehicles, unfit animals and slipshod loading had caused delay and disorder. I spoke concisely to the Camp Prefect and gave him two days to put matters right.

Next morning, after a bustling ride to the anchorage, I met Agricola before addressing the seamen. I was prepared for a description of a sullen, mutinous rabble whose discipline had completely dissolved. Agricola reassured me.

'The sailors are very tired, physically and mentally, after the rigours of their voyage,' he said. 'They have certainly had some ghastly experiences. They feel they've been made to overcome greater hazards than any commander should expect, and they have, at the moment, no intention of facing the same dangers on the return voyage. They're very bitter, and tend to distrust their officers who are, for the most part, loyally prepared to serve as you may direct.'

'What do you suggest I should say to them?' I asked bluntly.

'Praise and flattery, Legate,' Agricola said. 'Promise them the end of trial by wreck and tempest. Show them that, from this time forward, they can win reward and glory with comparative ease. I think they'll respond.'

The men were gathered in a clearing by the shore. From my rostrum—the beak of a bireme beached for repairs—I harangued them at length. I said that nothing less than the Prince's personal orders and the direst demands of military necessity had persuaded me to commit them to an undertaking which I well knew to be extremely hazardous. I told them that their voyage had made history: the annals of the Roman Navy recorded none more dangerous or more glorious in accomplishment. The names of their ships would be written in my dispatches to Rome and inscribed in the historic rolls of those whom the City honoured. Moreover I myself, in recognition of their courage and endurance, would donate to every sailor a sum of fifty denarii.

This roused the audience. When the cheers subsided I gave a firm assurance that, though they must sail again within two days, they would always be within sight of land and within a few hours' sail of a safe anchorage. Nor, I finished, would they have to make the return voyage to Boulogne until the onset of fair summer weather.

The trouble was over. My bodyguard ceased fingering their sword-hilts and relaxed. Sailors clambered to the deck, clapped me familiarly on the shoulder and promised unswerving loyalty. Pantera wore a relieved smile.

'As an orator, Legate, you are more persuasive than Cicero. I had feared greatly for the result.'

'Cash, not oratory, turned the scale,' I said briefly. 'A donation equivalent to four months' pay talks more convincingly than words. The money shall reach you from the treasury tonight. See it is distributed at once. There are no wineshops here where your men can get drunk.'

To Agricola, as we rode homewards, I added ruefully, 'I shall have to explain these gifts very tactfully to the Prince. In Republican times a general could reward his men as he pleased to the limits of his purse. Those days are gone. The Princes of Rome look askance on commanders who buy their men's allegiance with donations.'

'You've saved the campaign, Legate, and are half a million sesterces the poorer,' Agricola said hotly. 'What else should you have done? The Prince, when he learns the facts, will surely commend your resourcefulness.'

I shook my head gloomily. I was not so sure.

7

By next evening all was ready for departure. The barges had gone down river into Pantera's charge. I had held a final conference with my commanders and delivered orders for the morrow. Now, in my pavilion, while the camp slept and horns sounded the watches of a clear, starry night, I pored over one of Ostorius's maps by the flickering light of a single lamp, cursing gently to myself at the draughtsman's uncertain delineations. This pleasant occupation was interrupted by my orderly Secundus.

'A dispatch rider from Colchester, Legate.'

I took the sealed roll, questioned the man briefly about his journey and dismissed him. The message was from Aurelius Bassus. He wrote:

'The last ship from Boulogne has brought a number of agents from Roman banking houses. Several have arrived in Colchester and are busy recovering loans from clients among the Trinovantes. There is little money left here now, after the last exactions: the natives are being forced to part with goods and livestock. My spies report growing restiveness. A usurer has been killed by a mob in a village near Chelmsford.

'Annaeus Seneca's agents have been specially favoured. The Procurator has permitted them to enter Icenia and has provided them with a military escort. They passed through Colchester three days ago. Other creditors tried to join them, wishing to take advantage of the escort's protection. This, as they lacked authority, I forbade.

'Seneca's men tell me he has eight million sesterces invested in Icenia alone. He is recalling the lot. Obviously the mercantile community in Rome is apprised of the Icenian kingdom's imminent liquidation.

'I suspect the Procurator, also, has discovered this from his banker friends. He has come to Colchester and, impatient as a bitch in heat, awaits dispatches which are due from Rome within the next few days. If these contain his authority to expropriate the late king's possession he will presumably depart with all speed for Norwich.

'I prefer not to speculate on the cumulative effect of these exactions on the brittle-tempered Iceni. It is indeed a pity that the reinforcement of Colchester has had to be abandoned.'

I held the letter to the lamp and watched it burn. So much for Burrus's promise, on that long-ago day in Rome, that the Government would not foreclose on Icenia until my armies were free to prevent the consequences. Nero had been unable to curb his tongue and the whole pack was in full cry.

The flame scorched my fingers. I dropped the charred remnants to the floor, where they flickered with the dying whisper of a lost cause. The news changed nothing. The legions marched to Anglesey.

I bent again over Ostorius's ill-drawn map.

9

'Ah, Father Zeus, save us from this fog and give us a clear sky,
so that we can use our eyes. Kill us in daylight, if you must.'

                                                        THE ILIAD

1

Next day, the 10th of April, the army left Chester, marched fifteen miles and camped in foothills overlooking the estuary. The first six miles was easy going on the road we had just made to the fleet anchorage. Thereafter, guided by Britons from Chester who alleged they knew the main trackways leading west, we followed a native trail passable for horse and foot but awkward for wheeled transport. I had foreseen this and had sent legionary engineers and working parties to head the baggage-train. Our pace was not greatly slowed; the chief obstacles were scattered boulders, streams and minor landslides caused by winter rains.

We passed the ships riding at anchor a quarter-mile from shore, at a berth which gave good shelter from storms and was secure against seaward attack. The only craft used by coast-dwelling natives in these regions were small tubs made of hides stretched on wicker frames, carrying one or two men apiece. Pantera had all the deepwater seaman's contempt for these coracles as a means of boarding his galleys.

'And yet,' I reminded him, 'they say that Britons cross to Ireland in such boats.'

The Prefect sniffed. 'Tales told by the men who use coracles. They are all fishermen, and fishermen's stories—! My ships are safe. We keep watches aboard and the crews live in a fortified camp that commands the beaches.'

'You should be secure enough. I have ordered a patrol from Chester to visit you every day and see that all is well.'

Pantera's face plainly expressed his opinion of a superfluous precaution. I waved farewell and rode to overtake the marching army.

When the men started digging our first camp in Degeanglia they found hard rock under a foot or two of soil. The fosse had to be less than regulation depth and in compensation we built high rock walls surmounted by stone breastworks instead of a palisade. This was an expedient we often had to adopt during the campaign. Sometimes the ground was too hard for any pretence of digging; we then surrounded the camp with an outer wall set ten paces from the main breastwork.

Next day we began to build a road linking the fleet anchorage with our camp. The procedure of laying a road after we had traversed the ground rather than throwing a highway forward for the army's passage was inconvenient but unavoidable. So obscure were the enemy's movements and intentions that I could not risk sending working parties, however heavily protected, into country that had not been made good. Moreover, with a fort guarding each end of the stretch under construction I could reduce protective troops and release more men for roadmaking.

For this work the army was divided into two portions: guards and labourers. On the first day we worked backwards from camp, where I left a garrison of one milliary cohort and a cavalry regiment, and built a section five miles long. The units on road guard—five cavalry regiments and two auxiliary cohorts—occupied high ground whence they could watch all gullies and re-entrants giving access to the road. In the centres of the sector two legionary cohorts stood under arms in reserve. This left eight thousand men for road-building, an average of a man per yard. They worked in five gangs, one to the mile, under the direction of engineers.

After ten hours' work the first stretch was made. Naturally it lacked the finish of roads laid down at leisure under peacetime conditions. There was neither time nor materials for refinements such as mortared foundation beds, layered concrete and paved surfaces. The men dug parallel trenches twenty feet apart to mark the road's width and between them removed a foot of loose earth. On this they laid a layer of big rocks, unless, as often happened in these rockgirt regions, they had already reached a solid foundation. On a second layer of smaller boulders they put a thick surface of pebbles and flints. Large, flat stones laid on edge bordered the road and compacted the layers in place. Except in cuttings the three layers raised the road well above ground level.

Hitherto we had met no enemies. A few infirm and senile inhabitants still cowered in the coastal fishing villages where the only belongings left by the natives were their coracles, which lay like rotting oysters on the beaches below the round, reed-thatched huts. Farther inland our patrols swiftly investigated one or two small hill-forts and found obvious signs of recent occupation and hasty evacuation.

During the following day, while the road was carried back to the fleet anchorage, I interrogated some of the wretched old men we had caught. My inquisitors could twist little sense from them; they averred that all the warriors of Degeanglia were gathering in two great strongholds a day's march west. Ostorius's maps, which showed a river called Var some ten miles farther on, marked no native settlements; nor were they mentioned in his reports. I tried without success to extract information about defences and garrison strengths: the prisoners were aged and frail and, under persuasion, died too easily.

2

On the 13th of April we broke camp, turned our backs on the sea and plunged due west into the hills. I left five centuries of 1st Tungri and a cavalry troop in a small but immensely strong fort which the Tungri, helped by legionaries, had taken care to make nearly impregnable. In any event the Degeangli would have little time to waste on outlying strongpoints when an army was penetrating their vitals.

I aimed, in this day's march, to cross a ten mile stretch of hills to the Var valley. The nature of the ground dictated more caution than had been necessary on the flat coastlands and, from our captives' stories of the day before, it seemed we might meet trouble. We struck a trackway leading approximately in the direction we wished to travel; our surveyors, who also acted as navigators during marches with unreliable guides in unknown country, kept careful check on our course as we progressed.

The track mounted slantwise an escarpment overlooking the sea and used a deep re-entrant which eased the climb. Even so, after emerging on the high plateau above I had to halt to give the baggage-train some time to struggle upwards. This delay was extremely irritating: the van had not gone five miles and the rearguard had barely left camp. The incubus was our wheeled transport, particularly those cumbrous four-wheeled wagons carrying artillery. I rode back to investigate. The auxiliaries detailed as baggage-guard were showing little inclination to give any active help until, stirred by my caustic comments, they deigned to put shoulder to wheel. Their incompetence was then so remarkable that I summoned a legionary cohort who vigorously manhandled the heavy wagons to the top. Forewarned by this exhibition I appointed legionaries to guard the baggage-train on future marches.

The army marched easily across smoothly rolling tableland and dropped sharply into the Var valley. Before midday the men were at work fortifying the camp, which we called Varae. We had seen no tribesmen nor hill-forts. Did the Degeanglian strongholds exist only in the fishermen's imagination? The day was young; I decided to push on and reconnoitre.

With my bodyguard cavalry and two regiments of horse I followed the trackway's ascent into more rugged country. Steep hills deeply cleft by tumbling streams elbowed our route like curious strangers. Before we ceased climbing we saw our first armed tribesmen, little groups of warriors on distant hillsides who gesticulated and brandished weapons but came no nearer. Presently a scout returned from the vanguard.

'Enemy fort a mile on our right,' he reported.

The fort, perched on the escarpment's crest, overlooked a wide plain stretching to the sea. By ascending the escarpment farther inland where it edged the Var valley we had approached the stronghold on the landward side at an equal height and found ourselves separated from it only by a broad, flat-topped, mile-long ridge.

'Let us look closer,' I commanded.

Leaving Indus's Horse to cover our withdrawal I approached the place with my bodyguard and the Asturians, cautiously probing dense bushes which might conceal archers or spearmen. We halted well out of bowshot and surveyed the scene.

The fortress reared steep on its spur, and was guarded by double stone ramparts of tremendous height and breadth which combined with the natural scarps to give a truly formidable appearance. The entrance, directly facing us, was deeply inturned and flanked by stone guard chambers which, according to tribal custom, flaunted decaying heads and whitened skulls, trophies of internecine warfare. The battlements seethed with excited figures and glinting weapons; battle-yells and hornblasts shivered the air.

I examined the approaches. On the right the hill descended steeply to the coastal plain; in the centre was a flat tableland; on the left an easy slope to a shallow vale.

'How many defenders do you think those earthworks can hold?' I asked the Asturian prefect.

He pursed his lips, considering. 'Fifteen hundred comfortably; three thousand packed like olives in a barrel.'

'My estimate also.' I glanced at the sun and measured shadow-lengths. 'We can take this place before evening. Back to the track!'

I sent Agricola galloping to Varae with instructions. We left vedettes watching the fort, posted picquets for our own protection, dismounted and waited.

3

By mid-afternoon reinforcements arrived and, under cavalry escort, I took prefects and centurions forward to reconnoitre and explain the plan of attack. Guarded by 3rd Bracarii our three 'wild asses', or onagers, lighter and more manœuvrable than their big brothers the ballistae, trundled behind in wagons, to be off-loaded and assembled when they were within range.

To storm the fort I had gathered a combat group five thousand strong: four cohorts of XX Legion and five auxiliary cohorts. Three legionary and two auxiliary cohorts were to assault the entrance face. Auxiliary cohorts were to stage diversionary attacks on each flank, Tungri on left while Vardulli scaled the beetling scarp on the right. The thousand-strong veterans' cohort and 3rd Bracarii I held in reserve. The cavalry, meanwhile, was to seal the area and prevent interference from enemy bands roaming the hills.

I delivered a brief exhortation to the troops who then moved to their start lines. Onagers began lobbing boulders into the fort and a wild screeching signalled their devastations. I let the pounding continue for some time in the hope that the punishment might become unendurable and drive the enemy to make a sortie. The yelling, scurrying and horn-blowing on the ramparts increased; there was no other reaction.

'Sound the attack,' I ordered.

I unfurled my scarlet battle-ensign; the trumpets blared. XX Legion advanced at marching pace in century columns with Morini and Thracian detachments filling the intervals. On the left Tungri whooped to the attack in a turmoil of hornblasts and battle-cries; below on the right, invisible but not inaudible, Vardulli skipped and skidded along the hillsides. The onagers delivered a final volley, reloaded and waited.

Arrows whipped and stung the attackers, and men staggered and dropped from the ranks. The Thracians drew and replied; the twang of bowstrings thrummed on the breeze. Centuries closed on the outer rampart, raised interlocked shields above head and shoulders and broke into a trot.

'A critical moment,' I observed to Agricola. 'Will the auxiliaries be able to keep the enemy's heads down until the tortoises are over?'

They could. Morini had the reputation of being the best slingers in the Army of Britain, unmatched for accuracy and speed. Running between the shellback centuries they flung a leaden hail at the raging figures who assailed the tortoises with spears and stones. Wide gaps opened on the crowded battlements. With a heave and wriggle the flank tortoises were over; two in the centre, directed on the funnelled entrance, reared and recoiled.

'They're in trouble,' Agricola said.

'Shot at from both flanks,' I answered, 'while the enemy are defiladed from our own arrows and slings.'

Tungri on the left already flailed longswords at the inner ramparts. I did not seriously expect them to gain a foothold, still less penetrate the defences; but their impetuous onslaught had carried them through a storm of arrows and throwing-spears to pin the defenders on that part of the wall. The Vardulli, still hidden beneath the crest, sounded boisterously active.

The tortoises, momentarily hidden in the ditch between outer and inner rampart, reappeared scaling the steep glacis to their last objective. Morini and Thracians lined the outer earthworks and poured in missiles; the former, finding the targets out of distance—the double curtain had been designed to foil slingers—bounded into the ditch and hurled their shots almost vertically upwards.

'We're still held up at the entrance,' Agricola muttered anxiously.

'We are,' I said. 'And, if I were the enemy commander, I'd choose this moment to try a breakout. First centurion!'

'Here, Legate.'

'Advance the veterans and cover the fortress entrance. Stay beyond bowshot. Only engage if the enemy make a sortie.'

'Very good, Legate.' He turned and bellowed through cupped hands. 'First Cohort, close column of centuries. Advance! Double march!'

Before they had gone fifty paces a roaring horde erupted between the towering guard-chambers and engulfed the centuries struggling at the entrance. A new chord twanged in the battle-melody: the clash of blade on blade and piercing cries of mortal agony. The veterans swooped deftly from column to line and an iron hurricane smashed into the fight.

Our flank centuries had gained the inner ramparts, sweeping defenders before them like twigs in a torrent. Standards glittered on the battlements; trumpeters lifted their long horns skywards and bayed like wolves.

The fort was taken.

4

At the entrance legionaries prowled amid carnage, stooping over bundled bodies to dispatch enemies or recover our dead and wounded. At close quarters the stone ramparts were truly immense, and I marvelled that we had won them so easily. From one of the guard-chambers a wounded Briton hung head down; his dying convulsions pumped great blood-gouts from his mouth.

Inside the fortress Roman sword-blades hunted tribesmen through the riddle of sprawling hutments. All resistance was finished.

'Enough of this,' I said. 'Trumpeter, rally the legion.'

He sounded Valeria's call-sign, and the rally.

'Send runners to prefects of Vardulli and Tungri. Surround the fortress and cut off fugitives. Runners to prefects of Morini and Thracians. Collect prisoners outside the fort.'

Centurions quickly restored order. The tumult subsided. Auxiliary spear-points hustled a stream of captives from the fortress. Medical orderlies roamed the enclosure, bandaging wounds and improvising stretchers. Carrying parties took our dead to the onager wagons. Soon, except for native corpses and scampering livestock which eluded capture, the place was clear.

'Fire the huts,' I ordered.

Nearly a thousand men, women and children huddled together under guard. I examined the males with curious interest, for they were a pattern of our opponents in the struggle for Anglesey. A few were well enough attired in wool or linen tunics and trousers cross-strapped from knee to ankle. Others wore pelts of wolf or beaver above leather kilts; some were almost naked. Conical iron helmets were plentiful, sometimes adorned with ox-horns; but the only body-armour I saw was rectangular ringmail breastplates, and these were rare. Their weapons were spears, unpointed slashing-swords, short but powerful bows and round leather shields with metal bosses. The men were dark-haired and swarthy, short but muscular; the women blunt-featured and unattractive.

'Is there any man of rank among this mob?' I demanded.

A staff interpreter, who obviously found difficulty in comprehending the local dialect of Old British, repeated the question until after much argument, a Briton wearing a bright blue cloak was brought to my horse's head.

'Are you the King of the Degeangli?'

'The Degeangli have no king. They are ruled by a High Chieftain. I am not he.'

'Where does the High Chieftain have his dwelling?'

The man turned and pointed towards the setting sun. 'In a fortress near the sea.'

So, I thought, here was the second stronghold mentioned by our captives from the fishing villages.

'Take heed,' I said. 'You have seen what we do to those who oppose us. Look!' I pointed to the captured fortress, which sprouted a crackling forest of flame and smoke. 'This we have done with less than half our army—you know from your scouts that our main strength is still encamped at Varae. We have been merciful: we have spared the survivors of your garrison. They will be taken to our camp and cared for.'

The interpreter painfully translated. The Briton listened with sullen attention, striving to understand his own tongue so strangely accented. I waited impatiently.

'Now listen carefully. You and two chosen companions will go to your High Chieftain and deliver this message. At dawn tomorrow he will come unarmed to Varae with his princes and councillors and make submission to Rome. If within an hour of sunrise he has not appeared I will slaughter these captives, man, woman and child. Then I shall take his stronghold with my whole army and put every living creature to the sword. Do you understand? Then depart!'

We reached camp before sundown, penned the prisoners and burned our dead. Soon after dawn sentries sounded a needless alarm: the procession descending the trackway was that which I desired.

I received the Degeangli courteously and dictated terms. They were to cease all resistance to the passage of Roman troops through their territory. Any man carrying arms within sight of the road would be treated as hostile. They must immediately provide three thousand men of good physique for work on the road and bring us six cartloads of corn to replenish our supplies. I took hostages to secure these conditions and, in return, released our prisoners.

Seven legionaries and twenty auxiliaries died in the escalade: a small price to pay for quelling an entire tribe. We had no more opposition from the Degeangli.

5

We spent the next two days building the road rearwards to our previous camp, a task made easier by native labour. On the 16th, leaving Varae garrisoned by 3rd Bracarii and two cavalry troops, the army headed west into broken hills separating the Var valley from Conovium. This was Degeanglian territory, and although the Degeangli had submitted, the country's rugged nature dictated caution. Valens practised mountain warfare tactics rehearsed throughout the winter.

In essence his system was a chain of static flank guards protecting the army's passage when the terrain was so rough that mobile flankers could not operate. These picquets were posted in advance of the main body and so a picqueting force of mountaineers, Vardulli and Vascones, marched with the advanced guard. Century-strength detachments seized all hills that were dangerously near the track or commanded gullies and re-entrants likely to conceal ambushes and, after quickly fortifying their hilltops, remained on guard until the army had passed. They then descended and joined the rearguard.

Though a fairly certain insurance against ambuscades the method in practice had disadvantages. As we advanced the country became more tangled; so many hills had to be picqueted that the entire strength of both picqueting cohorts was consumed and 1st Britannic had to be brought forward. Apart from being expensive in men it slowed our march; the main body was constantly halting while picquets climbed the hills.

I voiced my opinions to Valens, who agreed. 'In really bad country a force might do twelve miles a day unopposed: half that if picquets had to fight for their ground,' he said. 'In Wroxeter we found the tactics chiefly valuable in transborder patrolling, to help detachments through defiles. On an army scale it's too slow and clumsy.'

The march that day was long and tedious, nearly twenty miles over switchback tracks which exacted toil and sweat from our engineers. The hills resembled a gigantic heap of debris flung from heaven and petrified in the chaotic disorder of its fall. Our surveyors were at odds with the guides, conscripted Degeangli, who were reliable in their choice of tracks but failed to understand the twin maxims of maintaining height and following the shortest distance between two points.

The artillery wagons and two-wheeled carts lurched and lagged; in desperation I detached a milliary cohort to escort vehicles, drivers and attendant legionaries and left them to follow at their own pace. We were still in Degeanglian territory; I scented little risk in separating my siege train under strong guard.

In late afternoon we dropped abruptly into the mile-wide cleft which forms the boundary between Degeangli and Ordovices and also divides the hill region we had traversed from soaring mountains beyond. We marched upriver, crossed by a ford and retraced our steps on the left bank, halting just below the river's tidal limits.

6

The camp at Conovium was set in the valley on a swell of ground between river and mountain. We were on soil already trodden by Romans: Ostorius had planted a cohort fort here twelve years before. The vast ramparts of our fortress soon obliterated the grass-grown mounds and silted ditch that marked his building.

During the previous summer Pantera had reconnoitred the river's estuary four miles downstream and proved it a safe anchorage. To my delight I found flood tide gave ample water for galleys to row upstream and moor directly beneath our ramparts. At low water the channel was strait and shallow; the anchored ships might be in danger of grounding. This did not matter; sailors, I knew, had methods of securing ships against damage under such conditions; and it was supremely important, in these hostile regions, that the squadron's berth should be heavily guarded.

I sent a messenger to Pantera with orders to sail at dawn of the 19th April for Conovium. The sea passage was fifty miles, the weather fair and winds light; he should reach Conovium by evening of the 20th.

This four days' respite gave time to make the twenty-mile road between Conovium and Varae. Work started at once, the soldiers being reinforced by Degeanglian labourers summoned by our noble hostages. Of forage there was no lack; grass grew green and lush in watery meadows. The grain levied from the tribe seemed nearly to have exhausted their supplies; foragers discovered only a few pitiful stores in half-deserted villages, barely sufficient to feed a cohort for a day.

Our transport, despite backbreaking toil in levelling trackways, had suffered both damage and loss. Several wagons, with wheels or axles smashed in headlong descent of some steep hillside, had been abandoned and their loads transferred to other vehicles which in turn collapsed or, precariously repaired, lurched into camp supported by their escorts' shoulders and prayers. Our carpenters and wainwrights worked all day and, by torchlight, into the night; we marched, eventually, not only with a full complement of baggage vehicles but also with five new ones, empty, in reserve.

We needed more draught animals both for the new wagons and to replace casualties. The hillmen did not use wheels. Mules were unknown; oxen were rare and had long since been driven to inaccessible valleys safe from marauding Romans. However, foragers and patrols found wild ponies wandering the lower hills and grazing in the valley; and cavalry horsebreakers, amid antics which raised ribald amusement and loud catcalls from watching legionaries, persuaded these reluctant and stubborn animals to accept bridle and collar.

Pantera, helped by a tranquil sea and following winds, made better time than I hoped. By noon on the 20th his leading bireme, towing a string of barges, nosed cautiously upstream with the flood and anchored beneath the fortress. Mooring the barges in these narrow waters was a tricky business. Fortunately the Frisiavones, watermen from Rhinemouth, were on duty in camp. They swam gaily to the barges, cast off towlines, paddled the unwieldy craft to the banks and made fast in orderly rows. The warships anchored in midstream, bow to stern. Pantera was ready with timber props to prevent his ships, stranded by a falling tide, from tilting on their beam ends; luckily the galleys remained afloat even at the lowest ebb.

Four days' work was not enough to finish the road to Varae. Surveyors apologetically explained that ups and downs caused by crossing the grain of the land had increased distances. I sent some of our forced native labour to the Bracarii with orders to work on the remaining three-mile gap.

With the fleet assembled there was no longer any reason for the army to linger at Conovium. Movement orders shook the troops into a bustle of preparation that was interrupted, for me, by the tragic outcome of a domestic comedy and by a letter from Aurelius Bassus.

7

At dawn of that last day in Conovium legionaries squatted in two facing rows in the latrines of XIV Legion's fifth cohort. Men grunted, strained and exchanged the bawdy gossip usual in such a place. Marcus Petronius, standard-bearer of Century XLV, was among those engaged in their morning duty; nearly opposite squatted a tesserar from another century. Between these two had lately arisen a bitter quarrel over the favours of a good-looking boy recently recruited to the cohort. The tesserar, disappointed in love, gave rein to his jealousy in a torrent of recrimination against Petronius.

Coarse insults and counter-gibes sharpened the amiable tenor of general conversation. One or two men shouted at the pair to cease bickering. Most of the spectators listened in contented silence to a quarrel which was none of their concern. The tesserar, goaded by Petronius's remarks, retrieved his latrine sponge from the freshwater runnel between the rows, carefully wiped himself and hurled it at his antagonist. Petronius received the stinking missile full in the face. Pausing only to wipe muck from his eyes he sprang dagger in hand at the tesserar. In a twinkling the latrine was in uproar.

Soldiers separated the fighting men but the damage was done. They hauled the tesserar, smeared with excreta and spouting blood from a severed jugular, out of the trench where he had fallen. He died before a medical orderly arrived. Petronius was clapped under arrest, cleaned, dressed and brought to me for punishment.

His offence was clear and abundantly witnessed; the penalty was death. Vettius Valens, in mitigation, said the dead man was a bad character, a muscular lout who provoked his seniors and bullied inferiors. The standard-bearer, on the other hand, was an outstanding legionary with, hitherto, a stainless record. His centurion also spoke on his behalf and pleaded for his life.

Every soldier is valuable during a campaign; Petronius was a particularly good one. I did not want to lose him when battles still remained to be won.

'Signifer,' I said, 'my plain duty is to send you to execution. I shall not do so because of the great provocation leading to your offence and because your legate and centurion have testified to your good qualities. It is not fitting that a brave man should be beaten to death. But you have committed a crime and must be punished.

'You will no longer carry your century's standard.

'Very soon your legion will be fighting, and fighting hard. You have the chance of an honourable death. See to it that you do not survive.'

(Marcus Petronius did not die. In the last battle his valour in search of extinction on Ordovican sword-points would have earned him decorations in other circumstances. Bleeding from a dozen wounds he came to me for sentence after the engagement. When I heard of his exploits I not only pardoned him but restored his rank.)

Hardly had I passed judgement on this squalid brawl when hoof-beats sprayed gravel outside headquarters' pavilion. A decurion entered and saluted.

'An immediate message from Colchester, Legate.'

I took the roll with foreboding and broke the seals. The letter was dated the 12th April.

'Gn. Aurelius Bassus to the Legate Propraetor G. Suetonius Paulinus. Greetings.

'Decianus Catus received orders from the Prince and departed for Icenia yesterday. He made no secret of his task: to sequestrate all Icenian royal property and treasure. He followed the trail of Seneca's agents like a dog-wolf scenting blood.

'Catus travels with a horde of secretaries and slaves. He has also taken every soldier in London and, to increase his escort, persuaded fifty retired legionaries in Colchester to don their rusty armour and accompany him. Those who went were mostly men of bad character and few scruples. Dissatisfied or unsuccessful farmers, they are attracted by promises of easy pickings. In the army they used to call it loot.

'The Trinovantes remain outwardly calm. They have become a nation of paupers and debtors: many natives borrowed from small moneylenders at exorbitant interest to meet obligations when the Claudian grants were recalled. The surface is comparatively unruffled; from the depths my spies dredge an ever-thickening sludge of disaffection and conspiracy.

'Should there still be no chance of stationing troops here I submit that you should command Colchester's magistrates to surround the colony with ditch and bank. I have already sounded them about this project: their replies were inimical and derisory.

'May the Gods favour your enterprise and protect your person. Farewell.'

I tossed the letter to Agricola. 'Read it. Another log on the funeral pyre of my ambitions. Some day someone will apply the torch. Secundus! Runners to unit commanders. Conference at headquarters immediately.'

8

Tribunes, prefects and centurions thronged headquarters' pavilion. Branched candlesticks on a trestle table plucked wavering colours from white and russet cloaks and splashed dull sparks on helmets and armour. Maps and papers littered the table—Ostorius's maps and twelve-year-old reports which from now onwards guided our steps and provided our information.

'Tomorrow,' I began, 'we start the last stage of our journey to the Anglesey straits. The distance is between twelve and fifteen miles across high mountains more tangled and complex than any region in Britain. Some of you have been there before.'

'I remember it well,' Valens rumbled.

There was a growl of concurrence from the older centurions.

'We have the advantage, then, of knowing the ground. Bad though it is, the Legate Ostorius Scapula cleared for his transport a path which he used going and returning. This path must still exist and should make things easier for our baggage-train.

'I wish we knew as much of the enemy. None of our patrols has made contact with Ordovican warriors, although they have captured some herdsmen who assert that all their war-bands have withdrawn to the west and crossed the sea. The Degeangli, you remember, likewise retired before us and concentrated in two hilltop strongholds. But, according to Ostorius Scapula, the Ordovices have only one citadel wherein they can assemble their fighting strength—a great fortress on a ridge of hills overlooking the straits.'

'We stormed and destroyed it,' Valens grunted. 'May have been rebuilt since.'

'Which makes it unlikely,' I returned, 'that they will again try to hold the same place. There and everywhere else in these mountains Scapula's legions routed the Ordovices. I therefore think that prisoners' tales of warriors crossing the sea are true; and that the enemy, warned by previous defeats, have put the straits between themselves and us.'

'You expect no opposition tomorrow?' Valens asked.

'Yes, I do. The region seems specially designed for harassing tactics. I expect we shall meet small, courageous war-bands, prepared to fight to the death in a succession of ambuscades. These people, remember, are fanatical Druids; they know that, whatever else we spare, we shall destroy their religion.

'Tomorrow, then, we march with a strong advanced guard and flank guards. No hill picquets.'

The Vettonians' tribune showed surprise. 'No picquets, Legate? In these mountains surely—'

'Have you seen the night?' I demanded curtly.

'Yes, Legate. Still and windless, and a thickening mist.'

'That mist, according to a defiant old goatherd a patrol took this morning, tomorrow will "clothe the mountains and blind the eagles". Which,' I added sourly, 'is native rhetoric meaning that visibility may be less than a javelin-cast. And in that case hill picquets will be masked and useless and the column will need close protection. Is your question answered, tribune?'

'Fully, Legate.'

'Good. Now to details. The army will march at dawn tomorrow. Indus's Horse and one cohort of XX Legion will remain at Conovium. Units of the advanced guard will be...'

9

Following an immutable rule of warfare in alien territory, the legions at first light levelled the ramparts and cast them into the ditch and so demolished our camp. I stood impatiently on a watchtower of the permanent fort that had been built in an angle of the fast-disappearing marching-camp. A chilly mist draped valley and hills and shrouded men and animals in opalescent haze.

Trumpets recalled invisible cavalry vedettes guarding the work of destruction. Legionaries thankfully ceased shovelling, donned cloak and helmet, shouldered javelins and joined their standards. The disparate elements of an army on fatigue duties sundered and fused in ordered ranks, cohort behind cohort, like sword-blades laid in rows. I raised a hand; horns bellowed; the vanguard glided out like the grey-scaled body of a venomous snake.

The column splashed through a muddy stream and started to climb. The mist curdled; I could barely discern helmets only thirty paces ahead. Fortunately the track was unmistakable, running wide and fairly straight, the margins periodically marked by big boulders. Ostorius's engineers, within the limits set them, had done their work well.

The ascent became steeper. I gripped my panting horse with calf and thigh, clinging to his mane to avoid sliding over his rump. When he stumbled to his knees I dismounted, threw the reins to Secundus and toiled upwards, envying the legionaries the javelins which they used as staves to aid their climb. Up we went, and up, clinging like flies to the side of an enormous mountain whose invisible bulk sheered like a toppling wave.

Still we climbed. Helmets pressed massively on throbbing temples; armour dragged at straining shoulders. The bodyguard's careless chatter had long since expired. Infantry and dismounted cavalry scrabbled upwards in a silence broken only by breathless curses when horse or soldier slid on loosened stones. The fog, like an ice-barbed strigil, scarified throats and nostrils and separated man from man in an enveloping cloak of melancholy loneliness.

Almost imperceptibly the slope eased until, where the track girdled a spur, we marched again on nearly level ground which on our right dropped abruptly to unseen depths. I breathed slowly, seeking to steady my voice.

'Agricola,' I said, 'the baggage will never ascend without help. Remain here, and when Valens arrives tell him to detach four cohorts to manhandle wagons to the top. I shall take the column on another two miles and halt until the train is up.'

When the army halted I rode on to speak with Saturius Secundus, whom I had detailed from my headquarters staff to command the advanced guard.

'Tribune,' I ordered, 'keep your points and flankers sharply alert. This will be a long halt. If the enemy are seeking us in the fog they will now have every chance to find us.'

'Very well, Legate.' He wiped moisture from his youthful beard: the whole army sprouted whiskers after ten days' campaigning. 'We are groping our way like blind men in a quicksand.'

'Grope carefully, Saturius,' I warned. 'How is your advanced guard disposed?'

'The 1st Tungri in the van, Legate, followed by 6th Thracian and two legionary cohorts. We are practically trackbound: the slopes are so steep and the mist so thick that centuries lose touch when I try to extend front.'

'That is inevitable.'

The 1st Britannic Cohort, our flank guards, were in the same plight. They marched alongside the column, sometimes on the track itself. I decided to replace them by Vardulli and Vascones, men accustomed to mountains who should be able to range farther afield.

While runners took my orders to commanders concerned in the changeover I stood in uneasy idleness, awaiting reports from the baggage-train. I drew neck-scarf tighter and tried to estimate how far we had come and how much daylight remained. In this opaque cloud maps were useless. I had no idea where we were.

Men came running from the mist. Commands boomed from invisible throats and re-echoed from every direction. Spanish, Basque and British auxiliaries met, mingled, diverged and disappeared on hillside and track. Presently orderlies came and reported the reliefs completed. Silence settled like a drawn blanket. A mutter of talk in the ranks drew a centurion's barking reprimand; leather creaked and iron clinked when men shifted their feet.

Tumult rent the stillness like a thunderclap. From the drifting blankness strident voices bellowed a tale of anger and triumph. Swords clashed on shields; a horn harshly brayed the alarm and stopped in mid-note.

Enemy were engaging the advanced guard; at any moment any part of our three-mile column might be attacked. I sent messengers running rearwards to shout my orders at each century as they passed.

'Outward face! Prepare to receive enemy!'

The six-file column split down the middle like a riven tree-trunk and formed two three-deep battle lines, back to back, one watching the shrouded hill-slope above, the other scanning fogbound ravines below. With a sleek, unhurried movement the bodyguard flowed forward and closed around me. They were just in time.

Battle-din rolled downhill towards us. A discordant spate of tribal yells drowned the high, lilting Spanish warcries. Somewhere amid the bush-scrub and heather, not fifty paces away and lost in fog, the flank guards fought for their lives. Arrows whipped overhead and thumped on shields. A man in the front rank whined shrilly and choked and scrabbled at the feathered shaft that quivered in his throat.

Vague forms like scurrying wraiths fell from the mist and shouted passwords that barely checked our javelins in mid-cast. Vascones tumbled into our ranks and the legionaries, snorting contempt, kicked them aside and peered grimly upwards, blinking moisture from beaded eyelashes, seeking targets for the weapons delicately balanced in ready hands.

Bowmen and spearmen came leaping from bush to bush, quick and crafty in using cover when the mist no longer hid them. A few impetuous warriors reached the track and ended their lives there; the rest stopped, loosed an arrow-storm and fled. Quickly as it had begun the fight was over. The mountains returned a final echo and drew cloaks of foggy silence about their shoulders. Some twenty contorted bodies lay in the heather. A javelin, embedded deep in ribs and backbone, flailed its shaft in convulsive arcs while the stricken victim writhed and twisted and strove to die.

Saturius Secundus returned from the vanguard and described a repetition of our own experiences: a sudden rush from the mist, picquets surprised and routed and his column scourged with arrows.

'We've lost thirty men, Legate. Some of the picquets were taken alive; we couldn't see to recover the wounded.' He lowered his voice. 'Do the Ordovices—?'

'Yes, they do,' I said shortly. 'Usually by fire, sacrificed to the Druid sungod Belenus. Don't get captured, Saturius. You'll find dying a lengthy and painful business.' I stared towards the rear. 'Almost as slow as our transport. Will it never climb this mountain?'

As though in answer a horseman loomed monstrous from the drifting vapour and reined with a scrape of flying pebbles. Agricola dropped from the saddle and saluted.

'Message from the Camp Prefect, Legate.'

'What is it?'

'He says that all pack-animals and bearers are up, but only a third of the wagons. Even with the help of four cohorts who are working there now he thinks it will take two more hours to bring the whole train to the top. The four-wheeled artillery wagons are particularly difficult.'

'You have seen this yourself?'

'Yes, Legate. In my opinion two hours is a hopeful estimate.'

I peered into the murk overhead. The white veil offered no clue, no radiance to show how far the sun had travelled. I summoned the navigator.

'How far have we come from camp?'

The tesserar displayed his stick, notched for every hundred paces. 'A little over five miles, Legate.'

'How long have we taken?'

The man glanced fruitlessly skywards and shook his head. 'Hard to say, Legate. We may have four or five hours of daylight left.'

'So.' I pinched my lip. Futile to postpone the unwelcome decision further. I turned to Agricola. 'Send runners to all commanders. Column will return to Conovium. Saturius, your detachment will guard the rear. Keep alert: you'll probably be harassed all the way.'

And so we returned ingloriously to the fort we had left that morning, marching with shields held high against arrows which whipped venomously from the mist. Twice during that weary retreat Saturius and his rearguard had to stand and repel attacks more vicious and sustained than any we had met before. The main body kept moving and did not retaliate. The men trudged sullen and watchful, javelins ready for the charge that never came; they heard only barbarian yells and twanging bows and saw only shadowy, distant figures and arrows flicking into crowded ranks.

Vascones and Vardulli, on the flanks, climbed like stags and fought like heroes against an enemy fighting on familiar ground and against the fog that sheltered him. But losses mounted; in desperation the auxiliaries edged closer and closer to the column they were protecting and arrow-flights whistled from the hillsides at ever-shortening range.

The wagons, manhandled with heartbreaking slowness up the slopes, rattled downhill easily enough, sometimes too quickly or the teams braced against brake-ropes. One or two hurtled over precipices and shattered from crag to crag, flinging loads and animals to invisible destruction.

We reached Conovium shortly before dusk. Legionaries worked into darkness throwing up the fortifications demolished only that morning; fortunately digging in earth already loosened was no great labour. And that night, in my tent, I re-read transcriptions of Ostorius's report on his Ordovican campaign and belatedly understood the full significance of one sentence therein: 'I left all baggage-wagons at Conovium and marched west with pack-animals alone.'

I have no excuse for this day's fiasco. A Roman army had been turned from its objective by terrain impassable to its equipment, by fog and by a handful of undisciplined bowmen. We had lost seventy auxiliaries and thirteen legionaries killed and as many wounded or missing. I, through crass stupidity, had lost the confidence of my army.

Head in hands, I sat brooding for a long time. Half-way through the second watch Agricola appeared.

'What is it?' I said without moving.

'Word from centurion of the guard, Paulinus. A wind is rising and dispersing the mists—'

I bounded to the entrance and thrust the curtain aside. High above a star gleamed fitfully, a beacon of awakening hopes. The sentry at the doorway stamped to attention; his cloak billowed gently in the breeze. I clapped the astonished man on the shoulder.

'A wind, duplicar! If this holds you shall see Anglesey today.'

I wheeled Agricola into the tent. 'Marching orders, Gnaeus! Get tablets and stylus.'

All through the watch Agricola wrote and I dictated; and candles flickered and tent-walls bowed to Aeolus's gift from the sea.

10

'Now terribly the brazen trumpet pealed its summons, and the war-shout rent the air.'

VIRGIL

1

Morning dawned bright and clear; sunlight gilded the mountains and a cold, invigorating breeze blew from the ocean. The river valley was still in shade when our column once more climbed the mountain track.

This time I was making no mistakes. I took only XIV Legion, two cavalry regiments and four auxiliary cohorts. Baggage was stripped to bare essentials; our strongest donkeys and mules carried no more than tents, mess equipment and packs. XX Legion's cohorts and other auxiliaries stayed in Conovium with orders to find and make passable for wheels a less arduous route out of the valley.

We marched with auxiliary skirmishers screening front, flanks and rear. I had told them to smash through light opposition but, against determined resistance, to feign flight and draw the tribesmen within the legion's reach.

The scene when we reached the crest was incredibly different. Mountains marched in stately grandeur to the horizon, and wild flowers, iridescent as multi-coloured jewels, blazoned their heather-covered shoulders with the colours of royalty. Small hill-forts, smokeless, lifeless and apparently deserted, perched on spur or summit too distant for investigation.

But we had little time to admire the view. The tribesmen swooped from ambush before our rearguard lost sight of Conovium crouched in her shadowed cleft.

Encouraged in estimation of their own valour by our ignominious retreat on the previous day, they needed little luring to close quarters. A shower of arrows and a loose-knit horde of shrieking savages rolled our Morini vanguard back to the legion's leading century. No orders were needed: I had explained the tactics. Four centuries charged in column. They crashed through the enemy, split outwards and hunted astonished Britons up and down the hillsides like raging demons. The legionaries, stripped of packs, rations, entrenching tools and other impedimenta, skipped the crags with goat-like agility. Meanwhile the column marched stolidly on. Presently trumpets sounded recall and panting Romans sheathed bloodied swords, reformed and fell in at the tail. Skirmishers again screened the van. We had scattered three or four hundred Ordovices at a cost of two Morini and two Romans dead; we counted sixty-five British corpses.

Another mile brought another attack which was so half-hearted and irresolute that the auxiliaries, rallying from the first shock, were able to prevent a break-through. After a sharp bout of hand to hand fighting they chased the tribesmen far afield. The entire Morini cohort joined in pursuit and, more excitable and less disciplined than the legion, failed at first to obey the recall. With my vanguard thus dispersed while the column plodded inexorably onwards I was forced to halt for a space and post Frisiavones in the van. The Morini, rejoining in scattered parties while we marched, endured a verbal flaying from an exasperated prefect who had already heard my opinion of his cohort's conduct.

We turned a jutting spur and saw the sea, far below and three miles distant, a shimmering sheet of liquid gold. A roar went up from the cohorts; standards thrust high; javelins twirled in the air. Scandalized centurions restored order with staff and tongue; and the army, poised and confident, began to descend from the mountains. My credit was in part restored.

Soon our aching legs found relief on the flat lands of the narrow coastal strip, a half mile wide, between foothills and sea. Here I halted and formed the legion in three columns, baggage in the centre, and surrounded ourselves with an auxiliary protective screen.

Two miles to the north-east loomed the mountain peak supporting Ordovicia's chief stronghold in this region, the great fortress which Ostorius had stormed and overthrown. Natives wounded and captured in the day's fighting had said the place was unoccupied. If it were held I should be forced to stage an assault; so formidable a concentration near my camp could not be allowed to remain. I had no artillery; an escalade might prove expensive both in casualties and time.

I indicated the peak to the Tungrians' prefect. 'Take your regiment, ride swiftly along the plain and try to provoke some reaction from the hill-fort on the summit. If the place seems empty dismount a couple of troops and send them to the top. If you find any Britons take them alive.'

The Tungrians pounded off. The other regiment, 1st Pannonian, I sent to explore the plain in the opposite direction and discover a camp site overlooking the sea.

Both returned within an hour. The Tungrians said the fort was deserted except for some aged natives and children cowering in rude huts; the stone walls were in disrepair. I handed their captives to inquisitors for interrogation. The Pannonian prefect brought equally welcome news: he had encountered no enemy and had found an excellent camping ground. Considerably relieved, I gave the signal to move.

We marched three miles in trident formation to a sandy bluff thrusting seawards and enclosed by the confluence of two streams. A mile across the straits reared the bulk of Anglesey. We found unmistakable signs that we were not the first Romans to fortify this place; traces of earlier ramparts with familiar rounded corners were plain enough. Veterans of XIV Legion recognized Ostorius's handiwork with wry affection. Our men dug wide and deep in willing soil. By nightfall the camp stood foursquare and massive, a darkening threat in the heart of Ordovicia.

2

Long before dawn I was in headquarters' pavilion dictating messages to heavy-eyed secretaries.

'The Legate Propraetor G. Suetonius Paulinus to Prefect of the Fleet Aufidius Pantera at Conovium. Greetings. You must sail on the first flood after receiving this letter to the northern end of Anglesey straits, where you will see our camp set on the mainland shore. The anchorage is sheltered but shoals on a falling tide. Use caution in your approach. The distance is little more than twenty miles; I shall expect you not later than tomorrow's dusk, the 24th of April. Farewell.'

'The Legate Propraetor G. Suetonius Paulinus to the tribune Flavius Longus, commanding at Conovium. Greetings. Dispatch at first light tomorrow the 24th of April to our camp opposite Anglesey these units: the first, third and fourth cohorts of XX Legion, 1st Vettonian and 2nd Asturian Cavalry, 6th Thracian, 1st Tungrian and 1st Britannic Cohorts, and all our artillery and siege train. Restrict unit baggage to pack-animals: send no wheeled transport except artillery wagons. You can expect only light opposition on the march. Farewell.'

These very important dispatches went on their fifteen-mile journey under escort of eight cavalry troops. Then I called a commanders' conference and issued orders for the day.

'The 1st Vascones escorted by 1st Tungrian Cavalry and Cavalry of the bodyguard will stand by to accompany me on reconnaissance. Vettius Valens, I shall want you with me.

'Five cohorts of XIV Legion and 1st Morini, under the Camp Prefect, will start enlarging the camp to contain our whole army less detachments left at lines of communication posts. This place is our advanced base; here we shall remain until we have met and defeated the enemy's main force; therefore the camp must be progressively strengthened to fortress standard. The soil is loose and sandy. You will have to revet counterscarp and glacis; clearance of woods around the perimeter will provide ample timber.

'The remaining two cohorts of XIV Legion will remain under arms as garrison ward; 1st Frisiavones will provide outlying camp picquets.

'A word of warning. Although we believe the enemy's main forces are concentrated in Anglesey he will almost certainly have left small parties on the mainland to observe and harass us whenever he can. See that you are not surprised. That is all. Valens, is your horse ready? Let us go.'

We left the camp and splashed hock-deep through a stream clear as crystal. Valens rode absorbed and silent. I clapped him on the shoulder, exhilarated both by the prospect of grappling the Ordovices and by the sunlit dawn promising another fine day.

'What ails you, Valens?'

'This scattering of our forces, Legate,' he answered in a troubled voice. 'Foraging parties here, roadbuilders there, all strung five miles or more from base in the heart of enemy territory. Are you so certain that the tribesmen are over the straits? Do you put so much confidence in prisoners' tales? Their statements may be part of a concerted plan to mislead you.'

I laughed. 'Valens, you take me for a half-wit. My inquisitors are skilful and thorough and usually extract the truth from the most stubborn captive. Even so, do you imagine I would rest the safety of an army entirely on such information?'

Valens growled. 'I have never thought you a fool, Legate. You are, if I may say so, sometimes over-bold.'

'Still thinking of my escapade on patrol? You judge me wrongly. I know where the Ordovices are because I have met and talked with one of our own intelligence agents.'

'Our own? Here?'

'We had three: natives with a grudge against their chieftains, willing to help us in return for gold, land and citizenship. Two,' I said soberly, 'have failed to make contact. The third was one of those old men taken from the ruined hill-fort yesterday.'

'You trust him?'

'Completely. So would you if you knew what his fellow-tribesmen have done to him and his kindred in the past.'

Valens looked happier. We jogged on, the point section a hundred paces ahead, cavalry drumming behind. We rode by the water's edge, below high-tide mark, and wet sand spurted under our hooves. The channel narrowed until the tree-covered slopes on the farther shore were almost within ballista range. I drew rein opposite a wooded promontory.

'How do you estimate the width here, Agricola?'

The tribune narrowed his eyes against the sun. 'Three hundred paces, Legate.'

'I agree. Less at low water. The shortest crossing we have seen so far. Ride on.'

The straits opened past the promontory and again closed their margins a mile beyond.

'Rather wider here,' I observed. 'Four hundred paces.'

No better crossings could be found although we followed the shore for five more miles to open sea. We returned in our tracks. Valens, on nearing the first of the two narrows we had discovered, waved a hand at the opposite shore.

'We are observed,' he said dryly.

Groups of natives appeared from the woods fringing the beach and ran level with our cavalcade, sometimes leaping in the air or clashing weapons and shouting war-cries whose faint echoes reached across the water. I watched their antics without amusement.

'We shall be seeing them at closer quarters before long.' I turned to a decurion of the bodyguard. 'Ride into the water as far as you can.'

The man legged his reluctant horse until the sea lapped his navel and his mount, submerged to the gullet, snorted in terror. He was then about thirty paces from shore. I signalled him to return.

'How is the bottom?' I asked.

'Firm sand and pebbles, Legate.'

I brooded over the scene for a while; then visited each of the narrows again, examining approaches and beaches, noting the state of tide and strength of current.

'This is the place,' I said briskly. 'Now back to camp. We need technical advice.'

After a meal of soup and bread in camp I returned again to my chosen crossing-places with a posse of engineers and Frisiavones' centurions who, being shore dwellers from Rhinemouth, were knowledgeable in the mysteries of coastal waters and tides. I stated my requirements. The Frisiavones examined tidal marks, flung branches into water to mark the current, glanced at the sun and, after abstruse calculations plotted with sword-points in wet sand, told me what I wanted. The engineers took longer; all afternoon they plodded up and down the beaches, waded neck-deep to take soundings, set marks opposite rocky obstacles on the bottom. Meanwhile I rode from one crossing to the other, measuring frontages and calculating distances while Agricola filled tablet after tablet with scribbled notes from my dictation. Britons on the opposite shore, in ever-increasing numbers, watched our activities and yelled defiance.

By evening my plan for the assault was complete in detail. I worked late into the night with my staff, expanding Agricola's memoranda into comprehensive operation orders. Early next day I countermanded orders for road-building and instead took the detachment to the crossing-places, where they felled trees and, while the tide was still low, drove piles into the shingle as far beyond low water as they could get. On each set of piles they fixed strong wooden platforms; and from high-water mark to each platform they laid a roadway—logs ranged in rows and staked to the beach—ending in ramps to the platforms. This work had to be done at speed to defeat the rising tide which, at full flood, submerged piles, platforms and roadways; and was not quite done during the day.

That afternoon the troops from Conovium arrived. The artillery was intact, thanks to the discovery and clearance of a much less gruelling route up the mountainside from Conovium. I thereupon summoned every prefect, tribune and centurion to the beaches in a gathering which provoked crowded and noisy reaction from the Anglesey shore; and explained on the ground the task of every cohort. I allotted frontages and planted stakes, notched with cohort and century signs, on the foreshore to mark unit boundaries. The commanders, used to straightforward tactical formations based on accustomed battle-drill, found, at first, the unusual dispositions and my insistence on hairbreadth precision a little puzzling. As the plan unfolded they quickly appreciated the need for exactitude in such a complex operation. Only the artillerymen looked dubious: their platforms, at that state of tide, were invisible beneath the waves.

To save our ballista platforms from destructive raids during the night I posted a sprinkling of auxiliaries on the beach with orders to build fires, sound watches and generally counterfeit the presence of a strong detachment left on guard. This simple stratagem proved entirely effective.

Barely were these dispositions settled when a galloper from camp reported the fleet's arrival. I returned speedily to find Pantera just disembarked. The Camp Prefect had guided the ships to their anchorage—a natural harbour, overlooked by our fortress, in the estuary of a small river—where the crews were mooring the barges. Daylight was fading;

I hustled Pantera and his shipmasters on board two biremes. Helped by the flooding tide we rowed cautiously through the straits towards our crossing-places.

Our warships' appearance instantly enlivened the tribal multitude on Anglesey's shores. Their strength, during the last two days, had fluctuated more or less according to the size and activity of our contingents on the opposite bank; now they poured from the woods in considerable numbers. Presumably they assumed the biremes heralded an immediate attack. From our course in midchannel I could study the native array in more detail than hitherto: the utter lack of military order they displayed and the riotous surge, like an ocean roller flooding the beach, which paced our movement to the narrows promised that we were unlikely to meet any drilled and disciplined phalanxes among the Ordovices.

Pantera flicked a contemptuous finger. 'A leaderless mob, Legate. Porridge for the legions' swords.'

'Hot porridge, Pantera. The Gods grant we don't scorch our lips,' I answered piously. 'Watch your helm, master! If we go aground on the wrong side both army and fleet will lack commanders tomorrow.'

The slow oarbeat ceased; blades lifted, dropped and held the galley stem to current.

'This,' I said, 'is the beach where you bring the barges at dawn tomorrow. Tide will be high, as now. The barges must be beached between those two tall posts you see yonder.'

Pantera examined the shore in the failing light, and pulled his nose. 'No question of turning the galleys,' he said. 'After we have loosed our tows we shall row on to the end of the straits, anchor and return after you have made your crossing.'

'That would be wisest. If you and your captains have seen all you want we had better return before it becomes too dark.'

Pantera hailed the other ship; carefully the two biremes backed, turned and rowed to the anchorage, accompanied by renewed yells and hornblasts from our persistent followers. On shore I held a final conference with shipmasters and men commanding barge crews, ensuring that each knew his task; and then went to headquarters' pavilion. Here cohort and regimental commanders were gathered for a final briefing. Item by item we went over the orders in minute detail, checking and counter-checking.

Before midnight they had gone. Agricola alone remained. I relaxed wearily in my camp-chair, staring at the flickering candle flames.

'You must sleep, Paulinus,' Agricola said softly. 'Shall I summon your servants?'

'I shall try to rest, Gnaeus.' I rubbed my eyes. 'Yes, fetch the slaves. If only sleep could be called as easily. One day, perhaps, you too will know the feelings of a general on the eve of a momentous battle.'

Agricola smiled. 'After all your planning, your forethought, your precautions, can the anticipation of certain victory be so disturbing?'

'It can.' I rose, unslung baldric and laid my sword carefully on the mess of papers littering the trestle table. 'One night your time will come, Gnaeus. You'll envy the criminal awaiting execution.'

3

I slept very little. Two hours before dawn Secundus roused me from troubled dreams. Servants ready with arms and armour received a curt dismissal and, waiting only to fling a cloak over my tunic, I left the tent and made my way through the camp.

The leather tents housing legionaries and auxiliaries which lined the Principal Way were dark and still. The daytime hive-hum of ten thousand voices was muted to a sudden snore or burst of unintelligible sleep-talk. The night was sultry with a breath of summer heat alien to the season. Turning into the Quintan Way I approached the cavalry lines where restive hooves thudded in sand and leather creaked and iron clinked and men murmured in subdued undertones.

I greeted the tribune Saturius Secundus, whom I had appointed commander of a force of four cavalry regiments which was to swim the farther narrows and attack the enemy's rear. He would have no artillery support for his crossing: all our engines were required for covering the main infantry assault at the nearer narrows. His success depended upon secrecy and surprise. Under cover of darkness he was to lead his regiments into position by a previously reconnoitred route which skirted foothills above the shore. When he reached his assembly area, a wood extending nearly to highwater mark, he was to remain concealed until the signal for attack.

We waited silently in the darkness. No torches flared; no voices whispered. Half-seen figures heaved blankets back, tightened girths, buckled headstalls and adjusted cloth-muffled bits. In shadowy procession the troopers led their chargers to parade in the space by the Praetorian Gate. The horse lines emptied and fell silent.

'Your men have rubbed themselves down?' I asked Saturius.

'Yes, Legate. And each troop carries a skin of wine. We shall dole it out when I see the artillery in action.'

I nodded approval. To ease the rigours of swimming in these icy seas I had ordered that each trooper should grease his body with lard and swallow a draught of wine before taking to the water. So, after four hundred and fifty years, I copied the Athenian general Iphicrates when he launched a picked force of swimmers across the Hellespont against Sparta.

The four prefects loomed from the darkness, saluted and reported.

'1st Pannonian Regiment on parade.'

'1st Vettonian Regiment on parade.'

'2nd Asturian Regiment on parade.'

'1st Tungrian Regiment on parade.'

Saturius acknowledged and turned to me. 'Permission to march, Legate?'

'March, tribune. The Gods go with you, Saturius.'

I climbed the watch-tower by the Praetorian Gate and listened. Hooves beat a muffled tattoo on rock and shingle beyond the sand; horses snorted and leather creaked. But orders passed in whispers and metal found no voice on metal. Like phantoms from a forgotten battle the cavalry faded into night.

Descending from the ramparts I went to headquarters, dismissed my escort and studied the water-clock. The camp still slept. I had forbidden all movement for yet another hour, for I wanted the cavalry to be well away before activity at our base aroused the enemy's interest.

I broke my fast on biscuits, soup and watered wine; then called Mannius Secundus and dressed for parade. I wore my battle armour, an exact copy of the new legionary pattern with two extra chest bands, for I am a tall man. Secundus buckled the baldric to my favourite sword, a blade forged in Mauretania whose temper and keenness were beyond emulation by our army smiths.

No hint of dawn tinged the sky when trumpets sounded rouse. Torches flared and orders crackled; men tumbled yawning from tents and stretched and groped for equipment. I walked along the crowded roads, through the Decuman Gate to the harbour. Here also was seething, torchlit alacrity. Pantera's white cloak glimmered on the headland like a pale ghost; but his commands, bawled through cupped hands at the crew of a recalcitrant barge, were salt-tanged and far from ethereal.

'Greetings, Legate.' He mopped his face with the end of his neck-scarf. 'Too hot! We shall have the queen of all storms before nightfall, if I smell the air aright.'

The sea, glass-smooth and black, lipped lazily at the strand. Wavelets of a flooding tide rippled to shore uncrested, too indolent to curl and break.

'Flat calm at the moment,' I replied. 'More than we dared hope. Does all go aright?'

'Very well, Legate, if I could only get these half-witted soldiers to secure their tows to the right galleys.' He seized a torch from his orderly and brandished it at a drifting barge. 'Hey, you! More to the right. Pass your line to that cutter. These landsmen!' he grumbled. 'Can't tell the difference between a trireme and a coracle.'

I regarded the harbour, brilliant as a Saturnalia with warships' lanterns and sputtering torches. This scene, far from the plodding cavalry column in the dark foothills, should certainly concentrate the enemy's attention.

'You don't sail until the first hour,' I observed. 'Things will be easier in daylight. I shall not see you again until after the battle. Farewell. May Fortune guide you.'

I walked back to the fortress, sweating under my armour in the unnatural heat. The bustle of preparation was subsiding. Men joined their standards, dressed files and stood at ease. Soldiers in rank upon rank packed the quadrangular space between barrack-tents and ramparts. I looked eastwards. Night was gradually slipping her cloak from the mountains' shoulders and dawn, like a furtive thief, crept silently into the sky.

4

The altars glowed lurid in an arc of spitting torches. The wavering flames gleamed on helmets, darted gold and blue from standards and javelins, burnished a centurion's seamed, tawny face and intent eyes.

In the centre I offered ritual prayers, made ceremonial sacrifice and waited while a diviner read auspices in a white goat's entrails. I had no expectation of unfavourable omens. Military necessity compelled the convenience of performing these solemnities before dawn, when there were no birds to fly in unfortunate directions and heavy clouds hit inconvenient meteors.

The diviner extracted the steaming liver, examined it closely and triumphantly showed it to his attendants. He turned to me and loudly proclaimed signs of the Gods' especial favour towards our enterprise;

then, bearing his carrion around the circle, he exhibited certain miraculous markings to the awe-struck soldiers.

I stood with upraised arms as though in prayer and repressed a smile. The diviner, a skilled and experienced fellow, used a preparation to inscribe certain letters, indicating victory, on the hand which he placed beneath the vitals of the sacrifice, so that the liver received the impress of these characters. The simple cunning of this ruse, which so impressed the religious minded, might have been suggested by the Gods themselves.

I dropped my hands, drew sword and saluted the massed standards. To the armoured ring I said, 'The omens are propitious. The Gods are with us. Go. Tell your men, and bid them fight like Romans.'

A man could just distinguish the ground beneath his feet when Vardullian horsemen jingled through the Praetorian Gate, swung right and forded the stream. Behind came three auxiliary cohorts, artillery, XIV Legion and other units of the assault force. In silence and half-light we reached the assembly beach marked with rows of numbered stakes. Under centurions' orders heads of cohorts and centuries diverged right and left, reached their allotted positions, formed line and stood at ease. I rode slowly down the ranks, intent for mistakes; and found none. With less fuss than a dinner-party seeking their couches ten thousand men arrayed themselves for battle.

Artillerymen and engineers urged wagon teams to the water's edge. Our wooden platforms, submerged by the tide, were invisible; only the log roadways protruded above high water. We had four ballistae and four catapults. I had caused four extra platforms to be made in case the enemy were not deluded by the activities of our auxiliary guard and crossed during the night to wreak what damage they could in the period of ebb tide. Crews offloaded wagons opposite roadways and began to assemble the machines.

A galloper came from Saturius Secundus to say that the cavalry had reached their assembly area unseen and unchallenged and were safely under cover. I breathed relief.

The light strengthened. The dark swell of land across the straits resolved into components of hillside, forest and beach. At this point a rounded peninsula jutted from the opposite shore, reducing the channel's width to three hundred paces; and this promontory, a bare half-mile across, seethed with Britons who spilled from the wooded slopes and crowded the beaches. A peculiar murmur, like the distant throb of river rapids, drifted from the throng.

A convex curve in the shoreline on our side hid from our view the farther crossing where the cavalry lay concealed. I could see no signs of the enemy extending their right to cover that area: they seemed, as I desired, to be concentrated against our main and plainly visible assault. Yet one had to make sure. I spoke to Agricola.

'Ride quietly along the beach until you can see where Saturius Secundus will cross. Find out whether the enemy has any forces opposite.'

Agricola meandered off, the picture of an idle horseman seeking privacy to relieve himself. Valens shifted in his saddle and muttered inaudibly.

'What ails you, Valens?'

He gestured upwards. 'The heavens have descended to watch us. Have you ever seen such a sky?'

From horizon to horizon, in fold upon fold, black clouds hung motionless. Sullen and menacing, they oppressed the senses and twisted nerves already taut. The dawn was breathless, suffocating like a crowded and ill-ventilated tent.

'Clouds cannot hurt us,' I said briefly. 'Where are those ships?'

As an actress answers her cue a galley nosed round the bend, her oars stroking the water in slow cadence. Behind, like barbs on a scourge, a string of barges dipped on the towlines. The noise from the opposite shore waxed like a river in flood.

Pantera, his white cloak gleaming on the poop, conned the leading bireme. As she drew opposite our beach he raised an arm, a trumpet sounded, axes flashed and the tows parted. The barge crews, eight rowers and a steersman apiece, heaved at the sweeps. They turned cumbrously shorewards; like ponderous beetles, oars flailing in true soldier fashion, they crept nearer. Keels grated on the shingle. Auxiliaries splashed waist deep and pulled barges to cohort frontages where they disposed them at pre-arranged intervals and, with hands on thwarts, held them afloat against the ebbing tide. Barely was this done before the next tow came ashore.

So the barges were gathered, some speedily, others with laborious slowness, some neatly aligned on their stations, others so clumsily manœuvred that they required much manhandling in the shallows; but all without accident. The procession of warships, freed from encumbrances, passed proudly down the straits. Then a cutter, the fleet's penultimate ship, went ashore.

What caused the error of navigation we shall never know. Possibly a cross-eddy seized her at the moment of shedding her tow and made her veer to starboard and run hard on a sandbank in a few feet of water, a javelin cast from the enemy beach. Her oars flailed in confusion, thrashing the water to foam. We saw her master run forward, gesticulating. The oars ceased milling, straightened, came parallel and beat in hard, purposeful strokes in the reverse direction, trying to back the vessel off the bar. She did not move.

The tribal mob, immobile for a moment as if incredulous of their good fortune, burst like a mill-race and pelted through the shallow water towards the ship. They swarmed around and over her like ants on dung. Swords glittered briefly. The oarbeats faltered. The blades died in diminishing harmony and trailed listlessly along her sides.

The last ship, a bireme, made a brave effort to save her sister. Cutting her tows, she swerved dangerously near the sandbank and her captain hurled a line aboard the cutter. Desperate seamen caught and secured the rope before they were cut down. The bireme's oars flashed in frenzy, the line straightened like a bar and the cutter yawed, muddy water churning beneath her bows. Then a sword flashed; the rope trailed in the sea and sank as it drew away from the stricken warship, dragging our hopes with it. A long sigh went up from the watching soldiers.

I turned roughly to their commanders. 'Tell your men to sit down and rest. We have several hours to wait.'

Orders passed. Rank after rank subsided on the ground, collapsing from front to rear as though felled by a hurricane.

'Prefects and centurions of the first flight, check your barges and report.'

Men went running to the water. With much heaving and straining they made some slight adjustments in alignment. I called the senior centurion of artillery.

'The tide is ebbing fast. Are all your machines assembled and ready?'

'Ready, Legate. May I put them on the roadways?'

'Yes. Hurry.'

I rode again through the squatting ranks. Men talked quietly, or gambled, throwing dice on shields; some lay supine, helmets tilted over eyes, apparently asleep. A centurion sat cross-legged, thoughtfully honing his sword-point; his standard-bearer, a dark-browed Etrurian, watched him idly. The standard, trident driven deep into sand, stood beside him; he kept a hand clasped on the shaft.

'Keeping warm in your bearskin, Signifer?' I asked.

The Etrurian threw the bear's mask from his forehead and wiped his sweating face. 'Warm enough, Legate. We shan't need your boats—a swim will cool us down.'

'Swim? We'll all be swimming before we're half-way over,' shouted an option from the rear rank. 'Craziest craft I've seen. Do you swim with us, Legate?'

'An aureus to a sesterce that I set foot on the opposite shore before you do,' I called back.

'Done!' cried the option.

'You've lost your money, you bandy-legged ape,' the Etrurian shouted. 'Old Upinfront goes with the leading auxiliaries. Where's your sesterce?'

The men chuckled. I moved on, smiling. The nickname, with its double meaning, was less scabrous than some applied by his men to the great Julius. The more flattering interpretation referred to my habit of seeing developments on a battlefield for myself rather than trusting to descriptions from subordinates. The soldiers appreciated this characteristic; my commanders often did not. Valens had protested violently when he heard my intention of crossing with the foremost troops. 'Rash and pointless!' he had exploded. 'Why behave like a new-joined tribune seeking glory? What good can you do?' Nor was he greatly pacified when I assured him my bodyguard would be in close attendance; I had no intention of becoming a casualty and I had to be up in front to assess the tactical situation when we landed.

Agricola appeared at my elbow.

'You've been a time,' I growled. 'Your report?'

'No enemy at all watching the far narrows, Legate,' he said quietly.

'Good.'

I regarded the opposite shore. The cutter burned. Thongs of flame flayed her decks and dissolved in towers of black smoke that mounted to the lowering clouds. The tribesmen surrounding her were losing interest and streaming back to the upper beaches.

The artillery centurion saluted. 'Ballistae and catapults on the roadways, Legate.'

'Very well,' I answered. The sea had receded. The timber roadways were exposed for half their lengths; an occasional lop and eddy in the water marked the platforms to which they led. 'Get your engines as far down the beaches as you can.'

Artillerymen hauled on ropes, levered and shoved and strained. Reluctantly the wooden monsters creaked forward on their rollers, pressing the corded logs deep into sand. Swaying perilously like drunken elephants they crept down the sloping beach foot by foot until, amid much shouting and play with braking ropes, the water lipped their forefeet.

The centurion returned panting, flicking blood from a crushed thumb. 'Barely two feet of water covering the platforms, Legate. With your permission we could mount them now.'

'Carry on, then, Centurion.' I beckoned Agricola. 'Time passes quickly. Send the trumpeters to their place.'

Three cavalry trumpeters rode slowly to the headland which hid the further crossing. Their business was to relay to Saturius's cavalrymen the signal for assault.

'Frisiavones, strip and grease yourselves.'

Amid catcalls and scabrous comments from their squatting comrades the auxiliaries stripped naked and rubbed themselves with lard. They dressed, fastening shields on shoulder-blades, throwing-spears athwart their backs, swords slantwise over stomachs, so that their weapons would not hinder swimming. Centurions passed down the ranks giving a few mouthfuls of wine to every man: an action which elicited sourly envious remarks from the legion.

Valens spoke at my shoulder. 'The enemy are lighting fires. Do you think they are preparing red-hot missiles or some similar unpleasantness?'

I turned and looked. At irregular intervals along the thronged beaches points of flame flickered like lambent spears. Farther up in the woods, partly obscured by trees, more fires glowed.

'Druids. Sacrifices. I hope they took no prisoners from that cutter,' I said sombrely.

Valens chewed his lip. 'We lost men during the march,' he reminded.

I abandoned an unprofitable subject. The artillery platforms were awash; crews stacked boulders and darts round their machines. The centurion reported his charges ready for action.

'The time has come,' I said. 'On your feet, men!'

Centurions came running at my summons and gathered in a wide arc round my horse. My speech was brief and to the point; and I do not propose to repeat it here. Versions have since appeared in Rome from the pens of writers whose imaginative genius exceeds their military understanding: no general valuing the respect of his army would utter such garrulous and irrelevant balderdash as they have reported.

'Man the boats!'

Century by century, cohort after cohort marched steadily to the sea, clambered aboard the barges and stood shoulder to shoulder, altering balance uneasily against the slight swell of the tide. The Vasconian rowers, kneeling amid booted legs, cursed softly and gripped oar-shafts. I turned for a last survey of the silent ranks remaining on the beach, raised an arm in salute and made for my barge, already packed with bodyguard infantry. I looked along the crowded shoreline, at the barges gunwale-deep, at the javelins springing like reeds above stone-grey helmets, at the Frisiavones shivering in water waist-high, at the centurion of artillery anxiously watching for my signal.

'Fly the standard!'

The scarlet battle-standard unfurled, flapped heavily and drooped in the stagnant air. A trumpet sang a single cold note and shivered into silence.

The ballistas' throwing-arms slammed on stopbeams with a force that rippled the water round their platforms. Catapults thrummed like a million angry bees. The first volley whirred towards Anglesey.

The fight had begun.

5

One of the many penalties of high command is that the exhilarating climax of battle, which ought to follow days of forethought and planning, often arrives in the guise of a remorseful foreboding indistinguishable from the gloom following a prolonged debauch. A general absorbs all his energies for months in devising his strategy, in training and equipping his army, in bringing his troops by long and arduous marches to a position where tactics, timing and terrain give them the greatest advantage and are least favourable to the enemy. The general is in complete control until the supreme moment. Then, like a soldier hurling a javelin, he releases his grip and watches the flight—but the weapon has gone from his control.

In theory an army should never be committed to battle until success is assured. The general, after planning in immaculate detail, should merely have to watch the fighting develop infallibly into victory. But we are not all Hannibals or Corbulos. Perfection, in my experience, is unattainable in war and the smallest mishap can bring disaster as certainly as a breath of wind can deflect a well-aimed arrow. Control is lost when battle is joined; yet unforeseen developments compel intervention. As a skilled checkers player with delicate finger-tip flicks his counters to the winning squares so the general in the raging confusion of a desperate battle must shift the pieces of his fighting-machine to oppose unexpected moves. In this he must be quick and cool-headed; otherwise his army sees a harassed figure, hunted by his mistakes, gallop the battlefield in sweating endeavour to retrieve his fortunes.

So, on the easy assumption that matters went exactly as I intended, I would sooner in this battle for Anglesey pass to the outcome, decided long ago, applauded for a short space and then forgotten. But I write history, not propaganda; and the ugly moments when success poised on an edge finer than the sharpest sword must be honestly told.

The operation, in broad outline, went more or less as I planned. Ballistae and catapults threw a preliminary bombardment on enemy positions and then covered our assault. The range was long, particularly for catapults; hence the erection of platforms at low water mark which advanced the engines seventy paces and more towards their targets.

The infantry crossed in three flights following closely one on the other. In the first flight were 1st Frisiavones who were towed on short ropes attached to the leading barges, and 6th Thracians and 1st Morini. Forty barges carried the three cohorts. Their task was to thrust the enemy from the shoreline, secure a foothold on the beach and cover disembarkation of the second flight.

The second and third flights, of sixty barges apiece, bore thirty-six hundred men of XIV Legion. With twenty-five paces between barges each flight stretched seven hundred paces from wing to wing. The enemy, crowded on his rounded peninsula, disposed a much longer line but because of the headland's narrow arc was forced to refuse his flanks and, short of plunging into the sea, could not envelop ours.

Against an enemy, therefore, whose numbers I had no means of estimating I launched a frontal attack of five thousand men of whom thirty-six hundred were legionaries. This slender force held the Britons until two thousand cavalry concealed at the farther narrows forded or swam the shallows and stormed the enemy's right flank and rear.

Left on the mainland were fourteen hundred of XIV Legion, the veterans' milliary cohort of XX Legion and fifteen hundred auxiliary infantry. The barges, recrossing after shedding the first three flights, picked up these men, legions first, and brought them to the enemy shore to support their comrades.

The Thracian and Vardullian mounted element and legionary horsemen did not cross: they remained on the beaches and paraded in single line to simulate a strong cavalry force lest the enemy should start looking elsewhere for our cavalry.

The fortress garrison—two cohorts of XX Legion and 1st Britannic milliary cohort—took no part in the operations.

So much for the skeleton of my design, which I must now clothe with the flesh of description.

6

The artillery engines were set at maximum elevation. At the first discharge all four catapult darts ploughed harmless furrows in the sea and plunged into the far shallows like flying fish returning to their element. The four ballista boulders, over-ranged, crashed into woods beyond the beach.

A pause followed. Artillerymen scrambled around the complicated timbers of their ponderous weapons and racked the throwing-arms, creaking against the resistance of twisted ropes, to loading positions, and heaved rocks into the slings. They altered traverse, turning the ballistae by stout bars slotted into rollers. Catapult crews racked back the power-ropes, like bowstrings of gigantic bows, to breaking tension, placed heavy iron darts in delivery-grooves, chocked the engine to gain more elevation and waited with hands on release levers. Decurions eased or tautened the racks to make final range adjustments and listened intently to the thrumming vibration of the power-ropes. Aim cannot be accurate unless both ropes of an engine are in tune: hence, as Vitruvius said, a capable artilleryman must have a good ear for music.

From the enemy shore rose an angry hum and the defiant blare of warhorns. An artillery trumpet yelped sharply; the stopbeams jarred and shuddered. A second volley whirled into the air.

This was better. The ballista shots sailed lazily to the peak of their high trajectory and descended with malevolent precision on the crowded beach. Only one dart fell short; by miraculous efforts the crews of three catapults had found the extra distance needed.

The range was registered. Two sharp notes from the artillery trumpeter signalled independent rapid shooting. Massive timbers shuddered under incessant shock of discharge; darts whipped over the water; boulders seemed almost to touch the stormclouds before plunging inexorably on their victims.

From the mainland it was difficult to assess the material damage although, from previous experience, one could picture the havoc created by our missiles. Ballista stones, the size of a wine-cask and weight of a man, want no better target than infantry so closely massed that they cannot avoid being hit. Nothing could be more unpleasant for the Britons than watching these brutal projectiles hurtling towards them and landing in an explosion of flying sand and spurting flesh. Catapult darts, on the other hand, struck unawares: flat trajectory and high velocity made them practically invisible until the yard-long bolts transfixed bodies as a cook spits quails.

I found it impossible to pick out any details of the enemy's battle order or to see whether they were arranged in organized companies. They crammed the opposite shore from waterline to woods; and the whole mass, in the fluidity of constant movement, shimmered like a desert mirage. Only around those mysterious fires, where the natives stood immobile as rocks in an angry sea, was there any appearance of discipline and control.

I waited patiently for our artillery pounding to take effect. For a long time, apart from a louder clamour and sudden surges and eddies of movement, the Ordovices showed no inclination to yield their ground. Then we heard horns blowing long, imperious blasts; and gradually the throng started to withdraw from the water, retreating step by step into the woods. Soon the foreshore was deserted except for a litter of bodies and those unmoving blocks surrounding the fires. Our missiles kicked harmless sand-sprays from the beaches. The engine-crews cursed, furiously handled rack and lever and increased the range.

This was the moment. A sharp order lifted the trumpets; the battle-call's ravening music slit the air like winged daggers. Oars bit water; boats lurched and gathered way.

These were no sleek war-galleys manned by seasoned rowers. The clumsy, overloaded wooden boxes gave perverse obedience to a false stroke and obstinately resisted efforts to correct their vagaries. Some turned broadside or collided in a flurry of splintered oars and frantic oaths; others lagged inert and ponderous like waterlogged hulks; a few incontinently filled and sank. The first flights, in ragged dressing fit to break a centurion's heart, crawled with agonizing slowness across the narrows. Still our missiles hurtled overhead, and still, save for those rigid groups by the fires, the beach in front was blessedly empty.

To this day my dreams remember the long-drawn strain of that crossing. I stood in the bows, hemmed by armoured bodies, afraid to stir for fear of unbalancing the boat, striving to control my legs' indisciplined trembling. Only the helmsman's time-chant and creaking oars disturbed the stillness. The barges, like a brood of gigantic water-beetles, crept over an ice-calm sea.

The wet, churned sand of the landing-beaches grew distinct—a wrack of dead men and abandoned weapons and embedded boulders and a catapult dart pinning a body whose limbs still moved feebly. And higher up, where sand gave place to pebbles, the smoke of those strange pyres climbed spear-straight to the clouds.

Our artillery sent a final volley crashing into the silent woods. I had told the centurion to keep shooting for as long as he could without endangering our own troops. We were still a hundred paces from our objective. I felt he was over-cautious.

Fifty paces. The stillness shattered like broken glass. Warhorns bellowed and a screaming multitude erupted from the trees, swarming over rocks, pebbles, shingle, pouring like molten lava to the sea. The scene trembled like an earth-shock in the roar of thirty thousand voices.

Twenty paces. The Frisiavones left their tow-ropes and swam ahead, gained footing in the shallows and plucked weapons. In the barges men gripped sword and spear and poised for the leap ashore. Arrows whipped; shields lifted.

All at once events cascaded and telescoped and extinguished thought.

The universe exploded in a tremendous thunderclap that slammed eardrums like a sledgehammer. Blue-white flame split the sky in flash after flash. Reason staggered beneath the onslaught. Sanity reeled and instinct commanded the body to hide, cower, seek safety in earth's deep bowels from the Gods' insensate fury. For the space of ten heartbeats we stood paralysed and the barges drifted gently to shore.

'Mars defend us! Look yonder!' Agricola's voice was cracked, unrecognizable. He pointed a shaking hand.

Furies with flaring torches, hair streaming wild, mouths agape in soundless shrieks, eyes wide and glittering, raced upon our shrinking auxiliaries in the shallows. The pyres beyond leapt high and triumphant; they were roaring furnaces in which nameless horrors writhed. Bearded men, black-robed, raised hands and faces in passionate supplication to the raging sky. Nightmare had broken the bounds of sleep.

My throat was desert and my bowels water. I trembled like any credulous barbarian while thunder rumbled and died and the balance tilted against a Roman army. Then an arrow flicked past my ear.

That hard, unambiguous sound restored thought and perception. The Frisiavones had recoiled in frantic disorder upon the barges in which our men crouched stark and paralysed. The barges drifted on the dying ebb of their momentum. We were all but defeated where we stood.

I whirled about, struck my staring trumpeter in the chest and shouted, 'Sound the charge! Sound and repeat!' I tore the scarlet banner from my standard-bearer, hurled a furious 'Follow!' at the bodyguard and leaped into the sea.

The water was waist-deep and cold. I gained the beach in a stumbling run, faced the barges and brandished my standard.

'Come on, you misbegotten cowards!' I shrieked. 'Thracians, Frisiavones, Morini, come! Do you leave me to fight alone? Are you afraid of priests and women?'

A foaming wildcat thrust her torch at my face. I dodged, struck deep in the belly and held her body as a shield against the gathering storm of spears and arrows. The bodyguard raced ashore, swords out. Centuries formed in line of battle at their standards, backs to the sea.

Somehow, in that pandemonium, the auxiliaries must have heard my entreaties. Horns whooped above my trumpeter's lonely wail; auxiliaries cascaded from the barges and met the enemy at the waterline.

All this had taken no more than the time needed to loose a dozen arrows, and already a good deal had gone wrong. That stricken hesitation in the barges had allowed the tribesmen to reoccupy the beach, temporarily swept clear by our artillery, before the first flight was ashore. Only four bodyguard centuries, a mere three hundred men, were formed in six-deep battle-line twenty paces from the sea and were fighting like tigers against an overwhelming mob. Already their wings had given ground so that they formed a crescent whose flankers fought in water knee-deep. I stood behind this arc and watched savage fighting develop for four hundred paces on either flank, half in the sea, half out, as the auxiliaries struggled ashore. There was no beachhead for the second wave.

I turned seawards. The long line of barges with the tall shields was fifty yards offshore. In the centre XIV Legion's golden eagle flaunted proudly. Vettius Valens stood alongside. I ran into the sea, cupping hands about my mouth.

'Hold!' I shouted. 'Hold! Form line in the water!'

Valens heard and raised an arm. I saw him turn his head; a trumpet blared; orders passed from barge to barge. Oarblades steadied, bit and held. Legionaries pitched into the surf, waded forward and formed line with waves curling beneath their armpits. Valens, back to the shore, watched grimly while his half-submerged centuries dressed ranks as though on the parade ground of Wroxeter. Satisfied, he turned about, sounded the charge and waded slowly to shore.

My bodyguard, the finest soldiers in Britain, still held their ground; but the auxiliaries, after meeting the enemy hand to hand with no time to form line, had fared badly. The fighting swirled, broke and engulfed struggling groups of Morini and Frisiavones; while the Thracians, misliking close-quarter cut and thrust, scattered into the sea whence they scourged the Britons with arrows. XIV Legion marched into this ferment like reapers to a cornfield.

They halted briefly, once, when the water was knee-height, and hurled javelins. Then swords rasped from scabbards, horns sang high and the legion crashed into the enemy in a splutter of white foam.

They gained forty paces before they were held. This was enough for the third flight, close behind, to form line on dry ground. The veterans' cohort stood quietly at the waterline in reserve; the rest doubled right and left to prolong the line or plug gaps wherever they found them.

Barges were already returning to the mainland to embark the second contingent. But I knew the day would be decided before they could arrive; five thousand Romans now battling on Anglesey must settle the issue. At this stage anything could happen. The tribesmen fought like wolves.

Slowly the half-mile battle-line hacked a passage up the beach. The ground they won was churned like a ploughed field and harboured a grotesque seawrack which jerked convulsively and bled and screamed. I followed the advance, step by step, until dry sand gritted underfoot and we passed high-water mark.

The enemy still fought fiercely and would not give. Time and again the bodyguard's rear files sidestepped and moved up to replace the fallen; as the ranks advanced they left a heavy trail of dead and wounded legionaries. A short space from the woods, amid a welter of rocks and loose-piled pebbles, we were brought to a standstill. Britons stormed from the trees and smashed against our shields. The line wavered. Centurions leaped to the front, swearing like madmen and roaring encouragement. The first centurion in the veterans' cohort flicked his gaze expertly from flank to flank, watching keenly for a break.

Far away to the left, behind the trees, cavalry trumpets howled like vengeful furies. Saturius and his horsemen were near. Now was the time for supreme effort. We won or lost this battle on the turn of the next few moments.

I waved to the first centurion. The veterans' cohort doubled up the beach, split into century columns, thrust through gaps in the line and struck like battering-rams. Horns whooped madly: that quick, treble-rise call which huntsmen use at the kill. I drew sword and plunged through the shouting ranks, the scarlet standard whipping behind. The bodyguard saw, gathered and swooped like a breaking wave.

Then all was wild chaos. Mad-eyed cavalrymen rode among the tribesmen, slashing and spearing and yelling. The legion, like a wrestler breaking a stranglehold, heaved and exploded in meteors of slaughter-crazed men and flickering blades.

The battle was finished and the hunt was up.

7

I set foot on the twitching body and jerked my sword free. Leaning on the hilt, head down, I gasped mouthfuls of air. Agricola put an arm around my shoulders.

'Paulinus, are you hurt?' he cried.

I choked, spat and stood erect, chest heaving. 'No, I am very well.' I looked about. Tumult raged in the woods. Here, above the beach, was comparative quiet. Waves rustled gently to the shore. Horsemen galloped from the trees, wrenched about and disappeared. Wounded men, crawling and stumbling, dragged reddened trails towards the sea. From a thousand agonized throats came that wailing moan which is the familiar dirge of hard-won battlefields.

'Get me a horse. Quick! And for yourself. And a mounted escort.'

Thunder rumbling overhead was drowned by the Strator Centurion's voice driving bodyguard legionaries to the beach. 'Rabble! Indisciplined scum!' he raved. 'Get back to the Legate's standard. Call yourself a bodyguard!' His swordflat whacked a legionary rump. 'What business have you chasing natives?' His staff whirled and struck. 'Your job is to guard the general. Double! In square about the standard!'

The chastened men dressed ranks. The Strator saluted stiffly.

'Awaiting orders, Legate. I shall give these scullions a month's treble drills for deserting you.'

'Let be, centurion. I set the example! Your men only carried it a little farther.' I pointed to barges recrossing the straits. 'Remain here and tell those troops to form on the beach and await orders. I shall go forward directly the tribune Julius Agricola returns.'

Agricola came with a troop of Pannonians and some led horses. We mounted and rode into the trees, a thickset woodland of numerous groves separated by patches of open grassland. In all directions, among the trees, across the open, Roman soldiers pursued and butchered.

The men were out of hand. I did not know what dangers lurked inland or whether the Ordovices had other forces in reserve: I must regain control at once. I flung up my hand and halted.

'Sound the rally.'

The call rang insistently. Some soldiers in the glade where we stood turned heads and checked momentarily; then plunged on. A dozen fear-crazed Britons raced past. Instantly, like hounds unleashed, the legionaries swerved after them. The trumpets called. They might have been deaf.

'What's the matter with the men?' I muttered. Vettius Valens and his staff, on commandeered horses, appeared from a tree-clump and cantered towards us.

'Gather your cohorts, Legate,' I said sharply. 'Have they forgotten what signals mean?'

'I have sent mounted tribunes to turn them,' he said in a tired voice. 'They are frenzied and beyond control. It will be difficult.'

'Difficult? A strange word from the Legate of Gemina. Why is this?'

'Come and see,' Valens said simply.

He led the way to woods overlooking the beaches, into a grove whose close-set trunks and matted boughs clouded the daylight. Here the thundery air seemed yet more stagnant, the gloom oppressive and tangible. Dead leaves muffled our hoofbeats; the horses stepped carefully over twisted bodies.

Valens said, 'There.'

A wooden platform, the size of an ordinary bed, stood in a slight clearing. The surface was a tattered mess of blood, bones and trailing entrails. Bloodstreaked eyeballs stared from heads jutting oddly between flayed legs and ripped stomachs.

Valens said, 'Look closer.'

I forced my trembling animal to the altar, for such it was. Dead eyes and twisted mouths, bitten tongues protruding in clench-jawed agonies of protracted death. Familiar faces contorted to grotesque masks. An option of Vardulli. One of Pantera's shipmasters—the price of a wrecked cutter. A centurion of Vascones.

Valens said, 'There.'

The oak-trees supported flayed and eviscerated caricatures of the human form. Broken bones protruded whitely through sodden flesh.

Valens said, 'And there.'

Over the remains of an enormous fire whose embers still glowed evilly in that dark place hung a wicker cage. Within the scorched frame-work was a blackened, coagulated mass. An acrid stench thickened the air and closed our throats.

Valens said, 'Our men—all of them. Every grove holds the like. Some were still alive when we found them.'

'These were the fires we saw,' I muttered.

'These were the fires,' Valens agreed quietly.

I sat hunched in the saddle, staring at those dreadful sacrifices.

'Has the enemy's resistance been smashed? Have they any forces still in being? Have you had any reports, Valens?'

'Enough to show that the whole British Army is in flight, Legate. There will be no counter-attack.'

'The day is young. Valens, take the tribune Saturius Secundus under your command. Your legion and his cavalry will pursue till sundown.' My voice shook. 'Kill, and burn, and destroy, Go.'

Thunder rolled. Raindrops pattered on the spring-green leaves of those unholy trees, poured faster, wild hoofbeats drumming to a charge. Heavy drips fell in the embers and hissed like snakes. I turned my horse.

'Druids' work,' Agricola said.

I said, 'Britons' work. This I shall not forget.'

8

That day was the 25th of April. For four days afterwards the army scoured Anglesey and met no resistance. The battle and extermination that followed destroyed not only the flower of Ordovicia's warriors but also her king, princes and chieftains. The Druids, most of whom were drawn from tribal nobility, nearly all perished in the massacre. Prisoners under torture revealed the identities of a few more: these we killed with the same barbaric mutilations they had practised on our soldiers.

I found no one to negotiate with; no authority to whom I could dictate terms, from whom I could exact reparations, tribute and slaves. Detachments rode from end to end of the island, surrounding forts and villages, herding hundreds of terrified captives into stockaded pens at our fort on the mainland.

I ordered the sacred groves to be felled wherever they were found; and into a lake revered by the Druids I cast a medley of articles and instruments connected with their religion: chariots, harness, ornaments, slave-chains.

We started to build fortresses for a permanent garrison in Ordovicia: one on the island and another, to hold two thousand men, at a place called Caernarvon on the mainland. This site was more suitable for a stronghold than our original camp: it held a strategic position on top of a broad, rounded hill and commanded the approach to Anglesey and the straits. Meanwhile, helped by prisoners, we finished the road from Conovium and extended it to Caernarvon.

On the 6th of May an 'Immediate' dispatch from London arrived at Caernarvon, whither I had moved my headquarters. It read:

'The Procurator Decianus Catus to the Legate Propraetor G. Suetonius Paulinus at Anglesey. Greetings. I have lately returned from travels in Icenia where I have been collecting money and properties bequeathed to the Prince under the late King Prosutagus's will.

'I found the Iceni recalcitrant and stubborn to the point of actively hindering recovery of our lawful dues. In some cases the soldiers of my escort had to take forceful measures against obstinate natives who resisted my just demands. The Queen Boudicca actively encouraged and exemplified this attitude. However, by determination and persistence I eventually extracted the funds we sought.

'It seems that Boudicca, enraged by her failure to prevent execution of the King's will, is trying to incite her nobles to revolt against our rule. I have this information from the magistrates of Colchester, whence yesterday I received a report of warlike assemblies at Norwich and elsewhere. I cannot conceive that this news, if true, denotes anything more serious than those oratorical orgies to which the Britons are prone: the Iceni have been disarmed for thirteen years and so are incapable of active violence.

'The magistrates' alarms are therefore groundless. Nevertheless in order to allay their fears, expressed to me in a request for military aid, I have dispatched two hundred soldiers from London. Though disposal of troops is a matter normally outside my province I thought it best under the circumstances to accede to the request and inform you accordingly. I trust you approve. Farewell.'

I re-read this pompous missive in some perplexity. Catus was most unlikely to view with equanimity a real threat of armed rebellion so near his own person; yet he made light of the matter and apparently considered two or three centuries of second-rate garrison troops a sufficient deterrent. On the other hand Colchester's hard-bitten veterans were not men to panic easily; if they were seriously worried something unpleasant was genuinely afoot. Yet, if the Iceni were on the verge of open rebellion, why had I not had word from Aurelius Bassus?

I bit my thumb and read the dispatch a third time. It rang false. Catus knew something or had done something—foolish or dangerous or disastrous—that he wanted to hide. How bad was the trouble? My instinct was to ride for London at once; yet I hesitated. The resettlement of Ordovicia and her incorporation in the province had hardly begun. Already I had given orders for detachments to search the mountainous country east of Caernarvon and make peaceful contact with chieftains to whom I hoped to delegate authority over the region. Organization of civil administration on a permanent basis would take at least another month. Meanwhile I had sent to Wroxeter for metallurgical experts and mining contractors to survey sources of lead and copper in the conquered territory. For mineworkers we already had slaves in plenty and more would arrive as we extended our control.

Now it remained only to extract the ores and start a river of wealth flowing towards Rome. The task laid on me by the Prince was nearly done and I could look to my rewards: Rome's approval and permission to expand Britain's frontiers beyond Brigantia. Must Catus's ambiguous letter undo all this?

No, I decided, it must not. I wrote to Petillius Cerialis and ordered him to send a detachment at least two thousand strong to Colchester with the utmost haste, irrespective of the situation in Brigantia. Couriers took the dispatch and started on the long gallop to Lincoln. Horses and riders would change at Conovium, Varae, Chester and at every fifteen-mile road-station studding the Frontier Way. They would reach Lincoln three days hence. Cerialis's force could enter Colchester four days thereafter. Seven days. And Catus's letter was three days old. Ten days. A great deal might happen within ten days. Half a province could be laid waste. I hesitated again, on the brink of reversing my decision.

No. I had heard nothing from Bassus.

9

Four days later, near dusk on the 10th of May, a troop of Indus's Horse galloped into Caernarvon fort. They supported in his saddle a tired, grey-faced man who tumbled from his horse in an exhausted heap. He gasped two sentences before he fainted.

For the space of ten slow breaths I stood immobile, staring sightlessly at mountain peaks bronzed by the last rays of a vanished sun. I gave orders and do not remember the words. Men began running. Riders leapt to saddles and flogged horses on feverish errands. I turned and walked slowly to my quarters, stepping carefully like a man bemused by wine.

The Prefect Aurelius Bassus had brought his message in person. The pyre was blazing.

11

'He rejoices to have made his way by devastation.'

LUCAN

1

Here was an emergency demanding speed above all. Here was an explosion to set an army hurtling eastwards in lightning marches in a move 'quicker than boiled asparagus', as the Divine Augustus used to say. Nothing, in this ghastly situation, could have been more desirable or more in accordance with my mood. Realities decreed otherwise.

The army was scattered across two thousand square miles of mountainous country from Anglesey to Chester. My first orders, given automatically with sense still numb from the shock of Bassus's news, recalled to Caernarvon both the island's garrison and the detachments penetrating Ordovicia. Messengers had gone. Like men pursued by demons they rode to bid commanders march full speed by day and night. Yet at best the whole force could not assemble until next afternoon; and then a hundred details needed attention before we could leave. Meanwhile, I had to decide what we were going to do.

Colchester was lost. Somehow London must be saved. To London the largest available force must go in the shortest possible time. Cavalry was the obvious answer. Horsemen were not the ideal garrison for a beleaguered town, but they might delay the insurgents until reinforcements arrived.

Of my six cavalry regiments two were in Anglesey, one somewhere in the Ordovican mountains with Vettius Valens, one at Caernarvon and one at Conovium. The Britannic Cavalry at Chester did not count: they could not be relied upon to fight against Britons. The last regiment to arrive, probably Valens's, would not reach Caernarvon before next afternoon; and they would be tired and needing rest. Even if this was denied them their horses could not traverse the mountain road at night. So our start must be postponed until dawn of the 12th.

The delay was agonizing; but I used it to ensure that everything was prepared in advance. All that night I worked in the new-built Caernarvon headquarters—timber-walled, cement-floored and shingle-roofed—so soon to be destroyed. A map of Britain lay unrolled on a big oak table, product of the legion's carpenters. I selected routes, measured distances and dictated to two tribunes, Agricola and Saturius Secundus, who noted mileage figures on tablets and calculated totals. Clerks with abaci clicked beads busily and translated miles to hours and days. From their calculations a complicated movement pattern slowly emerged which I wrote piece by piece on the operation roll.

The watches passed; dawn paled the candles. Like a mason filling the ultimate gap in a mosaic I penned the last line. The picture was complete. Nothing, so far as we were concerned, could happen very suddenly. We could not get any considerable force to London in under nine days.

When the day-guards' tesserar came for the watchword I called the Camp Prefect to conference and discussed administrative matters. He departed with his orders: to demarcate a camp for returning units, to stack rations and fodder in their lines, to load transport, to arrange conveyance for the wounded, to allocate an escort for our large prisoner-of-war slave train, to prepare the fort for demolition. He would have little rest for the next twenty-four hours.

At daylight escorted messengers took the mountain road with warning orders for Conovium, Varae and Chester and with urgent operation orders for Wroxeter and Gloucester. This dependence on horsemen for our communications accounted for no less than two of the nine days before a single legionary could reach London. The mountainous terrain was ideally suited for communication by signal, but we had had no time to build a hilltop chain of fortified towers.

In my quarters I found Bassus being attended by my personal physician, Hermogenes the Greek. The Prefect was deeply asleep.

'This man bears urgent news which I must know, Hermogenes. How sick is he? Can he be awakened?'

The doctor waved his hands. 'Better not, Lord Paulinus. The Prefect is utterly exhausted. He needs sleep; then food. By tomorrow he should be quite recovered.'

I stood for a moment irresolute, considering how much Bassus must know that was vital to my plans. Iceni and Trinovantes in revolt. Colchester surrounded. That was all I knew. Then I shrugged; a few hours would make no difference. I left the building and went to see Mannius Secundus about the choice and loading of my own equipment.

On campaign I have never allowed myself much lavishment in furniture, food and clothing. Officially, a Legate commanding a Province is limited by the Divine Augustus's iniquitous mule-and-tent allowance to bare essentials; unofficially there is no restriction on his scale of baggage. I have known a commander—who shall be nameless—to take the field with forty wagons piled high with gorgeous pavilions, silken hangings, quantities of bed-linen, furniture fit for a palace, wines, choice food. Behind trailed a cohort of freedmen and slaves, chamberlains, cooks, masseurs, barbers and entertainers. His troops laughed but, in the philosophical way of Roman soldiers on service, drew no bitter comparisons between their state and the general's: his extravagance, in fact, rather enhanced his prestige with the men. So it was personal preference, not a desire to propitiate my legionaries, that curtailed my baggage.

In the field I used as much as would fit comfortably in a four-wheeled wagon: a double-sized leather tent, folding camp furniture of my own design made of canvas, leather and wood, a canvas floor-drugget and enough clothing and linen to ensure a daily change. On campaign, like Marcus Cato of old, I drank the same wine as the men and ate the same food. In this was no special merit: I preferred it.

But twenty years had passed since I last confined my kit to the limits of a single pack-horse, which was the allowance for prefects and centurions of cavalry when marching without baggage. After anxious discussion with Secundus I chose as essentials a spare tunic, corselet and boots, some woollen shirts and drawers, an extra cloak and several blankets. The orderly, though accustomed to my austere habits, hardly stifled his shocked expostulations.

He was still more shaken when I told him to fasten a fleece over my riding-blanket and advised him to do likewise. My backside was hardened by many hours on horseback, but the next few days would bring riding of a pace and duration beyond the experience of most cavalrymen. Secundus, a legionary, was an awkward horseman and would undoubtedly suffer. Yet he insisted on accompanying me though I offered to take a temporary orderly from the bodyguard cavalry.

I went to headquarters where clerks were finishing written operation orders for every commander. I checked and signed. Cohorts started to arrive from Anglesey. A rear party, left to destroy the island's newborn fort, would not reach Caernarvon until later; and detachments had been left on the mainland beaches to burn barges, used in the battle, which now ferried everyday traffic across the straits.

Aufidius Pantera, an anxious man, arrived for consultation. He had received my message, announcing total evacuation of Ordovicia, wherein conduct of the fleet was left to his discretion. He seemed quite undecided what to do.

'I cannot stay here, Legate, without protection. If I return to the anchorage near Chester will any troops be within call?'

'No,' I answered. 'None nearer than Wroxeter.'

'Oh. The season is still too early to guarantee good weather for an open-sea voyage. After our experiences getting here—'

'You will have to make up your own mind, Pantera,' I interrupted brusquely. 'The Chester estuary should be safe enough. Your men can build a fort to protect the anchorage, as they did before, and you can lurk there until the weather is set fair.'

'It never is, in these waters,' he grumbled. 'I really don't know what is best.'

My patience ended. 'And I cannot tell you. Nor do I care. We seem likely to lose a province: the fate of twenty galleys is irrelevant. Do what you will.'

He flushed, started to speak, changed his mind and went, displeasure in every line of his body. I sighed, regretting my outburst. Pantera had an unhappy knack of ruffling my temper at crucial moments.

The long day wore on. I toured the fort, a broil of intense activity. Fatigue-parties emptied granaries, dividing the contents into separate fortnight-ration stacks for each unit. Carpenters made litters for the wounded: we still had over two hundred hospital cases from the Anglesey battle. Reserve equipment was being loaded on carts and wagons. All spare personnel were engaged in entrenching a camp outside the fort for outlying detachments who, when they returned, would have enough to do in preparations for departure without also having to dig their own fortifications.

I returned to my quarters. Bassus still slept and Hermogenes was equally obdurate against waking him. Thence to the praetorium, where I dictated letters to Rome. The laurelled dispatches announcing our victory over the Ordovices had long since gone; these were routine returns, casualty reports, reinforcement demands and recommendations for decorations. In the fight for the straits we had lost over three hundred legionaries and seven centurions, mostly from XIV Legion, and the same number of auxiliaries, of whom 1st Morini and 1st Frisiavones had suffered most. A cheap battle under the circumstances, for with five thousand men we had engaged and routed thirty thousand Britons and killed half their number. The landing-beach at Anglesey still stank of death.

I checked a nominal roll of men deserving awards for gallantry. The Prince, unlike his forbear the Divine Augustus, was not niggardly with decorations: I myself approved awards to soldiers of centurion's rank and below and had already granted a liberal quota of mural and golden crowns, neckchains, armlets and medallions. But those who received their commissions direct from the Prince were honoured by him alone; and so I sent him a list of tribunes and prefects recommended for golden crowns, silver spearheads or silver standards. I could request no fitting award for the most deserving case of all. Vettius Valens already held a golden crown and most other decorations. I wrote a fulsome report on his services and hoped that the Prince would see fit at some time to raise him to senatorial rank—a hope that was never fulfilled.

Hardly had I finished when, four hours before he was expected, Valens himself arrived. I flung my arms around him, never more pleased to see anyone in my life.

'Have you borrowed your eagle's wings and flown?' I demanded. 'Are your men with you?'

'They are not.' He wiped forearm across mouth. 'I'm dry as a desert. Have you wine? No. I handed command to the senior tribune and came on at top speed. Your message gave no reasons for recall—'

'Dispatch riders can be ambushed. We don't want the Ordovices to know our misfortunes.'

'Misfortunes? A mild word, if I guess truly. To me, the whole message reeked of the worst kind of trouble.'

'You smelt right.' A slave brought wine; Valens drank thirstily. I dismissed secretaries and guards and closed the door. 'Be seated, Valens. We have a full-scale rebellion on our hands.'

I told him the little I knew.

2

The Legate drummed fingers on the table when I ended. 'Bad,' he said. 'Colchester must be finished. Bassus got out just before the colony was surrounded?'

'So I gather.'

'And rode two hundred and seventy miles in four days. By the Twins, the man must be dead!'

'He was, very nearly. He will recover.'

'Where will the rebels move next? London?'

I tapped the map that lay between us. 'Today is the 11th of May. Colchester was invested on the 8th. For how long can an unwalled town, garrisoned by a thousand old soldiers and two hundred second-rate troops, hold out? A day? Two days? No more. We must assume that at this moment Colchester is in ruins and the defenders dead. What are the Iceni doing now?'

'Looting, if I know barbarians.'

I shook my head. 'On the 6th I sent a message to Cerialis telling him to march for Colchester. He must have started yesterday and is now somewhere on the North Way approaching Icenian territory. The Iceni at Colchester will hear of this threat and must turn to meet him.'

'And London is safe.'

'For a while. I do not know how many men Cerialis has. I told him to take not less than two thousand. Whatever happens to him he will provide a diversion which should give me time to reinforce London.'

'How long will you want?'

'Nine days.'

Valens did sums in his head and looked depressed. 'Cerialis had better win his battle. If he fails—'

'Even if he is beaten we might have just enough time. Listen. This is my plan. Tomorrow, with five cavalry regiments, I ride for London. A sixth regiment, Proculus's Horse from Wroxeter, joins us at Penkridge. We shall get to London by the 16th.'

'Five days? You can't do it!'

'We shall. At the same time XIV Legion with the veterans' cohort of XX Legion and three auxiliary cohorts will march by the Midland Way. They will collect road-station garrisons of 1st Vangiones as they go, which will provide another strong cohort. No wheeled transport and very little baggage. You will reach London on the 20th.'

'Nine days,' Valens said. 'Two hundred and thirty miles. Over twenty-five miles a day. Hard marching!'

'You march to save a province and ten thousand Roman lives,' I said sombrely. 'I sent an urgent dispatch this morning to Gloucester. On the 14th of May II Legion with one auxiliary cohort will leave Gloucester, collect 3rd and 4th Gauls from West Way road-stations and arrive in London on the 18th. A hundred and twenty miles in five days.'

Valens nodded slowly. 'A speedy concentration. By the 20th, nine days from now, you will have in London three thousand cavalry, eleven thousand legionaries and four thousand auxiliary infantry. Eighteen thousand men. Should be enough to smash the Iceni.'

'Perhaps.' I scrawled meaningless symbols on a tablet. 'Nothing spreads faster than a successful rebellion. We may have more than the Iceni to beat.'

'And the frontier?' Valens asked. 'The western fortresses will have been skinned naked.'

I explained how our forces were to be redistributed to guard our borders. Four cohorts of XX Legion from Wroxeter, warned by messenger, should be marching at that moment to reinforce Gloucester, and would be followed by two auxiliary cohorts from Anglesey. This, with the units left in Gloucester, would provide a garrison of two thousand legionaries and twenty-five hundred auxiliaries. Wroxeter would have five cohorts of XX Legion and thirty-five hundred auxiliaries, a total of six thousand men. The garrisons were small; some forts between the two fortresses might have to be reduced in strength or temporarily abandoned; but I was not pessimistic. We still held our Silurian hostages; and the Ordovices were in no condition to start a war.

Valens left to make his arrangements. By nightfall all outlying detachments had returned and I called a conference of commanders. They had received their written orders; only minor queries remained to be answered and administrative problems settled. Certain prefects were hurt and sulky because their units, detailed for dull garrison duties on the frontier, were not to march to a new war. I could not explain that I had chosen the auxiliaries most carefully, omitting from the field army all Gauls and Belgae who had racial affinities with the tribes of eastern Britain. I was taking no more avoidable risks.

I summarized orders for the morrow. 'The army will march in three detachments. The first, four cavalry regiments under my command, will leave at dawn. Night destination Chester. The second detachment—XIV Legion, First Cohort of XX Legion and auxiliaries, under command of the legate Vettius Valens—leaves directly afterwards. Camp for the night between Conovium and Varae. The third, two cohorts of XX Legion and five auxiliary cohorts, siege train, slave train, hospital convoy and wheeled transport, will demolish Caernarvon camp and fort before marching. Night destination Conovium.

'All detachments will carry a fortnight's rations on the man and two days' fodder for each horse. Valens, your men will travel light. Your baggage is limited to one mule or donkey to each mess of eight men, which will allow you to carry tents. Don't overload the animals; they have to go far and fast.'

I stumbled wearily to my quarters. Bassus was awake and seemed refreshed and well; but I had had no rest the previous night and was too tired for conversation. I fell on my bed and dropped into bottomless sleep.

3

Dawn came clear and cold. In grey half-light I rode to the fort parade-ground where four regiments and the bodyguard cavalry were drawn up in mass. Trumpets sounded in the camp where Valens's legionaries formed in order of march.

The prefects saluted and reported readiness. Valens appeared at my side.

'Jupiter guard you, Legate. Ride fast. We shall be at your heels.'

'We'll not linger, Valens. And you? Why are you not mounted?'

'I have to get eight thousand soldiers and a thousand pack-animals beyond Conovium today,' he said gloomily. 'Thirty miles over the mountains. The men might forget their corns if they see me also hobbling afoot.'

'We shall compare blisters in London. Farewell, Valens.'

I gave the signal. The vanguard cantered from parade-ground to road, sent scouts ahead, gained distance and slowed to a walk. I led the main body at the head of my staff and bodyguard. After allowing time for the rearguard's last files to get moving the trumpets signalled canter. I wanted to take advantage of the twelve-mile stretch of level going before entering the mountains.

The column, six files abreast, rattled and creaked and jingled in an easy, swinging rhythm. Horses pulled and fretted, tossing heads against the bits, curvetting in the dayspring's freshness. Auxiliaries sang snatches of song, high wild chants from far Asturias. I thought of the miles that lay ahead and wondered how long this gaiety would endure.

After five milestones we pulled to a walk and dismounted for a short routine halt to tighten girths, adjust bridles and correct any mistakes made while saddling-up in darkness. Among my staff an unfamiliar figure refolded his riding-blanket.

'Aurelius Bassus! How come you here?'

He straightened and saluted. 'My duty lies with you, Legate,' he said soberly. 'There is much information I've not yet given you.'

'Are you recovered sufficiently to go with us? By Hercules, you'll have ridden a long way before this war is ended!'

'I am well enough, Legate. Even if I were not I would tie myself in the saddle to hunt those savages who've murdered my friends in Colchester.'

'Colchester. Yes, there is a lot I do not know. You can tell me as we ride. Trumpeter, sound mount.'

We cantered on; and Bassus, at my side, began the story of Decianus Catus's incredible folly and the holocaust that followed. Some of the events he witnessed himself; of Catus's transactions in Icenia he was given full accounts both by agents secreted in the Procurator's following and by veterans of the colony who were with him. How Boudicca organized her revolt we heard afterwards from captured Iceni. Bassus could not tell me how Colchester died. That part of the narrative I had later from a freedman, one of the seven survivors, and include it here to complete the tragedy. A story obtained from such varied sources is bound to be disjointed, sometimes unreliable; and I shall not attempt to recount it in detail. The incidents did not affect the outcome: the fact of Colchester's destruction is what matters to this history.

4

Catus went into Icenia like the general of an invading army. The pretext for his action, for his irresponsible folly, was a copy of an appendix to Nero's document authorizing annexation of Icenia on the King's demise without male issue. The document, a highly secret, explosive text which contained full instructions for assimilation of the kingdom as part of the Province of Britain was, at that moment, being carried to Anglesey by Government couriers. Catus had received only a portion: an appendix covering financial matters that concerned the Procurator. For him it seemed sufficient excuse.

With an escort of three hundred legionaries scraped together from the London Arsenal and fifty scallawag veterans who joined him at Colchester, and a large retinue of freedmen clerks, slave secretaries, ox-carts and pack-animals, he crunched through Icenia. He met Boudicca at Norwich. Here, at a council of Roman civil servants and native elders, the Procurator laid before an astounded queen his astonishing demands. These went far beyond the bequests made to Caesar in Prasutagus's will. He produced Nero's authority for repayment of the Divine Claudius's gift—together with interest charges for eighteen years. Catus was an experienced official: he knew well that such a demand needed a legion's presence at his back. Yet he did this, supported by only a few hundred second-rate soldiers, in the heart of a country already tottering on the edge of hostility. Decianus Catus was never a brave man. He was merely the biggest fool in the history of Roman administration.

Boudicca did not refuse outright, although the exaction would absorb all her resources, beggar her chieftains and leave her and her daughters poor as the meanest goatherd in Icenia's forests. She asked for time to consider and retreated to her palace. Within a few days Catus heard that the Britons were stealthily departing from Norwich into the inaccessible marshlands farther west, accompanied—and this was the crux—by a wealth of gold and silver, coins, precious ornaments and bullion and jewellery and pearls. Seeing his booty being filched underneath his nose, he hurtled with his escort to the almost-deserted palace.

In this gloomy, ramshackle building he lost control of the riff-raff who formed the greater part of his train. In the search for treasure they found a wine-store. Within minutes a drunken mob had sacked the precincts and raped the female occupants, including the Queen's daughters. When Boudicca belatedly arrived on the scene she attempted, in a towering rage, to strike Catus. He had her seized and bound, and flogged her himself with a rod grabbed from his lictor.

Then, stunned by his own actions, pricked by the scorpion stings of panic, he fled from Icenia. His companions, however, had found the plunder from Norwich less than their expectations, and they ravaged far and wide during the return march. He passed through Colchester in a hurry and reached London on the 27th of April, panting with apprehension. For days thereafter Roman bands, laden with booty, filtered back from Icenia, leaving wreckage wherever they had been.

Behind him Catus left an outraged, rabid woman summoning her fighting men to a war of vengeance.

5

Ten days later the blow fell on Colchester. The rebel host swept from the forests, which they filled until the very trees seemed to be walking. They poured down roads and tracks like rivers in spate. They surrounded the colony in a vast coil, like a python contemplating its prey, and prepared for battle.

The men of Colchester had not been idle. The image of their gathering doom, painted from the reports of spies and traders fleeing from native wrath, was clear in their minds as lightning on the surface of still water. They made what preparations they could. Couriers on whip-scarred horses fled to Catus in London, to Cerialis in Lincoln. Bassus himself rode to Anglesey. From London the Procurator sent two hundred half-equipped soldiers, the scourings of depot and arsenal. And that was all. A thousand ageing ex-legionaries made ready to defend Colchester and her three thousand non-combatants against thirty thousand of the most savage tribesmen in the world.

The town had no wall, nor was there time to make one, so the settlement was abandoned, farms, houses, offices and forum, and the whole garrison withdrew to the Temple of Victory, whose precincts were guarded by a solid, stone-faced embankment. They shut the women and children within the temple and manned the walls.

On this target Boudicca launched the whole weight of her army. For two days, unbelievably, the Romans held their unlikely fortress. Then they broke, and Britons poured over the walls like water into a foundered ship. The men of Colchester fought like the veterans they were and died slowly and bitterly. Some were still fighting when the enemy battered down the temple doors and began the long slaughter within.

The end was fire: a raging holocaust that blazoned the earth with flame and scorched the stars in heaven.

6

Bassus had not ended his unhappy tale when we rode into Chester. There had been many interruptions on the line of march, and the futility of marching in continuous column soon became obvious: an accident to one troop inevitably halted everything behind. I extended the column to give a mile's interval between regiments; regiments allowed a hundred paces or more between troops. So, like beads on a ribbon more than eight miles long, we cantered, walked, climbed and slid from Caernarvon to Conovium—where Indus's Horse joined us—and thence to Varae and Chester.

Sixty miles of mountain road had punished men and horses. Casualties among horses were heavy, chiefly from sprains and falls; only a few files of led animals remained in regimental reserves.

Sunset was a memory. In semi-darkness I leaned on the ramparts of Chester fort and watched the last regiments plod wearily to the parade-ground, form mass and dismount. Many stragglers, I knew, still limped painfully on the nightbound road. I drove my aching legs to the close-packed lines. Men picketed, fed and groomed horses, stacked arms and saddlery and boiled soup over driftwood fires. Some already slept, cloak-wrapped on the ground, dead to the world. Prefects caught the torchlit flare of my scarlet cloak, hurried to report damage and loss, sought instructions for the night.

I led them to a wooden hut which was Britannic Cavalry's headquarters, where Bassus, grey-faced and breathing heavily, slept on a pallet. I regarded his beaten frame with compassion and admiration: the man had a constitution like tempered iron.

The officers announced their parade states. I said: 'Thirty-three horses have been left at outposts on the road. Seventeen more, and their riders, are stragglers and still lost. Twenty in camp here are unfit to march tomorrow. Not, I suggest, a good record for five regiments hardened by a month's campaigning.'

The barb stung, as I intended. The weather-scored faces showed surprise and resentment. I smiled grimly.

'Yes, I can guess your thoughts. Sixty-odd miles in one day on the worst road in Britain. Fortunate, you think, that the damage was no worse. Let me remind you of what lies ahead: a hundred and seventy miles at fifty miles a day. Tighten your march discipline. Look more carefully to your horses.'

I flattened a scroll on the table. The schedules written in Agricola's flowing script danced blearily before my eyes.

'Britannic Cavalry will make good your horse casualties. Give us your best, Prefect. We march at dawn tomorrow. Night destination Penkridge, where Proculus's Horse from Wroxeter will join us. Distance fifty miles; 2nd Asturians will be advanced guard for the day. I do not expect opposition but keep your eyes open in the forests beyond Mediolanum. Order of march…'

I finished reading and dropped the schedule. The five prefects, dark cloak-wrapped figures, stood gravely at ease. Centurions busily scribbled orders on tablets. A flickering oil-lamp planed shadows on oak-brown faces, graved deep lines from mouth to nostril. Good men, I reflected wearily, good Romans, dependable and strong. On those wide shoulders probably rested the fate of Britain. I surprised myself by the genuine pleasure in my smile.

'Today was the worst. The rest is comparatively easy. Good roads and shorter marches. We have finished with these accursed mountains, and we are all tired. Secundus! Bring wine.'

When they had gone I dropped on a bed beside Bassus, and Mannius Secundus, walking stiffly astraddle like a ruptured eunuch, insisted on massaging my aching thighs with oil. My last waking thought was a fleeting appreciation of Roman wisdom: we let alien soldiers do our horse-riding for us.

By sunrise Chester was three miles behind and we had settled to the regular pulse of a cavalry column of route on a good road: walk a mile, three miles canter, one mile lead, halt while the tesserar counted five hundred. Grudgingly the milestones lopped the distance to London.

7

My thoughts were sombre as the gloomy forests through which we rode. Bassus had told all he knew. He rode a length behind, slouched in the saddle like a man who, his mission ended, had surrendered strength and virtue. I remembered painfully my last question, and his answer.

'Can Colchester hold?' I had asked. A fool's question: a hopeless clutch at a straw of hope.

Bassus had shrugged wearily. 'Who can say? A thousand against ten thousand, or twenty thousand, or thirty thousand. I never saw the British army. I cannot judge.'

'Romans have often overcome great odds. Remember Quintus Cicero? For fourteen days his legion held against sixty thousand Nervii.'

'That was a long time ago,' Bassus had muttered. 'And Cicero had a legion—one of Julius Caesar's—and a fortress. Colchester commands a thousand stiff-jointed veterans within a temple.'

No more was said. I rode in brooding silence, unconscious of galled and aching thighs, sullen tree-ranks hemming the road, drifting rain beading cloaks and harness with evanescent pearls. The column forded a stream that swirled under the thrust of winter rain. The crowding trees retreated and our horses, leaning on their bits, plodded up a steep rise to the fort at Penkridge.

Proculus's Horse from Wroxeter were already in camp. Our own advanced party, sent ahead from the last halt, had pegged out an adjoining perimeter and guides led regiments to their lines. I rode into the fort, a small station garrisoned by a hundred Vangiones. The commandant's quarters were warm and well furnished: the centurion knew how to ease the rigours of outpost duty. I warmed my hands at a brazier, gazing abstractedly into the glowing charcoal. Little flickers of flame spurted and died behind the bars. Fire, that could comfort a man and destroy a city. Was Colchester burned?

I did not know.

12

'Did you meet hostile tribes and lawless savages, or did you
fall in with some friendly and godfearing folk?'

THE ODYSSEY

1

The Temple of Victory fell on the 10th of May. Of this disaster, as I
warmed my hands at the brazier in Penkridge fort three days later,
I knew nothing. My information ended with Aurelius Bassus's tale; and
he had left Colchester on the 6th.

Penkridge was a small station garrisoned only by a century and
troop. The square, stockaded rampart, rising from a wide ditch, stood
beside the road in a clearing of open woodland. A hundred yards on the
far side of the Midland Way was a cluster of round huts, the usual native
settlement which collects around a Roman station. Until a few months
ago, when my orders had removed them to a safe distance, these hovels
had shouldered the very ramparts of the fort.

The camp seethed in the twilight. The arrival of three thousand
men and animals had given to the quiet glades of Penkridge the complexion and atmosphere of a noisy horse-market. The fort, like every
road-station, overlooked the remains of old marching-camps, the
ditches silted and ramparts eroded; and in one of these Proculus's
Horse, the first comers, were comfortably installed. The other five

regiments, quartered around those crumbling banks, had to construct their own defences.

No power on earth will make cavalry dig. They carry only a few entrenching tools of a flimsier pattern than the legionary type. Normally, when a camp is being fortified, the cavalry are on outpost duties or reconnoitring or foraging. They seldom take part in the hard labour of fortification. Hence, on the rare occasions when cavalry are operating without any supporting infantry, the defences of their camps are a dangerous farce.

I regarded the scene glumly. The horses were picketed in orderly lines, head to head, and saddle-cloths, girths and bridles were neatly aligned in rows. Line-guards shook hay in front of their charges, rubbed backs, picked out hooves. No complaint here: the layout was exact and discipline good.

But with mounting amazement I watched their defensive arrangements. Fatigue parties ranged the woods, cut branches and dragged them to camp. Other details piled the timber in a leafy barrier along the perimeter and plaited and intertwined branches to make a firm breastwork which, when finished, was five feet high and two yards across. There was no vestige of a ditch.

The prefect of Indus's Horse read my feelings in my face.

'We have neither training nor tools to make a proper ditch and rampart, Legate,' he said apologetically. 'What you see is the kind of barricade made in war by Gauls and Belgae to protect tribal encampments. My men and the Tungri are the experts who construct the breastworks; the other regiments merely fell and haul wood.'

'A cattle-fence,' I said tersely. 'Jupiter help us if we are attacked in the night. Those twigs would not deter a two-year infant. Our cavalry have much to learn. Look there!'

I pointed to a corner of the camp where Gallic, Belgic, Spanish, Thracian and Pannonian troopers of the Bodyguard Cavalry lustily plied pick and shovel and patiently endured the jeers of their regimental comrades. A respectable rampart was rising around the bodyguard horse-lines.

'Those men are auxiliaries, like yours, but they've been properly trained. I shall sleep within your futile barriers tonight, to learn by experience the terrors of Domitius Corbulo's punishment—encampment outside the vallum. And some day I'll teach you and your cavalry the right way to build fortifications!'

I kept my word and spent the night on the ground, wrapped in a cloak. I slept badly, but it was not the lack of a bed nor the stamp and snort of horses nor the calling of the watches that kept me awake, for these things were familiar to me as my own name. My dreams were tormented, and always ended in fire.

2

After leaving the forest belt beyond Penkridge the highway pierced wooded, open countryside and the sun shone warm on our faces. My morose mood failed to respond to the soldiers' songs and cheerful chatter. A troop of the bodyguard preceded my horse—the guard always formed a self-contained tactical entity around my small headquarters—and I regarded the rumps of their horses despondently. Deep poverty-marks scored the animals' hindquarters; they moved sluggishly, often stumbling, and sagging heads bore heavily on the bits. We had marched six score miles in two days and the signs were plain. Ten troopers had been left at Penkridge because their mounts could go no farther; the regiments had no more led horses in reserve, and remounts taken from Chester and Penkridge had alone prevented a greater erosion of our strength.

The road swooped like an errant hawk, now flowing down the flank of a steep valley, plunging across a stone-paved ford, then rising triumphant to some rounded crest. The trees marched with us, scattered in copses or congregating across our path like dark ranks of a hostile army, impenetrable and impregnable. Their strength was illusion and the road clove them.

Sometimes we passed a cluster of wretched huts, wattled and thatched, surrounded by a timber palisade. A few bony cattle were tethered within, and a goat or two, and a swineherd tended his charges on the forest fringes and women dragged a wooden plough over a tiny field hacked from the scrub. Children ran to watch the column cantering by and men gazed beneath shading hands. These dwellers by the road were used to Roman troops. Deeper in the forests, in clearings, reached only by muddy trackways, the natives ran for cover and lay hidden until the iron helmets had gone.

We came to High Cross before dusk. This post, headquarters of 1st Vangiones, was the biggest and strongest on the Midland Way. An old legion marching camp opposite the fort quartered my six regiments. The auxiliaries, making no attempt to clear the bramble-choked ditch or repair the ramparts, solemnly crowned the bank with their ridiculous tree-branch breastwork.

And here the sack of Colchester was at last confirmed. Shocked and incoherent, the tribune in command told me the news.

'The colony fell four days ago, Legate. The whole place burned to the ground and not a Roman escaped.'

'Is this certain?' I demanded.

'No doubt at all,' he answered. 'High Cross is the intelligence and reporting centre for the entire Coritanian area. We have reliable agents—Britons—in Leicester, only twelve miles north. Their statements are explicit. And all today the burning has been common talk among natives in the settlement yonder. Traders from Verulam arrived this morning with the same story. I've studied and sifted all the reports most carefully. I'm afraid it's the truth.'

'Four days ago, you say? Where are Boudicca and her Iceni now?'

The tribune was less assured. 'I cannot say, Legate. The evidence is very conflicting. Some say she is still at Colchester. Others that she is marching on London or Verulam. Our Leicester spies think she is going north.'

'North?' I grunted. 'Straight into the arms of IX Legion? Most unlikely. Those Britons seek loot, not fighting. She'll be somewhere in the Colchester-London-Verulam territory. Haven't you any word from your posts nearer London?'

'Nothing positive, Legate. None has been attacked, nor seen any hostile Britons.'

I left him. I was tired after the ride, shocked by this confirmation of my worst forebodings and in no mood for careful and constructive thought.

High Cross was a luxurious outpost and contained a primitive but efficient bath-house. I sweated away my evil humours and emerged refreshed. The tribune provided a passable dinner: river fish, eggs, olives and sweet wine. After the meal I dismissed him and my guards and attendants, and called for maps, tablets, candles. Alone, jotting a note here, measuring a distance there, I tried to deduce, from meagre facts, what had happened and what was likely to happen.

At the end of an hour I frowned at the litter of scribbled tablets and crumpled maps, called for fresh candles, took a roll of paper and wrote:

The facts

Four separate Roman forces are converging on London, divided each from the other by at least two days' march.

For four days past we have lost touch with Boudicca.

The questions

Are the Iceni still at Colchester, plundering the surrounding country and quarrelling over the loot?

Or, satiated with slaughter and pillage, have they withdrawn into their own country?

Or have they marched to meet Cerialis?

Or, to avoid contact with IX Legion, are they turning south to sack London and Verulam?

I dropped the pen, rose stiffly from the table and sipped wine. Then I sent for Agricola.

'Study that,' I told him, indicating the paper on the table. 'Then try to answer those questions.'

The tribune read the paper twice with frowning concentration while I watched silently. At length he raised his eyes.

'You are Boudicca,' I said. 'You have just sacked and looted the capital of Britain, defeated a thousand Roman veterans and massacred three thousand civilians. You then hear that a legionary detachment from Lincoln, at least four cohorts strong, is only two or three marches distant. What would you do? Think, and take your time about answering.'

Agricola studied the maps, took measurements with a stylus. He straightened and smiled.

'I should go to meet the legion, without any hesitation.'

'Why?'

'My men are flushed with victory, confident, laden with plunder and now hungry for glory. I should take the opportunity of defeating this detachment, one of many that are converging, before the others arrive in support. Besides, two other courses open to me are both militarily impossible.'

'Which?'

'To retreat again to Icenia and await Roman vengeance. Out of the question. To turn on London or Verulam while a vexillation is bustling south and might find my men plundering and unready for battle. Madness.'

I walked to the window and flung the shutters wide. The night was warm, still, pricked by a thousand stars. I stood gazing into the darkness.

'I agree with you,' I said at last. 'Therefore Cerialis and Boudicca are about to clash or might already have fought. In either event she's more than forty miles from London—at least two days' march for a native army.'

'And so,' Agricola murmured, studying my notes, 'we certainly, and II Legion probably, will reach London before the Iceni—assuming that they are not routed by the Legate Petillius Cerialis.'

I shivered suddenly in the warm air and slammed the shutters. Trumpets sounded the second watch.

'It grows late, Agricola, and I still have work to do. How many horses have we lost today? Forty? Send for the tribune of Vangiones. He has six troops here and can provide those and more. I forgot to ask him whether he has noticed any unrest among the Coritani. Nothing spreads rebellion like success. Boudicca has had one victory already.'

3

People who have never seen war sometimes visualize cavalry as a glittering cavalcade, a pageant of flaring cloaks and streaming plumes and whirlwind speed that devours the miles in a headlong gallop. A day's march in Britain would disillusion them.

Towards the end of the fourth watch it had started to rain, and the men on-saddled in a steady, drenching downpour which continued with hardly a pause all day. In a grey, dreary half-light we left High Cross, muffled to the ears in sodden cloaks, water dripping from lanceheads and standards and spouting under the horses' feet. Soon afterwards we plunged into the forest.

This stretch of the Midland Way explored some of the thickest forest in the province. The trees, cleared to the regulation bowshot on either side, loomed like lowering scarps, dense as cornstalks in a field, tangled breast-high in undergrowth and brambles. The emerald leaves of young summer, decorating the branches like vivid gems, hardly softened those sombre precipices. Yet Britons lived in hidden clearings in the depths and hunted animals for food and shaped weapons from stone and sacrificed to gods far older than the ancient oaks. Those were the natives we Romans never found. Sometimes a patrol, lost in the forest, entered a glade where woodsmoke lingered and found the bones and skins of animals and deep pits roofed with branches. That was all. None ever saw the strange, shaggy men who used neither cloth nor iron and sowed no crops. The forest tribes—Coritani and Catuvellauni—feared and avoided them. Marooned by time, the last survivors of the people of the long tombs lived like wraiths in a haunted wilderness.

The rain teemed down. The advanced guard churned to a muddy morass the soft earth alongside the road where we normally cantered, three files a side, to avoid laming horses on the hard metalling. Nothing varied the monotony of this narrow lane, like a ravine cleft by some titanic axe—no huts, no grazing cattle nor rooting pigs, no still-faced peasants to watch our passing. Once we overtook a mule train plodding Londonwards from the Anavio lead-mines, escorted by a dozen sullen soldiers; and, a few miles on, a despondent road patrol of Vangiones.

Beyond Bannaventa the forest yielded. Men straightened shoulders, lifted drooping heads, stretched like prisoners released from shackles. During the midday halt I sought shelter beneath the dripping branches of a towering oak. The auxiliaries, whose cheerfulness had been subdued by the gloomy ride through the forest, began to recover their spirits and hissed and sang while they rubbed down their steaming horses. I chewed a soggy biscuit and told Secundus to fetch a dry cloak from the pack-saddle. Agricola, sanguine as ever, poured wine into a leather cup.

'What did the tribune of Vangiones say about the Coritanian attitude to this rebellion, Legate?' he asked.

'He thinks the Coritani are quite indifferent. His men report no change of manner among the natives they meet; they remain respectful and friendly as Britons can ever be. Nevertheless the station at Towcester was raided two nights ago.'

Agricola pondered with puckered forehead. 'Is that significant? Outposts are bound to be attacked from time to time.'

'Not in this area,' I grunted. 'It's most unusual. You're thinking of the frontier. No fort east of the Frontier Way has been raided for ten years.'

Agricola glanced uneasily at the long line of dismounted men and unsaddled horses, guarded only by mounted picquets prowling watchfully on the flanks.

'Should we not, perhaps, take extra precautions?'

'No need yet. The raiders were Catuvellauni, not Coritani. They inflicted no casualties nor damage to the fort. Loosed a flight of fire-arrows and ran. But in the native settlement they left quite a trail of slaughter.'

'We come to Catuvellaunian territory near Towcester,' Agricola said thoughtfully. 'Shall I warn the advanced guard?'

'No harm in doing so,' I said. 'The tribe as a whole hasn't yet joined the rebels, but Iceni and Trinovantes are their neighbours and they're probably becoming disaffected. We shall know more when we reach Verulam tomorrow.'

The column passed Towcester—where the garrison was helping villagers to rebuild burnt and shattered huts—and halted for the night at Magiovinium. Here was no convenient legion marching-camp and, as we had covered only forty-five miles that day and arrived well before dark, I compelled the auxiliaries to build a barricade double the usual width around their camp.

Magiovinium held two centuries and two troops of cavalry. I noticed with approval that the palisade had been recently repaired: freshly-cut tree-trunks replaced rotting timber and the rampart's scarp was steep and newly revetted. Working parties cleared nettles and silt from the ditch. Towcester's slight taste of war seemed to have ruffled our sleepy backwaters.

The centurion commanding the post was plainly worried.

'Can't put my finger on it, Legate,' he said. 'Ever since we had news of Colchester the natives have been queer. Shifty-eyed. Try to avoid you. Some of the British traders and shopkeepers in our settlement have quietly disappeared—think it's safer in London, I suppose. Still, we've had no nonsense from the Britons, nothing like that trouble in Towcester. They've been respectful, too—stand when our troops pass and so on. Until today. Today has been bad.'

'In what way?'

The centurion shrugged. 'Hard to say. The village seems frightened. Outsiders—natives who come from the forest to barter—have vanished like that.' He snapped his fingers. 'I made inquiries just before you arrived, from ancients who've lived in the settlement ever since the fort was built. No good. Nothing but nonsense about a legion being cut up. A muddled version of the Colchester business, of course.'

An ice-cold blade lay along my spine. For a moment I could not speak.

'Centurion.' My tone snapped him to attention. 'Return to those men and discover what they know. Use any means you like. If they won't speak call upon my inquisitors. I want results before the second watch.'

The man saluted and went. I found difficulty in unfastening my cloak, because my hands were shaking.

4

The night passed quietly. I slept very little. The centurion's investigations, helped by my inquisitors produced no more than he had already told. One man died under questioning; and a decurion of Vangiones, inexcusably forgetting all his sense of discipline, flung himself at my feet to plead for the Briton's life on the fatuous grounds that the old man was his concubine's father. I ordered him to be flogged.

The deep forests ended at Magiovinium. For ten miles the road climbed steadily to a great ridge of open down, a rolling stretch of coarse grassland raddled by stunted thorn-trees. The rainclouds had cleared during the night and left a blue and sparkling morning. We were approaching civilization. Sheep grazed on the slopes, native huts clustered on hilltops and sometimes a farmhouse built in Roman fashion, the steading of some retired veteran or wealthy Briton, gleamed whitely in a hollow.

Traffic on the highway had increased since the previous day. Carts and donkeys staggering under heavy panniers trailed slowly towards Verulam, escorted by servants. Faith in the power of Roman arms had sustained them till this moment. Now, for vague reasons they were reluctant to disclose, they were running. The spectacle was not comforting.

Around midday we reached Verulam, the only settlement of any consequence on the Midland Way between London and Wroxeter. This place, something more than a village and rather less than a town, was an example of competent Roman planning whose execution had been entrusted, without supervision, to British municipal decurions.

Verulam had been the Catuvellaunian capital. The overgrown ramparts of the tribal fortress on the hill, still partly inhabited, loomed above a formless jumble of buildings which swelled upon the finger of the road like an arthritic knuckle. From the shoulder of down where we stood I saw a brick temple amid walled precincts, a small tile-roofed basilica fronting a cleared space which did duty as a forum, and some substantial timber-framed houses standing back from a solitary paved street. The rest of Verulam was a haphazard collection of thatched huts, stake-fenced yards, muddy, rutted tracks and twin rows of shops, booths and stalls bordering the Way. The settlement had changed very little since the Catuvellauni, under pressure from Scapula's legions, had first deserted their hill-fort for the valley below.

We tried to enter the town and found the road, Verulam's main street, in impassable confusion. Carts, wagons, litters, mules and cattle blocked the Way. Women shrieked execrations at horsemen of the Tungrian vanguard who tried to force a passage. I ordered the column to halt and, assisted by bodyguard troopers and a lavish use of lance-butts, rode to the basilica.

Shopkeepers and others, loading baggage on carts, packed the forum. The basilica, whose appearance recalled a tribal chieftain's hall rather than a place for the dispensation of Roman law and justice, was empty.

I said curtly to Agricola, 'Find a magistrate and bring him here.'

The man came, a hard-faced, middle-aged Catuvellaun dressed in Roman habit.

'Who are you?' I snapped.

He gave his name, which I have forgotten, and added that he was a duovir of Verulam.

'Can you explain,' I said coldly, 'why your populace obstructs the highway and denies free passage to the armies of the Prince of Rome?'

'The people are going to London,' he answered.

'Why?'

The man hesitated; then spoke strongly. 'This is no time to bandy words, Lord Paulinus. The people have been leaving since we heard of Colchester's fate. Can you blame them? Three marches away a ruthless army is exterminating everything connected with Rome. We in Verulam have been loyal for a generation. We are a natural target for Queen Boudicca's wrath, our houses a ready-laid bonfire for her torches. So far as we know not one legionary cohort is nearer than a hundred and thirty miles. Do you blame us for seeking refuge where we can?'

'And where,' I said mildly, 'do you think you will find safety?'

The Catuvellaun spread his hands. 'The only security in Britain lies within a legion's fortress. But we go to London, because there is nowhere else.'

I looked towards the door. 'Judging by the congestion outside the whole of Verulam is taking the road. That, surely, has not been going on for the last three or four days?'

'No.' The duovir paused. 'We heard yesterday—I do not know the truth of it—' He stopped.

'Continue,' I said quietly.

'Forgive me, Lord Paulinus. This is probably a baseless rumour. We have been told the Iceni destroyed a legion.'

Noises from the forum drifted into the quiet room. A donkey brayed; a man cursed monotonously while he backed a recalcitrant mule between the shafts of a cart; wheels ground on cobbled pavements and a woman called shrilly to her child. Dust-motes danced in a bar of sunlight. The men within that crude basilica—tribunes, centurions, orderlies, troopers of the guard—stood like iron statues, like creatures frozen by an icy blast.

'Agricola.'

My companions stirred cautiously, as men who come alive after the stunning impact of a thunderbolt.

'Yes, Legate?'

'Orders.'

The tribune snatched a beneficar's tablet and stylus.

'Detach 1st Pannonians at Verulam for refugee escort duty. They will clear the road, restore order, organize convoys and guard them on the way to London.'

I examined attentively the garish mosaic at my feet, a typically barbarian representation of Ceres and the Seasons.

'The regiment will leave a standing patrol in Verulam. Strength, two troops. They will be quartered in the Vangiones' fort. Task, to observe northwards, particularly on the Colchester road, and to send to London immediate warning of enemy approaching from that direction.'

I rose from the wooden chair which was a magistrate's Seat of Justice in Verulam.

'The column will off-saddle now for the midday halt. And you, duovir of the Catuvellauni,' I added gently, 'do not believe all you hear. A Roman legion is not easily defeated.'

5

Not all the men of Verulam were fleeing to London. The duovir, when pressed, admitted that many of his people, chiefly impetuous youths irked by an uneventful existence under our rule, had vanished into the forests. He denied, too vigorously, that they were armed. If this were true of natives living close to Roman influence it boded ill for the loyalty of Catuvellauni living farther afield in the wastelands that adjoined Trinovantan and Icenian territory.

'When this revolt is crushed,' I told the magistrate bleakly, 'we shall know our friends. The others will wish for death long before they die.'

We marched later than I wanted, for the Pannonians found the task of collecting refugees, who clogged the road for miles towards London, a long and exasperating business. Late in the afternoon we left the last scattered groups behind and cantered down the slope from Verulam and entered the ultimate forest. In the depths, ten miles from Verulam, we found the ruins of the road-station at Sulloniacae.

It had been sacked within the hour. The barrack huts still blazed fitfully and smoke, dense and acrid, caught our throats. Bodies hung on the broken palisade, sprawled in the ditch, lay spreadeagled in the road. The litter of pillage was everywhere: shattered corn-jars spilling their contents, coffers split wide, torn clothing, helmets, discarded weapons. A dead horse, intestines trailing like twisted snakes, blocked the gateway.

I gazed mutely at the carnage while auxiliaries flung patrols to front and flanks and probed the impassive forest.

'What was the strength of this garrison?' I said.

A flurried consultation among my staff produced a decurion of Vangiones, one of the lucky few in their mounted element whose horse had not been filched to repair our own losses.

'The smallest on the Way, Legate. Twenty-five foot and ten horse.'

'Search the ruins,' I ordered. 'See if anyone is still alive.'

Nobody was. The bodies were collected and laid in a row. Some had been trapped in blazing buildings and were misshapen, blackened lumps. Only a few bore the marks of deliberate mutilation. That, and the signs of interrupted looting, indicated that the raiders had been disturbed very soon after they stormed and fired the fort. Their scouts had probably reported our approach.

A shout echoed from the forest. A patrol emerged dragging a tattered wretch whom they flung at my horse's feet. The decurion saluted.

'A Briton, Legate, badly wounded. Found him hiding in the undergrowth.'

I surveyed the man without compassion. A young face, I judged, beneath the muddy filth and blood-clotted beard. He wore the particoloured woollen trousers, bound criss-cross with leather thongs below the knee, common to Britons of the aboriginal tribes. A swordcut gashed his chest and bared the ribs; blood made a purple mess of the blue stripes on his body, the war-paint that no one east of the Frontier Way had seen for thirteen years.

I called the inquisitors. 'Take him away. Discover his tribe, where he comes from, who his leaders are. Get results quickly. We cannot stay here for ever.'

Auxiliaries found spades and buried the dead Vangiones in one long grave. Upon the road troopers on drooping horses stretched rank behind rank into the dim distances of the forest. Picquets stood rocklike in the clearing between road and trees and, beyond, patrols still beat noisily in a tangle of thorn and bramble and elder. Behind the smoking mound which had once been Sulloniacae a group of men, like skilful cooks carving a delicate dish, worked with swift, efficient movements on a thing that squealed like a butchered pig.

The chief inquisitor returned, wiped a clotted mess from hands and forearms.

'A Catuvellaun of the forests south of Towcester, Legate. Boudicca's secret emissaries have been busy there trying to gather allies for her rebellion. This man was travelling with a war-band by hidden trackways to Colchester. They crossed the road near the fort, watched from the trees, saw the gates ajar, the garrison careless and the sentries indolent. The temptation was too great.'

The inquisitor twisted his cleaning rag, a blotched horror of blood and ordure, and tossed it away.

'You wanted speed, Legate. I hadn't time to get more.' He paused hopefully. 'He's still alive.'

I lifted my gaze to the jagged ramparts. 'Nail him to the palisade. Trumpeter, sound march.'

The forest mockingly returned the trumpet's wail. The long column rippled into movement. For a brief moment a wind lifted and whipped the smoky murk above Sulloniacae into flaring streamers like a salute of pennoned lances.

6

The sullen gloom of the forest deepened after sunset. We were late and unlikely to make camp before dark. I extended the periods of cantering: troopers legged their weary beasts to prevent them faltering to a trot, that most uncomfortable and exhausting of all gaits.

We passed scattered groups of refugees, people who had forsaken isolated farms or villages to seek safety in London. Once we came across corpses and a broken cart, either the work of rebels or a gang of brigands encouraged by a spreading sense of lawlessness. We were approaching the core of revolt and the embers flung far and wide like a fire fanned by tempest.

The forest receded. The mighty causeway of the West Way strode from the darkness, engulfed our road and proclaimed on a milestone that London was three miles ahead. To our right the last gleams of twilight shimmered on a Thames curving in fantastic loops as though striving to escape from the imprisoning thickets, impenetrable as stone walls, which hedged her banks.

We forded a small, fleet river and saw lights and the massive bulk of crowded buildings. A house or two and a temple loomed from the dusk, the overspill of a growing town; and lamplight streamed from open doors beside the road and splashed colour on the dim ranks as they plodded past.

Our markers guided the column to a camp situated north-west of the town. The last shreds of daylight had gone. I dismounted and watched the inevitable confusion of tired auxiliaries making camp in darkness. Guides with sputtering torches led regiments to their lines and collided with other formations moving in opposite directions and horses stumbled and men swore and centurions cursed with the savagery of utter exasperation. Eventually the camp settled down; troopers picketed horses, off-saddled, rubbed backs and shook the meagre remains of the day's fodder before their mounts. Prefects paraded for orders.

'It's too late to fortify the camp,' I told them, 'even with your tree-branch walls. We shall take a chance and trust in the Gods. Double your sentries. Post outlying picquets two hundred paces from the perimeter, three to each face of the camp. If we're attacked fall in at alarm posts and form line: you'll have to defend yourselves without the help of barricades. Carry out an alarm rehearsal before you sleep.'

I gave the watchword, warned foraging parties and ration fatigues to parade at dawn, and went to my quarters in the bodyguard encampment. From some undisclosed source—probably a house in the suburbs—Secundus had obtained a sheet of canvas remarkably like a ship's sail and had rigged a shelter. Under the canvas was a wood-framed bed, another acquisition, upon which he was spreading blankets from my pack-horse panniers. This simple picture, framed in a lantern's mellow light, afflicted my tired body like a paralysing drug. Lassitude engulfed me like a wave, and sleep was a boon more desirable than fame or victory.

But commanders have no time to be tired. Soldiers carrying torches escorted strangers through the encampment. A message passed from the centurion of the watch to the centurion of the bodyguard, to the tribune of the guard, to the duty tribune and finally to Agricola.

'Magistrates of London beg audience to greet you, Legate.'

I mentally reviled a protocol which ordered ceremony at such forsaken hours.

'Send them along.'

The group approached. I stepped from the shelter, a torch-bearer at either hand and guards in station, and acknowledged salutations. A fat, cheerful face, red as wine, glowed from the nondescript crowd like a star.

This man announced himself as Aulus Alfidius Olussa, a Roman citizen of Greek descent, and a magistrate of London.

'Your authority is welcome,' I said. 'You can arrange certain matters for me.'

'I exist only to serve you, Lord Paulinus.'

'Some time towards morning, probably during the third watch, one of my regiments will arrive escorting refugees from Verulam. You will meet these people on arrival and provide food and accommodation.'

'It shall be done, Lord Paulinus,' Olussa said. 'Already many citizens and Britons have come here from the countryside. We are feeding them from municipal granaries and have provided timber to make temporary shelters. The grain, of course, is part of Government revenues.'

'And you want the amount remitted, I suppose. Never mind that now. You have only a few hours to prepare for the Verulam refugees. Certain other matters I shall discuss with you tomorrow.'

Olussa received his dismissal with a bow. 'Your chamberlain is waiting to escort you to the palace, Lord Paulinus. The palace is, I believe, understaffed—' He paused awkwardly.

'Because most of my officials and servants died in Colchester,' I finished grimly.

'So should you prefer it, my humble residence is at your disposal.'

'I sleep here,' I said definitely.

Olussa looked at the sagging strip of canvas, tumbled panniers, the narrow bed and trampled, miry floor. Rain dripped dismally; torches hissed and spat like wildcats. His face showed an incredulous amazement.

'As you will, Lord Paulinus,' he murmured.

The deputation of welcome was lost in the night. I sat on the bed while Secundus unlaced my corselet.

'Send to the centurion commanding London Arsenal,' I told Agricola, 'and warn him we shall want rations and tents for three thousand men. Also a special grain issue for the horses. When you've done that you can sleep. Tomorrow will be a very busy day.'

7

The Pannonians arrived with the scent of dawn and thoroughly disturbed the camp. They had taken twelve hours to cover twenty miles from Verulam to London. The Prefect reported no incidents on the march save the exhausting toil of herding an interminable column of refugees along a night-bound road and collecting stragglers who wanted to stop and rest whenever a load fell from a donkey, or nature called, or a goat strayed to the forest.

'Although,' the man added thoughtfully, 'they were less inclined to lag after we had seen Sulloniacae.'

So little of the night remained that there was no point in returning to rest. Secundus hung a horn lantern to a post supporting my canvas shelter. Agricola, who had slept wrapped in his cloak on a heap of straw at the foot of my bed, stretched and yawned.

'Chase the shadows from your brain, Gnaeus,' I said. 'Find your tablets and give me the dispositions of our forces at this moment.'

I reclined on the bed, hands behind head, and gazed at the stained ceiling. Rain seeped through the worn canvas and dripped monotonously. Agricola unfolded his notes.

'Vettius Valens,' he began, 'is at Mancetter, four marches away. II Legion should be at Silchester, two days from London. If, as we hope, Cerialis left Lincoln seven days ago his vexillation should by now have reached Colchester or London.'

'And the rebels?' I murmured, eyes closed.

'Last reported at Colchester seven days back,' Agricola answered firmly. 'Present whereabouts unknown.'

'Seven days,' I said. 'Plenty of time for them to have reached London or Verulam. Both towns still stand unharmed. Boudicca has met Cerialis.'

Agricola shut his tablets with a snap that split the wax. 'What do you really think has happened to IX Legion, Paulinus?'

I opened my eyes. The guards were out of hearing. Mannius Secundus sat cross-legged near by, polishing my helmet. He caught my glance and left the shelter.

'Cerialis,' I said slowly, 'has accomplished what I intended: he has diverted Boudicca to the north and given me time to concentrate my forces in London. He may even have defeated the enemy, but that I do not believe. His detachment is small, because I ordered it so. IX Legion must hold Lincoln and discourage Venutius from adventuring into Brigantia, therefore he could not have sent more than three or four thousand men to Colchester. Cerialis, I judge, has been smashed. Perhaps annihilated. But he has done his work.'

Agricola chewed the end of a stylus. 'Boudicca, wherever she is, still has four days to get here before Valens arrives.'

I nodded. 'That is the danger. She may also have time to interpose a large force between London and XIV Legion, so interrupting our concentration. But then Boudicca herself will be caught between hammer and anvil, between Valens advancing from the west and myself with II Legion from London.'

'Unless she first defeats us separately,' Agricola muttered.

'There is also that.' I swung legs from the bed. 'So we must try to find out where the rebels are. Fetch your maps.'

Agricola unrolled papers on the bed and brought the lantern closer. I traced with a finger the triangle of roads whose points were Colchester, London and Verulam.

'I don't think Boudicca's army, except for small raiding-parties seeking loot, is yet south of the Verulam-Colchester road. If it were we should have heard rumours from friendly natives. We must seek definite news. The Pannonians are already covering Verulam and scouting north. That leaves two roads: the North Way and the highway from London to Colchester. This will be dangerous work: the Britons may be anywhere. Whom shall we send?'

I stripped my crumpled, sweaty tunic, stood naked and shouted for Secundus. He took a clean woollen shirt from the panniers, a fresh linen tunic, leather breeches and leather over-tunic newly greased and smelling of lard. Over this he buckled the heavy corselet and dangling apron of iron strips studded with bronze. All the metal was scoured and oiled till the dull iron shone like silver.

'The Pannonians are our best cavalry,' Agricola said thoughtfully, 'but they've been marching all night. Next best are the Gauls: Indus's or Proculus's Horse.'

I stepped into thick-soled, iron-studded boots which Secundus laced calf-high. He fastened dagger-belt around my hips, slung a baldric over my shoulder and adjusted the sword against my left thigh.

'Make it Indus's Horse,' I said. 'Two patrols of three troops each, one up the North Way and the other towards Colchester. Depth of reconnaissance limited to twenty miles from London. Send me Indus's prefect. I shall give his orders myself. And summon the Camp Prefect.'

I donned a blue woollen neck-scarf, cloak and iron helmet and stepped into the rain clothed and armed exactly like the legionaries I commanded, with the difference that, like all officers above centurion, I carried neither shield nor javelins.

The Prefect of Indus's Horse came and went with orders to dispatch his patrols immediately. From the chief centurion of my staff, who acted as Camp Prefect, I demanded a parade state—and testily interrupted his tedious rigmarole of detailed regimental strengths.

'Add it up, Centurion! How many men are fit for service? How many horses able to carry them?'

The calculation showed that of 2,883 mounted men who had ridden from the frontier, 2,840 had reached London. Over two hundred horse casualties from exhaustion, lameness, colic and sore backs had been abandoned at road-stations and replaced from the Vangiones' cavalry wing. Of the latter, only a sprinkling had come with us. We had fought no battles. This was solely the price of riding two hundred and thirty miles in five days.

I gave the Camp Prefect his orders. 'You will fortify this camp properly today. No more cattle-fences. Draw entrenching tools from the arsenal. Send fatigues to the woods to cut palisade stakes. Dig a ditch and throw up a rampart to regulation measurements. Pave the streets with stones, river-gravel, anything you can find—otherwise the horses will reduce them to muddy quagmires.'

I took a paper from Agricola.

'Here is your authority to the arsenal. Draw rations for men and fodder for horses at marching scales. I want six days' reserves of both kept in camp. When we move from here—I can't tell you when—we won't be able to replenish from road-stations as we did on the Midland Way. Get tents for the men or, if the arsenal hasn't enough, buy hides and tell the saddlers to make them. Order these auxiliaries to clean accoutrements and look like soldiers again. Above all, get the horses fit. Plenty of grain, plenty of fodder—no lack of grass at this season—light exercise and careful treatment of wounds and sprains.'

I ate, standing, some wheat cakes and watered wine that Secundus brought. Then I mounted and with some staff officers and a bodyguard escort rode into London.

8

A wooden bridge over a brook joined the West Way to London's Principal Street. There I met Olussa, riding a mule fatter than himself, and a body of magistrates and councillors. He led us to the river.

On previous visits to London I had barely explored the town, contenting myself with short journeys between palace and basilica. Now it was expedient to examine the place thoroughly.

We rode through narrow streets to the Thames. Timber wharves lined the banks; stevedores loaded goods into ships moored alongside. Even now, in the first flush of dawn, the docks were active as any at Ostia or Marseilles. Warehouses behind the wharves disgorged merchandise—grain in bulbous jars, bundles of hides, lead ingots, bales of woollen cloth. From wicker cages resounded the savage baying of those huge hounds the Britons use for hunting; a column of slaves, chained and manacled, fruits of the campaign in Ordovicia, stumbled miserably up a gangplank. Here before my eyes was the farrago of riches wrung from Britain by Roman power and enterprise, the rewards of war and hardship and death, a cornucopia trembling on the brink of destruction.

Ships swung to anchor in midstream. A timber bridge stalked haughtily on oak-trunk piles across the Thames. A team of slaves hauled ropes and worked capstans to raise the central span and a bireme swam majestically to the sea. Beyond, on the south bank, the road to Richborough scarred the marshy waste like a swordcut.

'This,' said Olussa, embracing his surroundings with a wave of the arm, 'is the heart of London. This is her beginning and her end.'

I nodded assent. Here, certainly, was more energy, activity and obvious prosperity than was ever seen in the stilted streets of Colchester, in Verulam's muddy slums or Silchester's torpid rusticity. If Britain became settled and peaceful under our rule, like Gaul or Spain, this sheltered river-port must become her focus of trade, her highway for the traffic of nations.

'We shall ride the boundaries,' I told Olussa, 'and see what lies beyond.'

His mule bored phlegmatically through an argumentative party of Greek sailors and led us, hooves drumming hollow on the quays, to the confluence with the Thames of that brook we had crossed earlier, where a narrow estuary embayed a flotilla of small craft, fishing-boats, ferries and the like. In the angle of brook and river stood the arsenal.

I inspected forges, workshops, stores and barracks; then went out by a gate facing on the brook. The inner bank climbed to the remains of a rampart cavernously eroded, festooned with weeds, brambles and bushes.

Olussa explained. 'These are the ruins of native fortifications built long before the Conquest when London was only a fishing village. They have not been repaired since the Divine Claudius and his legions crossed the Thames. The stream, once a vallum to the ramparts, is to this day called the Wall Brook.'

We followed the rivulet and crossed the Principal Street. Occasionally I forced my charger up the rampart through tangled vegetation to the crest and looked across the stream. A scattering of thatched huts and wooden shelters, like flotsam rejected by the Thames, showed where London had begun to overspill the confines of Wall Brook. A quarter mile beyond was the firm, rectangular pattern of the auxiliaries' camp and the West Way vanishing in curtains of river mist.

The broken rampart, defeated by decay, petered out in a wilderness of reeds and marshy pools. The streets and buildings of modern London faded in the same discouraged fashion, for here began the marshlands of the north, a waste of slime and sedge and bog. Across it, carried on a high embankment, the North Way flung its haughty length to Lincoln.

We turned right-handed among humble shacks and rutted streets and crossed the Praetorian Way. Farther on we found a colony of newly-built huts, mere hewn-log frames, the bark unplaned, supporting turf roofs. The area was a fetid slum, a cauldron of humanity, livestock and smells.

'Refugees,' Olussa said dryly, 'from Verulam and a hundred farms and settlements for twenty miles and more around London.'

We skirted the encampment, followed by some hostile shouts which bristled my escort's lances. I surveyed the noisy throng thoughtfully.

'Are they giving any trouble?'

'Plenty,' the Greek answered. We can provide only the bare necessities, food and shelter, for which we receive neither payment nor gratitude. Very few are completely destitute. They have brought with them every denarius they possess—and the wineshops do a roaring trade and provide the stimulus for many brawls. Londoners are accustomed to strangers but prefer them to mind their manners. So the Council has enlisted a watch from citizens and freemen which patrols the streets and keeps order.'

'A wise precaution,' I said. 'But these people will not pester you for long. When Boudicca has been destroyed they can return to their homes.'

Olussa glanced at me sideways, opened his mouth and closed it again. His normal garrulity deserted him and, plunged deep in thought, he led in silence through the town's eastern fringes, sparsely inhabited, to the riverbank. The Colchester road divided this stretch and crossed damp, tussocky grasslands towards a distant line of wooded hills. After a brief contemplation of the Thames' shining waters, greenly translucent like fine glass, we returned through mean streets to the centre of the town where stood the basilica and, near by on the Principal Street, the Governor's palace.

This was London. I had inspected a settlement roughly six hundred yards square, confined on two sides by the Thames and an insignificant brook and on the others by marsh and wastelands. Within these limits houses sprawled haphazard, without plan or dignity, save for a few large brick-and-timber dwellings with wooden shingle roofs such as my palace, the basilica, the Procurator's residence and the manors of rich merchants—buildings which only emphasized a squalid vista of wattle-and-daub huts and thatched roofs. Main streets leading to the great strategic roads were tolerably paved; all others were meandering tracks of beaten earth, rutted in dry weather, muddy morasses in wet.

No proper earthworks guarded London; she was undefended and indefensible.

'We taught the Britons to build in stone,' I said, dismounting. 'Why have they not followed our precepts in London, Olussa? This basilica—a mean enough building—is of brick. So is my palace, and that was built by Romans. I have seen only two stone buildings, both temples.'

'Lord Paulinus, the nearest quarries are twenty miles away,' Olussa said. 'Furthermore, you can count on one hand the Romans of any importance who live here. London's citizens are lesser folk: traders, bankers, equestrians like myself.' He smiled. 'We are too busy making money to bother about architecture.'

I regarded him with amusement. 'You can hardly include yourself in the category of boors, Olussa. The fame of your establishment and the skill of your cooks have spread far afield. I shall visit your house, if that will not strain your hospitality too greatly. We have important matters to discuss. Besides, I'm told that your baths are more splendid than mine in Silchester.'

Olussa's bow nearly removed him from his mule.

9

I had intended, at the palace, to do no more than dictate letters and exchange my armour for easier garb; but a crowd seeking audience—

petitioners, lawyers and civil servants—besieged the forecourt. Nothing, it seemed, not even the threat of imminent annihilation, could destroy the British taste for litigation. Irritably I told Agricola to sift the most urgent business from this rabble, and went indoors.

The palace chamberlain's apologies for my reception were profuse. He had reason. The rooms were insufficiently heated for a chilly day; dust lay like a shroud on furniture and hangings. I did not rebuke the man. Rome gives official residences to her Governors and expects them to provide furniture and servants. Naturally I avoided the expense of maintaining a full complement both in London and the capital. The palace in Colchester was a heap of rubble; my servants were dead. Here only a few caretakers remained, and the public slaves the chamberlain had enlisted were unaccustomed to work in private houses.

I changed my clothes, summoned clerks and dictated letters to the Imperial Secretariat in which I told of the rebellion and its course and causes but for secrecy's sake made no mention of the counter-measures I had in hand. Then I wrote to the Prince and discreetly enlarged on certain details, particularly the Procurator's part. I knew full well that Decianus Catus, in his own dispatches, would by innuendo and lies minimize his own catastrophic errors and shift all blame to me.

Later I admitted the callers whom Agricola selected. A deputation of Treasury officials sought military escorts for lead and iron-ore convoys; the reinforcement of Colchester, they said, had denuded London of troops. A centurion from the Arsenal wanted to know whether bullion-trains should go as usual to fortresses. I ordered a complete standstill of convoys of all kinds until further notice; and privately marvelled at the utter ignorance, in London, about the true nature of what was happening in Britain.

Then I interviewed certain spies, ushered in quietly from a back entrance. These were my own private agents, carefully distributed in the arsenal, the Procurator's household and domestic staffs of prominent townsmen such as Alfidius Olussa. They were there to glean information on matters affecting my personal reputation and security and were not, except incidentally, concerned with politics. They told me nothing of importance about London's reaction to the Icenian invasion, but confirmed my suspicions regarding Catus's behaviour. The Procurator, I was told, was abjectly afraid. He seldom left his palace, drank enormously and indulged in abysmal orgies with his particular cronies. Drunk or sober he reviled the Governor. In conversation and correspondence he proclaimed me as the author of all Britain's troubles.

I listened grimly, re-wrote my letter to Nero in the light of this information; and left the palace for Olussa's house. My lictors had burned with Colchester, so bodyguard troopers formed an escort through crowded streets. Swarthy sailors from Syracuse chaffered noisily with Macedonian shopkeepers; hook-nosed Phoenicians, stately in trailing robes, stalked the roadway like ships in full sail; Greeks argued with Gauls; black Numidians bought wine from taverners of Egypt and Liguria. Arrogant legionaries on furlough elbowed passage to baths or brothel; Bithynian hucksters cheated gaping recruits from Narbonne. And through them moved the native Britons, tall, golden men of the Cantii and Regni and Atrebates, like a homespun texture underlying rich embroidery.

10

Olussa's mansion stood in extensive gardens within arrow-flight of London Bridge and boasted one of the few tiled roofs in the town. After a cup of wine the Greek conducted me to the baths, a long, low building flanking the forecourt. In the dressing-room the bath superintendent made obeisance; slaves removed our clothing and conducted us to the warm room, gently heated by murmuring flues. I lay on a couch and sipped mellow Samian from a silver goblet richly engraved.

'Tell me, my good friend,' I said comfortably, 'are your townspeople so favoured by the Gods that, as I have seen today, they can behave as though they were safe in Rome and need fear nothing from a rampant queen avid for blood and plunder?'

Olussa set down his wine cup carefully. 'Some days ago, Lord Paulinus, we heard of Colchester's sacking. Colchester is only fifty miles away. Our people were terrified.'

'Not for long, it seems.'

'No.' Olussa picked his words, his brow furrowed. 'At first the town was panic-struck. A mob filled streets and forum, calling on Rome, the Procurator, the magistrates for salvation. People ran to the docks, jumped aboard moored ships. A pinnace capsized and sank. Shipmasters cut cables and drifted downstream with the ebb. The arsenal shut its gates and manned the palisades. London was in uproar.'

Slaves lifted our couches to the hot room. Heat slapped my body like a blow. Steam blurred outlines; the attendants were misty shadows in a watery inferno. Sweat started from my skin in a million tiny fountains.

'I saw the same thing in Caeserea during the Mauretanian War,' I said. 'An ugly situation. What happened?'

'The Procurator took control. He came to the forum and spoke from the tribunal. He said Colchester had been surprised by a small war-band which, content with the capital's rich booty, had neither inclination nor resources to penetrate farther into the province. He said that messages had gone to you and to Petillius Cerialis. Within a short time the legions would sweep through Icenia and kill Britons in herds.'

A massive German slave turned me gently on my back and scraped my body with a horn strigil. My two personal guards, attending me from room to room, moved closer and watched his hands suspiciously. Beads of moisture coursed down their cheeks.

'You believed him?'

Olussa flicked a cascade of sweat from his chest. 'The Procurator was most convincing. He's an accomplished orator. He allayed the panic but the town was restless. Then refugees started pouring from the countryside with alarming tales, mostly false, and certain prudent merchants quietly took ship and sailed downriver to the sea.'

'At this season?' I asked.

'The storms of spring are abating. Ships can creep coast-wise to Richborough or Dover and await a calm day to sail to Gaul. Many merchantmen have already gone. You thought the quays crowded today: I assure you that traffic on London river is usually twice as much.'

The slave had finished. I rose and stepped carefully into the bath and lowered my body inch by inch into the fierce heat of the water. A few moments were enough. My couch was lifted to the oil room and the same German, cupping scented oil in his palms, massaged back and thighs, pummelling and rubbing with smooth, powerful strokes.

'I think,' Olussa continued, 'the ordinary riff-raff of the town are sceptical but resigned. Where can they go to save themselves? But many merchants and business men had trading connections with Iceni and Trinovantes and have a fair notion of Boudicca's power. These people are quietly packing and going by ship or by road to Richborough and Pevensey of the Regni.'

I lay face down, eyes shut, while the slave kneaded my spine.

'And you, Olussa?'

The Greek sighed. 'I am old and fat, Lord Paulinus, and my running days are over. I have lived in London for a long time and my home and all I love is here. I offer sacrifices to the Gods and make my vows and hope for the best.'

'Have you, as a magistrate, never thought of organizing some sort of defence, a garrison?'

Olussa cuffed a slave who bore too heavily on his buttocks. 'Who of us could build ramparts or handle weapons? A few soldiers, yes, from arsenal, transit-camps, palace guards. The rest of us are merchants and traders, soft-bellied, prosperous.' Olussa patted his own prominent stomach and laughed. 'No, Lord Paulinus. Colchester had her veterans; Silchester has Britons of fighting stock; London has only money. And money will not hold Boudicca; rather will it attract her hither as a lodestone draws iron.'

The German finished his work, bowed and retired. Five lovely Parthian slave-girls in filmy gauze tunics took his place. They trimmed, pared and polished my nails and plucked hairs with silver tweezers from armpits, belly and crotch so skilfully that I felt hardly a pang.

For the first time for many days I was relaxed and at ease. I scanned idly the elaborate floor mosaic that represented Ganymede and his green-veiled nymphs dancing in a setting of leaves and flowers. A coloured frieze decorating the walls depicted the romance of Dido and Aeneas. Every compartment of this bath-house was richly embellished in a manner rivalling the most opulent private baths in Rome. Olussa must have been immensely rich.

'How has London reacted to the arrival of Roman troops?' I murmured, half asleep. The breasts of the girl bending over my navel, tweezers poised, trembled enticingly beneath her transparent tunic.

'Confidence has returned, Lord Paulinus,' Olussa asserted. 'You are here and we know the legions cannot be far away.' He hesitated, plucking his lip. 'Have you had news of IX Hispana?'

'No.' I opened my eyes. 'Why?'

He would not meet my look. 'No particular reason, Lord Paulinus. One hears stupid and unaccountable rumours circulating in taverns and public baths at times like these. It is good to know they are unfounded.'

The Parthian slaves seemed less attractive. I waved them aside, rose and stalked to the cold room. The air struck like a wind from the north; the water in the plunge bath was blue and icy. I took a deep breath and slid under.

Slaves rubbed me down with shawls of softest Canusian wool. Then, muffled in a wrap of scarlet frieze, I was carried along a passage to the dressing-room and helped into my clothes, freshly pressed and warmed. Olussa at my side chattered inanities, unconscious of my abstraction. The bath superintendent approached, bowed and begged permission to speak.

'What is it?' I snapped.

'The tribune Julius Agricola awaits your pleasure, most noble Paulinus.'

I adjusted my cloak and went outside. Agricola's face was white and drawn. I led him beyond earshot.

'Yes?'

'An escort from the Pannonian patrol at Verulam has brought a soldier of IX Legion, one Gaius Saufeius.' He gulped, very near tears.

'Go on,' I said gently.

'Cerialis has been defeated, his army massacred. Four thousand dead—'

I gripped his shoulder. 'Control yourself, Gnaeus. Lower your voice. Have you spoken to this man?'

'Yes.'

'When was the battle?'

'Three days ago.'

'Where?'

'The North Way near Godmanchester.'

On the blank wall protecting Olussa's gardens I projected a mental image of the map of Britain, marked road-stations and counted distances. Under sixty miles from London. Three days' march for Boudicca. Within hours she could be at our throats. Yet we had no contact reports from Verulam nor from the patrol of Indus's Horse dispatched that morning. Why?

'Did this soldier—his name is Saufeius?—did he see where the Britons went after breaking Hispana?'

'They chased the remnants of Cerialis's cavalry northwards,' Agricola said heavily.

'All the rebels? Not just a detached force?'

'No. The entire army, horse, chariots and foot was heading for Lincoln. A general pursuit.'

So that was it. Boudicca was either unaware of the necessity, from her point of view, of a quick switch of her forces southwards, or had failed to control her men after their victory. Probably the latter, for I was beginning to respect her generalship. It might be a very expensive mistake: in three days my legions would be united in London and the war was virtually won.

We could only wait and hope. Nothing I could do would help Cerialis now.

'Listen carefully, Gnaeus. Saufeius must not be allowed to spread a tale of disaster through camp and town. Confine him in the palace and put Mannius Secundus in charge. Have a clerk write down his story in detail and let the transcript be ready for my perusal tonight.'

I paced the gravelled forecourt.

'Saufeius has probably chattered to his Pannonian escort. See they have no contact with anyone and return them to Verulam at dawn. And you yourself must keep a cheerful face. Smile, Gnaeus! We are safe, by my reckoning, for two more days at least.'

I touched his cheek affectionately and returned to the worried group whispering near the bath-house.

'Is dinner ready, Olussa? I have an appetite like a starving wolf!'

11

Olussa was only too pleased. Agricola's demeanour and the sudden sense of crisis must have convinced him that his dinner was wasted. Under his anxious eye—for Greeks, with all their cynicism and civilization, are intensely superstitious—I carefully crossed the threshold right foot first, and paused to admire a black and white magpie hanging in a golden cage from the lintel. Olussa's palace—I can call it no less— was built in a style and design that accorded more with the sun-baked shores of an Ionian island and offered few concessions to the peculiarities of Britain's climate.

Frescoes radiant with colour, depicting scenes from the Iliad and Odyssey, decorated the atrium. On one wall a gilded shrine displayed household Gods subtly wrought in silver and porphyry; on another a golden casket contained relics of Olussa's ancestors. Statues of Venus, Minerva and sundry deities lined the walls like a ceremonial guard. My host was in the forefront of an artistic fashion that disliked painted statues and preferred a newly-invented process of artificial colouring which impregnated the stone.

The guests, limited at my request to the duty tribune and the prefect of Proculus's Horse, both young men of good family, entered the banquet hall, a spacious room floored in red and white chequered marble surrounding an elaborate central mosaic. Rich hangings over doors and windows excluded the daylight; a hundred lamps in crystal chandeliers threw a brilliant radiance from the frescoed ceiling and sparked reflections glittering like diamond-dust from the floor, an effect produced by the sprinkling of ground mica and vermilion coloured sawdust. Soldiers of the guard disposed themselves around the walls, standing rigid beside the statues. The austere sheen of leather and iron contrasted strangely with a background of gaudy opulence.

I sank gratefully on a couch draped in purple silk, bolstered with cushions embroidered in fantastic designs. Alexandrian slave boys poured scented water over my hands. Musicians played a languid tune, a gentle melody set for lyres and pipes.

This was the first civilized meal I had enjoyed for several months and was the last for some time to come. It has stuck in my memory and I may, perhaps, be excused for savouring the details. Oysters and mushrooms, dormice stuffed with minced pork and flavoured with honey and poppyseed, black and white olives and pomegranate seeds, all served on silver dishes, provided an appetizer. A long-haired Ganymede—I felicitated my host on a mutual vice—poured a light honey-sweetened wine called hypocras.

Olussa's conversation was urbane and entertaining. He told ribald stories of love and peculation in London which tactfully excluded personalities of senatorial standing. He recounted startling scandals of current Roman life whose barbs stung every rank from the Prince downwards. No doubt I should have disapproved; yet the Greek was amusing, and I had an inkling that this was the last time I would laugh for many days.

'Poppaea,' Olussa said, 'holds the Prince securely in her hand.' He juggled with an olive in his palm. 'With the other she weaves a net of intrigue and calumny about poor Octavia. Gamblers in the clubs are wagering on the month of her elimination, with side-bets on the method—divorce, exile, drowning or poison.'

I stirred uneasily. This was strong meat. Not for a moment did I doubt the truth of Olussa's words: he had channels of information denied to me. My letters came by Imperial Post; my private correspondents wrote warily, barely hinting at the appalling wave of crime and corruption which had enveloped Nero's court since his mother's murder. Tribunes new-posted to Britain brought lurid tales whose broidery of scandal and rumour was difficult to unravel from the texture of fact.

Olussa gossiped on serenely. 'Seneca, they say, is losing his grip. The Prince avoids him and the unfortunate fellow is seldom granted an audience. He's starting on the slippery slope to perdition. With him goes the Praetorian Prefect. Burrus, you know, wouldn't allow the guard to liquidate Agrippina; Nero has never forgiven him. The State Council meets in an atmosphere cold as a Gallic winter, and only old Claudius of Smyrna, warmed by his financial juggling, remains placidly unaffected.'

I savoured a mushroom thoughtfully. So Burrus was losing power. A pity. He was one of my few staunch friends at court, and I would need every bit of influence to float my reputation above the tide of spite and criticism which must follow this Icenian rebellion. How far, I wondered, was he gone in disfavour? How long would he last? Was a successor already nudging the Prince's elbow? My interests demanded an answer to these queries, an answer to be sought through a medium other than the Imperial Post, whose censors scanned every letter and unravelled every cipher. Perhaps I could use Olussa's communications, that curious skein of traders, pedlars, sailors and thieves which flung news from Bithynia to Britain faster than the speediest couriers.

The musicians played a fanfare to the entry of the first course. Vast dishes, rare Corinthian plate, almost covered the elegant citruswood table reared on ivory pillars. I sniffed the exquisite aroma of fine food deliciously cooked: stuffed capons, roast hare (Olussa cared nothing for native prejudice), sows' papa, grilled fieldfares, grilled kidneys stuffed with pepper and coriander and fennel seed, garnished with beetroot and mustard dressing. The wine, poured from glass jars into crystal goblets, was Alban flavoured with a rare and extremely expensive herb grown only on the North African coast near Cyrene.

Being a lean man with a limited stomach I could not keep steward and carver occupied overlong. Olussa's requirements, despite his proportions, were also surprisingly moderate, so that much of the course went uneaten. His kitchen slaves, no doubt, were duly gratified. While servants washed our hands he quite casually let slide a remark stridently out of tone with our amicable conversation.

'How fares II Legion, Lord Paulinus? The Silures have been very quiet lately, one is told. Have you had word from the Prefect Paenius Posthumus?'

I regarded him speculatively. Augusta, at that moment, should be at Silchester, her hobnails worn by two days' quick pace marching; but I hoped that the world at large and civilian Britain in particular thought the legion was still in Gloucester fortress. How much did this cunning Greek know?

'As you have probably heard,' I replied blandly, 'we ensured that the Silures would be held in check for the duration of my campaign in Ordovicia. That truce still endures. Posthumus, I believe, is well and the frontier unusually peaceful. Why do you ask?'

Olussa's eyes met mine for a moment; then slid away. He waved a hand airily. 'No particular reason. II Legion has been out of the news lately; one is glad to hear tidings of our gallant troops. Have you heard, Lord Paulinus, Acte's retort to Seneca when…'

His anecdote was impertinently venomous and extremely funny, and I heard barely a word. Why, I pondered, in that brief moment when our glances met, had Olussa's eyes been full of compassion? Why should an equestrian merchant pity the Governor of Britain?

I recovered equanimity in contemplation of the second course: pastry shaped like thrushes and stuffed with raisins and walnuts; cream cheese flavoured with wine jelly; scalloped liver, pickled olives, figs and cakes. After a visit to the vomitorium I did fair justice to the delicacies and drained yet another cup of Alban. Then, warned by a shaft of westering sunlight glimpsed through the curtains, I rose and offered thanks for a banquet unique, in my experience, in Britain and seldom matched in Rome.

Olussa took his leave at the porter's lodge, where a huge brazen image of a chained dog excited my horse and made the process of mounting extraordinarily difficult. Preceded and followed by the guard I started at a sedate walk for the palace. Knowing that from their comrades in the banquet-room they had tallied to the ultimate cup my consumption of wine I looked sharply for amusement in their faces and found only respect. Soldiers appreciate a cask-proof head.

12

I intended to visit the camp before sundown. Secundus was absent from my dressing-chamber; the slave who armed me owned none of his deftness with buckle and lacing and changed my benevolent mood to black irritation. Armed at last, helmeted and cloaked, I strode down the corridors to the forecourt, passed the uncurtained door of a clerks' office and glanced within. Mannius Secundus lounged against a pillar. Seated cross-legged on the floor was a legionary, a small, dark, battered man with close-cropped head and alert, intelligent eyes. He talked volubly in a voice roughened by fatigue and emphasized his words by quick gestures like a monkey. A clerk scribbled shorthand rapidly; two others deciphered and transcribed, on fragile scrolls of Egyptian paper, a fragment of Britain's history.

The soldiers jumped to attention; the clerks rose and bowed. The little man answered my interrogative look.

'Gaius Saufeius, legionary, IX Legion, 3rd cohort, century of Babudius Severus, Legate,' he gabbled, staring fixedly head-height in true legionary style.

I examined him searchingly. His corselet was torn and daubed with mud. An armour-strip was missing from the shoulder whence a sword-less scabbard swung. A raw scar seamed his face from temple to chin. A dirty bandage swathed his forearm.

Saufeius had force-marched from Lincoln, fought a losing battle and escaped through enemy-occupied territory and terrifying dangers to safety. He was still a soldier, taut and disciplined, ready if necessary to march from the room and fight another battle on the doorstep. My legionaries were tough.

I said, 'The rebel strength and movements after the fight are important. Omit nothing. Secundus, see that Saufeius has everything for his comfort.'

I rode to the fort. The Camp Prefect had wasted neither time nor labour. The morning's vulnerable rectangle was now protected by ditch, bank and palisade. The scarp of the fosse was steep and well revetted, the counterscarp sharply angled, palisades stoutly embedded, sentry towers built and manned. The raw wood of gates and gate houses gleamed lividly. Tents newly issued from the arsenal stood in rows aligned exactly to a hands breadth; the pale, unused hides glowed in the sunlight like sheets of beaten gold. The streets were not yet gravelled, but at the central intersection thatch-roofed timber buildings marked the commandant's house and headquarter offices. Seldom have cavalrymen worked so hard for so long.

I spent two hours in the fort, inspecting, commenting, amending. Then, after designating the senior prefect as commandant, I left early in the first watch and returned to London. My head ached. Olussa's wine was sour on my tongue, his food a sodden sponge in my stomach. Secundus, once more in attendance, stripped my armour smartly, wrapped a soft robe about my shoulders and, after a probing glance at bloodshot eyes and pallid complexion, tactfully provided barley-water and biscuits. Agricola came for orders. I told him not to disturb me unless messages arrived from cavalry patrols or legions. Before leaving he deposited a roll of papyrus at my elbow.

This, a shorthand-writer's transcription of Gaius Saufeius's narrative, did not make cheerful reading. He had been on furlough in Colchester when Decianus Catus returned from his raid (I can call it nothing else) into Icenia, and had witnessed the stress and dismay of the period when rumours of Boudicca's impending invasion flowed into the colony. Then, because he had once been trained for the legionary cavalry, and rode well, he found himself, one bleak and rainy morning, galloping up the North Way to Lincoln with an appeal for help written on the lining of his scabbard. Changing horses at road-stations he made, at first, rapid progress. Beyond Water Newton he encountered roving Britons, armed and savage, and fled from the Way into forests, where he lost himself. This and other hazards so delayed him that he took four days to cover the hundred and fifty miles to the fortress, where he found a vexillation already mustering. Cerialis had received my orders from Anglesey.

Saufeius delivered his message. As a reward his centurion reprimanded him for dilatory riding, listened to no excuses and told him to join his century, already detailed and parading for the march to relieve Colchester. The wretched man had barely time to clean his accoutrements and swallow a meal before he was once more on the North Way.

Cerialis himself commanded the column, which consisted of three legionary cohorts, Petra's Horse and the 1st Cugerni: nearly four thousand men. The legate's plan, if correctly reported by Saufeius, was simple. Realizing that his infantry could not reach Colchester in much less than five days, he sent his cavalry on independently, riding hard, with the purpose of disturbing the besiegers—if the colony were invested—and drawing a substantial number towards his infantry marching in support. Once the Britons realized that legionaries were approaching, Cerialis considered that Boudicca would be compelled to raise the siege and turn to deal with the new threat.

His task, then, was to act as a bait, to attract the Queen from Colchester as a gladiator entices a lion from a wounded comrade.

He did not contemplate a major engagement. Once the enemy were committed against their new objective, himself, the vexillation would retreat northwards, luring the British forces to Lincoln and a leaguer of whose outcome he was confident.

A great deal, unfortunately, went wrong.

Petra's Horse, riding twenty miles ahead of the main column, progressed well enough, and on the second day reached Godmanchester. Here they left the North Way and turned east on the direct road to Colchester through Cambridge. Cerialis, however, arriving at Godmanchester next day, had to halt awhile and think very hard indeed, for the Lingones' road-station reported that the Catuvellauni had risen in support of their neighbours. The vexillation was then only a score of miles from the great belt of Catuvellaun territory which banded London on the north. An enemy thrust from this base, directed up the highway to Godmanchester, could sever his line of retreat.

The legate chewed the problem, decided the threat was too indefinite and continued his march, turning east in the wake of Petra's Horse. As a precaution, he told the Lingones to reconnoitre southwards.

Cerialis could not know how serious was his error. The temple had fallen the day before. His presence had indeed been reported to Boudicca. While his footsore legionaries tramped towards Cambridge the Queen was making frantic efforts to pull her loot-crazed army from ruined Colchester. Her successful execution of this feat was the most impressive exhibition of Boudicca's power and personality during the whole campaign.

That night Cerialis camped at Cambridge, a settlement already sacked by the fringe riders of Icenia's invasion. Soon after midnight a shattered and demoralized Petra's Horse reeled into the fort. They had met, head-on, a triumphant British host advancing from Colchester, and were badly mauled. Shortly afterwards gallopers arrived from Godmanchester, to say that Lingones' patrols had found a second army, Catuvellaun, sweeping up the North Way.

Cerialis knew his plans were wrecked and the campaign lost. His column broke camp in the dark and forced-marched, without halts, along the way it had come.

They made Godmanchester by dawn, to find the station still intact. They did not breathe easily for long. British horsemen from east and south showed on the roads. The hunt was up.

Lincoln, eighty miles away, was as inaccessible as the moon. Cerialis knew he would have to stand and fight. Ordering his infantry to make for a small hillock three miles away, the only tactical eminence in that flat land, he turned with Petra's Horse to delay his enemies.

The cavalry mêlée which followed annihilated that already badly battered regiment. The legate, wounded in the face, escaped with a remnant and joined his legionaries waiting on the hill.

Saufeius's account of the battle was vivid but disjointed: a soldier fighting for his life in the front rank has little time to assess operations as a whole. The outcome was inexorable. The combined armies, Icenian and Catuvellaun, swamped the little band on their diminutive mound. The cohorts fought, fell man by man, and died.

The Gods guarded Saufeius that day. Although wounded, he managed to seize a riderless horse, gallop from the slaughter and enter a forest, whence he watched the victorious Britons storming up the road towards Lincoln. When night fell he rode south, keeping direction by the stars, and hid during daylight. On the third day he found Verulam and the Pannonians.

Although Saufeius did not know it at the time, Cerialis again escaped. His guard surrounded him, hurt a second time and dazed, and hustled him from the battlefield. The legate was barely conscious during that appalling eighty-mile ride to Lincoln. A pause for rest, or to change horses at Water Newton and Ancaster, brought the rebels in sight. The last eighteen miles was a race. Men on foundered horses dropped behind and died while the better-mounted, thinking only of survival, galloped ahead regardless of their companions.

Swaying like a drunkard in his saddle, Cerialis gained the fortress only a few hundred paces in front of the pursuing lances. The gates slammed in the faces of Boudicca's frustrated horsemen, who swirled around the ramparts shrieking like madmen. From the stockades, secure in the knowledge that Lincoln was impregnable by any tribal army, three thousand legionaries regarded them with virulent hatred.

13

'We must steel our hearts, bury our dead, and let the day's
tears suffice them.'

THE ILIAD

1

Gaius Saufeius's narrative left me militarily no wiser. His estimates of the rebels' strength were uselessly vague, his description of the pursuit towards Lincoln quite unreliable. I could not believe the entire native army had followed a handful of demoralized cavalry all the way to Lincoln. Boudicca's main forces, greatly reinforced by Catuvellaun partisans, must have remained near Godmanchester and ravaged the countryside at will. How long would it take the Queen to reimpose her authority, collect her troops and prepare to advance on London? Boudicca had to regather a host diversely drawn from a thousand semi-independent war-bands each under a petty chief, himself intolerant of authority, plus more recent accretions that owed her no allegiance whatsoever. Under the spur of Cerialis's vexillation she had, after Colchester's sack, performed a miracle. Could she do it again?

Hispana's cohorts had died four days since. Where were the Iceni now?

Useless to speculate. I had eight troops of cavalry screening Verulam and London: they would tell me the worst when it happened. I extinguished the candles and went to sleep.

Awakening brought anticipations and recollections in a flood. This was the day when Paenius Posthumus would lead II Augusta into London. Because Augusta, like XIV Legion, was marching faster than carts could travel their limited reserves of food, carried on pack-animals, would need replenishment when they arrived. It would be well, I pondered, also to stack the corn needed by Valens's force, due in two days' time.

Government granaries in the town could hardly be expected to meet all these demands. A levy on private supplies might be necessary— an unpopular measure that would bear discussion with Olussa before promulgation.

The townspeople, aware that two legions were marching hotfoot to protect them, were relapsing rapidly into the comfortable routine of everyday life which events at Colchester had ruffled so sharply. They expected business to continue as usual, the law-courts to function undisturbed and the current of bureaucratic administration to flow unchecked. They would not welcome the short-cut, dictatorial methods which I foresaw to be inevitable. The exercise of my civil functions through normal channels was, in any case, going to be difficult. The London secretariat housed a scattering of low-grade clerks and unimportant records, all that was necessary to keep contact between the Procurator's offices and the Government at Colchester. The skilled and experienced staff of lawyers and accountants and administrators which accompanied my visits to London and other centres was gone, consumed in Boudicca's pyre. Gone, too, were the archives: that vast complexity of parchment and papyrus that embodied the decrees, rescripts and rulings which had directed affairs in Britain for over seventeen years.

The palace chamberlain had striven to regulate his domain since my unheralded arrival. A regiment of slaves that he had hired from the municipality or borrowed from private households cleaned the rooms, stoked furnaces, staffed kitchen, bath-house and bedchamber. Mannius Secundus, ousted by Gallic slaves from his brief tenure as personal attendant, glowered in the background and hissed unnecessary instructions while I dressed. The dawn was still grey when I went to the audience chamber through corridors which echoed like subterranean caverns, for the army of secretaries and advisers and scribes who usually people the palace were now pale wanderers in the Shades.

The morning audience, to my surprise, produced few civilian petitioners: perhaps Agricola's summary handling the previous day had discouraged all but the most persistent. I listened with a growing sense of unreality: a landowner's tale of robbery and assault by a lead-convoy escort; a merchant's protest against an order demolishing his warehouse to increase government wharfage space; a freedman pleading free status for a son born before his emancipation. What had these trivialities to do with Boudicca's whirlwind of terror and fire and death?

I dealt shortly with these and other matters, studied a list of cases awaiting my adjudication in the basilica and scribbled an order summoning litigants, lawyers and witnesses for the morrow. I seemed to have arrived at a hiatus in time, a lull when opposing forces gathered like thunderheads on a looming horizon and the world waited mutely for cataclysm. The pause must be occupied somehow: the processes of law were less tedious than fruitless cogitation in the sounding corridors of my empty palace.

Messengers came from the Pannonians at Verulam, from Indus's Horse on the North Way. The reports were negative. Indus's patrols, contrary to orders, had penetrated to Braughing and Chelmsford: at both places the road-stations were burnt and the settlements obliterated. But of Britons, hostile or otherwise, they had seen no trace save corpses. The countryside north of London was a plagueland of death and desertion.

Around noon a detachment of Indus's Horse brought to the palace a pair of ragged, emaciated creatures whom they had found on the Colchester road. They were the first of only seven survivors of the Colchester massacre to regain contact with civilization. I questioned the men briefly, ascertained they had no worthwhile information bearing on our present difficulties and instructed clerks to transcribe their statements. On this testimony is based nearly the whole of our information of the siege and sack which I have related earlier.

The hours crawled turgidly beyond midday. I rode to the cavalry camp, taking Agricola and Aurelius Bassus and a small escort. Bassus, after thirty hours' rest in London, was again his strong and vigorous self. Often during the long ride across Britain I expected him to drop senseless from the saddle. Day by day he had become more grey-faced and silent; at night he fell into a restless sleep and muttered and twisted in the torments of nightmare. A lust for vengeance sustained him; a taut determination underlay his grim, unsmiling demeanour.

Bassus had become a man of like mind to my own.

I spoke with commanders, decided some minor points of routine and departed. We walked our horses to the Way and regarded with quickening interest a trio of horsemen approaching rapidly from the west. Legionary helmets and shields bearing the capricorn—these were the outriders from II Legion whom I was expecting.

A tribune and two troopers pulled up and saluted. The tribune delved into his corselet and produced a limp roll of papyrus, tied and sealed.

'For the hand of the Governor, Suetonius Paulinus,' he said.

I broke the seal and read.

'Paenius Posthumus, Prefect of the Camp, II Legion Augusta, to G. Suetonius Paulinus, Governor of Britain.

'Greetings.

'I obeyed your orders and, on the 14th May, left Gloucester with II Legion Augusta and the 2nd Pannonian Cohort. Today, the 16th, we reached Silchester. Magistrates and decurions of the council say that the rebels have destroyed Colchester, have annihilated Legion IX Hispana near Lincoln, and are now besieging London.

'I therefore assume that the conditions prevailing when you sent your order no longer exist and that to advance farther will bring my force, totally unsupported, face to face with a greatly superior enemy and certain defeat.

'I have halted the legion. As Silchester lacks both defences and adequate supplies for my men and is also exposed to enemy interference I shall, at first light tomorrow, withdraw to Gloucester.

'I await your commands.'

2

The heavens careered crazily into a darkness shot with meteors and fiery whorls. The world reeled in a giddy vortex. Blood pounded in my ears and the bitter taste of vomit soured my tongue.

Reason clawed slowly upwards from the abyss. I was conscious again of sun and earth and sky and the tribune's frightened eyes and Agricola's curious glance and a centurion's impassive boredom.

Rage attacked me like a living enemy. I bowed my head and fought for sanity.

I stared unbelievingly at the crumpled paper in my hand. Sweat had smeared the ink. A fragment of dried river-reed—such an insignificant agent of catastrophe!

A biting-fly settled on my horse's neck. He shook his head irritably; yellow spume flecked my cloak. Just froth, I thought, like your careful plans, Paulinus, just so much froth.

Half your army has run away, Paulinus. What do you do now?

Gaius Suetonius Paulinus, you are the general. Think! You are Governor for the Prince of Rome in Britain. Think!

Sharp and blank, like memorials etched deep in sculptured marble, question and answer projected themselves on a livid mental screen that obliterated the sunlit landscape.

How many men did you hope to lead against Boudicca?

Eighteen thousand.

Without Augusta, how many are left?

Eleven thousand. Only six thousand legionaries.

Will you fight?

Unthinkable. The rebels probably number eighty or ninety thousand men.

So?

I want time. Time to break away and regroup, time to bring Augusta back to battle.

Here? In London?

No. Impossible. Boudicca is too close.

Then where?

I must withdraw to the west, to meet Valens and retrieve Posthumus.

You will abandon London?

Yes.

And all eastern Britain?

Yes.

And for two agonizing hours afterwards, while I wrestled, like Laocoön, in the coils of a crisis far more deadly and destructive than his fearful serpents, the catechism revolved and rested on that hideous affirmative.

Colchester has burned. Must London die, and Verulam?

Yes.

Enough, Paulinus. You have decided.

'Agricola,' I commanded, 'summon the prefects of horse, centurion of the arsenal and the magistrate Alfidius Olussa.'

I pressed my hands hard upon the table, and their trembling gradually ceased.

3

'I have resolved upon a course of action which is certainly ruthless, and may seem craven. Your judgement, or the verdict of history, is immaterial, because I have no other choice—and you, because the Prince has vested his authority in me, must obey when I command.

'So I have called you together to dispel your doubts and to harden your hearts. In what we must do we cannot allow pity or mercy to temper our resolution. By inclination we are neither callous nor faithless, but the extremities of dire necessity compel us upon courses which may seem to brand us cowards.'

Through shutterless windows an afternoon sun flung golden bars across the gravelled floor and slanted on walls of rough-hewn logs. Staff tribunes, prefects, senior centurions sat on wooden stools or stood, silently attentive, watching my face and throwing speculative glances at the map of Britain pinned to a wall. Olussa, chin on hand, hunched his rotund figure on a bench like some squat oriental god.

I paced slowly in front of the map, four paces forward, four paces back.

'I had hoped, two days from now, to assemble eighteen thousand soldiers in London. It was then my intention to advance swiftly northwards to meet the rebels before they could concentrate the forces they have scattered in pursuit of Cerialis's cavalry, to strike them while they were still looting every settlement between Colchester and Lincoln.'

I pointed at the tribune of Augusta, who stared haggard-eyed at the floor.

'That man has brought the word that killed my hopes. The Prefect Paenius Posthumus, terrified by a flood of rumours, lies and half-truths poured into his ears by rebel sympathizers, has seen fit to disobey orders. Legion II Augusta, due in London tonight, is actually forty miles beyond Silchester and retreating farther with every word I speak.'

Olussa's eyes met mine. Again I read that curious gleam of compassion. Understanding dawned in a blaze.

'You knew this?' I snapped.

He shook his head slowly. 'I could not be certain,' he answered heavily. 'Garbled and unreliable rumours travelled the trade-routes from Cirencester. They say Posthumus sought every excuse to stay in Gloucester. He was easily persuaded by our enemies in Silchester.'

My glance sought the tribune. He nodded sadly. I felt again the welling sickness of rage and shook my head to clear the deadly humming in my brain.

'To continue. The Legate Vettius Valens with seven thousand men is two marches distant on the Midland Way. In and around London we have three thousand cavalry.'

I gestured to the map.

'To defend London we must march north: the town itself is indefensible. Are you willing to face Boudicca with only one legion?'

A long silence. Faces incrutable, eyes seeking the floor, the walls, the reed-thatched ceiling.

Aurelius Bassus spoke. 'We go where you lead us, Legate.'

I rapped the table sharply.

'I refuse to lead you to slaughter. So we give London to the rebels.'

My words dropped like stones into black water, and men flinched in shock involuntarily so that a ripple of movement stirred the room from wall to wall.

'We have no alternative,' I said softly into the silence. 'This decision you must accept. In this sacrifice are embedded the seeds of victory.'

'We abandon London,' Bassus said abruptly. 'And then what?'

'Let us consider the choices. We could let Valens join us here and then march to Richborough, strengthen the fortifications and undergo a siege until reinforcements arrive from Gaul. Meanwhile the rebels will have wasted the whole Province.'

'Out of the question,' Bassus grunted.

Olussa raised a stricken face. 'You could doubtless evacuate your force by sea, Lord Paulinus. There is no lack of shipping at Richborough.'

'I have no intention of abandoning the Province,' I said coldly. 'The army of Britain prevails or dies in Britain.'

Heads lifted sharply; the attentive faces were taut with new expectancy and a kind of fearful relief.

'On the other hand we could return along the Midland Way to meet Valens. With what advantage? To be pursued by the rebels and brought to battle somewhere in the forests? Or, if we outmarch the enemy, to lock ourselves in Wroxeter and surrender the Province to barbarians?'

'Valens is marching light,' Agricola said. 'He intends to replenish his supplies in London. I doubt he carries sufficient corn in his pack train for a six-day retreat to Wroxeter.'

'A decisive argument: one that compels us to the only possible course that remains. My object is to unite my legions. But where? The place must be quickly accessible for XIV Legion, now nearing Magiovinium; for II Legion, which I hope to stop at Cirencester; for ourselves in London. It must be beyond immediate reach of the enemy and in a region where we can get supplies.'

I pricked the map with my dagger.

'Here is Silchester. Fifty miles from London, fifty from Cirencester, fifty from Dunstable.'

'Dunstable?' queried the prefect of Tungrians.

'Valens will reach Dunstable before noon tomorrow. At Dunstable a native track, the Icknield Way, crosses the Midland Way and brings him within ten miles of Silchester. Rough marching, but passable. I shall send a messenger to divert him.'

The dagger sheathed with a click.

'Nothing else is possible,' I said bitterly. 'Within three or four days the army can be regrouped at Silchester and supplied from her granaries. As for the rebels, we know they are not yet within twenty miles of London. They are unlikely to worry us at Silchester three days hence.'

I beckoned Agricola.

'Your tablets, tribune. Let us translate our plans into action.'

4

'The first part concerns you, Olussa.'

The Greek, hunched on his bench, brow on fist like a man dozing or drunk, slowly raised his head.

'You will immediately summon your decurions to the basilica. Tell them the facts. Conceal nothing: stark truth will do less harm than wayward rumours. London will be evacuated. All civilians will assemble beside the West Way, beyond Wall Brook, by noon tomorrow. This convoy, escorted by a cavalry regiment, will march for Silchester.'

Olussa regarded me with lack-lustre eyes. 'What of those who refuse to go?'

I made an impatient gesture. 'Presumably, after your council, you will address the populace in the forum. Death is the only alternative to flight. Leave no doubt on that.'

Olussa slapped hands to knees and rose, a stumpy yet oddly majestic figure.

'Lord Paulinus, I know the people of London. Many will leave, quickly and willingly: the merchants from Gaul, the businessmen who represent trading companies in Spain, Italy and Greece, the bankers from Rome and Alexandria, and others to whom London is no more than a shop, a booth where they sell their wares. And all those refugees who have fled to London for safety—they, spewed forth again, will run in desperation to any available shelter.'

The room was very quiet. An Asturian watering-detail passed the windows. Hooves scraped on gravel; a gabble of Spanish-accented Latin rang in the silence like bells.

'But what of those Romans, old men now, who came with the Conquest and settled here, who will lose all that makes their lives, who may account life itself of little value? What of the Britons in London who supported us from the beginning, who have trusted us for nearly two decades? They see the army going, their shield withdrawn, themselves, declared friends of Rome, exposed to barbarians who will hunt them to the sea. What have they to live for?'

'Olussa, you talk like a rebel.' I let my anger show. 'You chatter much of life and living. Your people can save their lives if they are prepared to abandon their homes and obey my orders. Houses may be rebuilt; life is lost for ever. I am trying to save the people of London, not the sticks and stones of an insignificant town. If any refuse salvation, let them burn!'

Olussa lifted his hands in a weary gesture of acceptance. 'Very well, Lord Paulinus. Yet I fear panic when the news is known, and rioting and looting. The dregs rise to the surface when a pot is stirred.'

'That has been foreseen,' I said grimly. 'The town will be policed by cavalry. Moreover, every ship on the river comes under my command forthwith. None will sail: guards will board all craft and remain aboard until further orders.'

I turned to the prefects.

'The 1st Pannonians will detail six mounted troops to patrol streets, squares and byways in the town. They will enforce order at all times, by any methods. They will also dispatch, immediately, dismounted guards to take over the ships; six men to each. The 2nd Asturians will escort tomorrow's convoy to Silchester. The rest of you will be at three hours' notice to march. You will get detailed orders in writing. That is all.'

Olussa's slovenly gesture of farewell was a deplorable contrast to the regimental officers' smart salutes. He went like a man walking in sleep, and stumbled at the threshold. Nagged by a mingled sense of exasperation and foreboding, I watched him go. He's lived too long in Britain, I thought—and dismissed the obstinate Greek from my mind.

If Boudicca must have London, I was determined she would gain very little material to help her prosecution of the war. I gave the centurion commanding the arsenal a Tungrian guard and authority to requisition ships to transport all Government bullion and coinage. Everything else—armour, weapons, grain, hides, clothing—he was to destroy by burning or dump into the river, saving only twelve wagon-loads of grain which would accompany the refugee convoy to Silchester.

I dictated a message to the senior tribune of II Legion, ordering Posthumus's instant arrest, and bade him turn Augusta in her tracks and return to Silchester by forced marches. This message, and another to Valens that diverted XIV Legion from Dunstable to the haven of Silchester, was entrusted to picked horsemen who carried authority to commandeer the best post-horses on their routes.

Lastly, dispatches went to Richborough, where the commandant was told to embark all military stores he could carry, destroying the rest, and sail all ships, naval and mercantile, to Boulogne.

'Poor old Pantera,' I mused aloud. 'Somewhere on the high seas, battling as usual with storm and tempest, littering the coast with wrecks, while rebels burn his base to the ground in his absence. However, he'll be bound to call at Portus—we'll try to send word there from Silchester.'

I rose and threw a cloak about my shoulders.

'Our horses, Agricola, and a half-troop escort. We will visit the Procurator. A pity we can't don togas and walk in procession behind the lictors. Our martial stench of oil and leather will offend that proud knight's nostrils. Yet, when I've had my say, I doubt he'd notice whether we wore wolf-skins or woad!'

5

It so happened that I did not speak to Catus, neither then nor afterwards. The forecourt of the Procurator's palace and the arcades of the Treasury offices resembled the aftermath of a sack. Boxes, chests, jars, clothing, files and furniture littered the paved yards; officials, scribes and slaves scurried in circles, like sheep scenting wolves, and flung luggage haphazardly on carts so overloaded that wheels splayed dangerously on axles.

Agricola strove to obtain some sensible information from this rabble. Time passed and my anger mounted. At last he returned. The Procurator had gone to the docks.

'So?' I observed bleakly. 'Let's follow him.'

We wheeled our horses, rode past the basilica, the mansions of prosperous merchants in coppiced gardens, down a street of shops to the blank posteriors of high wooden warehouses. Ships docked bow to stern jammed every mooring; a complex throng—Romans, natives, sailors, stevedores, shopkeepers and slaves—bubbled like boiling porridge at the river's brink.

'Somebody,' Agricola said tonelessly, 'is anxious to leave London. How could they know so soon?'

I scanned the scene and was reassured. Cavalrymen guarded the ships and dispassionately smashed sword-flats across the faces of any unfortunates who tried to scramble aboard. From the arsenal came columns of laden porters, moving through lanes which implacable Tungrians cleared through the crowd. They stowed their bundles in the holds of four large merchantmen.

'There's the Procurator,' Agricola said suddenly.

Catus stood at the wharf's edge, fifty yards away, arguing ferociously with a stony-eyed Pannonian decurion who blocked the gangplank like a tree. The shipmaster, red-faced and raging, flailed his arms. Disappointment and fear contorted the faces of the officials, Treasury scribes, hangers-on, whores and catamites who pressed round Catus. The decurion's lips were taut; his sword, held by hilt and blade, pressed across his thighs like a bar.

'Find out what's happening yonder,' I said.

I already knew the answer, had known it when I saw the wreckage at the Procurator's palace. Catus, at a considerable price in silver, had secured a passage to Gaul for himself, his senior officials and his favourites, together with quantities of the wealth he had amassed in Britain. Only a stubborn auxiliary stood between him and escape from Boudicca's swordsmen.

My fingers curved like claws, like the talons of a stooping hawk. I stretched my hand and patted my horse's neck, and I breathed out slow and deep, like a gambler who sees the dice roll for a fortune.

'Tell that decurion,' I said gently, 'to allow the Procurator and his people to embark. Tell him to give the Procurator every assistance, and see that he sails on the ebb, and report to me that he has done so.'

I turned my horse and rode away. Decianus Catus was finished. From her officers Rome will tolerate much—corruption, inefficiency, vacillation, lechery, venality. Only two sins are unforgivable: overweening ambition and desertion in face of the enemy. And so, whether I won or not, whether my army was ground in shreds beneath Icenian hooves and the Province surrendered and my name enshrined in the annals of infamy with Varus and Crassus and Flaminius, Catus was lost. This cowardly creature, this gross plebeian knight, was in the dust.

He sailed that evening. I never saw Decianus Catus again. He travelled speedily to Rome and arrived brimful of spite and a version of the revolt designed to discredit my part in the affair and justify his own. For a time no one knew what to believe: rumours of blood and fire and broken legions had already reached the City along the whispering trade-routes, and my own early dispatches spoke of rampant rebellion. The Senate suspended judgement. Then, when the truth was known, retribution fell like a swinging sword: Decianus Catus was stripped of his knightly ring, his property confiscated, and he and his family exiled to Seriphus, a miserable, rocky islet in the Aegean.

There he may still be living, or have died, and so vanishes from Rome's history.

6

My escort had difficulty in forcing a way through the crowded streets. I had not yet published the decision to evacuate London: Olussa was still in the basilica haranguing a hastily-summoned session of the town council. Nevertheless the matter was obviously common knowledge—Londoners poured into the streets and argued excitedly. The sight of my little group evoked some ugly looks and shouts and catcalls. Emotions curdled readily in an atmosphere that scaled all the passions from disbelief to terror.

Householders tumbled their belongings, packed in untidy bundles, from gaping doorways; men clapped panniers on pack-animals, backed wagons into courtyards. Mounted detachments of Pannonian cavalry, withdrawn and watchful, lingered at street crossings and squares. But the uncertainty bred from rumour prevailed above all else: nobody knew quite what to do.

Much depended on Olussa. When he called the citizens to assembly in the forum, his was the terrifying task of controlling the tension and channelling the dangerous impulses of the mob towards obedience and compliance.

Realizing that Catus had left his department in the slippery hands of fate I sent wagons from the camp, under strong guard, to remove to the arsenal wharfside all bullion and specie from the civil Treasury. And, remembering the angry look of that London crowd, I dispatched messengers to my palace, to military transit camps and recruits' depots, to the Treasury offices, bidding all soldiers and government officials to collect the baggage they required for the morrow's march and shelter in the arsenal for the night. These Londoners, if I could help it, would not be given any chance to vent their grievances on Rome's privileged servants.

Olussa, spent as a dry wineskin, came to the camp at sunset. He gulped his Setine thirstily, clasped the cup to his chest and stared broody-eyed into the brazier.

'What have you arranged?' I said abruptly, shattering his reverie and recalling both my presence and his manners.

'Arranged? Yes, of course. Your convoy will assemble, Lord Paulinus, beyond the Wall Brook bridge at dawn tomorrow. About eight thousand all told, men, women and children, so far as I can ascertain.'

He sucked at the empty wine-cup and once more sought his dream-images in the glowing charcoal.

'Eight thousand?' I rapped. 'There are over fifteen thousand in London. What of the rest?'

Olussa set down the cup carefully. His eyes were wide and bloodshot and glinted like spears.

'They have renounced Rome,' he said evenly, 'because Rome has forsaken them. Some are too old or ill or poor or resigned to care very much. They will close their doors, take to their beds and await what comes. Others are returning to their own lands whence, years ago, they travelled to live in this town with the encouragement and protection of Claudius Caesar, back to the great forests of the Regni and the forts on the bare hilltops. The brave and the desperate are staying to fight Boudicca, hoping for nothing but Rome's shame in their useless deaths. Many are lost, unable to decide, torn by greed for their property and fear for their skins, quarrelsome, hysterical and dangerous.'

His eyes clouded and he gestured tiredly. 'There may be riots tonight. May I have some more wine?'

A servant refilled his cup. I stared unseeing at the darkening sky, where a great streak of crimson, low on the horizon, flamed like a burning city. Camp fires flickered between the tents; a day guard, released from duty, tramped cheerfully past.

'You are tired, Olussa,' I said, 'and so I excuse you for words that are near to treason. You have accomplished a great deal and I can demand no more. You had best stay in the camp and sleep in peace. The town tonight will be noisy with the bustle of departure.'

He rose decisively. 'My thanks, Lord Paulinus. I cannot. There is much to be done and more to be prevented. Have I your permission?'

Agricola's jaw dropped in surprise when I saluted his departing back.

7

By midnight the tumult from the town, a full half-mile distant, roared like the thunder of surf. Sleep was impossible. I rose and dressed, donning tunic and leather riding-breeches without armour or weapons, and warned the Vettonians to stand to their horses. I sat at a table, conning returns and scribbling notes for future plans, and waited for word from London. Soon enough it came: a sweating decurion and a trooper with blood on his face.

'Legate, the Prefect wants help. The people are out of hand, rioting like madmen. The town is like a battlefield.'

Within moments I was picking my way in the darkness through the camp gates, and ten troops of Vettonians clattered behind. On the West Way we met a cart or two, laden donkeys and men and women who flinched from our approach and, illumined by the feeble glimmer of torch and lantern, hastened from London to the safety of their imaginations. A red glow reflected from the clouds over the town.

At the Wall Brook bridge I said to the Vettonian Prefect, 'Sort it out as best you can. Find and support our Pannonian patrols. Don't worry if you have to break a head or two.'

He grinned and plunged across the bridge. Three hundred horsemen followed. I turned right with my bodyguard troop and, in darkness and comparative quiet, traced the broken ramparts to the wharves.

All hell was loose.

Above a seething, shrieking mob torches tossed like flowers in the wind. A ship, moored to the dock, burned from end to end. On another a crowd surged like waters from a broken dam, piling haphazard on decks, into holds, climbing the rigging. I watched while the ship lurched, righted herself, listed again until the river poured over the bulwarks. The screams of drowning men pierced the tumult like thin slivers of glass.

Elsewhere the Pannonian ship-guards fought like marines to repel boarders, Swords gleamed sticky red in the firelight. Gaps at the dock-side showed where shipmasters, quick to sense danger, had cut cables and drifted to midstream and anchored safe from that murderous hysteria. Panic was not the only element—pillagers wielding hatchets and crowbars shattered warehouse doors and fought one another for a share of the worthless plunder.

It was time this finished.

'Clear the wharves,' I said to the bodyguard centurion. 'Use all the force you need.'

The troop formed line, shoulder to shoulder, hooves pounding hollow on the planks, and advanced at a walk. The long swords swung. The noise magnified and soared to a high-pitched scream. Then it was over.

The troop drummed back, compact and unconcerned, and horses stepped delicately over sprawled bodies and slipped occasionally in dark puddles. The centurion thumped pommel to thigh and awaited orders.

By some miracle the blazing ship, though burned to the waterline, had not fired the wharf and warehouses. Torches dropped in the massacre still guttered on the planks. I had them thrown overside.

'Tell all shipmasters to cast off and anchor in midstream.'

I watched the cables slipped, then turned towards the town. 'If this,' I observed to the centurion, 'is a fair sample of London's temper then Boudicca will be robbed of a burning.'

Humanity packed the streets beyond the wharves from wall to wall. Townspeople striving to reach the docks fought a counter-current of fugitives who had escaped our swords at the waterside. The guard stolidly beat a passage towards the forum. Flames licked high above roofs; dry timber crackled like Saturnalian fireworks and the smell of burning wrinkled our nostrils.

'The silly bastards can't wait for the Iceni,' the centurion said to his horse.

The wide streets near the forum were a battleground. Knots of Pannonians and Vettonians charged this way and that and cleared brief spaces which filled instantly with wild-eyed men who struck and bit and leaped on horses and grappled riders. Torches revealed lurid little scenes of carnage, glimpsed for a moment and obliterated, and the burning houses showered cinders and sparks indiscriminately on the fighters.

'To the forum,' I ordered.

The bodyguard closed and carried me through like a boat riding a wild and angry surf. At the forum's entrance arch I dismounted, climbed to a stone ledge that jutted saddle-high and surveyed the riot.

'Sound stand fast.'

The blaring trumpet, at first, had no more effect than birdsong in a gale. But the call, repeated again and again, gradually drew eyes towards my perch and my still figure and scarlet cloak. Like pale and restless foam-flecks on a heaving sea, the faces turned and noise and movement stilled.

I raised both arms and spoke at the top of my voice.

8

Hours later, unutterably tired, I returned to camp. Night was ending. I had, ironically enough, saved London from her own citizens. Order was restored; fires were under control; dead and wounded were being removed from the streets. I lay on my bed fully dressed, never properly asleep, and dreamed strange dreams until the trumpets of the fourth watch greeted the dawn.

The refugee convoy filtered across the Wall Brook in reluctant driblets and petered to a standstill beyond the bridge. The Asturian escort shoved and shouldered, cajoled and bullied, until the unruly swarm was disposed on the road in some semblance to a line of march.

Fugitives are seldom a cheerful spectacle. These were exceptionally depressed and surly and glum and frightened. From the ragged peasants leading half-starved goats, from fat merchants carried by slaves in silk-curtained litters, from harlots with paint smeared awry on their lips, from hawk-faced matrons riding mules, from podgy clerks still clutching useless documents, from Roman citizen or from British slave, from none in that shuffling column came a cheerful word or laugh or smile. Even the arsenal's legionaries, palace guards, recruits and furlough details marched sour-faced and dumb like men undergoing an unmerited punishment.

Axles squealed, hooves clopped on paving, a whip cracked, oxen grunted under groaning yokes, a child howled dismally; and the procession wound slowly to the west.

Olussa's estimate of numbers, I thought, was accurate. About eight thousand, in a column over four miles long. The Asturian Prefect disposed his troops, herdsmen rather than guards, at intervals along its length and made his farewell salute.

'All speed for the first twenty miles,' I told him. 'Collect the 3rd Gauls' road-station garrisons as you go. Do you think you can reach Staines tonight?'

The Prefect pulled a face. 'Not with this lot, Legate. Lucky if we make ten miles today. I reckon we shall cross the Thames after midday tomorrow.'

I concurred. 'Do your best. Destroy the bridge at Staines directly you've crossed. With luck we shall catch you there and increase your escort. Then for the last twenty-five miles to Silchester you ought to be reasonably safe.'

I returned to camp and re-read the previous night's messages from our cavalry screen. Verulam reported wandering brigands who fled on sight and who may or may not have been connected with Boudicca. Indus's Horse, sharply reprimanded for exceeding their limits of reconnaissance, rather sulkily described a brush with a small Catuvellaun war-band near the North Way. No prisoners taken and no further information.

I rubbed my chin. These signs, small in themselves, could be significant after the stark desertion of the countryside that the patrols had hitherto encountered. They might be the forerunners of Boudicca's return from Lincoln. Or they might not.

I threw the messages aside, summoned the prefect of Proculus's Horse and told him to take his regiment, dismounted, to prepare London Bridge for burning. When he had gone I remembered, with a wry grimace, the catalogue of litigation whose hearing I had appointed for this very day. Events had finally overtaken and overwhelmed the petty routine of provincial administration, and lawyers and litigants, their pleadings forgotten, had alike joined the scramble for sanctuary. How long since I signed that cause list? A mere eighteen hours—and the event seemed distant in time by as many days.

Grime caked my body; a scaling of sweat and smoke and cinders irked my skin. With Agricola and Bassus and a small escort I returned to London in search of a bath. At the Wall Brook gangs of men cleared undergrowth from the ancient native ramparts and planted stakes in a ragged palisade. Olussa's last ditch defenders, I thought grimly, flaunting their valour in mockery of craven Rome. I remembered a survivor's description of Boudicca's massed attacks at Colchester, and laughed without amusement. Suddenly a bath seemed less desirable and I swerved towards the docks.

Anchored in midstream were twenty seagoing vessels whose captains were prevented, by the Pannonian guards aboard, from following their natural inclination to leave London river as fast as wind and oars could carry them. To four treasure-ships, loaded with bullion from arsenal and Treasury, and two naval biremes I gave authority to sail on the ebb for Boulogne, and ignored anxious petitions from other shipmasters who clamoured, in a medley of languages that ranged from Hibernia to Thessaly, for permission to remove their craft from that doomed harbour. I had a need for their ships that was unlikely to earn their approval and saw no reason to anticipate a storm of protest.

I resumed my course for the palace and my bath. The streets were empty. Litter of the night's rioting lay in the ruts: torn garments, shattered wine-jars, staves, bricks, a broken cart, blood-pools dried and crusted and some desolate corpses. Fire had scorched houses and shops;

the blackened buildings gaped like decayed teeth. Life had retired within doors. From shuttered windows faces peered palely at our passing, and pathetic barricades—a pile of logs, an upturned wagon—shielded portals and defied the hordes of barbarism.

My bath presented problems. The palace was deserted—guardsmen dispersed a few wandering pillagers—and the furnaces dead. While guards chopped wood and kindled fires I paced the empty rooms amid a wreckage of torn hangings, battered furniture and broken statues. By mid-afternoon some wisps of steam floated in the hot room, sufficient to sweat dirt and fatigue from my body. A friendly pummelling from Agricola completed a mockery of a bath, and I left, somewhat refreshed, for the camp.

Men still worked on the Wall Brook ramparts. I stopped, paralysed by astonishment, at the sight of an extraordinary figure directing their efforts. Bulging from a tight brass corselet, an antique curiosity of Sulla's wars, and encumbered by an over-long baldric supporting a cavalry sword which clanged on tarnished greaves, Aulus Alfidius Olussa peered at me beneath the visor of a gladiator's helmet.

'What in the name of Apollo are you doing here?' I blared. 'Why are you not with the Silchester convoy?'

With a certain queer dignity the fat little man rendered a travesty of a military salute.

'I am no longer a magistrate of London, Lord Paulinus,' he said. 'The garrison has named me Dictator. We do what we can to prepare for siege.' He indicated the rickety palisade, now perhaps two hundred paces long, which surmounted the useless rampart.

A conflict of anger, exasperation and pity choked the words in my throat. He faced me calmly, fiddling with his ridiculous sword.

'We are short of weapons and workers. Few will stir from their homes. Last night's riots have broken their spirit. Do you know that over three hundred were killed, mostly by your soldiers?'

I stared at him dumbly.

'May I make a last petition, Lord Paulinus? Would you give me arms from the arsenal and send some of your men to help with these fortifications?'

'Most certainly not!' I exploded. 'Men will be sent, and within the hour, but not for abetting a bunch of madmen bent on suicide! They'll go round the houses and compel everyone they can find to embark on the vessels still in port. I want to save your wretched hides, not offer them as a sacrifice to Andate.'

'A sacrifice there will be, Lord Paulinus,' he answered softly. 'Men will die on these ramparts for the deities and faiths and beliefs of Britain, and for the gods of countries and provinces and tribes within and without the frontiers of empire, for London embraces them all. They will be sacrificed for the ashes of their forefathers and for their own self-respect and pride.'

He paused, then spat violently at my feet.

'Not one man will die for Rome!'

Olussa turned suddenly, tripped over his sword and sprawled in the mud. I laughed savagely and strode away.

In a little while I had to pause and wipe away the tears which blinded my eyes.

9

The rough compulsion of a dismounted regiment which scoured London drafted about two thousand frightened and unwilling townsfolk to the docks and herded them, packed tight as arrows in a quiver, aboard the anchored ships. To the shipmasters' objections the prefect in command offered the choice of compliance or of remaining moored, under guard, until Boudicca arrived. The tide was turned by the time everyone had embarked and the ships slipped cables, one by one, and drifted down-river. Two thousand Londoners were bound for exile in Gaul, temporary or permanent—who could tell?—taking only the clothes they wore and their lives.

That evening the cavalry screen sent long and ominous reports whose gist was that a number of apparently independent war-bands, varying in strength from a score to a couple of hundred warriors, were filtering southwards along the main roads and native tracks. They seemed anything but the spearhead of an advancing army. They were, I thought, as I pulled my lip and scanned the closely-written messages, the anarchical fringes of Boudicca's undisciplined hordes, escaped entirely from her control and ravening for plunder in territories as yet unpillaged.

Whatever their origins, they were too strong for our cavalry: the Pannonians had retired from their comfortable quarters in Verulam and were encamped in the ruins of Sulloniacae. Indus's Horse had likewise withdrawn ten miles nearer London and were bivouacked on the two main roads.

The net was drawing tighter.

So taut, indeed, that our warning could be very short—ten miles represented little more than two hours' grace. I resolved, then, to leave London on the morrow. My decision to destroy the bridge demanded more leisure than a hasty exit with Icenian chariots on our tails.

In the wooden headquarters hut, by the light of smoky oil lamps and flickering candles, I expounded my plans to the five prefects of horse.

'The enemy,' I said baldly, 'may be within two days' march of London, and it is time for us to go. Our forces are still scattered. XIV Legion should reach Silchester tomorrow night. II Legion, still retreating, is probably near Cirencester. One of our cavalry regiments is escorting refugees to Staines and the other five, less patrols, are here in London.

'You know my intention: to regroup the army at Silchester before meeting the rebels in battle.

'We march for Silchester tomorrow, and we shall avoid the West Way because the enemy is close to our northern flank and may cut the road. We shall cross and destroy London Bridge and head westwards along native tracks on the high downlands south of the Thames.

'Agricola, have you found guides?'

The tribune nodded. 'Yes, Legate. Two refugee shepherds from the hills above Crayford. Wild men who speak no Latin, but swear they know the ridgeway tracks to the valley at Staines.'

'Good, At Staines we meet 2nd Asturians and the convoy. They should get there tomorrow night.'

I consulted my tablets.

'At dawn tomorrow I shall recall the cavalry screen. Proculus's Horse will send detachments to smash or sink every small boat in London from coracles upwards on this side of the Thames. They will also provide fire-parties, with torches, ready to burn the bridge. The fords are too deep to be crossed easily, and a total lack of bridges and boats will discourage pursuit. We shall march when the patrols are in, probably around noon.'

The prefects' questions—rations and administrative details—I left Agricola to answer, and pulled on a cloak and left the hut. The night was black, cloudless, the stars gleaming like a million lancepoints. London lay dark, without lights, sunk in a deathlike trance—a sombre sepulchre of apathy and despair and resigned courage where men stared blindly from tottering palisades and waited, without hope, for their lives to end.

I walked wretchedly to my quarters, thinking of fat Olussa.

10

Three hours after sunrise the next day, the 20th of May, two sweating gallopers on lathered horses interrupted my gloomy contemplation of cavalrymen smashing boats in the Wall Brook estuary. The Pannonians at Sulloniacae, surprised at dawn by a spate of armed Britons who burst unheralded from the forests, were tumbling back to London. The messengers' disjointed sentences made one fact plain. The tempest that destroyed, in the end, London and Verulam and countless settlements of southern Britain was on the point of breaking.

Trumpets in town and camp sang high and clear. Within the turn of a sandglass the regiments were saddled, mounted and cantering in a clanging torrent across Wall Brook. London's pathetic garrison stood to arms at their palisades. Strong men and weak, old men and boys. Rusty swords and cudgels, reaping-hooks and slings. In a sullen silence they watched us pass, and sometimes spat contemptuous insults. The troopers scowled and stared ahead with set faces.

The planks of London Bridge drummed beneath our hooves. The water flowed fast and clear and limpid, and we saw on the riverbed, scattered like waste from a battlefield, swords and shields and javelins and helmets dumped from the arsenal. The arms I had denied to Boudicca, and denied also to London's defenders.

A high causeway carried the road across the river-bank marshlands. Beside it, half-concealed in an alder thicket as if aware of Rome's proscription, stood a small temple of Isis. I dismounted there, sat on the steps and waited.

The patrols of Indus's Horse had failed to return. The messenger, sent at dawn to recall them, had not reappeared. Had the Britons caught them, as they had so nearly caught the Pannonians? Had the galloper gone astray? Whatever the reason, six valuable troops of cavalry were lost in the forested hills north of London, among the tree-wastes that were now alive with Boudicca's rampant horsemen.

I could only wait and hope, and give them every chance before the bridge went down.

Fire-parties on the bridge lingered near pitch-soaked faggots tied by iron hoops to the timbers. In the bright sunlight their torches flickered like pale candles. The bridge tapered in perspective like a spear piercing London's heart. Metal glinted briefly on the ramparts above Wall Brook; a stray dog trotted purposefully along the wharves; the river eddied peaceably, a bright blue-grey, like a molten sheet of polished iron, and sea-gulls wheeled and quarrelled at sewermouths. Otherwise nothing moved nor showed, neither man nor beast, and no smoke from hearth or furnace drifted in friendly ambience above London's roofs.

The hours dragged by. On the causeway long ranks of dismounted horsemen chattered and yawned and guffawed and shouted nonsense from troop to troop. Tribunes, centurions and orderlies lounged and gossiped. The sun rode higher in a cloudless sky. I gazed over the river with aching eyes, dozed a little in short half-trances, studied the inscriptions on Isis's forbidden shrine and tried not to think of the past.

A call from the guard disturbed my profitless reverie.

Distant specks crawled on the West Way. I gazed beneath cupped hands till my eyeballs prickled.

A decurion on watch said, 'Legate, they are not Romans.'

'How can you tell?'

'Horse and foot intermingled, Legate. Infantry running ahead of the horsemen.'

The faraway blobs dissolved and coagulated on the embanked roadway and shimmered hazily in the strong sunlight.

'There's a chariot!' Bassus exclaimed.

Tiny as a child's toy, the definite, unmistakable mark of the barbarian. Where were the apple-green cloaks of Indus's Horse?

'Burn the bridge.'

An orderly sped to the fire-parties. Torches dipped and plunged. A hundred fire-points breathed black smoke which coiled languidly in the windless air. We smelt the pungent reek of tar and heard fire take old timber in a crackling embrace. Horses stamped and snorted. The torch-bearers flung their brands in the river, streamed from the bridge, ran to the standards.

Fire gripped the bridge and threw furious tresses of flame from pile to span and wreathed and caressed the spars like a lover. Timbers tottered, collapsed and smashed into the placid waters in a welter of spray and steam.

I returned slowly to the road.

'Mount!'

A warhorn wailed, faint but clear, above the crackle and crash of the falling bridge, calling across the Thames like a derisive salute.

I did not look back.

11

When downlands barred the horizon we left the road and followed a native trackway, narrow and rutted, that wound in pointless deviations to the west. Then we marched in the eye of the setting sun until, at evening, we came to a deserted hill-fort. A few rotted stakes, leaning like tired old men, remained of the stockade; grass-grown ramparts slid wearily into ditches choked with thorn-scrub and nettles. The place was huge, eerie in the dusk; the hill wind whispered like ghosts of dead warriors.

The regiments made camp within the perimeter, picketed horses, posted sentries and collected firewood. The men were subdued and depressed, the groups around the cooking-fires oddly silent. Of the town that once throve within these ramparts only some tumbledown wooden huts remained: in the best, renovated from time to time by shepherds or wandering pedlars, Secundus spread my blankets on a mattress of grass and bracken.

I craved sleep, but could not rest. Stars twinkled through a dozen rents in the ruined thatch, yet the hut seemed hot and stifling. I donned my cloak and walked through the sleeping camp to the ramparts. A sentry challenged and my guard answered; challenge and countersign clanged in the silence like gongs.

Hillside and forest were a dark avalanche cascading from my feet to the rim of the earth. A solitary wolf howled mournfully. Far away a tiny halo of light glowed and dimmed, kindled and faded like a dying spark.

I watched it for a long time.

14

'The season of caution is past when we are in the midst of evils.'

SENECA

1

We climbed another rise and looked on Staines. The broken stockades and ravaged huts of a native settlement sprawled in a clearing. The gates of the road-station hung drunkenly from their posts; the portal gaped like a dead mouth. Timbers of the shattered bridge trailed in the swollen river like broken bones.

The prefect of Asturians, those guardians of London's refugee convoy, toiled up the slope towards us. His shoulders sagged; his body hunched loose in the saddle; and the bloody rag wrapping his arm was a tattered banner which signalled defeat.

He told his miserable story. A few miles from Staines the road passed through a deep belt of forest. The road-swathe through the forest was like a mountain pass, the Britons thundered from the trees like avalanches from cliffs.

The Asturians had a chance of escape, and took it, but the refugees had none. The roadway became a slaughter-house. Eight thousand people who had obeyed me and left London, who had trusted my word and my protection, had died there.

About half the regiment rode from the massacre, galloped to Staines and destroyed the bridge in a frenzy of haste. Then, concealed in trees on the farther bank, they watched exultant savages destroy the settlement and road-station. That done, the rebels seemed content; they made no attempt to ford the river but returned, whooping, to the forest and the place of carnage.

They were a small, errant war-band, no more than two or three thousand strong, escaped from Boudicca's control and gone loose like a pack of rabid dogs, slavering for blood and pillage. They had found their victims. Eight thousand helpless fugitives from London. Fugitives by my orders.

For the torn corpses heaped on the road beyond Staines I alone was responsible.

In a bustle of false energy which, fragile as a paper mask, barely concealed my sick weariness I set about choosing a camp site and issuing orders for a depressing and dangerous night.

2

At the tenth milestone from Staines Agricola reined his horse sharply.

'What a perfect battleground!' he exclaimed.

I threw him a sour look. The sun had barely risen, and promised a perfect day, but I was in a mood to appreciate neither weather nor talkative tribunes. Least of all at that time, with my legions scattered and a trail of massacres, defeats and disasters hounding my thoughts, had I any desire to speculate upon battles.

'Your tactical genius is the envy of the whole army,' I snarled. 'Do you propose that we wait here and fight Boudicca with five and a half cavalry regiments?'

Instinct, nevertheless, compelled me to examine the landscape. The West Way, bursting through a straggling wood, leaped on a high causeway across a thousand yards of waterlogged heath pimpled by tussocks of dead-yellow grass. The heath ended in a firm, gravelled slope which rose gently to a ridge swelling at each end into a rounded hillock. A dense mat of thorn-trees and bramble undergrowth crowned the whole of these heights. The Way pointed like a spear across the heath, cleft the centre of the ridge and vanished beyond the thickets, leaving a gash in the tree-line on the horizon to mark its course. A mile to the north towered a conical hill which wore, like a ruined crown, a once-formidable hill-fort.

'Certainly a hard position to take,' Bassus observed. 'Very heavy going across the heath—see how the horses are slowed.' He pointed to the vanguard troop, plodding fetlock-deep in sodden tussocks.

'Can't turn the flanks, either,' Agricola said, unaffected by my surliness. 'Those wooded knolls at either end look quite impenetrable. One would have to attack head-on, on a front no wider than the length of the ridge. A comparatively small force could hold the position against considerable odds. What do you think, Bassus, would be the minimum required to occupy the ridge in reasonable depth?'

'About a legion,' I answered, while Bassus pulled his lip. 'And this is no time for tactical exercises. That hill-fort will do for our first beacon-station. Detach a troop, Agricola, and see they understand their duties.'

I had left at Staines a section of hard riders and fast horses to carry warning to Silchester of a rebel advance in strength on the West Way. In addition I had decided to establish a chain of signal stations along the twenty-five miles between Staines and Silchester which could send the same message by fire at night and smoke by day in a tenth of a galloper's time. Had there been a third and a fourth means of conveying that message I would have used them: I could not know too soon when that terrible woman and her bloodstained horde, like hounds recovering the scent after a fault, would come baying upon my trail.

When, shortly before noon, we entered the forests which enclose Silchester the vanguard was instantly challenged by vedettes of XIV

Legion cavalry: a welcome sign of Vettius Valens's relentless efficiency. Farther on we met the legate himself, prowling his outpost line. His grim, bristly face, brown and seamed like old leather, crumpled in a grin of welcome as he clasped my wrist.

I was glad to see him. We rode into Silchester together, my arm about his shoulders.

3

Epaticcus awaited us with his magistrates and decurions at the east gate. I cut formalities short and promised to meet the council later in the basilica, for Epaticcus seemed burdened with news and I could sense troubles seething beneath the mask of an expressionless face. Probably the legionaries, relaxing after a hard march, had rioted in the taverns.

Gemina's camp was on a heath a half-mile west of the town. Within two days Valens had converted marching-camp to fortress. Ditch and bank were cut perpendicular and revetted; stout tree trunks hewn from the forest replaced the regulation palisade stakes. Watch-towers topped the stockade at regular intervals; the noonday sun glinted from sentries' helmets. Wooden huts, roofed with tiles levied from Silchester's brick-makers, replaced the tent-lines.

Centuries marched and drilled on the parade-ground or, stripped of corselets and weapons, jumped and ran and wrestled. Javelins thudded in targets; sword smacked shield in thrust-and-parry. Words of command ripped the air like catapult-bolts. I realized, suddenly, how much I had missed my legionaries. The long fortnight which had separated me from my heavy infantry, from these swarthy, stocky, dependable fighters, was permeated with a succession of disasters, and unreasoning instinct argued a chain of cause and effect. Moodily I regarded my companions of the march from Caernarvon, the auxiliary cavalry filing to the horse lines which Valens had far-sightedly provided. Their gaudy cloaks, azure, emerald and saffron, blazoned the sombre parade-ground like a riot of summer flowers. I tried to convince myself, against reason and justice, that the constant proximity of such second-rate troops fostered second-rate generalship and explained, in part, the trail of bloody horrors which had dogged my heels since leaving Ordovicia. Conviction's grip was loose. I knew my military history, and remembered many instances of brilliant victories gained by shoddy troops.

I hunched my shoulders, shedding introspection as a dog shakes water from his coat, and said to Valens, 'You've marched two hundred and fifty miles in ten days and built a fortress. Do your men never rest?'

He laughed—a short, throaty bark. 'They're hard as nails and fighting fit. By Hercules, if I didn't keep them occupied they'd drink all the wine and rape every woman in Silchester. So I make certain they go to bed too tired even to think.'

In camp headquarters, a roomy hut adequately furnished by the legion's carpenters, Valens shed his sparse humour and became grimly businesslike.

'I'm out of touch, Legate. A lot seems to have happened since we left Caernarvon that I know nothing about. Deluged with rumours, of course, at every halt. Epaticcus has told me a little, but you can't trust a Briton for truth. Would you bring me up to date?'

I gave him a synopsis of our setbacks: Colchester's sack, Cerialis's defeat, Posthumus's defection and the fall of London.

The legate frowned. 'So. A veritable avalanche of catastrophe. And I bring you little comfort.'

'You bring yourself and a strong fighting force, Valens,' I said amiably. 'I don't find the thought depressing.'

His mouth drooped at the comers. 'You'll see. First, the muster roll. Encamped here are XIV Legion, the veterans' cohort of XX Legion and your bodyguard infantry. The auxiliaries are 1st Vardulli, mixed milliary; 6th Thracians, mixed cohort; 3rd Bracarii, infantry cohort, and about five hundred of 1st Vangiones, collected from road-stations on

the Midland Way. March casualties from sickness and exhaustion, total-
ling twenty legionaries and ninety auxiliaries, were left at road-stations.
I doubt we shall see them again. We met no enemy and suffered no
other losses. I have in Silchester six thousand legionaries, three hundred
auxiliary cavalry and two thousand auxiliary infantry.'

I knew most of this and suffered the rigmarole patiently: Valens
could never shed his centurion-on-parade mentality. I said, 'You can
add six cavalry regiments I brought from London.' I remembered the
ambush at Staines. 'No, five and a bit. Something over two and a half
thousand. We have nearly eleven thousand in camp. Why this preoccupation with numbers?'

The legate paused, drummed fingers on the table.

'Are any refugees from London, Verulam or elsewhere following
you?'

I told him what had happened to the convoy. Valens's comment was
an explosive sigh.

'That's a relief, anyway.'

Valens was a hard man, but he was not callous and in this context
his rejoinder was completely out of character. I stared at him, astonished.

'What do you mean?'

He gave me a long, considering look. 'Only this, Legate. We have
rations for three more days. Silchester has no supplies. What do we eat?'

I gaped in wonder. 'No supplies? Nonsense! The Atrebatan corn-
levy for the past year lies untouched in Silchester's military granaries.
Has Epaticcus not told you?'

Valens's face wore a crooked grin. 'He told me that Paenius Posthumus, commanding II Legion, took the whole lot back to Gloucester
with him.'

I was speechless.

Valens said, 'When Posthumus decided to retreat he declared that
the Government's corn, at least, should not fall into enemy hands. He

commandeered every cart and wagon in the district, scraped the granary floors to the last grain and marched away.'

A rage akin to epilepsy shook my whole frame with uncontrollable spasms. Vision blurred and phlegm flooded my mouth. When sense returned I was trembling as with fever, and Valens's hand was on my arm. Words came with difficulty, like a man rehearsing a half-forgotten language.

'We must seize native supplies, scour the countryside.'

Valens dropped tiredly into a chair. 'Useless. I've already searched every private and tribal grain-store in Silchester. Sent foraging parties to farms and villages as far as Winchester. The natives have probably managed to hide a little, but this is May, and corn-supplies are running low. I've obtained barely enough to feed half my force for an extra day, no more. What did you bring?'

'Seven days' rations,' I answered dully. 'We can redistribute to your men.'

Valens's lips moved in calculation. 'That will give two more days' supply for the whole force. So we can exist for five days, with care. What, Legate, are your plans?'

'Briefly, to wait here in Silchester until II Legion, Jupiter burn them, return from Gloucester; then march to seek Boudicca.'

'And now?'

I shrugged. 'We can go to Portus. If we find enough ships, and if Pantera's fleet calls there, we could embark the legion and sail to Gaul. Or retire to Gloucester and lock ourselves up with that coward Posthumus. But why talk nonsense? In fact we shall do neither. I shall stay here, send messengers to hurry Augusta, and order detachments to the forests to hunt food, boar and deer, and to drag the rivers for fish.'

'The legionary detests meat.'

'He does. After five days he can make his choice: whether to hear his belly rumbling from indigestion or from starvation. I think his tender stomach will adapt itself to flesh. So detail your hunting parties at once,

Valens. Above all, tell your supply officers to keep our ration shortages secret: a hint dropped in Silchester today will reach Boudicca tomorrow, for the Atrebates stink of sedition. And as I've marched for two days, sweated like a Titan and stink worse than a slave I'm now going to have a bath.'

4

The garden of my mansion was gay with flowers, the hedges trimmed, lawns scythed, and blossom caressed the fruit trees like sleepy butterflies. The house was swept and polished, and servants and chamberlain waited at the porter's lodge. Someone had sent a night-rider from Staines to warn Silchester of the Governor's approach.

I dawdled over bathing, thankfully soaking Thames valley mud from my skin, and deliberately emptied my mind of all thought beyond enjoyment of the moment. Afterwards, wrapped in soft towels, with a cup of sweet wine and a dish of preserved figs at my side, I relaxed on a couch and allowed calculation and consideration to invade my brain.

Today was the 23rd of May. Two days previously the rebels, presumably under Boudicca, had reduced London to a stinking heap of cindered buildings and charred bodies. Verulam, likewise, was in ruins. The Icenian hell-bitch had ravaged unchecked for nineteen days, sacking three towns, defeating a vexillation, burning countless farms and villages and slaughtering every Roman and most Britons in her path. The Britons doubtless accounted her a successful warleader; they probably saw in her the personification of their accursed Andate; yet she had failed in what must be her chief object: to bring the Roman Army to battle. Boudicca, or her chieftains—I never discovered whether she was the sole author of our chapter of defeats—was no fool in the business of war. She must seek her main enemy without delay. Otherwise her army, as is the way of tribal levies, would speedily disintegrate in search of loot and spread like locusts over the defenceless lands below London, bringing ruin and death to Cantii and Regni alike.

Could she find me within five days? That was the limit of our existence as a fighting force: afterwards we must march west, bellies flapping like empty sacks, to the nearest supplies at Gloucester.

Would II Legion return to Silchester within that time? I reckoned on my fingers: my vehement messenger should have reached Augusta three days since; had they started immediately they could now be within a day's march of Silchester. I shook my head sadly. It hadn't happened, for outriders and native gossip, which travelled faster than horses, would already have told us. Posthumus was likely to resist arrest; he probably headed a clique of tribunes and centurions who shared his preference for fortress life above the hazards of campaigning in the field.

I robed myself slowly and with care. Mannius Secundus entered and tendered distastefully a small leaden seal which a furtive creature, lurking in the shadows of the slaves' quarters, had given him to support his petition for audience. The disc proved his status as a Government spy. The rebellion, fortunately, had not yet rent the intelligence network in territories south of the Thames. This agent was head of espionage among the Atrebates, and I was very pleased to see him.

I need hardly say that it is not my practice, except with the small regiment of private agents who guard my security, to interview spies personally. That is the function of my chief of intelligence, who collates and abbreviates reports from the whole Province and submits them for my perusal. My chief of intelligence had been in Colchester when Boudicca came. The Atrebatan spy who now sought admission had the sense and hardihood, luckily, to appreciate that his information was worth a direct approach to the overpowering personage who ruled Britain.

In an inner room, with Secundus as guard, I heard his report.

'The Atrebates as a whole have no sympathy with Queen Boudicca and her doings, most noble Paulinus,' he assured me. 'My fellow-tribesmen are well-fed, prosperous and happy. We grumble about taxes—who doesn't?—but Rome does not bear too heavily on our necks.'

'There is no doubt of Epaticcus's loyalty?'

The spy shook his head vigorously. 'None at all. We, the common folk, revere Epaticcus. He is still, to us, King of the Atrebates in all but name. Many impugned his honour when he first swore allegiance to our conquerors; nobody has doubted his wisdom since.'

'That statement, to my mind, has two edges.'

'The sharper edge is the one least used. Britons rate honour above expedience and though, as I have said, the common ruck can endure Rome, certain noblemen among the Atrebates are plotting a secret deputation to the rebels, to agree upon terms before they invade our territory.

'As you are well aware, most noble Paulinus,' the spy interpolated tactfully, 'two factions within the Atrebates have created discord ever since our conquest by Epaticcus. The descendants of the old kings, the true Atrebates, resent his usurpation of the throne and the overthrow of Commius's dynasty. For too long, in their opinion, a Catuvellaun, supported first by the mighty Cunobelinus and later by Rome, has ruled this tribe. Rome's conquest obscured these differences for a time, and the Atrebates became one nation against Vespasian's legion, but long years of peace have again uncovered the split. On one side is Epaticcus; on the other are nobles of Commius's family who would pay any price, even submission to the Iceni, to see an Atrebatan ruling the Atrebates again.'

'You know these men?'

'The leaders are Pertacus, Lucilianus and Campanus, three high-born princes of Commius's line, who are willing to talk treason when the time is right.'

'The time is not far distant when all three will fall silent,' I said savagely. 'You have done well to come so quickly with your news—my chamberlain will give you gold. For the future, local intrigues are less important than information of the enemy. Provide your agents with horses and send them east to spy the rebels' movements. Let them pretend to be emissaries of this treacherous Pertacus and so obtain forewarning of Boudicca's intentions.'

I left the mansion and walked to camp headquarters at a pace that troubled my guards. I summoned Valens and the Prefect commanding Proculus's Horse.

'I have left a party of Atrebates—inhabitants of the destroyed settlement at Staines—to watch the river. They are certainly unreliable, and our signal stations depend on them for warning,' I told them. 'We must stiffen that front quickly. Proculus's Horse will send six troops to Staines at once. Co-operate with the Atrebates but don't trust them: watch the West Way and fords for three or four miles upstream and down.

'The West Way, moreover, is not the only route open to the enemy. We must guard all approaches. So you will also send two troops northwards on the Icknield Way and two troops south along the ridgeway. Limit of reconnaissance will be twenty miles from Silchester. Patrolling will continue until contact or recall. You will not fight for information: I want no casualties.'

When the Prefect had gone I told Valens of my conversation with the spy.

'Intrigue and treachery, not blood, flow in British veins,' he snorted contemptuously. 'Do we know where the three principal traitors are?'

I pulled an ear thoughtfully. 'I shall sound Epaticcus after the council. Perhaps this is a case when inaction would be prudent. We don't want to make arrests and precipitate a revolt. If we can ride the wind here for five days, or less, traitors can be dealt with at leisure.'

Valens grunted agreement.

'When we have to go, in whichever direction, we must move sharply. Your men are dispersed all day foraging and hunting. How little notice do you need?'

'Three hours,' Valens said at once.

'Three hours be it. Pass the word to all commanders. And now for Epaticcus and his decurions.'

5

Nothing of note emerged from the meeting. Councillors spouted oratorical fountains which expressed ascending loyalty to Rome, homage to the Prince and righteous horror at the rebels' iniquities. Two of the most vehement speeches came from decurions named Lucilianus and Campanus.

I delivered a brief address and expressed gratitude on the Prince's behalf for their support in troubled times and promised a speedy finish to the revolt. I dwelt with some care on the penalties to be enacted on the persons and property of traitors and rebels. Rome, a tolerant ruler, I reminded the audience, never forgot a wrong and never forgave.

The councillors seemed properly impressed. Campanus's face was impassive. Lucilianus smiled faintly, as at some secret thought.

The setting was worthy of a meeting whose ceremony and conduct was without fault. The basilica, a complete masterpiece of warm, rose-red brick, was a building fit to house the government of any town in Nero's provinces. I told Epaticcus so, while we strolled in the busy forum.

'Your approval is an honour, Legate,' he murmured.

His manner was pensive and withdrawn. I rallied him, only half in jest. 'Perhaps your faith in our victory is not so confident as your decurions' speeches suggest?'

The old man's face was grave as he drew me beyond hearing of the guard. 'Legate, I am afraid. I don't know your plans and don't dare to ask. I only know what I can see: all Britain's terror and power and hatred reared like a stupendous wave that will obliterate for ever the name and memory of Rome from this land, while a single legion, marooned near a defenceless town, awaits starvation.'

I suppressed a flare of anger, an incautious retort which might have exposed my intentions. I no longer inclined to trust any Briton, even one so old, distinguished and apparently loyal.

'Your concern for our well-being is gratifying but quite unnecessary, I assure you,' I answered bleakly.

'My own safety worries me also, Legate,' Epaticcus said with a wry smile. 'Even at my age life is precious. If you lose I die. Indeed, I may be killed before the matter is decided.'

I said calmly, 'I do not understand you. Explain.'

'Hasn't your spy told you?' He cackled briefly at my discomfiture. 'A good man! He's bailiff on one of my farms near Speen. You've had a visit from him. Yes, Pertacus and his faction must remove me somehow before they start negotiations with Boudicca. They know they'll never carry the Atrebates with them while I'm alive.'

'If you know of this plot,' I said impatiently, 'why don't you deal with the plotters?'

'With what proof? You forget, Legate, we're all Romans now, and accusations must be supported by testimony and witnesses, argued by lawyers, backed by precedent and decree and tried before magistrates or by the Governor himself. Twenty years ago,' he said viciously, 'I'd have flayed those swine alive and impaled them through the crotch on blunt stakes.'

'When I have beaten Boudicca,' I said, 'will you do precisely that? You have my authority.'

'If you defeat Boudicca,' Epaticcus said, 'I will.'

6

For four days eleven thousand soldiers idled in Silchester. Valens's men cleared the forests of every edible creature within a five-mile radius, skinned, cooked and ate them, complaining the while more loudly than professional mourners at an equestrian's funeral. Strangely enough the legionary's hatred of meat proved more serious than a soldier's fad. If senators enjoyed fish and game why, I argued, need Marius's mule be so fastidious? In fact an epidemic of disordered bowels, loose or costive, crowded latrines and hospitals and alarmed the doctors. Slightly worried, I ordered a reversion to wheat rations and directed the meat to be dried and smoked and held as emergency supplies.

Gallopers searching for II Augusta found the roads empty as far as Cirencester: Posthumus, collecting auxiliaries in his fortress like a fussy hen gathering her chicks, had even withdrawn 3rd and 4th Gauls from the road-stations. A message sent farther, to Gloucester itself, commanded the legion to bring with it all the corn stolen from Silchester. The bearer never returned, and we could only speculate whether he and his escort had been murdered by rebels or detained by Posthumus. The Camp Prefect, I was now convinced, was a traitor; his treason was greater than Boudicca's; his punishment, the slow death of the rods, I anticipated with relish.

The hours crawled; daylight lingered like the eternal dawn of legendary Thule and the nights were a dark limbo wherein doubts squirmed like maggots in festering meat. I dreamed nightmares, of myself helpless and trussed with cords while my executioners remorselessly converged, swords in hand; and one of the killers was Boudicca, the other Starvation; and a third, the dilatory Eagle of Augusta, lingered chuckling in the shadows.

Outwardly I displayed a splendid indifference, pretending a carefree demeanour as became a confident general surrounded by trusted troops. I attended parades, mingled with the men, jested happily with centurions. Grasping diversion from necessity I galloped, lance in hand, after boar and deer and followed the hunting dogs with a reckless ardour that earned scarcely veiled reproof from Valens and Agricola. The Atrebatan nobles, who sometimes hunted with us, disapproved also, for different reasons, because I speared the cornered beasts with utter disregard of the Britons' ancient rituals of the chase.

My wanderings, attended only by a couple of guards, through Silchester's streets became so much a habit that townsfolk hardly turned their heads. Buildings flourished like flowers in a well-tilled garden and blossomed like petals from the proud calyx of basilica and forum. But the Atrebates, with their rustic proclivity for open spaces, imposed country-house gardens upon a town's narrow confines. Each building was a small island in a vast field. Good building land was wasted. Native huts still disfigured the new houses and often nudged some imposing mansion so closely that it seemed the owner was reluctant to discard entirely the simple farm-huts of his youth.

A glance at the ramparts dispelled any notion of making Silchester a fortress against Boudicca. Time and weather had consolidated the high earthen banks; part was revetted, but the crest wore no palisade and the entrance, lacking gates and gatehouses, yawned like tired old men.

In the evenings, after the first watch mounted and the camp gates closed, Aurelius Bassus and Valens and his principal centurions generally visited my mansion. Over supper and wine we talked the talk of soldiers immersed in their trade: tactics and armour, ballistas and boots. Inevitably the conversation drifted to our current difficulties and incited discussion of measures against the dangers which, as all these senior officers recognized, were quickening against us hour by hour.

At the close of our fourth day in Silchester we met as usual. The evening was warm; we lay on couches in the cloistered arcade overlooking the garden. After supper I dismissed servants and guards beyond earshot so that we could talk freely. In gathering dusk the scent of flowers drifted like incense; the western sky glowed lemon-pale and early stars blinked timidly from a blue-dark vault. For a time we lay without speaking, quietly resting, absorbing tranquillity and peace, relaxing in that treasured calm which Silchester wore like an old and comfortable garment.

Valens poured wine.

'One more day,' he said without emphasis. 'Then the men eat pig. Three more days—no more pig. What then?'

'Only two days' meat after all this hunting, Valens?'

'It takes a lot of flesh to feed eleven thousand.'

'A vast appetite for such a small army. But two days is time enough.'

Valens set down his cup with a vigour that made the crystal ring. 'Legate, what are you going to do?'

Lazily I flicked an olive stone into the lily-pond. 'Wait another day.'

'Wait? For what?'

'Boudicca. Or Augusta.'

Valens grunted, drank, belched noisily. Hoofbeats drummed in the distance, faded and swelled, a rhythmic pulse that beat in our ears.

Bassus said gently, 'And if neither appears, Legate?'

'We march.'

A moth blundered from the garden, hit the candelabra and fell to the flags. Agricola set his foot on the small, velvet body. The tiny crunch sounded loud in the stillness. Valens sighed, a long, slow exhalation.

'So. To Gloucester, or Portus?'

'You mistake me, Valens. We march east, to seek Boudicca.'

The legate came to his feet like a sprung blade. His cup shattered and sprayed slivers which glinted in the candlelight like diamonds.

'By the Twins! Here's defiance! Hark to old Rome! With half an army, nothing to eat—! Magnificent!' He capered wildly, a grotesque parody of a Grecian dance. 'You can depend on Gemina. If Britain can be saved—'

A sentry challenged. Feet scuffled the gravel, a voice protested, loud and urgent. Into the wan circle of light tramped a decurion of the guard, a tribune of XIV Legion at his heels.

'Duty tribune carrying urgent news for the Legate Suetonius Paulinus.'

'Yes, tribune?'

The youth's face was flushed; he breathed jerkily after the brief fury of his gallop from camp.

'The signal beacon is ablaze, Legate.'

I examined my nails. Valens swore softly, a long string of Gods. Agricola swallowed, gulped and spoke.

'Boudicca is at Staines.'

'So we must believe,' I said idly. I took my cup, held the wine to the light. 'Or at least approaching the river. Valens.'

'Legate?'

'All your men are in camp. Within an hour it will be quite dark. Until then routine must continue as usual: no parading, shouting or trumpet calls. Give a written message to your commanders to that effect, by the hand of this tribune. Tribune, you rode here through Silchester?'

'Yes, Legate.'

'At a frenzied gallop. I heard you. Return the same way, at a walk, and sing. You haven't a care in the world, understand?'

He nodded mutely.

I looked at my guests. 'We shall not be returning to the camp before dark, so make yourselves comfortable. Secundus! Tell the servants to fetch more wine, then prepare my armour.'

With his eyes Valens implored explanations. I smiled at him, shook my head and went indoors. Had he known that by the hand of a trusted spy I was about to send a message hurtling through the night to Boudicca he would probably have clapped me under arrest.

7

The candles guttered and smoked vilely. The corners of the big, bare room in legion headquarters retreated behind shadows. Men coughed and cleared their throats. The time was two hours before midnight. No gallopers had come from Staines to amplify the beacon's warning.

I studied the encircling faces, elusive in the flickering light as shadows on water.

I said, 'We have a fifteen-mile night march before us. The army's immediate object is to leave Silchester without anyone being the wiser: my hope is that nobody outside this camp will know, until dawn tomorrow, that we have gone.

'Half a mile of open country separates us from the town. To make certain that nobody is watching the camp we shall send patrols at once to sweep a quarter mile radius from the stockade, to seize anyone found and bring him in. Detail the Thracians for this work, Valens: they move quickly and quietly in the dark.

'Nobody else will leave camp, on any pretext, until the army marches at midnight. No man will leave his barrack until one hour before that time. All preparations must be made in silence and without lights. Your camp guards will remain behind, Valens: they will sound watches throughout the night as usual, change sentries, follow the normal routine.

'We will make a detour northwards around Silchester, following a forest path which rejoins the West Way two miles east of the town. I myself know this track well: my hours of chasing boar in the woods were not solely for exercise. I shall lead the vanguard.

'The army will march straight to battle. No preliminary camp. Therefore you go stripped for action, without transport, mules, pack-horses or followers. Rations will be carried on the man: one day's corn that is left and two days' meat.

'The bodyguard leads, Valens; then an auxiliary cohort. Cavalry in the rear. Otherwise arrange the order of march as you think best.'

The commanders departed, leaving only staff officers in the room. I stayed at the table, scribbling idly on a tablet, drawing from memory an area of heath and ridge and woodland, erasing and redrawing, tracing thereon the stylized symbols for cohorts and cavalry. With a quick sweep I obliterated the whole sketch, and stared into the candle flames.

This was the definitive moment. Irresolution and fear suddenly swirled in my mind like a tide-rip. Was my judgement right? A beacon had flared in the night; a middle-aged general, apparently glowing with a confidence inspired by good wine and congenial company, was committing his army to an onset which would be decisive and could be utterly disastrous.

Grimly I examined the record of the past fifteen days. My movements had been dictated by a ruthless, energetic and successful enemy. I had desperately sought the initiative and had been ceaselessly harried and always frustrated. I had resolved to fight only when all the components of my field force were united and had seen the concept shattered by an agile foe and a subordinate's ineptitude. Was this the way in which great issues were decided?

In this case it was. For mine was no time-split decision taken in the heat of wine. During all those long days in Silchester, during my solitary walks in the streets, in pauses of the chase, in wakeful hours in the silence of my bedchamber, I had probed all the chances, weighed all the factors of every possible contingency and had forged a solution to every single one. Fate and Boudicca had made this move: my counter-move was automatic, a response pondered, checked, cross-questioned and proved more rigorously than a lawyer's lie.

There simply was no other answer.

I sighed, shook my head like a diver breaking surface, walked to the door. The night was warm and starlit. The camp throbbed like a gigantic heart, alive and pulsing, but quiet, quiet and dark. To Valens's troops the bonds of strict discipline were accustomed clothing; orders at any hour, however bizarre, they accepted and fulfilled. Away towards the Sinister Gate only were there identifiable sounds, faint enough, but loud-seeming in this controlled hive of silence.

'The cavalry lines,' I said aloud. 'Agricola, send at a run. Quiet them.'

The cavalry alone, who had been under my direct command for the past fortnight, were lax in discipline. I smiled wryly in the gloom.

Valens and his senior centurions came to the praetorium and begged my attendance at the sacrifice and auspices. I sighed again, and went with them to the Temple of the Standards. By dim lantern light the standards were hastily blessed and distributed, the goat slaughtered the diviners were Valens's men, with whom I had no understanding. Mentally I composed a speech to combat unfavourable omens, to twist the signs to our own advantage. Somewhat to my surprise the diviners, after long deliberation over the steaming liver, declared that the Gods favoured our design. So, after a brief exhortation to the officers, I returned in relief to the bare wooden-walled room, sipped a last goblet of wine and hoped for a rider from Staines.

None came.

When the water-clock showed a half-hour to midnight I donned helmet, sword and cloak and walked to the Praetorian Gate. The streets were clear, but soldiers in rank upon rank crammed the seventy-yard space which separated barrack-huts from ramparts on all four sides of the camp. At the gate I found Valens.

'Awaiting parade states, Legate,' he said. A tribune alongside held in one hand a candle, in the other a sand-glass. Valens threw the glass an anxious glance.

Tribunes, prefects, centurions, decurions reported, low-voiced, strengths and readiness. At last Valens turned towards me, saluted.

'XIV Legion Gemina and attached troops, as ordered, await your commands, Legate.'

The gate creaked, swung open. I rode across the causeway into the night.

8

In starlight the forest track was distinct and easy to follow. We forded a shallow stream, emerged from the trees, plodded across fields, skirted a sleeping farmhouse and struck the West Way. I led on for four mile-stones and halted. Units closed up, passed reports to the van. I sent auxiliaries, 3rd Bracarii, ahead and moved forward.

The individual backs of marching auxiliaries coalesced into a long wedge which narrowed like a dark sword-blade and obliterated the grey ribbon of road. Behind my horse iron-nailed boots crunched the metalling with a cadence like the repeated surge of eroding waves; the sound reached down the four-mile column and died with a whisper like wind in the grasses. The stars shone clear and steady, throwing a strange violet glow on bushes and mounds beside the Way, and farther off the forest trees, as though spurning the gift of light, flung black curtains across the silvered landscape.

We halted at every third milestone. The second halt brought a commotion among the vanguard, the rap of challenge and countersign. Hoofbeats thudded, horsemen loomed dark on the road. The body-guard closed and waited, challenged in turn.

'Proculus's Horse.'

The decurion spoke his message, rapid and succinct.

'Several thousand hostiles reached Staines just before dark, Legate. Horse, foot and chariots. They were starting to cross the river when I withdrew. No losses among my troops. Our native allies, the Atrebates'—he spat—'have joined the enemy or dispersed this side the river, I don't know where.'

I said, 'Get your men off the road. Fall in at the rear. Be silent. Then rejoin me here.'

We moved on. The decurion reappeared at my side.

'Tell me what happened,' I said. 'Keep your voice low.'

'They came along the West Way, Legate. Only a few hundreds at first. Tried to cross the river. The Atrebates showed themselves and shot some arrows. The enemy turned, splashed from the water, lined the bank, yelled their lungs out. Soon they were reinforced: several thousands, I judged. I told our signallers to fire the beacon.'

He coughed, dry throated, and rubbed his lips.

'That Atrebatan leader, Pertacus, began to parley, shouting from bank to bank. I couldn't follow his gab but he seemed remarkably friendly. Plenty of smiles and laughter. The Atrebates were all crowded up where the bridge had been, Pertacus in front, thigh-deep in the river, and opposite the enemy swarmed, happy as you please, looking ready to burst across at any moment. Gangs of rebels were hunting up and down the banks, wading into the water and out again, looking for fords.'

A pale sheen touched the horizon ahead, the faintest sigh of colour, evanescent as mist on a mirror.

'I didn't like it. I couldn't see round the bends in the river. A lot might have been going on I knew nothing about. You understand, Legate? I sent word to our patrols at the fords to fall back on the road.

'Some of his Atrebates obviously disagreed with Pertacus and his arrangements with the rebels. Much argument and arm waving. Presently Atrebates began slipping away from the river and vanished in the trees, leaving Pertacus to his dirty work. A good number stayed with him, though.'

The decurion sucked his teeth reflectively.

'I was busy collecting my men, out of sight of the bridge, and couldn't watch all the time. When next I looked the press on the opposite bank was so great you'd have thought each blade of grass had become a warrior. Among them, on the road, was a woman in a red chariot.'

'Boudicca?'

'Who else? Pertacus stretched his arms towards her like a lover, splashed deeper and waded across, followed by some of his men. Then our beacon flared on the hill, and the natives saw it.'

The eastern sky glowed a delicate pearl-grey, the translucent tinge of burnished iron.

'They swept into the water like wild boars running from a forest fire, and filled the river from bank to bank. I didn't wait. Ordered files about and galloped. And here I am.'

'You have done well, decurion. Join your men.'

I had staked my decision on a fire-signal that might have heralded no more than a raiding party seeking loot, a war-band escaped from Boudicca's control, or merely a reconnaissance in force. This nagging fear was ended. Where the Queen went her army followed. All the rebels in Britain—Iceni, Trinovantes, Catuvellauni, Coritani—awaited us over the rim of the horizon, where the dawn etched ridge and hill and tree-scape like bleak precipices against a primrose sky.

From the saddle a man could see ground underfoot. I halted the column.

'From here, Valens, I am going on fast with a cavalry regiment. Send 1st Tungrians from the rearguard. You will bring the army on. Put out flank guards before you move, though I don't think there's much likelihood of contact yet.'

Valens broke his night-long silence. 'How much farther?'

'Three miles. Let the men talk. We can be seen now from farther than voices carry.'

The Tungrians, all iron-clash and leather-creak, pounded from the rear, sent point troops scouring ahead, swept onwards at a canter. With staff and bodyguard cavalry I followed close, and loose flints sprayed beneath our hooves.

Soon we climbed a long slope, breasted a ridge and looked upon that empty expanse of sodden grassland where Agricola, days before, had delivered his lecture on tactics.

The place, though not perfect, was the best killing-ground between Staines and Silchester. Here we must fight our last battle.

9

The Tungrian cavalry posted vedettes a mile beyond the ridge where the heath dissolved in a welter of straggling woods. I galloped from end to end of the position and examined the ground in detail. The ridge curved like a bow, concave side towards the enemy, with the horns swelling into knolls on either flank. That on the left was a small spur, six hundred yards across, jutting from the main ridge. The feature on the right was more extensive and extended for a thousand yards southwards, being separated from the ridge itself by a narrow valley. This flaw in a good position was hidden by a projecting spur of the right-hand hill which curtained the re-entrant and almost concealed it from the enemy's view.

Thorn, briar, hedge-oak, elder and scrubby pines covered the crest and reverse slopes from end to end. No one could describe this as forest: the soil was too poor and sandy to support big trees. But a better hindrance to movement could hardly be imagined than this tangled vegetation which was dense enough to baulk a hungry goat.

My flanks and rear were thus secured by nature. The forward slopes presented a bare, gravelled scarp extending like an apron for three hundred paces to the soggy heath where horsemen, as I soon proved for myself, could ride no faster than a trot. Only on our extreme left was the ground firm enough for horse and chariot to manœuvre.

My sketches from memory on the tablet in Silchester had been reasonably accurate and required only minor alterations to correspond with reality. To staff tribunes and centurions I explained our dispositions and frontages, stationed guides on the reverse slope, by the roadside, for each unit, and hurried back to meet the army.

The long column filled the road beyond sight. I greeted Valens, drew him aside and stood to watch the cohorts pass.

Cavalry first, jingling and clashing, flaunting gay cloaks like banners, lances twirled and flung aloft in salute. Auxiliaries, tough little Bracarii, leather-capped, unarmoured, flat square shields bobbing on their backs as they jogged in that characteristic, shuffling half-trot which could cover fifty miles in a day. Infantry of the bodyguard, tall, proud-stepping men whose gleaming armour and glossy leather scorned such dim preservatives as oil and grease. The Eagle-escort of XIV Legion Gemina, a taut phalanx surrounding the glittering standard presented, nearly a century before, by the Divine Augustus. Headquarter tribunes in gilded cuirass and complicated helmets, brash gallants prancing on curvetting chargers.

Looming through dust-haze tramped the Legion, the heavy infantry, the splendour of Rome and the hammer of her enemies. Six abreast, javelins sloped, they swung rank upon rank in measured harmony: boot-crash on gravel, cuirass-creak, scabbard-thump and, like a dominant chord, the metallic susurration of bronze-studded apron strips swinging and clashing in unison. From their passing rose an aura of dust and oil, greased leather and sweat, a scent sweeter to my nostrils than spikenard of Syria. And as they marched they sang a nonsensical ditty with a rhythmic tune:

> *Cras amet qui nunquam amavit.*
> *Quique amavit cras amet.*

Suddenly I was no longer afraid. These short, swarthy, arrogant men ruled the earth. No one could beat them. I grinned at them. They laughed back. Their confidence enveloped my chilly fears with the warm comfort of a furred cloak. At this moment I knew the long tale of reverses was ended.

'Jupiter, how they stink!' Vettius Valens, always short-tempered in the early morning, snorted and wiped nose on scarf.

'No matter, Valens. Here are the true auspices of victory—five thousand of them. They're better omens, much better, than your gut-poking diviner could provide.'

I smiled at his shocked expression and turned to follow my men. I was humming a little song.

> *Cras amet qui nunquam amavit.*
> *Quique amavit cras amet.*

15

'In the capacious urn of death every name is shaken.'

HORACE

Extract from a letter written three months later to Sextus Afranius Burrus, Praetorian Prefect.

1

You ask me, Burrus, to embroider the baldly official dispatch which reported my last battle against Boudicca. What more can I add? What is there to say about an action which went exactly according to plan, where the sequence from contact to pursuit flowed without pause or dislocation in the ordered cadences of a poem by Horace or Catullus? But I know your avidity for military detail and so, to gratify an old friend, and because of certain matters which could be of technical interest to the Prince's War Minister, I pen for your eyes alone the account that follows.

The army's deployment from column of route to line of battle was a smooth and fluent operation capably managed by the guides I had provided for every cohort. XIV Gemina, extended on the left by XX Valeria's first cohort, held the main position: the brow of a ridge which curved in a gentle arc. The length of their line was something under fifteen hundred yards, thus allowing a six-rank depth. Behind them, athwart the road, I placed my only reserve: the bodyguard cohort of horse and foot.

Cavalry held the wings. The left, on a somewhat narrow knoll, was guarded by Pannonians, Vettonians and Indus's Horse. The right, a broader plateau, gave more room for Proculus's Horse, Asturians and Tungrians. The latter, at this stage, were a mile ahead, covering our deployment and seeking the enemy. Both places were constricted, the left especially, so that the regiments, tightly massed, were packed so close to the forest that rear-rank horses bucketed and kicked against the brambles. The inconvenience was temporary: these hillocks were mere assembly areas; I had no intention of fighting on them.

I posted my skirmishers—Bracarii in the middle, Vangiones and Vardulli on the flanks—nearly a thousand paces in front in a straight line covering the whole ridge. Thracian archers, mounted and afoot, I distributed my troops and centuries along the line. You will understand that my screen was very tenuous, only three hundred cavalry and two thousand infantry. This, in Britain, is our usual handicap. Until our auxiliary strength is greatly reinforced you will never hear, from this Province, a repetition of a not uncommon event in Rome's military history: a battle fought and won by auxiliaries alone, while the legions stand and watch. But this is an old bone, one that we will not chew now.

An engineer squad tore a gap in the causeway within bowshot of the skirmishers. For chariots the highway alone gave access to our front; a simple demolition prevented any irruption by those overrated fighting vehicles.

The dispositions, then, seen with a bird's eye, were like an archer's bow whose string was the auxiliary skirmish line; the curved stave was a legionary crescent holding the ridge, and the West Way, like an arrow, cut through the centre.

The men dressed ranks and stood at ease and leaned on their javelins. I rode along the entire front, sometimes extending the intervals between centuries—centurions in battle-line are always prone to contract their manœuvre-gaps—and called commanders to conference. Away ahead, tiny in the distance, Tungrian vedettes unhurriedly scoured the woods. A chorus of birds filled the air with song. The sun's first rays sucked a drifting haze from the damp heathland.

I had secured my objective. Now all we had to do was wait.

2

You will certainly have heard, Burrus, various criticisms of the methods by which I seized the ground where I wanted to fight. Some of these grumbles, conceived in the minds of amateur strategists and ventilated during sterile debates in the Senate House, have already floated by devious routes to my ears. The only aspersion that, lacking inner knowledge, might stick in your mind is the accusation that after a fifteen-mile approach march I committed my army to battle without supplies or transport, without a base and without the certainty that the enemy would indeed offer battle on that or any subsequent day.

All but the last of these charges are true; and the last is only partially false because in war is no certainty. But grant the extreme probability that Boudicca would certainly meet me on the day and place I had chosen and then the other moves are revealed as vital to my plans. And I was convinced that she would be there because I had offered her a bait more compelling than bloody meat to a shark.

I dined in my house with Vettius Valens and other companions on the night when beacons signalled the alarm to Silchester. My first action was to send two trustworthy Atrebatan agents, well rehearsed in their parts, at full gallop to Staines. They rode by different routes, to lessen the chances of interception or capture, and were to pretend they had been sent by malcontents of the anti-Government faction among the Atrebates. Their message to the rebels was brief: the Roman Army had no supplies and, half-starved and despondent, was due next day to retire from Silchester towards Gloucester.

A gamble, you may think. True, but the risk lay in the ruse's execution and not the outcome. A fall in the dark or interception by our cavalry at Staines might have prevented either messenger from reaching the Queen. In fact both arrived, were accepted, their stories believed. No general in Boudicca's position could have failed to react with the utmost vigour. Her object was to catch and destroy my small force before it could reach safety in a fortress or be reinforced by other legions. Here, it seemed, was her god-sent opportunity. A quick move, a rapid march and, somewhere on the road beyond Silchester, she could overtake and force me to battle on unequal terms and unfavourable ground.

You see, Burrus? I *knew* on that morning of the 27th May Boudicca would be whipping her rabble towards Silchester like a huntsman cheering hounds to the kill. Therefore I *had* to reach my chosen battleground before her and, to make surprise effective, she must have no inkling that I was anywhere but on the road to Gloucester and salvation.

Hence the night march without transport because, as you well know, our supply-trains are the most undisciplined and uncontrollable element of the army. Indeed, I have often considered the wisdom of enlisting a special corps of supply and transport drivers under the same rules of discipline that govern our soldiers. I am composing a treatise on the subject for your perusal. In this instance a pack of slaves, freedmen and mules, stumbling around in the dark and losing their way, would have advertised our course throughout the countryside. I could not afford to sacrifice surprise for the sake of the soldiers' comforts.

What, in fact, did we lack? The men carried entrenching tools and palisade stakes, so we could fortify a camp. They had three days' rations. Only tents and reserves of arms, equipment and food were missing. I realize, nevertheless, that the expedient is unprecedented in the annals of Roman war. You can rest assured I shall not strive to repeat it.

All military teaching and all the manuals of tactics insist on a firm base, a fortified camp at least, within easy reach of the battle-ground where our forces, if worsted, can retire to reorganize and recoup. I had none nearer than Silchester, fifteen miles away. Granted. But I had no time for digging ditches. Boudicca was approaching: my army must be in line of battle when she appeared. Was I, for the sake of a hastily-dug rampart, to be caught as the Nervii caught Caesar at the river Sambre?

So, my dear Burrus, you can meet my critics, if you feel so inclined, with the assertion that I may have been unorthodox but was never rash. Yet I feel, such is the conservatism of the Roman military mind, that whereas the battle might in time find mention in our text-books the approach march, of which I am secretly proud, will be ignored or dismissed as a regrettable aberration on the part of an otherwise competent general. Am I not right?

3

Commanders met me near the road, in view of the battle-line. The men, for some reason, like to see the general delivering his orders before battle, even if they cannot hear what is said. The group was large and unwieldy, nearly half a cohort strong: more than twenty tribunes and prefects, a hundred centurions and over ninety cavalry decurions. I think, Burrus, we should consider a different system for giving battle-orders. Ours, with the merits of speed and personal impact, has the obvious disadvantage of separating junior commanders from their units for too long, and often by a considerable distance, when contact with the enemy is imminent or already exists.

My audience was in fact so large that I had to shout, which I dislike intensely. I told them we should see the Britons very soon, and that they were impressive only in their numbers. Lest they be dismayed when they saw the plain before them swarming with warriors, I emphasized our advantages. We were on higher ground; our front was exactly suited to our strength, so that we had sufficient depth; our flanks and rear were unassailable.

For the conduct of the battle I gave detailed orders which I shall not repeat here—you will recognize them as the action unfolds—and delivered the usual harangue. Army custom nowadays demands less in this line from a general than in the old days: Scipio's prebattle speeches, if his histories can be trusted, must have taken longer than the conflict itself.

In my exhortation I again warned the men not to be intimidated by the sight of the enemy's massive strength or by the noise they made. Spectacle and clamour were their only assets. The vociferous multitude they were about to see were no more than badly-armed, ill-led natives the like of whom they had thrashed on the hills and plains of Britain from Richborough to Anglesey, from Lincoln to Exeter. If our men kept their ranks close, attended to their centurions' orders, pushed with their shields and hewed a passage with their swords then victory was certain. They must not, I warned them, stop to plunder during the battle: they could loot their fill when the rebels were dead.

When the commanders had gone I turned to survey the army. The men were stripped for action. Packs, cloaks and palisade stakes had been discarded and shield covers stripped. This impedimenta, normally removed by followers to the wagon-train, they dumped in precise, orderly lines behind the ranks. Because my battle-plan permitted only a single javelin volley I had ordered everyone but the front rank to plant his javelins upright among the piled baggage, so that the enemy should still receive the visual effect of a forest of spears.

The legionaries rested, without breaking ranks. Some gambled or chattered or sang; others squatted or lay supine, arms across faces, apparently asleep. The sun had not yet escaped the enshrouding clouds which mounted with him as he climbed the sky, and this was fortunate, for otherwise the light would have struck full in our eyes.

4

I confess to you, Burrus, that with three hours elapsed since dawn and no sign of the enemy I was becoming nervous. Had my agents failed to reach Boudicca? Had she ignored them? Was she marching by another route? I suffered a long agony of suspense which endured until an agitated flurry among the Tungrian vedettes ejected a messenger who careered along the road towards us.

He reported contact with chariots and native horse. I directed the Tungrians to fall back to their battle positions: it was no part of their work to hinder the enemy's advance.

The cavalry plodded troop by troop over the heath to the right-hand hillock. Enemy was close upon the rearguard's heels. Chariots spurted from the woods, converged and mounted the causeway, rattled in pursuit. The Tungrians, irritated by such rude hustling, turned about and charged, scattering chariots and horsemen.

This was the first clash.

For the next hour the spectacle resembled nothing so much as an audience slowly filling the auditorium of a vast theatre. First came cavalry and chariots, like eager playgoers hurrying to secure the best seats. The heavy mire forced the shaggy British ponies to a walk; the chariots, entirely baffled, scrambled for the causeway where they jammed like midnight traffic at the Appian Gate, or edged to our left where the ground was firmer. One and all, at first sight of our army on the heights, silent and formidable as a city wall, halted at a respectful distance and flung distracted cries one to another and then, forced onwards by the concourse filling the heath behind, edged reluctantly nearer.

I sounded battle stations. The men stood, shook themselves, slipped arms through shield-straps, adjusted helmets, loosened swords in scabbards. Centurions, immensely busy, disposed distances, intervals and manœuvre-gaps to a hand's-breadth. The cavalry, with a ripple of movement as if shaken by a sudden windgust, swung into the saddle.

I rode slowly to my place upon the road where the bodyguard massed exactly behind Gemina's left cohort, and raised my scarlet battle standard.

5

The skirmishers engaged. The Britons in the van were not eager to come to grips, but the tide of warriors which was filling the plain thrust them within arrow and slingshot range. I have no doubt that at this stage the enemy were utterly surprised by the physical fact of our presence and preparedness. They had advanced from Staines in the natural manner of tribal armies: a disorderly mob which scoured the countryside and gave hardly a thought to the retreating foe whom they had not expected to meet for another twenty miles. The sight of our battle-line checked them like a horse reined on his haunches.

The auxiliaries were able to enjoy themselves. In this kind of long-range missile-fight they were unsurpassed: they shot faster, more concertedly and more accurately than the Britons. The Bracarii in the centre delivered a tempest of slingshots that actually forced the natives to give ground—a feat which, against the pressure at their backs, seemed physically impossible. The Vangiones and Vardulli horsemen periodically flung short, fierce charges from the wings against little bands that encroached too near, while their infantry hurled arrows and throwing-spears in alternate volleys. The Thracians ranged behind the line, individualists to a man, each seeking his target and dispatching arrows that seldom missed.

But experience had taught me that Thracian archers would not stand when their arrows were gone, and so I told a tribune to mark and watch a particular Thracian and to count his shots. A quiver held thirteen arrows. When these were finished the bowmen would be looking over their shoulders and the skirmish line, a spent force, was ready for recall.

Meanwhile the rebel army, like a river bursting through a broken dyke, flooded the field of battle. The sight was nearly beyond description or belief. The plain became a ferment, an ebullience where colour and movement gyrated and intermingled and ebbed and flowed until the turbulence passed beyond the limits of human vision or comprehension. I could distinguish no set divisions among this host, no order, no formation; the whole array seemed in perpetual flux and commotion. I can give no conception of the noise. Battle-cry and war-chant competed with a thousand bellowing horns; horses neighed; and those huge hounds which the natives use both for hunting and war strained at their leashes and bayed and howled.

For what it is worth, I was told later that the Iceni, the largest contingent, held the centre, with Coritani on the right and Catuvellauni on the left. We never discovered where the Trinovantes and Pertacus's insurgent Atrebates were stationed.

Only one indication of system and forethought was apparent. The better-armed warriors were in front. From our elevation we could see a broad band of multi-coloured cloaks, brightly-enamelled shields and painted helmets which fringed the host like the foaming rim of an earthquake wave. Picked fighters, these; mighty men of huge stature, tall as a javelin, blue-eyed and bearded and long-haired, and their hair was the tawny colour of sunlit autumn oak-leaf. I saw them afterwards, in their hundreds, when they were dead.

I have often thought, Burrus, that the massive physique of western barbarians engenders in them a false confidence, a mistaken belief that they cannot fail to overcome, in war, the stocky, cut-rumped dwarfs who fill our legions. Otherwise a hundred years of defeat in Gaul and Spain, in Germany and Britain, must surely have sated their appetite for death upon our swords. A Celtic aristocrat is a warrior and little else; fighting is the only trade he knows. Fortunately for us, perhaps, he is an amateur, disinclined by custom and temperament to that incessant practice which alone can perfect his art. He neither understands nor admires the discipline and drudgery, all and every day throughout twenty years' service, which transforms our puny little Romans to a killing machine which inevitably destroys him at every successive encounter.

The fight on our skirmish line was closing to sword-length when a tribune called my attention to an astounding development at the enemy's rear. From the woods debouched long columns of wagons and carts, pack-ponies and laden donkeys and straggling herds of cattle. The warrior-mass upon the heath prevented them from advancing farther, and they spread right and left in ever-increasing numbers until they enclosed the plain like a concrete wall, a tightly packed crescent a mile long, a ten-fold barricade of animals and vehicles whereon, like spectators at the Games, mounted a shrill multitude—the wives and mothers and concubines of Boudicca's teeming army.

For a moment I was worried. Was this some new and crafty tactic? The obstacle, solid as a cliff, effectively closed the battlefield and changed the nature of the terrain.

I remembered tribal habits. When Britons go to war they take their possessions with them, down to the last-born babe and newest-fledged cockerel. Sometimes, when particularly certain of victory, barbarians will bring this version of a baggage-train to the very battlefield itself. You will remember, Burrus, a similar incident which Caesar recorded during his campaign against the Helvetii. But never yet, to my knowledge, had they so uncompromisingly hemmed the contestants that retreat for their own men was made impossible. Were they acting thus by design, ignorance, or simple over-confidence?

I shrugged. The thing was done. I had not foreseen the movement and I could not visualize its effect upon the battle. I switched my attention to a curious procession on the causeway.

6

This was the last time I set eyes on Boudicca, so it is a pity she was too far away for me to study her expression or hear her voice. To my middle-aged eyes she was a tiny golden doll in a small red chariot, noticeable among a hundred thousand crowded bodies only by the fervour she excited among her followers. For what ensues, then, I am indebted to the keen vision of young staff officers and to stories told later by captives.

Stationary chariots thronged the road where the Queen's conspicuous war-car, drawn by two white horses, threaded a wary passage. She wore, as usual, a yellow cloak and golden ornaments to match her hair, which flowed unbound over her shoulders. Beside her in the chariot— which must have been uncomfortably crowded—stood her two daughters, those unfortunate victims of Catus's slaves.

During her slow journey towards the front she harangued her warriors. Whatever she said could not have been heard by more than a small fraction of those she addressed, but her appearance alone aroused sustained roars of acclamation and waving spears and much beating of swords on shields. Nor have her words been recorded by anyone I met afterwards: an omission that will certainly be repaired by our own historians in the future, when deathless words will be put in Queen Boudicca's mouth.

Her exhortations had one positive effect. From somewhere within that vast rabble men who held aloft long spear-shafts struggled to the front. They appeared to be some kind of standard-bearers: the spears were garnished and the bearers well-accoutred. They pushed beyond the foremost ranks, shouting, and the tangled fighting at the skirmish line died away; the British warriors withdrew, leaving these native vexillars, two score and more, standing clear in the space, brandishing their burdens.

Standards they were indeed, Roman standards. Cohort and century standards—Hispana's 1st, 3rd and 6th cohorts, Petra's Horse, the 1st Cugerni—tarnished and damaged, the pitiful emblems of a murdered vexillation. Each standard spiked a head, mouldered and unrecognizable, and the bearers wore Roman armour, ill-fitting and slipshod, as though to emphasize their mocking travesty of everything our soldiers held most sacred.

A terrifying sound exploded from our ranks: shame and horror expressed in a deep groan, and anger, which turned the groan to a rising growl, and enormous rage which burst in a roar that sent the sham vexil-lars reeling for shelter to their own shield-wall. Our line bulged ominously. It seemed for a second that the legionaries would charge the enemy there and then. Centurions turned about, plied their staves like servants beating draperies. The surge subsided.

I, who had watched this performance in grim silence, gave thanks to the Gods and Boudicca. She had supplied the ultimate insult, the last unbearable stab of the goad that drives good soldiers beyond sanity. Nothing, absolutely nothing, could hold this legion now.

Events moved swiftly. The Britons flung a headlong attack on the length of our skirmish line. I sounded recall. The auxiliaries yielded, broke and ran, skipped agilely to the flanks and cleared our front, pur-sued by a storm of arrows. The tribal army gave one stupendous shout and raced towards us in a torrent that raged like a stampede of wild animals.

I raised my arm. Every horn and trumpet sounded. The pealing clangour quelled all sound; for a moment the Britons faltered, lost cohe-sion. In that silence ten thousand swords rasped from scabbards with a whisper like the husky voice of doom. Shields up, sword-hands low, the legion moved down the slope at a steady, controlled run.

7

You will recall, Burrus, Domitius Corbulo's little pamphlet, published after his first campaign against the Parthians, in which he advocated certain changes in our battle tactics. Corbulo being who he is no one could dismiss his ideas as merely the private fads of another successful general: you yourself, if I remember right, used the Praetorian Guard to experiment with his more promising theories. The sequel gave an important addition to our training manuals: the cohort wedge was introduced as an alternative to line or to century echelon in attack.

I recollect that many experienced soldiers in Rome disapproved strongly. Vespasian was particularly vehement. 'We'll be reverting to maniples next,' he declared bitterly. He saw in it an attempt to restore the cohort as the tactical unit, a practice outmoded decades ago when Pompey established century manœuvre as the basis of battle-drill. But, so far as the army was concerned, the movement was in the text-books and had to be practised.

By and large I have small admiration for our Parthian conqueror, as you are aware. Yet the more I watched this evolution practised on parade grounds at Gloucester, Wroxeter and Lincoln the more convinced I became that against an undisciplined and incoherent enemy such as we fight on all the frontiers of Empire the cohort wedge was a battle-winner. I encouraged my legates to perfect the technique.

One small alteration I made for the occasion. Corbulo, as you know, recommended one century at the apex and two echeloned rearwards on either flank. The sixth century, detached, he held in tactical reserve. I had no reserve other than the bodyguard; I therefore stationed the sixth century at the base of the wedge, ready to support and reinforce wherever required. An improvement in some ways, don't you think?

8

The legion, I need hardly say, advanced in line—you cannot deliver javelin volleys from wedge—and checked at twenty paces' range. The front rank flung their javelins, light and heavy following point to haft. The Britons wavered. Their foremost warriors, spitted like bullocks, fell as a spent wave collapses on shingle. The rest leapt the bodies and came on.

Javelins gone, the wedges struck like fangs. Along the whole front Roman and Briton met shield to shield, sword to sword, with a crash that shivered to the skies.

I sat my horse, still as a rock, and the sweat was cold upon my temples. In a clash of this kind, where you cannot manœuvre, outflank, or throw in massive reserves at the crucial moment, when you cannot execute any tactics of open warfare, when you can only hew straight ahead, nothing counts but the training and discipline of your soldiers and the strength of their sword-arms. In such battles the issue is usually won and lost within an hour.

The first shock carried our wedges deep into the British ranks. The enemy rallied and a standstill combat raged from wing to wing. The rebels caught in the V's between the wedges, forced to fight on two fronts, showed a disposition to disengage from what they regarded as something of a trap. On the other hand our spearhead centuries could make no headway against the enormous press of infuriated natives battering at their shields.

Valens's men fought beautifully. His centurions—contrary to the usual practice where individuals called on covering files for relief when they were tired or hurt—were taught to relieve the entire front rank whenever the fighting allowed, before weariness or wounds curbed their vigour. The neat, sidestepping movements whereby each century's front suddenly produced twelve fresh legionaries to oppose a tiring enemy were a delight to a soldier's eye.

You have realized what was happening, Burrus. In this fight, a hundred thousand against six—for our cavalry were not yet engaged—my selection of ground where no outflanking was possible, my choice of a cut-and-thrust battle, permitted no more than a thousand Britons—the precise man-power of my battle-front—to engage at any one time. Each of our men had to fight ten tribesmen, but he could deal with them singly, in succession. The result was never in doubt.

Gradually, at different places, at varying speeds, the front began to move. First, the centuries flanking the wedges found opposition weakening and thrust forward. The apex angles widened, flattened until our battle-line was all but straight. Frenzied by this reverse the Britons fought back fiercely. Our advance ceased.

The hour-glass was two-thirds run.

Away on the right, opposite Gemina's sixth cohort, the enemy suddenly gave ground. The cohort followed, steadfast and controlled, re-forming wedge and flinging the reserve century into a dangerous gap that opened at the junction with its neighbour. Soon the enemy facing the second cohort began to retreat, more slowly, and then elsewhere, and then the entire line was moving, not fast, a step at a time, steadily, and there were no more checks.

I watched the wings closely, for you must understand that once our flanks had pressed beyond the sheltering horns of the ridge they became exposed to attack and could be turned. Compelled by the pressure in front, large numbers of enemy had already splayed to right and left rather than retreat. They hovered there, impotent but eager, like wild dogs watching a fight between leopards. On our left, where the ground was firm, the disengaged elements contained many chariots and cavalry.

The time had come to disperse these separate threats. The tribune Julius Agricola commanded our horse on the left—his first command—and the prefect Aurelius Munatius Bassus on the right. I sent gallopers to both.

A scream of trumpets sped the cavalry down the slopes. They hit the Britons with the unexpected force of a mill-race. The flanks dissolved in an instantaneous swirl, a chaotic welter that contrasted vividly with the plodding, remorseless battle of the centre.

Like a door burst from its hinges the whole enemy front collapsed. A stubbornly resistant battle-line changed without warning into a frenzied rout. The reason is hard to explain. Perhaps the rebels, severely pressed by the legion, already knew themselves half-beaten and the sudden convulsion on the wings finally broke their nerve. A ferocious and tenacious warrior army was transformed within ten pulse-beats to a featureless rabble that strove madly to escape our swords.

The battle was over. Nothing remained now but the killing.

9

I had never moved from the ridge. This is the only occasion, Burrus, when I have taken no personal part in an action where I was present; the only time I had belied my legionaries' nickname. An exemplary general presiding over a model battle!

Soon after the enemy broke I rode from the hill in order to keep contact with the pursuit. After fifty yards I paused in surprise. The rout was on; all organized resistance had ceased; nevertheless our line advanced hardly faster than they had against the Britons' spear-studded shield wall.

On the flanks the cavalry mellays boiled like turbulent seas. Troops charged, rallied, wheeled and streaked in pursuit of flying chariots and scurrying horsemen. In the centre the legionary ranks skewed crookedly across the heath, and gaps opened in the line wider than reserve centuries could fill. Through these gaps, like water spirited between our fingers, spewed frantic Britons who sought refuge on the wooded heights where we stood.

I ordered my bodyguard to deal with the fugitives. While this minor massacre progressed behind our battle-line I scanned the field, seeking a reason for our sluggish advance.

You must realize that the line was now fully a thousand yards from my command-post. Looking ahead I saw, first, the guard hunting their prey over a corpse-littered heath; then, beyond the saw-edged corrugations of the legion's line, a huge mass of humanity raged like a great splotched sea rent by cross-currents and tide-rips. The battle-din sounded a sharper note; the crazy tones of terror drowned trumpet and death-yell and battle-cry.

I put heels to my charger, skirted the cleft in the road where broken-backed horses still struggled among shattered chariots and dead men, regained the causeway and hurried to the front. Valens saw and joined me. Our combined staffs and guards clustered on the road; horses stamped the paving and tribunes chattered excitedly.

My brief query met an equally succinct reply. The legate explained that the enemy were trying to run but couldn't. They, and we, were checked by the wagon-barrier that stopped the rout like a dam. Like reapers scything corn, our men could advance only over the bodies of those they killed. Valens added, unamusedly, that it was slow and tiring work, but not dangerous.

I rode closer to the sweating backs of our centuries and saw the truth. In the distance the banked wagon-lines, many yards deep, were marked by a rising wave of flying bodies which scrambled across baggage, carts and cattle as a torrent swirls over a fallen log. Between this barrier and our cohorts a broken army was being systematically butchered. Beyond the wagons, where the woods began, our cavalry were closing from the wings and killing furiously amongst the trees. The heathland was one vast slaughter-house.

Valens espied a disarrayed cohort and left precipitately, trailing a stream of oaths. I stayed a long time, surveying the carnage. The legion reached the wagons, climbed across. The screams and shouting faded. Far away in the woods cavalry trumpets sang, hallooing to the chase.

I sent gallopers to Valens, to the cavalry commanders. Orders for the cohorts to stand, re-form; for the cavalry to pursue to the river ten miles away, and no farther.

Strewn on the heath's expanse the dead lay piled in heaps, in rows, in tattered strings like seaweed on a beach. Among them the wounded crawled and staggered and thrashed and moaned. Auxiliaries, disregarding my ban on plunder, flitted like hungry wolves from pile to pile, their daggers busy. Broken chariots, dead and hamstrung horses, shields and weapons littered the trampled tussock-grass like the shredded wrack of a hurricane. At the wagons a wall of corpses towered yoke-high; and women and children, cattle, donkeys, goats sprawled in a shambles of twisted limbs and blood and spewed entrails. From ten thousand separate agonies the aftermath of battle plucked its tune, and a wailing moan that was a litany and hymn of mutilation throbbed to the skies.

10

The sun shone high in an azure heaven where golden clouds drifted lazily like ragged sails. Two hours, I reckoned: two hours had smashed the scourge which had ravaged Britain since that terrible dusk, nineteen days before, when Boudicca descended upon Colchester. Where was she now, I wondered idly. Dead? Buried somewhere beneath this carnage? If alive she must be found.

Trumpets insistently repeated their brazen commands. Centuries rallied to standards, ranked and dressed, detailed parties to search for missing comrades. The men moved wearily, like sleepwalkers, drunk and numb with slaughter, blood-streaked from heel to helmet. The marching squads were ochre blots upon the yellowed grass, black checkers on a hideous game-board.

Prisoners appeared, stumbling groups herded like animals, driven by sword and spear. I regarded them speculatively, tempted by the idea of total extermination, a battle with no vanquished survivors. These people were rebels; they were criminals guilty of the crime of treason; they had forfeited the boon of quarter which custom and the usages of war allow to defeated enemies; they deserved no mercy and merited a felon's death. But I put the thought aside. Our men would demand their rewards, and the industries of Britain wanted slaves.

11

My letter is overlong, Burrus, my script imperfect and tiring to your eyes. The bare statistics you already know. From battlefield to river my inquisitors counted over seventy thousand native corpses. Four hundred and ten Romans died; as many again were wounded. Losses among auxiliaries, chiefly in the skirmish line, were nearly double: over seven hundred were killed.

You, old friend, know I am not a squeamish man. But never since great Julius's wars in Gaul have so many dead been heaped within so small a space. I wonder if he ever felt such sick disgust, as I did on that day when the sun was warm upon my face and the rusty stench of blood flooded my lungs like a corrosive acid, such shuddering revulsion from slaughter and the slaughterers?

He was not the man to admit such weakness. Nor must I.

Farewell.

BOOK III

Aftermath

A.D.
June 61 – February 62

16

'The whole people must be wiped out of existence, and none
be left to think of them and shed a tear.'

THE ILIAD

1

'When do we march?' Vettius Valens demanded.

We stood on the soft earth of a newly-dug rampart guarding
the camp which crowded beneath the old hill-fort. The ridge of our
morning battle-line hid the corpse-strewn heath from sight. Stretcher
parties tramped through the gateways bearing dead and wounded
Romans; squads departed to scour the field for others who had not
answered the roll-call. Beyond the Dexter Gate captives were herded
within a stockade of raw timber cut from the woods.

The camp hummed with life and yet seemed curiously empty. We
had neither tents nor baggage. The barrack-lines were meagre tokens,
scantily delineated by discarded packs, helmets, shields, all meticulously arranged in cohort divisions. The principia of camp headquarters
was a vacant space; a wooden shack represented my praetorium.

'I can't tell you,' I answered. 'Everything depends on supplies which,
in turn, depend on II Legion.'

Never had the victor of a very considerable battle felt less victorious.
I was quite exhausted, half asleep, unable to think coherently. Valens, on

the other hand, showed smart and alert like a man newly risen from ten hours' sleep. He was a true praetorian, a typical First Centurion, an iron frame with no feelings at all.

He said briskly, 'We should find plenty of corn in the enemy's baggage-wagons.' He pointed to a trail of vehicles which lumbered over the ridge, making for the camp.

I grimaced wearily. 'Those are more likely crammed with gold and silver and jewels and every conceivable kind of plunder, the spoils of twenty days' ravage from Lincoln to London. All quite uneatable. And you won't get many more carts into camp today because we've killed the cattle. No lack of meat, at all events. The wolf packs will feed well this night.'

'Will you summon our baggage-train from Silchester?' Valens asked.

'I don't know. We may have to return there ourselves tomorrow. With barely two days' rations what is the point of advancing into a ruined countryside scraped clean of supplies? I don't know. All depends on Augusta.'

The time was late afternoon. The sun, sinking over Silchester fifteen miles away, hid behind black and angry clouds.

'We'll have wet backs before nightfall,' I added. 'Come, let's visit the wounded.'

I walked tiredly to the hospital lines. Doctors and medical orderlies moved quietly and efficiently amongst stricken men who lay upon crude mattresses of leaves and bracken. The supply of bandages, salves and unguents, no more than the medical staff carried in their packs, was inadequate.

A legion's battle hospital is a comparatively quiet place. The Roman soldier, by training and habit, is inured to pain and contemptuous of noisy agonies. Even so, some hurts are so far beyond the controls of conscious thought that man is reduced to the animal, a raw bundle of shrieking anguish. Death claws at the vitals, and in the act of dying is no dignity.

I saw these twisted bodies and longed for my physician Hermogenes and his magical poppy juice that deadens pain. He was far away in Wroxeter; here we had nothing, not even wine, to soothe the tortured wrench that bridges life and death.

I told Valens to send legionary cavalry speedily to Silchester for medicines, bandages and drugs, spoke to as many wounded as could listen, and went to the praetorium hut. On a native cart Mannius Secundus had found a carved ebony couch, a richly inlaid object pillaged from some wealthy villa, and this he had set in splendid isolation in the middle of the floor. I lay back gratefully, tried to formulate plans and orders for the morrow, dozed, slept in brief snatches.

The sky was darkening when I woke. Men waited outside the doorway and horses stamped impatiently. Secundus, seeing my eyes open, stirred and spoke.

'The cavalry has returned, Legate.'

Bassus and Agricola entered: Agricola pale and fatigued, bloody bandages wrapping leg and arm; Aurelius spry and lithe, an exultant smile curling his lips.

'Is all well?'

'Very well, Legate,' Bassus said. 'We chased the remnants and killed hundreds. We hunted them to the river and slew thousands at the fords. No resistance anywhere. They ran like hares.'

'Very good.' I pondered for a moment. The six cavalry regiments had marched and fought almost without ceasing for fifteen days. I had studied parade states and watched their effective strengths, particularly in animals, dropping steadily. 'Send your units to the horse-lines. I shall want detailed fitness-rolls tomorrow, at the first hour.'

I studied Agricola's drawn features. He was young; the responsibility of his first command, excitement, strain and wounds had drained him. 'Bassus, take over command of all cavalry. Agricola, you revert to headquarters duty.' I pointed to the flamboyant couch that squatted like an exotic animal in a commonplace cage. 'Sit down. Open your tablets. Note these orders.'

Perhaps that short doze had unfogged my mind. Perhaps, while half-conscious, my brain had responded to the training of many campaigns and formulated answers while my body slept, so that certain immediate problems which had seemed insoluble now demanded solution and would not be deferred.

'Tell Valens to send engineers under escort—one auxiliary cohort will be enough—to replace the bridge at Staines. A temporary job will do so long as it's ready by midday tomorrow.

'The Camp Prefect must find wagons and draught oxen to evacuate our wounded to Silchester, starting at dawn.'

I then dictated, in rapid sequence, summons for reinforcements: to Mamilianus in Wroxeter, demanding that he dispatch to London, by forced marches, my headquarters staff, 2nd Vascones and 1st Frisiavones. To Gloucester for 1st Thracian cavalry and 1st Tungrian milliary cohort—messages addressed to prefect and tribune personally, for I could not trust Posthumus. To 2nd Nervii on the Cirencester-Exeter sector of the Frontier Way.

Agricola wrote rapidly. I rubbed my brow, thought furiously. 'Not enough cavalry,' I muttered. 'One fresh regiment only, and we're woefully short.'

The tribune's stylus paused. 'Auxiliaries in the frontier garrisons will be dangerously thin, Legate.'

'I know. Can't be helped. Wroxeter will still be garrisoned by five legionary and two milliary Britannic cohorts. Gloucester? Let me see. I told Posthumus to bring 2nd Pannonians and to collect 4th Gauls from the West Way. If he ever appears I shall take those off him. Gloucester then will still have II Legion intact, together with 1st Morini and 1st Baetasii. No cavalry. He must manage without. And 1st Nervana will still be patrolling the Frontier Way from Cirencester to Lincoln, though I doubt whether any of their forts north of High Cross, in the heart of Coritania, have survived.'

Agricola frowned, figured on his tablets. 'I total the auxiliary reinforcements ordered to London as six hundred cavalry and three thousand infantry.'

'Add those we've got here: twenty-five hundred cavalry and two thousand infantry, allowing for casualties. Very little for the task before us.'

'What do you intend, Legate?'

'To seek, pursue and destroy. Work for light troops, not legions.'

'You haven't mentioned Lincoln.'

I shrugged. 'What do we know? Only, for certain, that Cerialis has lost two thousand legionaries, an auxiliary cohort and probably the best part of Petra's Horse. Quintus himself is likely dead. The fortress may have been overrun by Iceni, Coritani or Brigantes. We can count on nothing from IX Hispana. Until we know more I regard Lincoln as a void.'

'Any marching orders, Legate?'

'Nothing yet. Nothing until I hear from Posthumus.'

I stretched and yawned. 'Get those messages off, Agricola. Then go to bed.'

2

The first watch mounted. Night descended on the camp, a heavy blackness rent by lightning and shivered by thunderclaps. Camp fires, defying the gathering storm, blazed strong and cheerful. The first raindrops, heavy and warm as fresh-spilt blood, plopped around the lounging soldiers like spent arrows.

By the middle of the second watch the storm raged like an explosion of Olympian anger. Thunder-volleys crashed unceasingly; rain cascaded in solid sheets; vivid flashes revealed cloak-wrapped men lying prostrate in sodden rows. Rain pools extended, joined, became miniature lakes fed by gushing streamlets.

I splashed through darkness, mud and water, found Valens likewise going the rounds.

'Our punishment for marching without baggage,' I said. 'The penalty for breaking rules. A miserable reward for our men after their exertions.'

A searing flash showed Valens's face split by an enormous grin. 'By Jupiter!' he roared above the hiss and rumble. 'D'you think Gemina cares for a little wet? This don't disturb them. Look!' He prodded a hunched bundle with his foot. The man never stirred. 'They've won a famous victory and dream of booty. An hour's sun tomorrow and they'll be polished fit for Caesar's guard!'

The Camp Prefect's forethought had given a meagre cover to the hospital lines: wounded sheltered beneath captured native wagons and stayed reasonably dry.

I turned and splashed to headquarters, where two mired horsemen, couriers from the details left in Silchester, waited with the centurion of the watch. Outriders of II Legion, they said, had entered Silchester before sunset; the legion was encamped at Speen, ten miles west, and would reach Silchester by noon next day.

I asked questions.

The decurion answered, 'The Prefect Paenius Posthumus commands, Legate. He has brought all the corn taken from Silchester and more besides. I don't know what light troops accompany the legion.'

'Return to Silchester,' I commanded, 'and tell Gemina's baggage-train and followers to join me here tomorrow.'

I said to Valens, 'I want a reliable, intelligent centurion to take a message to Speen. He will leave within the hour.'

I dictated a letter, addressed to the legion's senior tribune, ordering Augusta to send to our camp all supply wagons and auxiliary units under command. The legion itself was to return forthwith to Gloucester.

Valens, listening to my dictation, raised an eyebrow. I gave him a straight look. 'No glory for Augusta in this campaign,' I said bleakly. 'Those who began the work shall finish it.'

The second letter I wrote myself.

'Paenius Posthumus, Prefect of the Camp of II Legion Augusta. Greetings.

'Under the authority vested in me by the Divine Nero Claudius Caesar, Prince of the Roman people, I command you to surrender yourself, disarmed, to the bearer of this letter. Obey his orders, which are mine.

'On the evidence available to me I hold you guilty of disobedience, of cowardice in face of the enemy, and misappropriation of military supplies whereby the army's safety was endangered.

'You will present yourself to show reason why, for these crimes, you should not be publicly degraded in the army's presence, flogged and dismissed the service. Farewell.

'G. Suetonius Paulinus, Legate and Propraetor in Britain.'

I suspended the letter between my fingers and reflected. The punishment proposed, which relied on the somewhat doubtful precedent of Corbulo's treatment of the Prefect Aemilius Rufus, was legitimate and within my powers. But I wanted this man dead, and only Nero himself could sign his death warrant.

'Where is your centurion?' I asked Valens.

The legate beckoned a short, broad-framed soldier. Raindrops sparkled on his helmet and dewed his cloak like rime.

'Centurion Sempronius Sempronianus, 4th century, 1st cohort,' Valens briefly announced.

'Come with me,' I said. I led the centurion outside the hut, in the dark, beyond hearing of the sentries. The downpour was lessening; thunder growled and muttered far away.

'Centurion Sempronianus, you will personally deliver this message to the Prefect Paenius Posthumus before Augusta breaks camp at Speen. The legion marches at dawn; you have five hours to ride twenty-five miles.'

I raised my chin, gazed at the teeming skies.

'Give him the letter when he is alone. Take his sword when he has read it. Posthumus may question you. He may not. In either case you are to make clear to him that a tripod has been erected here, in this camp, for the punishment of death under the rods.'

I studied the centurion's face, sought his eyes in the darkness.

'You will tell Posthumus the tripod is for him. Do you understand?'

'I understand, Legate.' Sempronianus's voice was quite expressionless.

'You will then return his sword.'

'The Prefect is to be permitted to settle his affairs?' Sempronianus inquired tonelessly.

'Yes,' I said. 'Now go!'

3

By dawn the rain had ceased and the skies were clear. The men relit camp fires, made racks of javelins and sword-belts and slung cloaks and accoutrements to dry.

The duty tribune reported an attempted break-out from the prisoners' stockade during the night. I strolled from the Dexter Gate to investigate.

The tribune described how, under cover of the thunderstorm, a party of captives had flattened the stockade—the fence was hastily-constructed and flimsy—and fled into the darkness. Fortunately the guard was alert. Helped by lightning-flashes they had retrieved most of the fugitives and killed others. Some had got away. Those recaptured, two hundred half-naked Britons, were separated from the remainder and penned under close guard in a corner of the enclosure.

'They want to escape,' I said. 'They shall. Bring them out.'

The Britons were led from the corral and stood before me in shivering wretchedness.

'Hamstring them,' I told the tribune.

Ten soldiers with drawn swords worked down the line. Two swift cuts, just above and behind the knees, felled each man as if he were jerked by invisible ropes. They lay moaning, crawled their several ways, left red trails on the wet grass. From the stockade, where the prisoners watched, arose a horrified wail.

'Let them go where they will,' I said tersely, and returned to camp to organize the stripping of the battlefield.

All day long carts came and went, laden high with spoils from the enemy baggage-train. Squads quartered the field, turning over the dead, collecting jewel-hilted swords, enamelled shields, torcs, necklaces. Signifers—experienced managers of cohort funds—helped by staff accountants, notars and librars, supervised distribution to cohorts, to centuries and troops and thence to individual soldiers. The total plunder, while not magnificent by the standards of famous triumphs in Rome's past, was unique in British warfare, for it yielded the wealth of the province's most civilized territories. The men seemed very satisfied, though I forbade captives to be distributed as slaves. There were not enough to go round; they would be required for Government tasks; and plenty more would be forthcoming in the near future.

The spoil was divided at a formal parade which, for the first time since Boudicca's defeat, allowed me to address the army, bestow praise for their conduct during the battle and, in return, receive their acclamations. I had purposely postponed this occasion to allow time for enthusiasm to cool. Men who have snatched victory from the teeth of enormous odds have been known, in the immediate fervency of relief and thanksgiving, to wish unwanted honours upon their commander. To be hailed as Imperator by the troops may be gratifying to one's vanity but is highly dangerous politically. Life was simpler a hundred years ago.

That done, I attended the ceremonial burning of our dead: a melancholy business which entailed great labour and a vast expenditure of firewood that, both rain-sodden and green, burned reluctantly and merely charred the bodies so that they had to be buried anyway. Soldiers are conservative creatures: when time or timber is short they will inter their dead without protest; otherwise they insist always on the ancient rituals of cremation. In Rome nowadays, among patricians, the fashion is turning more towards burial.

Inquisitors of my staff, whose work it was to count the enemy killed, identify dead chieftains and extract any general information of value from the carnage, reported positively that Boudicca was not among the slain. I shrugged. She was no longer important, a general without any army, a queen without a realm. Of more interest was the news that Druids, identified clearly by their robes, figured among the bodies. In Anglesey I had driven a stake through this Hydra's head, but the contagion still lived, the poison still festered in the remote wildernesses of Britain.

Late that evening a long column of wagons—XIV Legion's baggage and the contents of Silchester's military granaries which Paenius Posthumus had stolen—rolled up the West Way and trundled into camp. Tents burgeoned like mushrooms, and a rapid check by Gemina's Camp Prefect and his assistants proved that our supply problems, for two months at least, were over.

With the wagons marched the 2nd Pannonian and 4th Gallic cohorts who had accompanied II Legion, and a deputation of noblemen, Silchester decurions, who came from Epaticcus to convey congratulations on our victory. I scanned their faces, discovered certain absentees.

'Where are Campester and Lucilianus?' I inquired politely.

They were imprisoned, they explained, and awaited trial on the morrow for treasonable conspiracy. Pertacus had already been condemned in his absence. The decurions seemed embarrassed: I did not press the point. I thanked them graciously and they withdrew.

Last of all, a bare fraction before our gates closed for the night, entered centurion Sempronius Sempronianus, a weary man after his fifty-mile ride. He dismounted stiffly and saluted.

'I delivered your message, Legate, as you commanded.'

'So?'

'The Prefect Paenius Posthumus bade me tell you three truths.' Sempronianus hesitated, ill at ease.

'Continue, centurion.'

He braced himself, stared fixedly over my shoulder. 'First, your orders to him were hazardous and unsound. Second, his disobedience was not cowardice but common sense. Third, only the Luck of Rome and Jupiter's favour have preserved a bad general from his deserved retribution.'

'Very interesting,' I said softly. 'Is the Prefect coming to say this to my face?'

Sempronianus gazed blank-eyed into space. 'I didn't have to tell lies about the tripod. He asked for his sword when he'd read your letter; then went alone to his tent. Paenius Posthumus is dead, Legate.'

I fingered my lip. 'So be it. And understand, Sempronianus, as you value your rank, that not one hint of your mission, or the instructions I gave you, will be disclosed to anyone.'

'I realize that, Legate.' He tendered a paper. For a moment his eyes met mine in a look of the most astounding dislike. 'I have retrieved the evidence. Here is your letter to Posthumus.'

He saluted, swung away, saddle-galled and limping.

So passed Paenius Posthumus, Camp Prefect of II Legion Augusta, bequeathing to posterity the question: how does it happen? How do such men degenerate? For Posthumus came up the hard way from legionary to centurion: not for him the accelerated promotion granted to broken equestrians and municipal magistrates who enlist for want of a better job. His qualities, a sound brain, a ruthless mind and a tough physique, raised him through sixty centurionate promotions to First Centurion and, at the close of an outstanding military career, Camp Prefect. How does such a man decay so swiftly, become so flabby, so unreliable?

Not a coward? He was condemned by his own action, or rather inaction. Anyone could understand that. Why, then, should Sempronianus regard me with hatred?

I walked slowly to my tent, wondering.

4

Next day the army marched. The column of route, vastly extended by corn-wagons and carts full of booty, was ten miles long. Beyond the frontiers so lengthy a train would have invited attack: here I had no fears. Britain was at peace again.

The wreckage of pursuit festooned our progress. At Thameside the grim garlands lay deep, and bodies heaped the banks, littered the shingle, choked the reeds. Our cavalry, while executing this carnage, had not lost a man.

Across the river we passed the scene of the refugees' ambush. One might suppose that to men sated with killing, inured to the sight of corpses in thousands, the spectacle would be unremarkable. This was different. Time had decayed the carcasses; decomposing flesh weighted the air with a charnel smell. More revolting than all were the mutilations.

The Britons had had leisure to do their worst. Hardly a body bore only its death wounds; most were split, disembowelled, de-sexed, and many had been tortured. The spectacle, a loathsome putridity that fouled the roadsides for three miles and more, was one to haunt a lifetime of dreams. I saw soldiers—young legionaries and hardened veterans alike—retch and vomit.

The army marched on, morose and angry. I welcomed this change of mood. Victory induces in troops a sense of well-being, a certain mellow contentment, a benign contempt for their enemies, which was not the attitude I wanted during my campaign of retribution.

Everywhere lay the scars of devastation. It was as though every habitation, every man-made fragment, had attracted some supernatural vengeance, a God-sent perdition which had laid them simultaneously in ruins. Fort, mansion, villa, farmhouse, hut and byre alike were charred heaps ringed by swollen corpses. We glimpsed birds and beasts of the wild but saw no other living thing, human or animal, in that wasteland scourged by Boudicca's armies.

The men did not sing on the march that day.

The army camped ten miles from London and, in a tense and dangerous mood, reached the outskirts early next forenoon.

London repeated on a larger scale what the countryside had already shown: a grey-black desert, humped and jagged, whence a few half-burnt houses jutted like rock-pinnacles in an empty seascape. We fortified our camp a good distance away from the huge, sombre tomb. When guards had been mounted on the ramparts, and a cavalry sweep found the environs deserted, I permitted leave details to enter the town. I rode there myself.

A town that is thoroughly sacked and burnt covers her mortal wounds under a mantle of ruin, the layers of ash and rubble that once were her being. So it was with London. The burning had been thorough; some stone walls and marble pillars stood; otherwise the Province's biggest community had been reduced to a pile of cindered rubbish wherein the ghastly relics of massacre were immolated and concealed. Within the devastated precincts was much to sadden, little to horrify.

We found the Britons' handiwork outside.

Lining the river-bank like palings of an outsize fence were rows of stakes and crosses. On these hung shrivelled bundles, still recognizably human. The men were crucified and castrated, sometimes with eyes and tongues torn out, the women impaled through the crotch and their breasts severed.

This was the veritable mark of the beast whom I had sworn to exterminate. I put the spectacle to use. I returned to camp, paraded every soldier not on duty and marched the whole army, legionary and auxiliary, horse and foot, slowly past these terrifying remnants of Roman men and women. Then we reverently gathered the bodies, built a great pyre and burned them.

One corpse was doubtfully identifiable as Alfidius Olussa. With my own hands I poured his ashes in a jar and ordered a stone to be inscribed and set upon his sepulchre.

The troops' reaction was more vigorous than I had foreseen. After returning, quiet and oddly subdued, to their quarters, four cohorts of Gemina suddenly drew swords, trampled their centurions and rushed the prisoners' stockade, where they slaughtered every Briton and flung the bodies into the Thames. Three thousand slaves wasted.

But this was only one raindrop to quench a bonfire. My object was realized. The army was ravening for revenge.

5

Many questions begged stridently for answers while I waited in London for reinforcements. Where had the residue of Boudicca's army fled? Were other insurgents loose in the countryside? Were the half-committed tribes, Catuvellauni and Coritani, permanently subdued by our victory? Or were they taking measures to invigorate the rebellion? Above all, how did Lincoln and Hispana fare?

Some of the answers materialized during the days following. Frightened, half-starved fugitives, survivors from the sacks of farms and manors, stumbled to our camp to tell that rebels were active and ravaging territories of the Cantii south of London. Mere bandits, these, marauders who had deserted the main army before the battle, unaware of the cataclysm that had swept their comrades out of existence. I detached a vexillation—a legionary cohort, one cavalry and four infantry auxiliary cohorts—to destroy the pests.

Patrols which probed north and west discovered very little. The countryside was deserted and ruined. They brought captives to London, but the prisoners, fugitives from the battle or wandering pillagers, told nothing useful. Naturally, every Briton swore he was but a peaceful peasant going about his business.

I employed the troops in clearing the rubble and preparing London's site for rebuilding. Engineers built a new bridge across the Thames. On the fifth day of our wait I was, in desperation, preparing a strong vexillation for Lincoln when Quintus Cerialis himself, with no more than three troops of Petra's Horse, swept into camp like a tempest.

His first sentences set my mind at rest. The fortress stood; IX Legion Hispana Triumphalis Macedonia, though shorn of her three best cohorts, was battleworthy and bursting for revenge. By that extraordinary agency which carries news faster than sound among the natives Cerialis had heard, only two days afterwards, of our victory, and realizing that contact between his force and mine was vital, had set out on a hurricane four-day ride.

I scolded him gently on the risks of his journey.

'No danger at all,' he asserted. 'We saw hardly a soul. You'd think the country had been cleared by a pestilence.'

Cerialis told me of his march to Colchester and the disaster that ended it: an account which, alloyed with that of the legionary Gaius Saufeius, I have given earlier. He added another startling piece of information.

'After the rebels had chased me into Lincoln they lingered around the fortress for two days. Only three or four thousand men, but I feared a trap and decided against a sortie. Remember, I had no idea where their main army was. Then they left, and a messenger arrived from Cartimandua of the Brigantes.'

'Cartimandua?' I said. 'Was she threatening—?'

'No,' Cerialis said. He grinned at me impudently. 'Your diplomacy is too good for that, Paulinus. She was in trouble. Her late escort, Venutius, was marching on York.'

I frowned. 'No coincidence, I imagine. The Iceni had shared plans with Venutius and required his co-operation.'

'Precisely. You'll appreciate the problem's delicacy, with a revolted Province at my back and a tribal army looming, as it were, over my front garden.'

'What did you do? Promise assistance when you could?'

Cerialis stared. 'By Apollo, no! Promises wouldn't have halted Venutius. I cleared every man from Lincoln and went to York.'

My eyes bulged. 'You evacuated Lincoln? You left the fortress empty?'

'Stark,' he nodded. 'Why not? Sitting on our backsides behind ramparts helped neither you nor Cartimandua. To march south after Boudicca invited annihilation. Stopping Venutius was the only useful thing to do.'

He sighed. 'I'd hoped for a battle.' His eyes grew dreamy, and I remembered Cerialis's fixation on Brigantia, his visions of conquest. 'But it was not to be. Venutius heard we were advancing from York, turned tail and fled home to his fort in the north. I thought it foolish to follow: we'd averted the threat and the dangers were great. Rome will deal finally with Venutius one day and, despite his great reputation, I don't think he'll give much trouble at the end.'

He yawned, stretched. 'That's all. We were back in Lincoln within ten days.'

I gazed at him, admiration mingled with consternation. Only a Cerialis could have taken his life, army and reputation in both hands in a fling which, gone awry, would have fired the Province from end to end. And only a great soldier could recognize the limits of that enterprise; a lesser man, exalted by success, must have courted disaster in pursuit of his quarry.

'Now you're here,' I said at last, 'we can discuss what must be done to finish this business for good.' I led Cerialis within the praetorium, gestured to a chair, paced the room as I talked.

'Rome,' I began, 'is at war with Iceni, Trinovantes, Catuvellauni and Coritani: those tribes which have themselves declared war upon the Roman people.

'The instigators, fomentors and leaders of the insurrection are the Iceni. We will exterminate them, so that their name shall never again appear in the history of this Province.

'The Trinovantes have given such help, by treachery and liaison with our chief enemy, as their small numbers and cowardly nature permit. Their lands are forfeit; they shall be sold as slaves and vanish from Britain.

'Catuvellauni and Coritani are less embroiled. Both have sent forces against us, but the tribes are not, I believe, totally committed. That remains to be proved. Their lands shall not be sequestrated, save for those who have borne arms against Rome, but we shall demand compensation in slaves, corn and treasure.'

I paused, awaiting comment. Cerialis, listening intently, said nothing.

'That is my policy. For the execution, the army in London will divide into four vexillations. One for the Iceni, to kill, burn and destroy. Another against the Trinovantes, to enslave every man, woman and child. The third for the Catuvellauni, to seek those clans, villages and settlements whence warriors have gone to fight us, to enslave all able-bodied men and confiscate all property. The last, a reserve formation, will remain in London.'

I swung to face Cerialis.

'You, Legate, will return to Lincoln and detach two vexillations: one, to take the same measures against the Coritani as I have decreed for the Catuvellauni; the second will march to the Icenian fenlands and kill every man it meets.'

I studied his face, and weighted my words.

'You will be harsh, ruthless. You will remember, day and night, that these savages, these animals with men's faces, have killed, tortured, raped and ravaged without mercy; that eighty thousand Romans and friendly Britons have died and that we have, so far, barely exacted an equal return. Against such people leniency is only another name for weakness.'

The stern, helmet-shaded face nodded approval. I struck my hands together.

'When the auxiliaries from the frontier arrive we shall move simultaneously. I shall send you word.'

I ordered wine and we talked of other matters. Years afterwards, Cerialis told me that he had never been able to forget the venomous ferocity which impregnated those short phrases of judgement and condemnation, and the bitter hatred which marked furrows deep as scars upon my face.

6

Three days after Cerialis had returned to Lincoln the frontier auxiliaries arrived in London. The detachment sent to liberate the Cantian territories also returned, and brought a respectable number of prisoners who were promptly penned in our slave-corrals. The vexillation reported widespread devastation but no organized enemy: the damage was done by wandering, independent marauders. Canterbury was burned; the enemy had not, luckily, penetrated to Richborough which, though abandoned, was intact.

The vexillations departed on their errands of retribution. I placed Aurelius Bassus, a man without mercy, in command of the Icenian detachment. Agricola went to Trinovantia; his mission was easy; the practice would do him good. Vettius Valens commanded against the Catuvellauni because his task, which involved sorting sheep from goats, punishing the guilty without alienating the innocent, demanded knowledge and experience. The vexillations, while differing in strengths, comprised roughly equal proportions of auxiliaries and legionaries, with an inevitable shortage of cavalry.

No sooner had the troops gone than the wan features of the Commandant of the British Fleet appeared in our depopulated camp. Aufidius Pantera, never a cheerful man, was exceptionally woebegone and brimful of grievances.

'The survivors of the Anglesey flotilla made port at Richborough two days ago, Legate. The harbour and town is deserted, but an auxiliary guard told me you were in London and the road was safe. I borrowed a horse and escort from the soldiers and wasted no time on the way.'

'I'm happy to see you again, Pantera. Since we parted in Ordovicia our army has written a bloodstained page in Britain's history which you have not yet read. I trust your voyage has been fortunate?'

'Fortunate!' He snorted bitterly, gazed venomously into his wine. 'Fortunate? The rigours of campaigning have affected your sense of time, Legate. Nearly a month ago I sailed from Caernarvon. A month for the passage!'

'What delayed you?' I inquired innocently.

Pantera exploded. 'By the Trident! Gales, Legate, storms and tempests! Wreck after wreck. For days on end we cowered in some wretched cove, crept out when the wind abated, sailed for a few miles before the next blast struck, ran for shelter and lost another ship or two.' He banged his goblet on the table. 'Do you recall how many vessels sailed from Richborough for your campaign against the Ordovices?'

'Twenty biremes,' I said simply, 'and ten cutters.'

Pantera glared. 'Correct. Not all reached Chester, if you remember. Then, when you had to leave Caernarvon so hurriedly, you gave me the choice—choice!—of remaining in Chester's river, with no protection at all, or of returning to Richborough. Naturally, I sailed at once.'

'You met trouble, I gather.'

'Disasters!' Suddenly all his aggressiveness went; his face crumpled and he seemed on the verge of tears. He stretched both hands to me across the table. 'Legate, four ships are moored at Richborough.'

I stared at him. 'The rest are lost?'

Pantera nodded, dumb, his eyes entreating compassion.

I pulled my lip. Twenty-six warships sunk. No Actium, certainly— yet nearly half the British Fleet's complement had gone. But new ships could be built and fresh crews soon recruited. A fleet was not like a legion: no great prestige was involved in naval reverses—at least, not in these waters. A calamity, but far from catastrophe.

I reflected glumly. The ultimate responsibility was mine; yet this incompetent could hardly escape censure. The executive command was his. Vitriolic sentences formed on my lips and died unsaid. No reprimands could raise ships from the sea-bed.

I loathe weak men. Pantera was one of those undecided, unconfident creatures who should never have commanded anything bigger than a coracle. Someone in Rome, probably thinking he could do little harm on such remote frontiers, had foisted him on Britain. I wished I could send that man the account.

The damage was done. Vituperation was no help.

'A bad business,' I said briskly. 'Still, four ships are better than none. Urgent dispatches await carriage to Rome; without ships we could not transmit them to Boulogne. You will be good enough to take these letters back to Richborough.'

Pantera raised his head, gazed at me in unbelief. 'Is that all you have to say?' His voice was a whisper.

'What do you expect?' I said wonderingly. 'Would you prefer a lecture on seamanship?'

He stood whitefaced, seemed about to speak, turned and walked jerkily from the room.

I noticed, with disapproval, that he failed to acknowledge the sentry's salute.

7

I sent no laurelled dispatches to Rome announcing my victory, which I preferred to regard as a mere police action against tribes already conquered. On the other hand I was lavish with recommendations for honours and awards, both individual and regimental. Some the

Prince accepted, others not. Chief of those subsequently granted were the additional titles 'Martia Victrix' to XIV Legion Gemina. The legion had already bestowed upon itself an unofficial soubriquet: 'Domitores Britanniae', the Tamers of Britain. By obstinate insistence upon its use both in correspondence and conversation the legion, with the passing of years, made that bombastic appellation more authoritative than the Senate's more dignified honours.

XX Valeria, in recognition of her 1st cohort's part in the battle, received the cognomen 'Victrix'. I tried to secure Roman citizenship for several auxiliary units: only 1st Vettonians and 1st Loyal Vardulli, both present at the victory, actually received this honour. The rejection of 1st Cugerni's claim was particularly disappointing: the cohort, virtually annihilated during Cerialis's foray to Colchester, had fought more than well enough to deserve recognition. Moreover, as citizenship is granted only to those men actually serving at the time of the award, the twenty-odd survivors would not have unduly diluted the Roman plebiscite. One hopes the cohort will win distinction at some later date in its career.

With a forceful pen but little real expectation I pressed for reinforcements: four thousand legionaries, six cavalry regiments, ten infantry cohorts. Equally important were administrative officials and clerks. In Boudicca's holocaust the Province's civil service, together with all her files and records, had been wiped out. The whole civil establishment awaited replacement and, from Rome's archives, copies of decrees, edicts and accounts relevant to current issues must be provided. When military pacification measures ended trade and agriculture would have to be re-started. I quailed from the nightmare thought of competitive claims on intestate property and the contentious litigation that must inevitably follow.

Shortly afterwards long droves of captive Britons, the first substantial rewards of our punitive expeditions, began to reach London. I set these creatures to work, supervised by legion engineers, at rebuilding London, and summoned the tribune Sextus Frontinus from his cosy command of Britannic cohorts in Wroxeter to direct town-planning and architecture.

Restoration of everyday communications with the Continent was immediately vital. Merchantmen would not readily cross the straits unless they saw our fleet in being and vigilant, for the Frisian pirates were an ever-present menace. In a dispatch to Pantera I ordered transference of the British Fleet from Boulogne to Richborough, and told him to organize a building programme in Boulogne's shipyards to replace our losses. I commanded the return to London of stores, bullion and refugees sent to the Continent for safety and, with the promise of naval protection, encouraged merchant captains to resume trade. On this last point I was not overly anxious: three or four trading vessels moved cautiously up the Thames within days of our arrival; crews disembarked to stare aghast at the ruins of their familiar port.

Then, bored with inactivity, I left a token garrison in London and I removed myself and the reserve vexillation to Colchester.

8

We marched through the drearily deserted territory of a proscribed people. Settlements which Boudicca left intact Agricola's vexillation had destroyed as being obviously suspect. Old men and women too ancient or ill-favoured to appeal to the soldiers were all we encountered. They either fled from us or, if too weak and ill to run, fawned prostrate and begged for mercy.

Colchester, in death, was queerly impressive. A dark, broken stratum of ruin was all her remains, but from this, like a tall ship land-locked in black rocks, soared the Temple of Victory, smoke-streaked, indestructible, gleaming pallidly triumphant.

Stone and marble had defeated the fire-raisers. Within, shrines lay smashed and defiled; Agricola's men had removed the skeletons but not the stains of massacre from floor and walls, so that the interior was like a disused slaughter-house. Yet the temple, the very symbol of Rome's Imperial Power, the hated emblem of her sovereignty in Britain, stood virtually unscathed when the tide of insurrection had ebbed. This was an omen to shake sceptics and confute agnostics. Even I wondered.

Agricola, lately returned from a raid on a fishing village, confessed his task was all but accomplished. Seeing the enormous stockaded enclosures packed with enslaved Trinovantes, I could easily believe him.

'Use part to clear and rebuild Colchester,' I told him, 'and send the rest to London. We must soon start slave shipments to the Continent. Any treasure?'

He shook his head. 'Very little. I'm told the wealthy Trinovantes fled to Icenia before Boudicca marched. The gold is there. Bassus should find it.'

'We shall soon see,' I said, 'because I'm going on.'

After a day's rest I marched northwards with a strong escort. At once the country changed; open fields submerged under forest; roads degenerated to cattle-tracks. We saw the marks of Bassus's passing: farmhouses sacked and burned, wrecked huts and a casual litter of rotting corpses. The country, nevertheless, was not quite lifeless. Figures flitted like ghosts at the forest's edge and vanished; sometimes arrows whistled from the trees—the bowmen were never caught. We marched with guards and flankers alert and took pains over fortifying our camps.

After a two-day journey through this unnerving forest, unbroken save for clearings where dead settlements reeked, we made contact with Bassus's scouts and found him with part of his vexillation on the point of storming Norwich. I had visualized the Icenian capital, once the seat of the wealthiest king in Britain, as a township like Silchester, crude and smelly, perhaps, but enriched by fine houses and noble public buildings. I was unprepared for the squalid reality: a native settlement on a large scale, a conglomerate of round thatched huts and rectangular wooden byres, all surrounded by a stockade and shallow ditch. On a near-by hill the ruins of Prasutagus's elaborate two-storied palace smouldered like a dying beacon, and soldiers rummaged for loot in the wreckage.

The attack was about to begin. Cavalry roamed the untilled fields and muddy pastures that ringed the town like a bedraggled skirt. On one side a marsh-bordered stream flowed beneath the stockades. The horsemen hovered like stooping hawks, poised to strike anyone who fled from the shelter of those rickety defences.

An infantry column—auxiliary cohorts—emerged from the Roman camp and massed in battle-line beyond bowshot of the town; a legionary cohort ranged itself in reserve and stood boredly watching proceedings, leaning languidly on javelins: a demeanour plainly indicating their assessment that auxiliaries alone could settle the business.

I brought my little force to the camp gates and greeted Bassus. His face was deeply lined, his bearing taut and irascible.

'I have spent ten days,' he said, 'harrying the tribesmen in this area, beating the forests, scouring the settlements and, in ever-narrowing circles, driving the natives inwards to Norwich. I'd hoped to make a big killing here.'

'What went wrong?' I asked.

'A big break-out two days ago, in the thickest part of the forest. A mass attack, a narrow thrust, carefully conceived and directed. Caught us by surprise.' He shrugged. 'Nobody to blame. The troops on these herding operations have to cover a very wide front.'

'Did you follow?'

'I've sent a detachment in pursuit but it won't get far. Everyone who escapes our net makes for the same area: the fens. Impossible country. You could mislay a legion there without noticing it had gone.'

I compressed my lips. 'Bassus, you were sent here to kill Iceni. Instead you are letting them escape to a natural sanctuary and that, on the face of it, implies a serious dereliction of duty. However, this is neither the time nor place to pursue the matter. Continue your operation against the town. How many tribesmen have you trapped inside?'

Bassus's face was gaunt and his lips trembled. 'A thousand or two, men, women and children. We won't take long.'

He turned, signalled; the trumpets pealed. Vascones, Nervii and Tungrians trotted towards the stockades, which suddenly seethed and loosed a storm of arrows. The auxiliaries plodded on, shields raised, while their own covering parties replied with slings, bows and throwing-spears. The columns dipped in the ditch, vanished momentarily as though in the trough of a wave, leapt at the palisades.

The auxiliaries, in deference to text-book assault tactics, carried a few ladders. A token gesture: they quickly discarded these encumbrances; scrambled upwards on their comrades' shoulders or hurled one another to the top as a groom lifts a rider to the saddle. The wave of men poised briefly on the stockade's crest, broke and crashed within.

'That's that,' Bassus observed soberly. 'Shall we go closer and watch the fun?'

We rode our horses to the edge of the ditch. Through broken gaps in the stockade I could see clear into the town. Resistance had ceased at the perimeter. Inside, the auxiliaries ran berserk.

They were head-hunting. They felled the enemy; then decapitated him neat and clean. A Tungrian, in no way incommoded by the staring head gripped between his teeth, exchanged lively cut and thrust with a powerful Briton. Another, clutching three prizes in his shield hand, paused to skewer them through the temples on his throwing-spear, like onions on a stick, and waved the streaming trophies triumphantly.

Presently I rode away. The sack was nearly over; huts were alight, timbers crackled, smoke billowed skywards. Across the pastures troopers galloped whooping in pursuit of scurrying wretches trying to escape from the town. The legionaries, whose support, as they had foreseen, was not required, marched disgustedly back to camp. Auxiliaries began to pour from the burning wreckage of Norwich, and each man carried a severed head.

'A new departure,' I remarked, indicating these bloody relics.

'A Vasconian custom,' Bassus said. 'Our Pyrenean mountaineers are still pretty barbaric. Because we take no prisoners the fashion has spread to other auxiliaries: a kind of competition among cohorts. Crude but harmless.'

In Bassus's tent I put some searching questions and pondered, somewhat perplexed, over his replies. Two things became clear: the Iceni, knowing themselves condemned, were gathering for a last stand somewhere in the fens; this concentration was being shrewdly and ably directed by a central command.

'Is Boudicca still alive?' I demanded abruptly.

Bassus spread his hands. 'I can't tell. Evidence from captives, whether voluntary or extracted, is contradictory. No one admits to having seen her since the battle. I can't decide whether she or a surviving chieftain or even a Druid is rallying the Iceni. Whoever does it is too competent for my liking.'

I stared glumly at his tired face. 'The marshes, you say, are a certain refuge. Will you be able to penetrate them, find the enemy and bring him to battle?'

Bassus rubbed his brow. 'No, I don't think I can.'

I rose to my feet. 'Nevertheless, the Iceni will be destroyed, even if we have to drain the swamps to find them. I shall go to the fens and see for myself.'

9

I did not leave Norwich for some days. Bassus, after his semi-abortive sweep, had to overhaul his plans and scheme afresh. I interfered very little and offered no suggestions.

Close contact with his detachment produced an impression, confirmed later when I met other troops of the vexillation harrying Icenia, that all was not well with the men. The legionaries seemed sulky and indifferent, performing their duties without enthusiasm. The auxiliaries' blind ferocity in action matched an insolent, ever-increasing lawlessness in camp. In short, morale was dropping fast.

Bassus was well aware of the situation. He ascribed the cause to long spells on detached duties.

'I have three main divisions working the territory, each roughly the same strength: one legionary, three auxiliary cohorts and some cavalry. They work under my directives, largely on the initiative of their separate commanders—we seldom meet. In addition, I have planted forts at strategic points to control the swept areas and deny reoccupation. All these scattered garrisons and field forces suffer from a relaxation of control and a loosening of discipline.'

'Nonsense,' I said sourly. 'We've had to police countries and hunt fugitives a thousand times in the past. That's no reason for morale to go bad.'

Bassus stroked his jaw. 'There is another point, Legate. This endless killing. The men daily see good slaves wasted. We've taken enough Britons in Icenia to supply every man in the vexillation with a personal servant five times over. They feel entitled to a native apiece or, of course, his value in the slave-market. But we've killed them all, because you ordered it so. The men get nothing and are promised nothing.'

'They have an ample share of booty,' I replied savagely. 'Icenia was rich: you have sent much wealth to London already. The vexillation's portion was presumably deducted.'

Bassus was silent and the subject dropped. Later, against my beliefs, I was persuaded that men engaged in prolonged, continuous slaughter become degraded, lose their self-respect and, in the eyes of others, assume the status of public executioners rather than soldiers.

After much interchange of messengers Bassus reunited, at Brancaster, two of his detachments and began a sweep into the fenlands close to the seacoast, while a third battle-group probed the marshes northwards from Cambridge. Cerialis wrote that a vexillation of Hispana, with supporting troops, was swooping from the north. This three-pronged manœuvre, we hoped, would drive the Iceni into a bag where they could be held and destroyed at leisure.

I watched the start of the operations and saw enough of the fen country to fill me with dismay. The vast, muddy, reed-infested wastes, flat and featureless, criss-crossed by innumerable streams and rivers, could for years conceal forces far greater than the Iceni possessed. Depressed, I left Bassus to his unpromising campaign and, with my escort, turned south along the Icknield Way. Arrived at Cambridge I summoned the tribune Sextus Frontinus from his rebuilding activities in London.

'I have a project in mind,' I told him, 'which may or may not be feasible and will certainly demand all the engineering skill you possess. Briefly, I want to drain these accursed fens.'

Frontinus gasped, and with reason. Official opinion regarded the fens as a lost land beyond knowledge or reclamation.

I said, 'I think it possible, at least, to reduce the swamp area very considerably. If you think the plan workable you need not be deterred by lack of labour: I shall send you, if necessary, every prisoner we have taken since the rebellion. You are permitted, for your preliminary reconnaissance, to collect from the London garrison such engineers and advisers as you require. You will also need an escort. See to it. Do your work and report to me speedily.'

I left Frontinus scratching his head doubtfully and departed from Cambridge to meet Vettius Valens.

10

At Verulam I found Valens had moved his headquarters north to Towcester. Verulam, like Colchester and London, was a burned-out wreck wherein slave-gangs were busily clearing rubble. The dingy settlement of pre-rebellion days was, I felt, no great loss: my business was to ensure that a worthier township arose on the site. The legionary engineer-option in charge seemed to know his business and so, after a brief pause, I travelled on to Valens's camp.

Unlike Aurelius Bassus, the legate looked relaxed and cheerful. Both Catuvellauni and Coritani, he said, were thoroughly cowed and submissive, only too anxious to provide slaves, corn, hides and treasure lest they should meet the treatment decreed for the Iceni.

'Though I don't know how long this happy state will last,' he added. 'I suppose you know the natives are on the edge of starvation?'

'Why?' I asked. 'You haven't confiscated all their supplies, and you have no authority to destroy standing crops.'

Valens smiled dourly. 'There aren't any standing crops. The rebellion started, you remember, in seed-time. The rebels were in such a hurry to cut our throats that they forgot to sow before they left home, or else they hoped to subsist on our granaries when we were all dead.'

'Remarkably short-sighted.'

'Undoubtedly.' Valens smoothed his chin. 'But have you considered the implications? The survivors of the rebellion are back in their settlements, living on the meagre remains of last year's harvest. When that's gone, they starve. And the good boys, the clans which took no part in the revolt, will be no better off because we'll demand their harvest to pay the indemnities decreed for Catuvellauni and Coritani as a whole.'

Valens rasped his stubble again. 'Policy is not my affair. But do you mean, Legate, to compel these people to another outbreak, a revolt bred from despair?'

'You have your orders,' I said shortly. 'If you need more cohorts I shall call the reserve from London and, if required, strip the frontier.'

He looked at me oddly, a long, searching inquiry. 'No,' he said at last. 'I have enough men to hold this territory and Cerialis has a vexillation at Leicester. But I foresee fighting again very soon. You accept that?'

'I accept all consequences stemming from my decisions.' I tapped a finger on the table between us. 'I am concerned with the future. Rome

will stay in this Province for a very long time, Valens, long after we are
both dead and forgotten. I mean to ensure that never again, in the whole
history of our dominion in Britain, will the Britons east of the Frontier Way rise against us. I intend to teach them a lesson they will never
forget.'

Valens glanced at me, averted his eyes, sighed. His cheerful gaiety
had faded.

11

The political situation here, among tribes who had only partially committed themselves to the revolt, differed from that in Icenia where the
sword alone ruled. Many notables, princes and chieftains submitted
to Valens, either protesting innocence or casting themselves upon his
mercy. He dealt with such men according to their deserts. Those proved
to have borne arms against Rome were enslaved, the guiltless released to
their homes. Many intransigents, however, fled northwards and, as we
learned later, took service under Venutius. That troublesome warrior,
encouraged by this accretion, began raiding from his fortress into Brigantia, and soon I received woeful letters from Cartimandua. I returned
promises and encouragement; our forces were fully occupied and, at
that moment, I could provide nothing more substantial.

I went to Lincoln, met Cerialis and told him Venutius was ram-
paging again, which he already knew. After a stern admonition against
any expeditions in Cartimandua's support I returned to Verulam, dismissed to London all my escort except staff and bodyguard, and rode
for the frontier.

I entered Wroxeter on a sun-baked day in mid-July. The civilized
security of a great fortress was like a soothing balm to mind and body.
Since leaving Silchester a month and a half earlier I had lived in petty
forts or marching-camps set in wasted fields, beside derelict towns,

overlooking dreary marshes. So for two days I discussed no business and allowed prolonged baths, massage, sleep and luxurious victuals to restore my nerves and vigour.

For this proceeding I had an enthusiastic ally in Titus Pomponius Mamilianus, legate of XX Legion Valeria, soon to be Victrix. Hitherto I had found little in this man's character worthy of commendation: on my arrival as Governor his control, as I have described earlier, was so lax that it seemed his centurions, not he, ruled the roost with advantage to none but themselves. Contemptuous of his military qualities I had left him to command in Wroxeter during the Ordovican campaign: he had guarded the frontier ever since with complete success. My earlier judgements were mistaken.

Not that Mamilianus regarded himself as a soldier. Long, thin, languid, aristocratic to the last tendril of his overlong hair, he dabbled in philosophy, wrote passable verse and was passionately interested in gastronomy and beautiful boys. I had sometimes wondered at his assignment to such a turbulent Province. His offhand account of frontier crises during the Boudiccan rebellion reminded me that Rome does not entrust her legions to men without iron in their hearts.

Our withdrawal from Ordovicia had been followed by a period of calm while the tribesmen sought assurance that we had really gone. Then they assembled their forces and a combined Degeanglian-Ordovican raid struck deep into Cornovian territory south of Chester.

'Two forts were overrun,' Mamilianus said negligently. He nibbled an olive stuffed with chives, delicately savouring the flavour. 'Fortunately some survivors reached Wroxeter very quickly and I flogged a vexillation on a night march northwards. We cut the tribesmen's line of retreat and killed several thousands. They've been quiet since—occasional cattle-raids, no more.'

Thus, in a few words, he dismissed an operation which, I learned afterwards, was a masterpiece of quiet, determined interception.

'And the Silures?' I said. 'Have they troubled Gloucester at all?'

'I believe not,' Mamilianus said. 'The tribesmen respect the hostages you hold. The frontier from Chester to Gloucester is, as you might say, torpid. Try these thrushes' tongues in shrimp sauce, Legate—they're quite delicious.'

I sipped my wine reflectively. 'What is your opinion of Wroxeter as a fortress?'

'Very comfortable quarters indeed,' he answered promptly. 'I know no other place in Britain I'd rather live in.'

'I don't mean that,' I said testily. 'How do you rate its strategic value to our military purposes nowadays?'

He eyed me shrewdly. 'Very low, I'm sorry to say. Ten years ago Wroxeter was a natural frontier terminus for the Midland Way. Today it faces a mountain waste inhabited by comparatively unwarlike tribes. The fortress is too far away from the Ordovices—our real problem—and distance tends to breed disrespect.'

'Exactly. And the Ordovices, thanks to Boudicca, have to be conquered all over again. For that campaign we shall again require a base in the north. I think that base should become a permanent fortress, an ever-present menace to the territory we have won.'

'Chester?'

'Yes.'

I reflectively savoured a tasty morsel on my palate. 'Wroxeter is still necessary. Until all this mountain land from Ordovicia to Siluria is subdued we shall need a fortress facing the central regions. And a garrison here can quickly support either Chester or Gloucester. I shall therefore leave XIV Legion here and transfer you and Valeria to Chester.'

Mamilianus groaned. 'A deadly place. Too far from the Severn, which spawns the tastiest trout in Britain. However—'

'A detachment with engineers, within the next day or two,' I said. 'We shall go to prospect a site for a legionary fortress. You're quite right, Mamilianus: these thrushes' tongues *are* delicious.'

12

From the Cornovian elders I acquired for Rome the small sandstone plateau of Chester in perpetuity. Legionary engineers wielded measuring-chains and groma, plotted and figured, sketched plans for my approval. With Cornovian labour, Ordovican slaves and an advanced party from Wroxeter the construction began. I told Mamilianus to have the place built and garrisoned within a month.

In Britain my name may be honoured or execrated—I neither know nor care—but two permanent memorials of my rule remain: a Roman town in Silchester and the Roman fortress of Chester.

13

At Gloucester II Legion, subdued and ashamed, strove to rehabilitate itself by energetic patrolling on a frontier void of foes and glory. The warlike Silures might not have existed. Our patrols met none but peaceful herdsmen; our foraging parties roamed unhindered. Augusta, commanded by a tribune, was in low spirits and badly needed a strong legate to restore her morale, a fact I had recognized months before and petitioned Rome about. I let the men know that, with Posthumus's death, bygones were bygones and the legion itself still stood high in my estimation. Nevertheless, the fortress' atmosphere was depressing. After some searching inspections I left for Cirencester where, in a mansion lent by a wealthy Dobunian landowner, I halted to take stock.

Pantera's speedy restoration of communications with Boulogne had allowed a backlog of correspondence to reach me from Rome. This, however, dealt with pre-rebellion affairs, the routine of a Province at peace, fiscal decrees concerning corn-dues—the corn was never sown—rescripts attached to petitions from citizens whose skeletons mouldered in wayside ditches. Everywhere I and the clerks on my staff, used largely to dealing with military affairs, felt the lack of background, of references, of files perished in the flames of Colchester and London. Though Boudicca had failed to seize Britain she had thrown its administration into chaos.

In the west, Cirencester, Dorchester and Exeter, important civilian settlements untouched by the revolt, possessed government revenue and juridicial offices staffed by civilian clerks. I summoned many of these to my headquarters in an effort to form the nucleus of a civil service until properly trained accountants, jurists and scribes arrived from Rome, With this slender corps I tried to establish some sort of administrative order; and began with a circular letter to tribal and cantonal magistrates that demanded nominal rolls of those who had perished in the rebellion, plus a statement of property destroyed. It was no good demanding taxes of the dead or assessing revenue from burnt-out farms.

Answers to my dispatches after Boudicca's defeat began to arrive: flowery congratulations from the Senate, a brief recommendation in the Prince's own hand, a terse note of praise from Burrus. More important, perhaps, was information about reinforcements: two thousand legionaries, two regiments of horse and eight cohorts of auxiliary infantry were heading for Boulogne. Also, a Senatorial letter told me, a new Procurator, to succeed Catus, had left Rome for Britain with a complete actuarial staff. I sighed in relief. I knew nothing of the new man, Julius Classicianus; he could hardly be worse than Catus and would relieve me of the unaccustomed burden of civil accountancy.

I convened an assembly of tribal magistrates, decurions and rural magnates representing unaffected tribes of the west and south: Cornovii, Dobuni, Durotriges, Belgae, Regni and Atrebates. Epaticcus of the Atrebates, I heard with concern, was gravely ill. From this gathering, met in Cirencester's insignificant basilica, I obtained in conversations public and private a political sense of those settled areas which had been beyond Boudicca's influence. The general opinion, one gathered from a consensus that barely flattered Roman sentiment, was disappointment because she had failed, mingled with profound relief because they themselves had escaped the consequences. Relief and joy were expressed openly to my face; disappointment, I need hardly add, was discovered only by my spies.

I distributed gifts to the principal officials—money, horses and slaves—and promises of recommendations to the Prince for grants of citizenship. I had to use the Prince's name because, in outlying provinces where the name of Caesar is all-powerful and the Senate merely a vague, unknown entity, to pretend that such awards are still the Senate's prerogative is meaningless.

While the sweet music of praise still lingered in their ears I divulged the real reason for their convocation. Half the Province's arable land was unsown or ravaged; the army's corn supplies for the coming winter were in danger. The normal taxation system would not answer. The instigators and victims of the rebellion could not provide their quotas; the unaffected tribes must make deficiencies good. I explained these facts gently and in detail, saw dismayed faces and heard a gale of protest. I raised my hand.

I said, 'You never knew peace and security until Rome came. And peace you cannot have without soldiers, and soldiers you cannot have without food, nor food without taxation. If you value your present well-being you must make sacrifices to ensure that it endures.'

With which piece of logic I dismissed the assembly.

Our tax-gatherers accordingly received fresh instructions; Gloucester, on my orders, sent soldiers to the tribal revenue-collection centres. One cannot take too many precautions where taxation is concerned.

14

In mid-August I returned to London. The rubble had been removed, the streets cleared and building-foundations laid. Docks and wharves, completely restored and in full working order, harboured a satisfying complement of ships. Shopkeepers had erected booths where they conducted a brisk trade; a fresh influx of merchants and bankers, undeterred by their predecessors' fate, conducted business in temporary hutments of timber and thatch. A new London was growing, fast as a fungus, from the old.

News from the revolted areas was not altogether happy. Agricola had finished his work among the Trinovantes: the tribe, sold into slavery, had ceased to exist. Valens, still at Towcester, reported widespread famine in the midlands coupled with sporadic fighting against outlaw gangs which had taken to the forests. Cerialis and Bassus in the fens had made little impression upon the hard core of Icenian rebels, those elusive outlaws who, knowing themselves doomed, were fighting to the end with the bitterness of despair.

Only one item relieved these gloomy reports. Bassus wrote that Boudicca was dead. Hopeless, heartbroken by the spectacle of her people being hunted like animals and butchered on sight, she and her two daughters had swallowed poison.

I felt no elation. The Icenian Queen had ceased to mean anything from the moment her army broke before Valens's swordsmen. She was no Caratacus, this rabble-rouser. Her presence would have cheapened an Imperial triumph; a furtive end in a miasmic swamp was better than she deserved. Yet I had an uneasy sense that her legend would remain in Britain for a very long time.

I recalled Agricola and his vexillation to London and replaced him in Colchester with a small military detachment and a skeleton civil staff to administer the reconquered territory. He was too young and untrained for complicated civil administration. Nevertheless, supported by tough and experienced centurions, he had made a thoroughly good job of reducing Trinovantia. Anyway, I missed the boy. The tardy progress of pacification seemed less depressing when he once more shared my tent and table and listened, grave and intent, to my schemes and discourses.

Sextus Frontinus returned from his reconnaissance with a drainage plan of leviathan proportions. His scheme involved, in the main, cutting a navigable canal or dyke, over eighty miles long, from Lincoln to Cambridge. This, connecting two river-systems, would open communications in the fens and through subsidiary ditches would drain immense areas of swamp.

He slapped his maps enthusiastically on my table.

'A feasible and worthwhile project, Legate,' he declared. 'No deforestation problems in that country. Once we've drained the marshes we have an enormous area of fertile land ready for the plough. The soil is wonderful, where it's not under water. These fens could become the granary of Britain.'

I regarded the maps dubiously. 'We should certainly need a good return for such a vast undertaking. Have you calculated the time and labour involved?'

Frontinus smiled confidently. 'Give me twenty thousand slaves, Legate, and within three years I'll have barges moving between Cambridge and Lincoln and corn growing where marshes stank.'

'Three years!' I began rolling the maps. 'No help to Bassus and Cerialis. No immediate profit.'

Frontinus's face fell. I visualized the huge slave-pens that lay around London, the steady though diminishing inflow from Valens's operations and the long chain-gangs travelling the roads to Rome.

'Twenty thousand is too many. Half that, possibly, and double the time. A legacy I may bequeath to my successors. In any case I cannot sanction such a task without studying the layout myself. Agricola, when do the first reinforcements arrive?'

'Eight Batavian cohorts await shipping at Boulogne. Legionary details and cavalry regiments are seven days' march from the port.'

I unrolled the map, traced the course of Frontinus's canal. 'This avoids the war area in the fenlands, I see, so we shall not be embroiled in fighting if we go and look. Nothing to hold me here: no Continental troops will reach London within ten days. Let's start tomorrow.'

Frontinus gave a pleased grin and departed to make arrangements. With a sufficient escort and a staff that included all the engineering and agricultural experts I could find, I made a leisurely journey to Lincoln and back, diverging frequently from the North Way to examine the proposed line of the canal. Nothing in the plan seemed impossible; the technicians' recommendations were unanimous.

'You can begin your dyke,' I told Frontinus as we jogged down the North Way to London. 'I shall sign an order allocating to you ten thousand slaves from the pens, a supervisory staff of engineers and an auxiliary detachment for guards and escort. You will begin digging from Lincoln and will not, on any account, start work in the fen country proper until operations there are ended. The risk of slaves absconding to the enemy is too great.'

In these short sentences originated an engineering feat which completed seven years later, opened inaccessible country and provided far-reaching cornlands for Britain's granaries. Frontinus, posted elsewhere in the natural course of his military career, could not finish the project. The scheme in its inception was mine; a subsequent Governor, when the canal was opened to traffic, received the credit. As the man was, and is, a spineless nonentity under whose rule Britain stagnates, who has made no conquests and advanced no frontiers, I grudge this undeserved laurel placed upon his brow.

However, these events lay in the future. The present, upon that sunny afternoon of the first day of September when I entered the fortified camp outside London, saluted the new Procurator's appearance in a comfortable enclosure near the river-bank, where tents and huts housed his considerable entourage of civil servants, clerks and slaves. Julius Classicianus awaited, so a respectful chamberlain assured me, the pleasure of an interview at my convenience.

I sighed. His arrival would relieve me of much unwelcome work; but Procurators, agents of the Prince and answerable to him alone, were always a nuisance, if not worse.

This one was to prove worse, much worse.

17

'There will be no common faith between those who share power, and each man will be jealous of his associate.'

LUCAN

1

Gaius Julius Alpinus Classicianus, Procurator of Britain, was an able administrator, obstinate and tough, who represented a new type of official. Unlike Catus, born and bred in Italy, he was a Gaul of Belgica, a man whose outlook and sympathies were provincial rather than Roman. Physically he looked not unlike myself: tall, lean, hawk-nosed and hardbitten. There all resemblance ceased.

At our first meeting, because his own department was so particularly concerned, I gave him a frank and friendly exposition of the administrative and financial breakdown caused by the rebellion. He listened politely to my summary of the measures I had taken to quell disorder and secure, so far as was possible, a balanced budget. My remedies were, in brief, heavier taxes from the loyal tribes allied to savage reparations from the insurgents.

'It would seem best,' he murmured, attentively examining his finger-nails, 'that I should establish my offices in London and then, with your permission, make a tour of inspection through the devastated areas. Only personal observation will enable me to judge how much, or how little, revenue can be expected from those cantons.'

I agreed, and provided an escort. Next day Classicianus departed for Colchester, leaving instructions with his chief officials to put the Province's fiscal machinery in motion. The Procurator's palace and revenue offices were still being rebuilt: I housed the Treasury in camp, under guard, and the secretariat in wooden huts beyond Wall Brook. And forthwith I set about planting spies within Classicianus's household and offices.

The task was not easy. The Gaul had brought an integrated secretariat, complete to the humblest copying-clerk. Vacancies existed only for menials and slaves, whose value as spies was small because they were barred from access to important documents and high-level correspondence. But a quick death from natural causes—within a few days a commentar succumbed to the British climate—and a mysterious accident which drowned two principal notars allowed me to insert, in important and confidential positions, three freedmen clerks who were practised intelligence agents.

Classicianus's household was not difficult to penetrate. His Celtic affinities disposed him to engage without suspicion native chamberlains, porters and slaves; and British domestics soon flooded the chambers of his wife, Julia Pacata. Many were on my payroll: in a little while the Procurator could hardly sneeze without my knowing it.

Classicianus's counter-intelligence, unfortunately, provided vexatious problems. A troop of commentars, notars, librars, scribes and copyists, replacements for my own secretariat, had travelled from Rome with him and crossed in the same flotilla. He had had plenty of opportunity for subversion. I had the new arrivals thoroughly screened, posted some doubtful characters to obscure town-halls in the west, and still felt uneasy. Only after a radical alteration of office routine, whereby the newcomers were relegated to the outer fringes of security and all secret correspondence, civil or military, was handled by a trusted body of centurions and beneficars, did I feel safe.

Before this espionage-web was thoroughly woven the reinforcements that the Prince had sanctioned and Burrus had assigned from stations in Gaul and Lower Germany disembarked at Richborough. Four legionary cohorts went straight to Lincoln to replace Hispana's losses. Of the eight Batavian cohorts I sent three to the frontier and five to help Bassus against the Iceni. The cavalry, Sebosius's Horse and a Spanish regiment, likewise went to Bassus.

Vettius Valens, whose opinion I valued, had made me doubt the wisdom of my policy in the midlands. As the days passed and dispatches from his Towcester headquarters continued to report severe famine, an incipient breakdown of civilian administration and intensified guerrilla fighting in the forests I realized I should either have to commit more troops to pacify the territory or else disengage entirely. If I withdrew my forces we could re-establish our lines of communication with the released cohorts and strengthen the frontier garrisons. The danger was that our enemies, spurning this declaration of peace, might continue to harry us from the forests.

There was no question of relaxing in Icenia. Twelve thousand troops—more than the army that defeated Boudicca—were engaged in the fenlands against half as many Britons. Apart from my own determination to eradicate the Iceni, Roman prestige was at stake.

Agricola finally persuaded me, after much thought, to order Valens and Cerialis to withdraw their vexillations from the lands of the Catuvellauni and Coritani. In the same dispatches I declared a public amnesty: anyone who had marched with Boudicca could return to his home without fear of punishment or persecution. Payment of reparations would cease. Corn would be sent to granaries at Towcester and Leicester for distribution in the famine areas.

'And where,' I asked Agricola, 'do we find this corn? There's none in Britain.'

'There are enormous stocks in fortress granaries,' he answered. 'Wroxeter alone has three years' reserve for her garrison.'

I was horrified. 'Give army supplies to rebels? Impossible! In this year's military corn levy the loyal tribes have supplied not only their usual quota but also surcharges to repair war damage and the rebels' deficiencies. How will they react when they see their taxes used to feed people who have defied Rome? Do you want another revolt on our hands?'

'They needn't know. Send the food, without advertisement, from the fortresses. Replenish at leisure through emergency requisitions on the Continent, from Belgica or Lugdunensis.'

I frowned. Imperial decrees allowed a Province, in emergency, to obtain men, arms and supplies from a neighbour without prior reference to Rome. But such requisitions had to be ratified afterwards by the Prince, repaid in cash or kind, and were unpopular with recipient, donor and the Roman Government.

'You'll get me recalled,' I grumbled.

'If the midland trouble flares into another rising you will certainly be recalled,' Agricola said quietly.

I glared at him and he returned my look without flinching.

'Call a clerk,' I said at last. 'I'll dictate the dispatches immediately.'

2

Classicianus's tour, of whose itinerary the army kept me closely informed, accelerated to whirlwind speed as it progressed from Trinovantes to Iceni, from Catuvellauni to Coritani. Within a fortnight he was back in London; inside the hour he pleaded admittance to my council.

A formal request of this nature meant a full-fledged debate, the protagonists supported by respective panoplies of advisers, jurists, accountants, experts and scribes. I appointed a day distant enough to cool his ardour and meanwhile sought enlightenment from my spies. What I learned assured me that, once again, the Governor and Procurator of Britain were at loggerheads.

The meeting opened with the usual preliminary prayers and courtesies; then Classicianus read a long, tedious statement of revenue losses due to the rebellion and its aftermath. Item by item, lead, silver, tin, wool, cloth, hides, corn, jewellery, pearls, dogs, slaves, he compared income and export figures with previous years and found, not unnaturally, deficits in each. He concluded by asking how I, as Governor, proposed to balance the accounts.

I yawned openly. 'For two months and more,' I said distinctly, 'Britain has been torn by a war which killed nearly two hundred thousand people and inflicted immense damage upon her economy. The revolt and its consequences are regrettable but nevertheless a fact: we cannot undo it. We can, however, reorganize, rebuild, recoup until the Province is again solvent, progressive, contented and returning to Rome more than the City expends on her upkeep. I am doing this now, but these things take time and you, my dear Classicianus, have been in Britain a bare twenty days.'

'Long enough, Legate,' he replied in a voice like silk, 'to recognize that no peace, security or revenue can be expected in this island until our armies stop killing the inhabitants.'

My face froze. 'You speak of matters beyond your jurisdiction.'

Classicianus's pale eyes glinted. 'Directly, yes; consequentially, no. My office requires certain calculated revenues to be secured from Britain. The natives cannot pay taxes while they are being harried through swamps and forests, hunted like animals from Lincoln to London.'

The enemy had exposed his ribs; I gave him the point.

'Tribune,' I said unhurriedly to Agricola, 'show the Procurator copies of the dispatches I sent yesterday to the legates Vettius Valens and Quintus Cerialis.'

Classicianus flattened the rolls, read frowning, laid them aside. He was a good dissembler; no hint of chagrin showed in his face.

'Admirable,' he said, 'apart from the matter of free corn distribution, whose sources I cannot at the moment fathom. Doubtless you have given similar orders to your officers in Icenia?'

'No.'

'Why not?'

I stirred. Agricola, standing beside me, moved quickly towards the Procurator, collected the dispatches, hid the Gaul momentarily from my sight. I relaxed in my seat; the sudden throbbing in my temples subsided.

'I see no good reason, Classicianus, why I should explain military policy to you. The operations in Icenia will cease when no Iceni are left alive.'

His eyes, cold and intelligent, searched my features for long moments. A paper rustled; metal clinked as a guardsman eased his stance.

'That is your last word.' The sentence was a statement, an expression of formed opinion. The Procurator stood, gathered his robe. 'The consequences, in misery and money, you realize and accept. I must warn you, Legate, that my recommendations to the Prince will be very different.'

He departed, trailing his entourage, leaving me faintly puzzled. I knew men; I had spent years judging them in court and war; Classicianus was honest, a man of rock-like integrity. He knew, from reading my dispatches to the legates, that our punitive operations in the midlands were ending; that the revenues from those tribes would soon be restored to him. Why should he be so concerned about Icenia, a land that first Catus, then Bassus's soldiery, had sucked dry of wealth—a kingdom that had never paid tax to Rome? For a venial Procurator I could have found a dozen reasons: for Classicianus, none.

I hastened to urge vigilance upon my spies.

3

The long-drawn hostilities against Boudicca's remnants began to worry me. Autumn was upon us; winter conditions in Britain, especially in the fenland morasses, would soon put an end to active campaigning.

Goaded by anxiety I again rode north and conferred with Cerialis and Bassus at Cambridge.

Our forces had penned the Iceni within a rectangle, fifteen miles by thirty, backing on the Wash, and had ringed this waste of reeds, mud-flats and tidal watercourses with a chain of forts. The quarry could not get out; nor, unfortunately, could our troops get in. So intricate was the country, so waterlogged, that our operations were necessarily amphibious; the men had to construct barges and boats, a difficult undertaking in a treeless wilderness. The Iceni, on the other hand, unhindered by armour, unhampered by static bases, moved amid the marshes with the speed and venom of watersnakes, luring our men into ambushes and then vanishing, never standing to fight.

Whereas a dead Briton was a phenomenon, we suffered casualties daily, a steady attrition which unsettled the men and, combined with unspeakably dreary surroundings, created a feeling of futility and exasperation. The campaign, in short, was practically at a standstill.

A journey around the fort-cordon confirmed the incredible difficulties facing cohorts and commanders. Active fighting in such terrain was nonsensical; the circumstances demanded a change of plan.

'No more punitive expeditions into the marshes,' I told Cerialis and Bassus. 'We must contain the enemy in the net and at the same time draw it tight. Advance your forts, two or three together; consolidate; advance others in turn. Mutual support is axiomatic; the enemy must not slip through gaps. Thus we shall force them into an ever-narrowing compass until they are driven to the coast and the beaches.'

'And then?' Cerialis interjected.

'Send me word when you have them with their backs to the sea.'

'Your programme is bound to be slow,' Bassus said doubtfully. 'In these quagmires the siting and building of a single fort sometimes takes days.'

'Conditions will be tolerable here until the end of October,' I said amiably. 'If you haven't finished by then your campaigning, during a British winter, will be rather uncomfortable.'

They saw my point and grinned wryly.

During the tour I made it my business to visit and encourage the fort garrisons and reserve cohorts stationed farther in rear. I praised their fortitude under trying circumstances and promised a return to winter quarters in the near future. I have never yet broken my word to soldiers, and I think they believed me.

4

After the arsenal, the Governor's palace in London had first priority for rebuilding. When I returned from Icenia my residence, designed on a more magnificent scale than its predecessor, was partly inhabitable. I changed quarters from camp to palace and was immediately depressed by cavernous space, vast echoing emptiness, absence of furniture and decoration and a pervading residue of builders' litter. Constructional noises from other parts of the premises disturbed my councils.

The still ruinous state of London, the lack of proper offices for my staff and secretariat, the need for a basilica where I could dispense justice, and the discomfort of my new palace decided me to move headquarters temporarily to Silchester. Civilian officials do not take kindly to shifts of domicile: the transfer required more drive and organization than a prolonged war. But among Silchester's autumn-tinted woodlands I was able without distraction to assess impartially both my own predicament and the condition of the Province.

Thanks to efficient agents I had copies of all Classicianus's important correspondence. They contained little solace. He had written to Claudius of Smyrna, to the Senate, to the Prince himself, repeating in essence the facts and figures, with adverse comments on every discrepancy, that he had proclaimed in council. He adduced that no improvement in the state and revenues of Britain could be expected until operations in Icenia were abandoned, the natives pardoned and their lands restored.

His remedy was drastic: the Governor, a man who owed all his disasters to his own misconduct, whose few successes stemmed from his legions' valour and the Luck of Rome, must be recalled.

In anticipation of the Procurator's damnatory diatribes I had already sent well-reasoned explanations of my pacification policy to the Roman authorities. In their replies neither the Senate nor Burrus expressed any dissatisfaction. The trouble was that I could make no personal counter-attack upon Classicianus; the Gaul's conduct, both public and private, had hitherto been exemplary.

Now Valens gave me a weapon.

The legate, according to my orders, had withdrawn his vexillations from the midlands, established granaries and distributed corn. This had failed to pacify the renegades. Suspicious of our motives and incurably hostile to Rome, they stayed in the forests and started harrying road-stations, rest-houses, ore convoys and any other manifestations of governmental authority. I was forced to direct two extra cohorts to the country between Leceister and Towcester where the gangs were active.

Valens reported strange rumours pervading the countryside that I was soon to be replaced by a new Governor, a man who bore nothing but goodwill towards the natives, who would pursue a policy of moderation and humanity, who was not inflated by the pride of victory. The tale in itself was not remarkable: men struggling in the abysses of adversity will snatch at any rumour that gives them hope. But Valens, or rather his tribune on the spot, found a pattern and persistence which indicated deliberate dissemination. He confirmed discreetly from my secretariat that the story was unfounded; then proceeded determinedly to track the source. For a long time he groped in the dark, until a native's hint and a quick cavalry swoop intercepted a Catuvellaun war-band. Among them were two strangers, Cantii from Rochester.

The pair, under interrogation, confessed to being in Classicianus's pay.

Their depositions, witnessed by a tribune, I promptly forwarded to Burrus. My covering letter—a brief document, for the testaments were self-explanatory—asked for the Prince's commands in a case where a high Roman official, in collusion with the enemy, had tried to undermine the power and authority of the Prince's representative in Britain.

5

Soon after arriving in Silchester I had visited Epaticcus of the Atrebates on his bed of sickness, but the old man was in a coma and too far gone to recognize anybody. Within a few days he died. To me he entrusted the administration of his will, leaving 50,000 sesterces for my own use; the remainder he bequeathed to Silchester for financing erection of some public edifice or to institute five-yearly games.

I had lost a friend, and Britain was a poorer place.

And here let me say that Epaticcus's bequest and my own annual salary—250,000 sesterces—were the only moneys I received in Britain from any source. I state this not from pride but as a corrective to one of the many malicious slanders which have since pursued me. Large-scale extortion by provincial Governors, after the pattern of Republican times, is no longer possible; but even nowadays a Governor has only to let it be seen that he is prepared to grant favours or stretch a point of law, in return for money, to make a fortune within a year. I am a wealthy man; I have great estates in Etruria; if I wished for more I could invest in banking, shipping, mines or some other form of trade which, though technically forbidden to senators, is becoming increasingly lucrative. I despise, with all my heart, the squalid venality practised by men like Decianus Catus.

Epaticcus's death coincided with information from my spies at fleet headquarters, confirmed by those in the Procurator's secretariat, that a curious intrigue was brewing between Pantera and Classicianus. The two had been corresponding and had met recently at Richborough. What they said was unknown; their letters revealed that Classicianus, sparing no weapon in his fight to get me recalled, was using Pantera's grudge over the loss of his ships to send a two-pronged complaint to Rome. The Procurator bemoaned the cost, and the Fleet Commandant the waste, of men and material. Both insisted that my dictatorial overruling of Pantera's professional advice was the supreme cause of an expensive disaster.

I suddenly felt overwhelmed by a sense of impotence. I could find no satisfactory means of retaliation. My dispatches giving the full story of the fleet's expedition to Anglesey had long since gone to Rome where, so far as I knew, they had aroused no adverse comment. Pantera's intervention was exasperating. Was I now to write a defence against a subordinate's spiteful accusations—accusations that the Prince might well reject without my intervention?

One never knew: it had better be done.

I began to compose a letter but was interrupted by the arrival of a special courier, the last of a relay which had ridden night and day from Rome. The weight of the news he brought reduced my differences with provincial officials to the level of petty quarrels between barbarian decurions of some uncouth rustic settlement. For the burden of the courier's dispatch could change the pattern of life up to and beyond the frontiers of the civilized world.

Afranius Burrus wantonly ignored the canons of discretion enforced by Caesar's agents. After the customary polite courtesies and inquiries he wrote:

'Palace politics are moving fast to a crisis. The Prince in Council is increasingly intolerant of his old advisers: men like Seneca, Claudius of Smyrna and myself. His dissipations multiply; his companions become wilder, more vicious and worthless. Ribald suggestions from his dissolute troupe are too often adopted and subsequently masquerade as Imperial edicts.

'The conduct of government under Nero is such that I cannot claim, myself, to have fostered the Senate's privileges or bolstered their relics of power. But we have always displayed, hitherto, a frail façade of decency, a kindly pretence which maintained an illusion that the Senate, in matters of everyday government at least, was the executive and legislative assembly of the Roman people. We all knew how shallow was the deceit, how for years Rome has been ruled by one man and that the Senate was but a mouthpiece for his decisions. We nevertheless kept the outward forms of a republic and pretended that the Prince was indeed no more than the principal of his senators.

'All this is going, disappearing with a rapidity that makes me afraid. The Prince's scabrous companions openly deride the Senate and mock their solemn deliberations and weighty conclusions. They aim at power; they hope to destroy the last vestiges of republican rule and they aspire to supremacy under a potentate whose control is absolute; who is, in fact, a king.

'The last of the Claudian line is going mad. The taint in his blood has infected his reason. I worried little about Nero's personal depravities—his lyre-playing, poetry, play-acting and his strange love for chariot-racing and charioteers—when his sense of public responsibility outweighed his private vices. But he is no longer responsible.

'Men of courage and integrity will oppose his aspirations, will fight against the rapacity of his companions. I see myself among them. The mad ruthlessness of creatures like Tigellinus will crush them, and I foresee a reign of terror, a delator's paradise, which will make Caligula's proscriptions seem a happy memory of a golden age.

'Chief among Nero's profligates is one Ofonius Tigellinus, a fishmonger and horse-coper who has now become Prefect of the Watch. I fear this man. He is ambitious and wicked beyond belief; his influence upon the Prince is enormous. And he is aiming, without any doubt whatever, at my position.

'I believe you know how taut my relations with Nero have been since that day, four years ago, when I refused the Praetorians' help in Agrippina's murder. He has never, I think, quite trusted me again. His attitude lately has been markedly cold; my advice is disdained, my opinions ignored. My prestige has waned; my fortunes are sliding rapidly downhill.

'I offer you, however, not querulous complaints but a warning. Julius Classicianus has sent the Prince a spate of letters which vehemently and viciously attack your conduct and administration. What has attracted this man's malevolence I know not. The point is that, when Nero throws these letters to his Council and invites their views, anything I say in your defence is not only disregarded but may even prejudice the Prince against you.

'The real trouble is that two successive Procurators, of quite different character and outlook, have come to much the same conclusion about you and your government. Catus's diatribes were discounted as spiteful vituperation from a discredited coward; Classicianus, an able and upright man, repeats more forcibly and with stronger evidence what Catus has already said. The Senate begins to doubt: Thrasea said yesterday that when two winds carry the same smell it is time to remove the carrion.

'The Prince wanted you recalled. I pleaded with all my strength on your behalf while he fiddled impatiently with his model chariots. With Seneca's support I persuaded him to wait until a disinterested observer could assess the situation in Britain and make a report.

'The independent observer is on his way, may already have reached you. Polycletus, one of the Prince's freedmen, is to decide your fate. He is extravagant and vain, also shrewd and capable and deep in Nero's confidence. Treat him with respect; flatter him; but do not try to deceive him. Sink your pride, Paulinus. Remember he is the Prince's person in Britain.

'I wish you well, old friend. For me the sands are dwindling. Do not grieve too much when the glass is empty, for I shall be ready to go and too tired to be sorry.'

6

Burrus's reckless language horrified me nearly as much as the contents of his letter. The Prince's agents, as he knew very well, haunted posting-houses along all the great roads from Rome and pried into message satchels, tampered cunningly with seals, read and noted treasonable or subversive correspondence. I examined the seals and stitchings of the oilskin wrapper with minute care. All seemed secure. Nothing could have saved the Prefect's head if Nero's spies had read this letter; my own would be none too safe. Burrus was sunk in the carelessness of despair.

Cautious hints in private correspondence and gossip from newly-joined tribunes had all tended to show that the Praetorian Prefect was out of favour. I had paid little attention. Burrus's fortunes had fluctuated before; at one time Nero, in a fit of rage, had dismissed him and only Seneca's urgings secured his reinstatement. The situation which he now disclosed was different and very dangerous.

I was profoundly depressed. I burned the letter, gave my chamberlain orders for a return to London. My Silchester mansion, a provincial Governor's country house, was no fit residence for the Prince's envoy. The fleet must be warned to provide an escort for his crossing, the new, raw palace in London prepared for his reception, Richborough, Canterbury, Rochester—any place where he might halt or sleep—furbished and provisioned for his comfort. Civil dignitaries, magistrates and decurions must be notified so that Polycletus should be greeted with suitable ceremony in every town. II Legion, the nearest garrison, would have to send troops for ceremonial guards and escorts.

Rome sent me no official notification of the freedman's visit, nor did I receive any until he reached Boulogne. It seemed that Polycletus wished to reach Britain unheralded, to catch me unawares, though when he landed he showed no discomposure on discovering the elaborate preparations made for his reception. But that was later.

The visitation had come at a most inconvenient time. Cerialis's latest dispatches stated that his fort-chain now ringed the Iceni within a narrow belt of coastland, a maze of tidal creeks, which was impenetrable without ships. This I had foreseen. Three thousand soldiers waited in London; fifteen requisitioned merchantmen were in port; Richborough harboured the British Fleet. My plans envisaged a small sea-borne expedition, a short three-days' sail from the Thames to the Wash. There we would disembark behind the enemy and, in conjunction with our land army, finish the Iceni for good.

Because of Polycletus my intention of commanding the expedition myself had to be abandoned. Otherwise there was no reason for postponement. I called Pantera from Richborough, outlined the plan and told him to anchor twelve biremes and ten cutters in London.

As usual, I met objections. At that season the onshore winds, combined with contrary currents and tides and the uncharted shoals of the Wash made navigation in those waters extremely hazardous. A squadron was already detailed to escort Polycletus. The end of the cruising season was near: autumn gales were imminent. His new crews were untrained. The new ships were not fully equipped. And so on.

I heard him without patience and said, 'Pantera, you complain at large that I never take your advice. I shall try to be consistent. Bring the ships, completely manned, rigged and provisioned, to London in six days, that is by the 5th of October at latest. You will command the flotilla in person.'

Not that I had any faith in Pantera's seaman-like qualities, but policy demanded that he be kept out of the way until I had put my case to Polycletus.

The warships rowed upriver on the 4th; the troops embarked and the convoy, thirty-seven vessels carrying six cohorts, sailed next day. I appointed Flavius Longus, a tribune of XX Legion seconded to my staff, in overall command. Gallopers went to warn Cerialis.

Two days afterwards word came that Polycletus was at Boulogne. I hurried to Richborough to meet him.

7

During the following month Nero's ex-slave dominated my life. I make no apologies. Senators of our generation mournfully acknowledge the power wielded by Palace freedmen: lowborn creatures whom they at once despise and conciliate. My father treated such men with cold disdain; my grandfather would not have recognized their existence.

Polycletus, to do him justice, was not an unpleasant personality. A big, dark, fleshy-faced man, he was a good listener and pungent speaker. In other circumstances I could easily have made him a friend.

His equipage was magnificent, far beyond the requirements of his mission. He crossed the straits in the fleet's only trireme, *Radians*, and five transports carried his retinue and baggage and fifteen warships cruised in escort. At Richborough his camp was a town within the fortress; magnificent pavilions housed his followers and a gilded timber building of pre-fabricated, wagon-transportable sections was his travelling-palace. He journeyed in a mule-litter curtained with cloth-of-gold and, when ceremony demanded, mounted a four-horsed, silver-plated chariot whose panels were inlaid with pearls and ivory. Three hundred slaves, besides numerous chamberlains, stewards and major-domos attended his wants, and a large and competent chancery transacted his business.

The Procurator, of course, also received Polycletus at Richborough and vied with me in obsequious servility. The long procession, swollen by my bodyguard and Augusta's legionaries, rolled unhurriedly to London.

I had summoned dignitaries and chieftains from near and far to do him honour. Cogidumnus of the Regni was there, and princes of the Belgae, Atrebates, Durotriges and others. Cartimandua, pleading preoccupation with Venutius's irruptions, deputed her sulky lover Vellocatus. Polycletus treated them well; his manners were gracious without condescension, affable without familiarity. The elders responded with a grave, reserved dignity that concealed their outrage at being compelled to treat as a superior being one who, in their aristocratic eyes, was little better than an animal. To them a slave was always a slave; the smell of the pens was ineradicable.

The entire concourse departed for Colchester where, on the 13th of October, we celebrated the anniversary of the Prince's accession with prayer and sacrifice at the Temple of Victory, ceremonial parades and games on the camp parade-ground and speeches in the partly-rebuilt basilica. In due course we returned to London and the tribal heads returned thankfully to their homes.

Then the meetings began.

Polycletus was intensely thorough. He called conferences attended by myself and Classicianus, each supported by a bevy of advisers and secretaries, and threaded a skilful course through an ocean of conflicting evidence which was sometimes so minutely detailed that an hour passed in the exposition of a single point. The conferences lasted for days. The freedman was patient, persistent, even-tempered; he pursued the truth with the tenacity of a skilled and experienced lawyer; his questions were always pertinent and shrewd.

The scales tilted against me. The measures I adopted, in the light of circumstance, were seen to be ineluctable; the material results nearly always proved damaging to Rome's exchequer. I challenged my opponent to suggest alternative expedients; he replied coldly that while the past was unalterable he had a complete remedy for our present ills. Remove our troops from the fens, resettle the Iceni, those who still survived, in their old domain, placate the Catuvellaun outlaws.

This, making prestige the reason, I blankly refused.

Polycletus, after he had drained these exhausting inquisitions of the last dregs of information, spent hours in solitary discourse with me and Classicianus in turn. How he treated the Procurator I know not. At my table, toying idly with a flagon of wine, he was the well-mannered guest who seldom pressed an opinion and never asked embarrassing questions. Gently, inevitably, he guided the conversation in the direction he wished. I was frank with him, concealed very little. I think by the end there was nothing he did not know, or had not guessed, about the strains and stresses, the checks and balances, that influenced my conduct of affairs in Britain during my short and stormy tenure of office.

Then, politely refusing my company, or Classicianus's, Polycletus and his retinue departed on a leisurely tour of Britain. He went to the fenland borders, spoke with Cerialis; drifted through the midlands and watched our men flushing Catuvellaun brigands from the forests; conversed with Mamilianus in Chester, with Valens in Wroxeter; and returned by slow stages through Cirencester and Silchester. Wherever he went, so my agents in his train reported, in town or village or farm he spoke with the Britons and questioned high and low, decurion and cowherd alike.

The natives, well aware that Polycletus was a manumitted slave, were both contemptuous of his status and puzzled by the deference which Romans, from the Governor downwards, accorded him. The rough tribesmen of the west, Cornovii and Dobuni, found his magnificence pretentious and his inquiries impertinent. At Wroxeter and Cirencester the native magistrates and elders showed the Prince's emissary so little respect that the tribune of his escort had to intervene very sharply indeed. Polycletus was unperturbed: when the officials were recalled to their senses he treated them civilly, and coolly pursued his examination.

I, meanwhile, faced a bitter disappointment. The expedition against the Iceni, favoured by following winds and a calm sea, had made a swift passage to the Wash. Then, by a series of appalling navigational blunders, Pantera had grounded no fewer than eleven ships on sandbars five miles distant from the coast. Only four were refloated and, after cruising haphazardly about for another two days, seeking a clear channel to the shore, Pantera refused, unless directly ordered, to risk any more losses. After an acrimonious argument Flavius Longus commanded him to close upon the beaches. Three transports promptly went aground; the tribune in despair ordered the fleet about and set course for London.

No failure could have been more ignominious. We had not come within miles of the enemy. We had lost thirty men by drowning. The operations inland, timed to coincide with a vigorous sea-borne assault, had been a total failure. Not one native was killed.

When Longus had dispiritedly made his report—I could not bear to see Pantera—I had to consider what must be done in Icenia. The season, late October, was far advanced; the time remaining before winter's onset was too short for protracted fighting. The Iceni, I decided, must be penned in their watery fastness until, in the spring, those who had not died of starvation could be flushed out and killed.

I wrote to Cerialis: 'Your forts within the fens are too remote to be manned and maintained during winter. Withdraw your strongholds to the marshland borders, to a line whence you can cover Frontinus's work on the canal and at the same time confine the enemy to the marshes. They must not be allowed to filter inland. Units of the field army which are not required for garrison duties will be quartered in Lincoln. The area will come under your command: tell Aurelius Bassus to join me in London.'

For a time the accidents of nature, of impassable marshes and winter weather, had saved the Icenian savages from the sword. But by every means in my power I would ensure that they froze and starved during the icy months that lay ahead.

8

I went to Colchester to offer, at the Temple of Victory, the triple sacrifice of pig, sheep and bull that marks the official end of the campaigning season. The colony was recovering fast. Colchester's demesne lands, absorbing the forfeited holdings of rebel Trinovantes, had increased enormously. The normal wastage of time-expired veterans, combined with an influx of retired soldiers who were attracted from other parts of Britain by the lure of expansive farmlands, was re-populating the town. Reconstruction, aided by hundreds of slaves—captives of the rebellion—

progressed rapidly; the veterans, with ample Trinovantan labour to till their lands, were well content.

Polycletus, busied with complicated preparations for his departure to Rome, was in London when I returned. He showed no inclination to discuss with me his provincial tour nor any desire to conduct any other business. His behaviour, during these last days, was frivolous: he attended the slave-market in person and chose twelve beautiful Trinovantan boys and twelve girls; he celebrated, with particularly debauched rites, a festival of Isis at the river-bank temple which the rebels had unaccountably spared; he gave a succession of dinner-parties where the entertainment was of Alexandrian licentiousness; finally, on the eve of his departure, he borrowed my palace for a state banquet, magnificently opulent, extremely correct, and very dull.

The procession to Richborough outshone in splendour and ostentation the pageant of his arrival. On the second day, soon after leaving Rochester, Polycletus invited me to share his litter. Rather reluctantly I dismounted, parted the shimmering curtains, reclined on scented cushions and wondered what the freedman had to say.

He was not a man whose origins and training had encouraged directness in thought or speech: I had to endure massive courtesies and meandering small-talk while he plied me with wine, fruit and sweetmeats. Patiently I replied in kind until he came circuitously to the point.

'The Court, I am told, is changing its character,' Polycletus said in the careless tones of aimless gossip. 'With increasing experience the Prince becomes, shall we say, more liberal in his views, feels less bound by the conservative principles and prejudices of his divine predecessors, is less amenable to the advice of his old counsellors.'

'I have heard something of this,' I replied cautiously. 'The world does not stay still, and a wise ruler trims his sails to the winds of change.'

Polycletus pensively sucked a sugared fig soaked in wine. 'Quite so,' he agreed. 'The Prince, to continue the metaphor, is taking the tiller in his own hands and setting a new course.'

'What of the old helmsman?' I said.

Polycletus snapped his fingers decisively. 'Enough. Let us be plain. Burrus is on the way out. Seneca's influence no longer counts. Claudius of Smyrna is a clever accountant who does what he's told and knows better than to dabble in politics. Your friends in the Senate are powerless.'

I glanced apprehensively through the curtains at the eight sturdy slaves who bore our litter with practised smoothness.

'Deaf-mutes,' Polycletus said. 'We can talk freely. The state of Britain, most noble Paulinus, will be considered in a climate of opinion quite different from that prevailing in the Prince's Council when you took office a year ago. The tough, expansionist frontier policy is dying, and a trend towards consolidation, towards a better understanding with the natives, is now in favour. The Prince becomes more liberal.'

'More lackadaisical,' I grunted. 'Anyway, I don't believe a word.'

The freedman grinned. 'Never forget I am the Prince's agent. You're quite right, of course. I'm merely quoting the official version. The truth is this. Listen carefully.'

He spoke at length in a low voice, occasionally rapping my knee with a forefinger to emphasize his points. He talked of the present with knowledge and insight, of the future with prophetic accuracy. I knew horror and dismay, but no longer disbelief: Polycletus's manner forbade all doubt.

'The Prince's friends are no longer yours,' he finished. 'The Prince's interests and yours are diametrically opposed: your frontier wars, your expensive soldiers, your costly Province are to him a wearisome burden, a bore and vexation. You are not the man for palace intrigue, for poetry, music or complicated vice; you will not help him to kill his opponents. You are, on the other hand, a general of distinguished merit; you might, on this uttermost frontier, become too powerful, too much admired by your legions.'

He tapped my knee again. 'Above all, most noble Paulinus, you have failed in your mission.'

I said nothing.

'Why were you sent to Briton? To make the Province pay.'

'The books are not balanced yet,' I said wearily. 'Before Boudicca's rising our exports of lead, textiles and slaves were the highest in Britain's history. Since the rebellion I have sent to Rome over thirty thousand slaves and a huge treasure.'

Polycletus shook his head. 'Not that, nor twice as much, will meet the human and material deficit that Boudicca has bequeathed. In the profit and loss account you are a debtor.'

'Temporarily, perhaps,' I admitted. 'The campaigns I plan for next year will restore—'

'No.' He raised a peremptory hand. 'You and I are not taxgatherers, most noble Paulinus, like our friend Classicianus, who wants you recalled because your oppressive policies sap his revenues. A profitable return from taxation is very desirable and yet, in the long view, quite incompatible with a most perilous sentiment that I have discovered in Britain.'

'Hatred,' I said laconically.

Polycletus was surprised. 'You know it?'

'Naturally. I am neither blind nor deaf; my intelligence system is competent. The Britons hate me for suppressing their religion, desecrating their sacred groves and killing their priests. They hate me for defeating Boudicca and slaughtering her eighty thousand followers. They hate me for enslaving one whole tribe and exterminating another. What of it? I shall kill more Britons next year and incur yet more loathing. When has a victor ever been popular with the vanquished?'

Chin in hand, Polycletus watched me. 'Is that all you know?'

'What more? Is it not enough?'

He shook his head again, sadly. 'No, it is not. And that is why I must recommend to the Prince that you be recalled. Not for your judgements in law, which are unshakeable; not for your administration, which is thoroughgoing and efficient; not for your campaigns, which were brilliant;

and not because the people you rule in the Prince's name implore their gods for your death.'

'Then why?'

'Because you hate them.'

9

I waited five irksome days at Richborough until the choppy seas and savage November winds abated sufficiently for *Radians* and her retinue to put to sea. Polycletus kept to his wooden house and said no more: I was left wondering at a shattering misjudgement by an otherwise intelligent man.

His astonishing verdict restored my confidence: Princes of Rome do not reverse policies nor recall able Governors for mere trivialities. Although I foresaw some argument in Council and an actuary's balancing of gains and losses, Polycletus's assessment of my administrative and military virtues—which I had no doubt he would present to Nero precisely as he had stated it to me—would convince that hard-headed libertine in my favour. And the freedman's whimsical deduction was a product of his imagination, not only fantastic but also abysmally false. Does a sane, sensible, educated man bother to *hate* an animal? He does not. How, then, was it likely that I should hate the Britons? Even if, by some improbable quirk in my character, it were true what in Hercules' name did it matter?

I returned gaily to Silchester, to law-suits whose burden was lightened by Classicianus's insistence on dealing with all fiscal cases himself. An enactment of the Divine Claudius gave him this jurisdictive right which, in my view, made the Procurator both judge and party in his cause. In Catus's time the Procurator's inertia in any litigation that did not offer a fat bribe often compelled me to call fiscal suits to my own court. With the energetic and upright Classicianus I was content to observe the cautionary maxim that, if a case is one which involves the pecuniary interests of the Treasury and concerns an agent of the Prince, a wise Governor will refrain from trying it.

December's onset, ice-barbed gales and rainstorms in the van, reduced Britain to a frozen, muddy waste. Fort and fortress alike snugged down for the winter; only patrols, double-cloaked and mired, moved like forlorn phantoms on the bleak frontier roads. In my Silchester mansion I studied pleadings, wrote reports, planned operations; and warm air from the hypocaust snored gently in the flues.

The Saturnalia came and went, the snow melted and I returned by easy stages to London. The town was an excoriated patchwork, desolate in winter's grip, depressing in spirit and appearance. The population's growth outstripped rebuilding: huts, shacks, hovels and tents outnumbered the rawly-new houses and infested the confines like a verminous swarm. The revolt had deprived many countrymen, farmers and peasants, of their holdings and livelihood; now they flocked to the nearest towns to seek subsistence. And merchants, bankers, slavedealers and shopkeepers, doggedly persistent in the pursuit of money, had returned in droves to the Province's wealthiest settlement.

London since reoccupation had been under military government administered by the commandant of the fort. Now, with the situation less fluid and the populace more settled, I appointed a council of decurions who elected magistrates and resumed the forms of municipal government. In Colchester a steady influx of Roman veterans had long since begun the normal routine of civic administration without any prompting from me.

Regularly, through the medium of my spies, I read copies of Classicianus's dispatches and private letters to Rome. His propaganda against me was constant, unwearied and dangerously reasonable in tone. To the Prince, to the Finance Minister, to influential senators and equestrians he reiterated the one argument, supported by skilfully selected facts, that Suetonius Paulinus was the sole hindrance to Britain's safety and prosperity. I read the letters unamusedly, and reluctantly admired his clever pleading. Agricola, when he saw them, was frankly alarmed.

'You should counter this, Paulinus. You must write to refute his arguments, or send a representative from Britain to state your case to the Senate.'

Aurelius Bassus was more direct. 'It's time Classicianus met with a fatal accident. Would you like me to arrange it?'

I laughed at both suggestions. Polycletus, not the Procurator, decided my salvation or damnation; my fate rested in hands more ignoble than a knight's. I was impotent to disturb but could still resent a system which gave manumitted slaves and enfranchised Belgae power to affect the destinies of senators and patricians. I have since learned to curb my prejudice: the years that divide me from Britain have taught the value of a smile or nod from an actor or gladiator—if he be a Princely favourite.

Pantera also, I discovered, was now in direct correspondence with the War Ministry, though his letter-writing seemed mainly confined to details of ships sunk, crews drowned and stores lost. I guessed that the Prince's Council or the Senate, or both, were conducting a very searching inquiry into the profit and loss account of my government.

On a bleak day in February, while I was compiling in Silchester a list of the supplies to be accumulated for the summer campaigns, an Imperial courier handed me the slender scroll, oilskin-wrapped, stitched and sealed, that ended my rule in Britain.

The letter was no crude dismissal. Politely-worded official prose invited me, in view of the unprecedented losses of fighting ships during the year, to come to Rome for discussion and reappraisal of Britain's naval requirements. My early departure was requested so that decisions could be put into effect before the campaigning season began.

Burrus's familiar monogram was missing. Tigillinus's franking scrawl, which I could not then decipher, became all too familiar later on.

The letter's content did not deceive me. This was a final recall. From the black flood of stunned despair that drowned my mind for days there emerged, like a slimy reptile, the image of peril. I became afraid, for I had failed the Prince; and fear, my constant companion and bedfellow in the humiliating years that followed, never left me until Nero died.

To maintain the pretence of a temporary absence I collected for the journey only a small retinue of servants and baggage; secretly I told Agricola to arrange for the rest of my household to be shipped in the spring. The subterfuge was a waste of time. That strange and accurate instinct for information which Britons possess had spread throughout the Province, within days, the rumour of my recall. I did not bother with denials.

Classicianius, cold, polite, formal, without triumph, outwardly accepting the official reason for my journey, came to wish me well. Cogidumnus, less tactful, came as President of the Council to say good-bye. He expressed the Council's gratitude, on behalf of their tribes, for the benefactions of my administration. He was sorry that a recent Senatorial decree forbade his Council to send to Rome the customary solemn declaration which thanked, in the name of the Province, a Governor on expiry of his term.

I had never heard of that Senatorial decree. An inquiry to my offices disclosed that it had arrived with the same dispatches which carried my dismissal. I was inclined to regard the prohibition as a piece of petty spite, a pinprick engineered by an unfriendly senator; but the decree applied to all provinces and is in force to this day.

The legions' reactions were both flattering and dangerous. From Lincoln, Chester and Wroxeter came deputations of centurions on lathered horses, ostensibly to salute my going, to escort me to Richborough. The reality was different. They well knew that the weak-kneed policy advocated by the Procurator would replace me by a conciliatory Governor, a man of peace, a lurker behind frontiers. The issue was plain: no wars, no loot. And in my brief years of command the Army of Britain had looted as never before.

In a secret conference they begged me to stay, to make excuses for delay. There was wild and treasonable talk of naming me Imperator, of seceding from Rome, of proclaiming the Province independent. The legates, they promised me, were in favour: Cerialis, Valens, Mamilianus would support my elevation.

I felt cold with fear. If word of this reached Nero's ear my life was worth not a counterfeit denarius. In an impassioned speech, meaning every word I said, I recalled the men to their duty and loyalty to the Prince. I bought their silence with a valuable donative, 7,000 sesterces to each centurion; and flatly refused their last request to send a cohort from each legion to escort me on my way.

Only II Legion had held aloof from this ill-advised plot. Poor Augusta. She had not the spirit even for sedition.

After this alarm I transferred, in a brief interview, the Province's administration to Classicianus. I did not reveal my plans for the summer, my hopes of annexing Brigantia—hopes which have never yet been fulfilled. Seven years afterwards the frontiers of Britain rest exactly as I left them.

The bodyguard, in review order, escorted me to Richborough. The countryside was a stark and snow-sheeted landscape sulking beneath an iron-grey sky. Magistrates and decurions of war-scarred towns on the route paraded as in duty bound, without enthusiasm. At Richborough a small, storm-tossed flotilla rode to anchor: one bireme, a transport for my servants and baggage, four escorting warships. No *Radians* trireme for the departing Governor: Pantera, with a smirk, declared the seas too rough to bring her from Boulogne, the winds too strong to cross that day.

I took the grin off his face by straightway embarking and ordering him to put to sea. I should certainly be very ill, but physical sickness would be an anodyne to the aching pain in my heart. I clasped hands with Agricola, soon to rejoin me, and with my faithful Mannius Secundus, whom I never met again.

The oarblades dipped, backed water. The bireme sidled from the wharf. The sail flapped, filled, strained at the sheets. With a sharp clatter the rowers shipped oars. The thunderous clash of the bodyguard's salute roused sea-gulls from their storm-shelters to wheel and cry like souls in torment.

The vessel rolled savagely as she cleared the shelter of the break-water. I stood in the stern, gripped a mast-stay, gazed at the dimming ranks of the soldiers I loved, and the salt spindrift stung my eyes to tears.

A sudden rain-squall swept viciously between ship and shore and blotted the land from sight, and I saw no more of Britain.

APPENDIX

Order of Battle of the Roman Army in Britain

Notes:

1. The four legions were definitely in Britain at the time of Boudicca's rebellion. None of the auxiliary units, however, is mentioned in literary sources: their presence is known only from archaeological and epigraphical evidence. Since they were all in Britain before A.D. 180, some considerably earlier, we can reasonably assume that the majority marched with Suetonius Paulinus's army.

2. The strengths shown are full war establishment: numbers generally tended to fall below this.

THE LEGIONS (each 5,600 men including 120 cavalry).

II Augusta, originally formed by Octavian after Philippi. Capricorn and Pegasus on standard.

IX Hispana (also Triumphalis, Macedonia: the latter title probably gained at Philippi). Originally Julius Caesar's 9th Legion, reconstituted by Octavian. Neptune on standard.

XIV Gemina (also Martia Victrix after A.D. 61). Formed out of two legions (hence 'Gemina') by Octavian. Capricorn and eagle on standard.

XX Valeria (also Victrix after A.D. 61). Formed by Octavian, and called after his general Valerius Messalinus. Boar on standard.

THE AUXILIARIES

Cavalry Regiments

	Composition	Calvary	Infantry
Classus's Horse	Gallic	500	
Petra's Horse	Gallic	1,000	
1st Asturian	Spanish	500	
1st Thracian (archers)	Thracian	500	
1st Pannonian	Pannonian	500	
Indus's Horse	Gallic	500	
1st Tungrian	Belgian	500	
Proculus's Horse	Gallic	500	
1st Vettonian	Spanish	500	
2nd Asturian	Spanish	500	
		5,500	

Mixed Cohorts

	Composition	Calvary	Infantry
4th Lingones	Gallic	120	360
1st Loyal Vardulli	Spanish	240	760
6th Thracian (archers)	Thracian	120	360
1st Nervana	German	240	760
3rd Gauls	Gallic	120	360
4th Gauls	Gallic	120	360
1st Vangiones	Rhineland	240	760
1st Lingones	Gallic	120	360
2nd Lingones	Gallic	120	360
		1,440	4,440

Infantry Cohorts

	Composition	Calvary	Infantry
1st Cugerni	Rhineland		500
1st Celtiberian	Spanish		500
4th Dalmatians	Dalmatia		500
1st Morini	Boulogne		500
1st Baetasii	Belgian		500
3rd Bracarii	Spanish		500

Infantry Cohorts (cont)

2nd Pannonians	Pannonia	500
2nd Vascones	Basques	500
1st Tungrian	Belgian	1,000
2nd Asturian	Spanish	500
1st Frisiavones	Rhinemouth	500
2nd Nervii	Gallic	500
		6,500
	Total: 6,940	10,940

Grand total for the Army: Legions 22,400, Auxiliaries 17,800 = 40,280.

About the Author

George Frederick Morgan Shipway was born in 1908 in India. He attended the Royal Military College at Sandhurst and was commissioned into the Indian Army in 1928. He was attached the 2nd Battalion The Prince of Wales's Volunteers (South Lancashire), and then to the 13th Duke of Connaught's Own Lancers. He spent two years (1936-1938) as Adjutant of the Mekran Levy Corps. In 1940-41 he became a General Staff Officer, at General Headquarters, India. He remained on the staff until 1944 when he was posted to serve with the Hyderabad Lancers. Shipway retired as a Major and honorary Lieutenant-Colonel on 9 January 1948, following Indian independence. After retiring he became a teacher at Cheam School in Berkshire for 19 years before becoming a novelist at the age of 60.

Also from Santa Fe Writers Project

Muscle Cars *by Stephen G. Eoannou*

A powerful journey through the humor, darkness, and neuroses of the modern American Everyman...

"Eoannou's debut collection is all—all—heart."
—Brett Lott, *author of* Jewel,
an Oprah Book Club Selection

Ordination *by Daniel M. Ford*

For generations, warlords fought bitterly for dominance in a land without a king, leaving a fractured, war-torn country plagued by thieves, slavers, and the servants of dark gods and darker magic until disgraced knight, Allystaire Coldbourne, finds himself on a dangerous journey to defeat an ancient evil.

"Ford's debut offers compelling characters and sharp dialogue."
—Publishers Weekly

Fatal Light *by Richard Currey*

A devastating portrait of war in all its horror, brutality, and mindlessness, this extraordinary novel is written in beautifully cadenced prose. A combat medic in Vietnam faces the chaos of war, set against the tranquil scenes of family life back home in small-town America.

"One of the very best works of fiction to emerge from the Vietnam War.."
— Tim O'Brien, *author,* The Things They Carried

About Santa Fe Writers Project

SFWP is an independent press founded in 1998 that embraces a mission of artistic preservation, recognizing exciting new authors, and bringing out of print work back to the shelves.

Find us on Facebook, Twitter @sfwp, and at www.sfwp.com